"This is from the brave girl who gave you life," Tess said quietly. "She wanted you to have it. Open it. Then we'll talk."

Liz picked away the tape around the bundle and slowly unwrapped yards of white silk. It was old, yellowing in places, apparently undisturbed for years. Suddenly, gold spilled out—coins, she thought at first, then realized it was jewelry. She held up what appeared to be a great multistringed necklace, although it was unimaginable that anyone could wear the heavy ten or twelve strands, each of them bearing gold coins too numerous to count at a glance—they would cover the chest like chain mail, reaching to the waist of a tall woman. Liz lifted the mass of gold—belts, necklaces, bangles, cuffs. Soft yellow antique gold of such purity that some of the ornaments were bent from the years of being piled together. A silk kerchief revealed smaller pieces—rings, long, intricately worked earrings, strange pins, ornaments for the hair.

"Ma."

Tess turned to look at her.

"Who was she, this girl who gave you all this?" Liz asked.

"Her name was Fateema. They said she was thirteen...."

Watch for the newest blockbuster from
NELL BRIEN

Coming in October 2000
Only from MIRA Books

A VEILED JOURNEY

NELL BRIEN

MIRA

ISBN 1-55166-528-X

A VEILED JOURNEY

Copyright © 1999 by Shirley Palmer.

All rights reserved. Except for use in any review, the reproduction or utilization of this work in whole or in part in any form by any electronic, mechanical or other means, now known or hereafter invented, including xerography, photocopying and recording, or in any information storage or retrieval system, is forbidden without the written permission of the publisher, MIRA Books, 225 Duncan Mill Road, Don Mills, Ontario, Canada M3B 3K9.

All characters in this book have no existence outside the imagination of the author and have no relation whatsoever to anyone bearing the same name or names. They are not even distantly inspired by any individual known or unknown to the author, and all incidents are pure invention.

MIRA and the Star Colophon are trademarks used under license and registered in Australia, New Zealand, Philippines, United States Patent and Trademark Office and in other countries.

Visit us at www.mirabooks.com

Printed in U.S.A.

This is a work of fiction, and to serve the story being told, some liberty has been taken with the order of actual events. The Anvil of Allah exists only in the imagination of the author, and the *fatwa* described was issued by the Taliban in Afghanistan, not in Saudi Arabia.

Acknowledgments

It is a pleasure to be able to thank the people who are such an integral part of my writing life. My buddy Marge Karlin, herself a fine writer, has seen this novel through from bud to blossom. The input from Dell Coleman, Phyllis Spiva and Margo Bauer smoothed a lot of ragged edges. Ken Atchity of AEI in Los Angeles has been a patient mentor. Peter Miller of PMA Literary Management in New York, agent and calming friend, has loved my work from the beginning, and always returns my phone calls. Thanks, Peter. And then there are the folks at MIRA, Dianne Moggy and Amy Moore-Benson, who have brought *A Veiled Journey* to life. No writer could ask for more enthusiasm and support. You've been terrific.

This brings me to the guy behind the scenes— Dan Palmer, husband and unwavering fan. Thank you.

For my mother

There were no footmarks on the ground
for each wind swept like a great brush
over the sand surface, stippling the
traces of the last travellers till the
surface was again a pattern of
innumerable tiny virgin waves.

—T. E. Lawrence
The Seven Pillars of Wisdom

If any of your women
Are guilty of lewdness
Take the evidence of four witnesses
Against them, and if they testify
Confine them to houses until
Death do claim them
Or Allah ordains for them some other way.

—The Holy Koran
Sura 4
Verse 15

Prologue

"Her name was Fateema. They said she was thirteen...."

Jeddah, Saudi Arabia
1958

The wind was picking up, another *shamal* on its way. Somewhere in the house a shutter had torn away from its fastening and banged against the wall with every gust. Tess Ryan lifted herself on one elbow, the better to listen. Below the noise of the wind and the maddening shutter, she thought she could hear a deeper pounding. Light from a passing lantern brightened the room from beneath the door, then faded. Hassan, muttering to himself in Arabic, making his way to the courtyard.

Tess glanced at her husband, asleep in the bed next to hers, and thought how much she hated not being able to sleep cuddled against him. Thrilling though this posting had been, for newlyweds Jeddah certainly had its drawbacks. No refrigeration, no plumbing, no shops to speak of, food she hardly recognized in those that did exist. And a deadly climate, the city either blanketed by the unnerving moisture of the Red Sea, causing heat rashes in inconvenient places, or buffeted by the *shamal,* a dry and crackling wind that swept in from the desert, bringing sand into every corner, every fold of cloth. Afterward, it took days to shake it out of the household linens and their clothes.

Not this time, though. One more day and they'd be on their way home—back to air-conditioning and a big double bed.

Silently, Tess swung her feet to the floor, felt around for her slippers, then put on one of her loose caftans. She opened the bedroom door, slipped through, closed it silently behind her. Not that she would awaken Jim; he could sleep through anything, even a *shamal*.

"Hassan. What is it?" she called softly. The houseman had opened the small iron grill in the front door and was peering through it.

"Someone is outside, madam, attempting to awaken the keeper of the gate."

Tess crossed the tiled entry and opened the door. The tamarisk trees tossed violently, sand devils whirled around the walled courtyard. Through the noise of the wind, she could hear more clearly the pounding at the wooden gates that opened onto the narrow alley outside.

"That son of a camel who calls himself the keeper of the gate is sleeping. As he does nightly, madam, when he is supposed to be awake, protecting the household."

Protecting them from what? Tess thought, irritated. Burglary was unknown. Justice was swift in the kingdom, and primitive. A thief lost his right hand, the clean hand, to the sword, and in a close-knit tribal society that made him an outcast—even family would not allow a left hand, the dirty hand used for bathroom duty in a world where water was more precious than blood, to be used to scoop food from the communal bowl.

Tess held her impatience in check. Hassan had been feuding with the old gatekeeper for the entire year they'd been here. No doubt there was a relative somewhere that Hassan wanted for the job.

"Then go wake him up," she said. "But gently."

Hassan did not move. "That old man is too feeble for the great responsibility that has been given him—"

"Oh, for God's sake!" Tess started across the fifty feet of courtyard at a run. The wind whipped at her caftan, and she held a hand to her hair—it felt as if it were about to be snatched from her head. She bent over the doorkeeper, huddled against the outside wall, his head wrapped in his *ghutra*, the ubiquitous Arab headdress that was held in place by camel hobbles. The old man was hard of hearing at the best of times and half blind. But he'd come with the house and he was a pleasant old boy.

"Mansour." She put a hand on his shoulder. "Mansour, wake up. Someone wants to come in." Tess turned to the gate, tried to lift the wooden bar from its slots.

Mansour looked up, obviously startled at the sight of the Western woman wrestling with the heavily barred outer door. He struggled to his feet and hurried to help. The door swung open, helped by strong thrusts from whoever was outside.

Before she could protest, two figures swathed in black slipped through the opening. One of them pushed the door wider, enabling a litter carried by four large Nubians to enter. A woman, shrouded like the two men and veiled, walked by the side of the litter, murmuring what sounded like encouragement to whoever was hidden by the drawn curtains.

"What are you doing?" Tess shouted. The wind blew her words back in her face. She tried to bar the way. "You can't come in here. This is the property of the United States of America."

"Do not be alarmed." One of the cloaked men detached himself from the group and came toward her. Close behind him a tall, broad figure carried a screened lantern. The wind pinned their desert robes against them. "We have come to ask your help."

The noise of the gusts made it hard to hear the words. "Who are you?" Tess shouted.

"That is of no importance." The speaker kept his *ghutra* wrapped around his face, revealing only his eyes. The voice was that of a young man.

"We can't help you," Tess said. "You'll have to leave. I'm sorry."

"I bring this woman to you for help. She cannot bring forth her child."

He'd been taught English by an Englishman, Tess thought, not an American. A cultured voice, not that of a tribesman. And he was going against every tradition of his people by coming here. Men in this part of the world cared little for the well-being of women. He must love her.

The young man saw her hesitation. "She is very young."

There was no hospital in Jeddah, nowhere to send them. Tess glanced at the litter, noticing the submissive posture of the woman beside it. The lantern flickered in a sudden intense gust and went out. She looked back at the young man. God knows what Jim would say. "You'd better bring her in."

The young man gestured to the Nubians carrying the litter. They waited until he turned to follow Tess into the house, then fell in behind him, the woman still at the side of the litter. Tess struggled to close the front door against the wind, not surprised that no one moved to help. She called for Hassan to take over, then turned to the small waiting group.

"There is no doctor here," she said.

"But you can get a Western doctor," the young man said.

A moan came from inside the litter. The black-shrouded woman slid a hand between the curtains and murmured softly. Tess walked over to her. "How long has she been in labor?"

The woman shook her head, not understanding, and

glanced warily at the young man. He did not look at the litter, or seem to hear the moans coming from inside. The Nubians stood like statues, their dark features impassive. They were slaves, Tess knew. Slavery was widespread throughout the kingdom.

"She has been struggling to give birth," the young man said. "This is the third night. She is young, and it is her first child. Her strength is failing."

"How old is she?"

"Thirteen years."

Tess bit back sharp words. A child struggling to bring another child into the world. The marriage of twelve-year-olds was common, as were thirteen-year-old mothers. Who knew how many deaths there were of children too young to bring their babies into the world? Who cared?

Tess touched the woman's arm, gave her a smile, then gestured to the Nubians to lower the litter. They looked at the young man, and he nodded. Tess knelt, opened the curtains. Although she was moaning, the girl was not conscious. Tess put a hand on her distended belly, then saw the blood soaking the white pads beneath her. Her heart sank. This girl needed more than a doctor. She needed the facilities only a hospital could provide. Even then, she could very well die.

"What's going on here?" Hair tousled, Jim Ryan stood in the doorway. "Tess, who are these people?"

Swiftly, the young man adjusted the *ghutra* covering his face, making sure only his eyes were visible between the black-and-white checkered folds. The man with him, the lantern carrier, did the same. What little of his skin could be seen, the bridge of his nose between his eyes, his hands, was blue-black. Obviously, he, too, was a Nubian. A slave.

The loosened shutter still banged back and forth, the sound invasive and irritating. Jim spoke sharply in Arabic to Hassan, who stood in the shadows cast by the flickering lanterns Tess had lit—Jeddah had no electricity, either—his eyes darting from face to face, storing up enough drama for a year's worth of gossip. Reluctantly, Hassan turned to leave.

Tess got to her feet, hurried to close the door behind him. "When you've fastened that shutter, please check all the others in the house," she called. "Then go to bed, Hassan. We won't need you any more tonight."

Hassan started to argue, and Tess checked him in midsentence. "Good night, Hassan. *Shakrun.*" She closed the door firmly, went back to stand close to her husband. "Jim, this girl is dying. We've got to get her some help."

"Tess, who are they? My God, Tess. There's nothing we can do—"

Tess opened her eyes wide, indicating the young man, trying to send Jim the message that he could speak English. In the light of the house lanterns she'd seen his robes, rough Bedouin cloth—he looked as if he'd just come in from the desert. But he hadn't. She'd noticed his hands. They were not those of a desert tribesman, a herder of camels or goats from one remote well to another. She took her husband's arm, turned him away from the group watching them.

"Listen, Jim," she said softly. "He brought her here because she can't give birth. She's going to die if she doesn't get help—"

"This is not our business, Tess. We can't help her. If she dies in our care, all hell will break loose. The least of it will be our having to pay blood money to her family, God knows what else—"

"They're not ordinary Bedouin. Look at them. Look at the slaves. They're well fed, good clothes. These are not people likely to demand blood money. She's dying—"

"This is the sort of situation we have to stay out of. We can't do anything."

Tess put a hand on his arm. As a boy, Jim's imagination

had been fired by all things Arabic—the stories of desert warfare fought by Lawrence of Arabia; the drama of the young Ibn Saud unifying the peninsula with the sword; the Arabian journeys of Wilfred Thesiger. His fluency in Arabic had secured this posting at a crucial time for the United States, even got him permission to bring his new wife. It was understood at State that he had a brilliant future. What she was asking him to do was to risk that future to save the life of an unknown girl.

"Yes, we can. I'm taking her down to the *Murphy*."

The USS *Murphy* was in Jeddah harbor for a courtesy visit and to pick up a party of Saudi princes and their servants for the long journey to the United States for talks about the development of the Saudi oil fields. One of the few Arabists at State with a degree in international law, Jim Ryan was to be part of the negotiating team.

"Are you crazy? If he is from an important family, and she dies, it could be an international incident. My career will be over before it starts. You've got to get her out of here."

"They've got a fully equipped hospital on board that ship."

"For the use of important Saudi princes. For diplomats, not charity cases."

"For all we know, he could be one of the princes—"

The girl in the litter shrieked, the sound bubbling into a moan. Jim Ryan went pale.

Tess reached up, kissed him, something she normally would never do in front of a Saudi. Displays of affection between the sexes was taboo, although it was common to see men strolling about, holding hands. "Jim. I love you. I can't let this girl die. I'm taking her. Please understand." She turned to the young man. "We'll take her to the ship." He'd know what she meant. Everyone in Jeddah knew of the visit of the *Murphy*.

"No," the man said swiftly. "She cannot go to the ship. She must stay in this house."

Tess stared at him in shock. "But she cannot stay here! She needs a hospital!"

"The ship has only men. You must help her here."

"Well, I can't. I'm not a doctor, I'm not a nurse. If she doesn't get to the hospital on that ship, she will die."

"Then that is the will of Allah." He gave a sharp command in Arabic to the Nubians. They picked up the litter. The girl inside screamed. The woman reached a hand inside the curtain, withdrew it covered in blood. Struggling to understand what was happening, her eyes went from the young man to Tess and back. She spoke softly. The young man shook his head without speaking.

"Have the mercy of Allah," Tess said to him.

"If she dies, it is the will of Allah," he said again.

The girl was moaning now, nonstop. Tess wondered where she got the strength. The black veil of the woman by the litter was wet with tears.

For the first time Jim Ryan spoke to the young man in his own language.

The man turned, stared at Jim as if considering his words, showing no surprise at Jim's fluent Arabic. Then he said in English, "We will go to the harbor."

Tess started toward the bedroom. "Good. Oh, good. Give me just one minute to change."

Jim followed her, closed the bedroom door, grabbed his pants.

Tess snatched the pants from him, threw them back on the chair. "Don't even think it! You're a man! We'd only have another problem with him if you try to come with us, and that girl doesn't have the time for arguments about Arab honor." Tess pulled on her own trousers, a hooded sweatshirt, socks, tennis shoes. The State Department was meticulous about respecting Saudi customs, particularly now with

the United States jockeying for control of Arab oil fields—
loose caftans, arms and legs covered to wrist and ankle, only
hands visible, hair shrouded in public; they'd stopped short
of demanding the veil, at least, thank God for small mercies.
But if they were caught tonight, wearing pants would be the
least of her problems. Penalties were harsh and swift for any
infringement of law—and she couldn't even begin to imagine what the head of the U.S. negotiating team would say.
Jim's boss. "I'll be safe. You know that."

"Yes, but it—"

Tess cut him off. "Jim, please, don't argue. There's no
time." Tess thrust her passport into a pocket in case she
needed some ID. "What did you say to him to change his
mind?"

"I said if the girl died, the son she could be trying to
give him would die with her."

"Oh, sweetie, good thinking." Tess gave him a quick
hug. "Don't worry, I'll be back soon."

Jim went with them across the courtyard, helped Mansour
open the gates. They went through, and Tess heard the bar
drop into place behind them. Uncertainty grabbed her. The
alley was a wind tunnel—sand stung her face and got into
her eyes. She pulled the hood of her sweatshirt over her
hair, down as far as she could to shield her face.

She touched the young man's arm to get his attention,
then reached up to put her mouth against his ear so that he
could hear her over the noise of the *shamal.*

"Can you get us down to the harbor?" She would never
find her way alone. Jeddah was a maze of streets and alleys,
unnamed, unpaved, unlit except for the torches on the main
thoroughfares.

Silently, he pointed to the tall Nubian carrying the lantern
at the head of the small procession. Tess nodded. The Nubian set a sharp pace. They turned from alleyway into alleyway, their feet soundless on the packed earthen streets.

Within minutes, Tess realized the young man was no longer with them. She looked around, but he'd faded into the swirling brown night as if he'd never been.

Twice they came to a main street. Torches flickered eerily, a dim glow seen through a curtain of blowing sand. Each time the Nubian led them quickly across, into darker, narrower lanes. He was eager they not be seen, Tess thought. Women, out at night, with men not their husbands. Dangerous in this society. Then she remembered that slaves were considered neuter. Nonpersons.

So he had to be protecting the identity of the young man who'd left them.

The smell of camel dung gusted toward them. They emerged into a large square filled with camels, couched with their backs to the wind—a caravan waiting to leave as soon as the *shamal* ended, the drivers, heads wrapped in untidy turbans, huddled against their animals for protection from the stinging sand.

The Nubian shrouded the lantern with his cloak, motioning them to keep close to the buildings as they made their way around the square, the moans from the litter lost among the sounds of camels belching and groaning. They turned into the darkness of another alley, and minutes later, they were at the sea.

The *Murphy* was moored at the end of a pier used by the *dhows,* double-sailed merchant vessels of an ancient Biblical-era design that still plied the Red Sea, and by the ships that brought the devout to Jeddah to start their overland journey to Mecca, a pilgrimage every Muslim who could was required to make at least once in his lifetime. The large open space fronting the harbor was edged by mud-brick warehouses, and the few torches attached to the buildings danced wildly.

The square was empty, no one prevented them from getting close to the American ship. Two American sailors, their tropical whites streaked by the sand, stood guard at the end of the gangway. Tess could see them square their shoulders, move their feet anxiously as they watched the small procession approach.

"Hold it. Right there."

Tess moved forward. "Good evening. I am Mrs. James Ryan of the American legation here in Jeddah." She felt ludicrous, in the middle of the night shouting the niceties of the diplomatic corps in the teeth of a roaring *shamal* at the two stone-faced sailors. Doggedly, she plowed on. "I wish to speak with the medical officer."

The sailors shifted their eyes to her. "Ma'am. Sorry, ma'am," one said. "No way I can disturb the ship this time at night."

"I will take full responsibility for the disturbance."

"Well, that's as may be, ma'am." The sailor looked at the Saudis behind her. "This don't look like official business to me."

The girl in the litter screamed. Both sailors reached for their sidearms. "Jesus! What's that?"

"There's a girl here who needs help from the hospital. She's trying to have a baby. You have to call an officer."

"Ma'am, civilians aren't allowed on U.S. Navy vessels," the young sailor said. "There's no way—"

"Please. Get the doctor. Let him decide."

"Ma'am, I can't leave my post. I'd get thrown in the brig for sure if I left my post, ma'am. I can't do that."

The big Nubian spoke to the other slaves. They started to turn back to the city.

"Wait! Wait a minute!" Tess turned to plead with the sailor who hadn't yet spoken. "Let me go on board. I'm an American—"

"What's going on down there?" A figure in white stood at the top of gangway. "Who are these people?"

"Chief, this lady wants the doc. Lady having a baby,

chief.'' The young sailor sounded relieved to pass the problem over.

The chief came down the gangway. ''Who's having a baby here?''

''Chief, there's a lady in that litter—''

The girl moaned. The chief bent down, put a hand on the curtain. The Nubian leapt at him. One large black hand gripped the chief's wrist, the other was on the dagger at his belt.

The young sailors unlocked the holsters of their sidearms.

''Chief,'' Tess said swiftly. ''You can't look inside that litter. Their women are taboo for anyone outside the immediate family. He'll kill you if you try. Please, I am Mrs. James Ryan of the American legation.'' She fumbled in her pocket. The young sailors unholstered their weapons. ''This is my passport.'' Tess waved the document. ''Look, please. Trust me. There's only a very sick young girl in that litter.''

The chief, hard eyes challenging the Nubian, moved to reach for the passport with the hand the man held. The Nubian released his hold, kept his own hand on the hilt of his dagger. The muscles around the chief's mouth twitched as he took the passport, glanced at it, handed it back to Tess. He turned to one of the sailors. ''Get the doc. On the double.''

They waited in silence except for the howl of the wind and the sound of the sea slapping against the seawall and the hull of the ship. And the constant moans from the girl in the litter.

Finally a young man ran down the gangway.

''Lieutenant Gould, U.S. Navy,'' he said. ''What's this about a baby?'' He sounded incredulous.

Quickly Tess explained the situation, Gould nodding as she spoke. He bent toward the litter. The Nubian stepped in front of him, blocking his way. Gould held his eyes for a long moment. Then the Nubian stood back, and Gould looked inside the curtain, putting his hand on the girl's head. He stood, studying the harbor, the blowing sand. "I can't do anything here. I'll have to take her on board."

"Sir. Begging your pardon, sir—"

"It's okay, chief." Gould cut him off. "Just the girl. We can't take the litter." He reached inside to pick the girl up. The tall Nubian pushed him aside. The moans were whipped away into the wind as he lifted the girl, holding her carefully against his chest.

"The rest of you, wait," Gould said. He turned to the gangway.

Tess started after him.

"Hold it," Gould said. "This is a naval vessel, not a cruise ship."

"It's okay. I'm going home on her tomorrow." What difference that might make tonight she wasn't sure, but Tess put her foot firmly on the gangplank. From behind her, the veiled woman grabbed her arm. "And this is the girl's mother," she improvised, unsure of the relationship but it sounded right.

"Jesus!" Gould said. "Okay, make it snappy. Come on."

He raced up the gangway. The silence of the sleeping vessel was a relief after the howl of the *shamal*. They met no one. Gould led them deeper into the ship, finally opening a door. A young medic put down the magazine he was reading and jumped to his feet.

"Lieutenant." He looked over Gould's shoulder at the Nubian with a very pregnant girl in his arms, the front of his white robe staining slowly with blood, then at the two women crowding behind him. His eyes bulged.

"Ted," Gould said. "No time for explanations. We've got an emergency." He gestured toward an inner room, and the Nubian brushed past the astonished medic, placed the girl gently on an operating table. Gould hustled him out, talking over his shoulder to the medic. "We're going to have to deliver this baby by C-section. She's going to need blood. You women wait in that room outside.'' He was stripping off his jacket as he spoke. ''And get this man off the ship.'' He poked his head around the door of the operating room as he closed it. ''Or it's my ass.''

Tess looked at her watch, saw that it was only 2:00 a.m. Her eyes stung from the blowing sand, and she felt as if an aeon had passed since she'd been awakened by the banging shutter, but it was little more than an hour. The woman sank onto her haunches by the side of a chair, her green eyes watchful above her veil. For the first time, Tess noticed the circlet of gold coins around her forehead, another beneath her eyes, binding the veil in place.

''You will have to leave.'' Tess spoke slowly to the Nubian, relying on the old belief that if one spoke slowly enough it somehow created a common language. She opened the door, peered out. The passageway was empty. She beckoned. ''Come with me.''

''I will stay, madam,'' the man said. ''I cannot leave these women of my master's household alone in this place.''

Tess looked at him in amazement. His voice was deep and rich, his English perfect. ''You speak English!'' It infuriated her that he hadn't made that known before. ''Why didn't you say?''

''It was not necessary.''

''Who is your master? The young man who brought her?''

''I cannot tell you.''

''Your name, then.''

''That, also, I cannot tell you.''

''Oh, for God's sake.'' Tess turned to the woman. ''Do you speak English, too?''

The Nubian answered for her. ''She does not. I was taught with my master, so that he could practice the language with me.''

"Well, you've got to leave, you heard what the doctor said. Stay on the dock. When you're needed to take her home, I'll call you. Let's go."

The man folded his arms. He took a position behind the outer door to the passageway, as hidden as it was possible to be in the small cabin, and sat on his heels. "We will wait."

Tess hadn't the energy to argue. What difference did one more presence make? If someone came in and saw her, plus a shrouded Saudi woman squatting on the floor, there would be hell to pay, anyway. And if the girl died, it would be better all around to have them both here, either to dispose of the body or to help with the inquiry if it came to that. Let them stonewall a naval investigation if they could. Tess looked at the woman, shrouded in black. With her face covered, by *shari'ah* law she was literally a nonperson in this Arab world, and Tess knew she would not be allowed to testify.

An hour dragged by with no sound from the operating room. Tess sat in the chair next to the woman. Once she placed a hand on her shoulder in an attempt to transmit some kindred female feeling, but the woman didn't react. Tess knew she had to be deep in misery, but there was no way to communicate. The Nubian's face, too, was hidden by his *ghutra*, his eyes wide above the folds.

The door to the operating room opened. Tess jumped out of her chair. The woman beside her rose to her feet in one graceful, fluid motion, and Tess realized she was young, probably not much older than Tess herself.

Gould beckoned. "You can come in." The Nubian started forward. "Just the women."

"My master wishes me to stay with—"

"Listen, mister," Gould said. "I don't give a shit what your master wishes. This is the United States Navy. And I say just the women."

Tess looked at him, surprised at his anger. His face was set and grim.

The medic stood just inside the door of the operating room, a bundle wrapped in a sheet in his arms.

"She won't take her, ma'am." He looked down at the baby. "Pretty little red-haired girl and her mama won't have anything to do with her."

The girl was lying on the table. She was conscious, her green eyes enormous in a white face. By her side was another wrapped bundle.

"She had twins, poor little kid," Gould said. "Years too young. Her body couldn't take it."

The woman pushed past Tess, hurried to the girl's side. The language she spoke to the girl was not Arabic. Tess felt tears spring to her eyes at the gentleness in her voice, the hand on the girl's forehead.

"She's okay, she'll live, but she won't have any more kids," Gould said. "She was too small for this. I'll eat my uniform if she's even thirteen. Goddamn these people."

Tess put a hand on his arm. "Thanks. You saved her life." But for what? If she couldn't have more children, Tess wondered what the future held for her. In this world, a woman's value was in the sons she could bear. "Is the other baby a boy?"

"Yes. They should both survive, although the boy's much stronger. For some reason she won't even look at the girl."

The woman left the young mother's side and came to put a hand on Tess's arm. She spoke in Arabic, and Tess shook her head. She knew only a few rudimentary words—*please, thank you, hello.* The woman took the baby from the medic, looked down at her briefly, then pressed the child against Tess's chest. Tess took her gently, looked into the small face, the unfocused blue eyes, then back at the woman. Her green eyes were luminous with tears.

"She's a lovely little girl," Tess said. "Look at her, lieutenant. Isn't she lovely?'' She held the child out to the woman. The woman shook her head, pressed the baby back into Tess's arms and spoke rapidly. She kept patting the baby's head, pressing her deeper into Tess's arms. Tess felt her stomach clench. Jim should be here to translate, to back her up. She didn't know what this woman wanted.

But she did.

"What's she saying? Do you speak Arabic?'' she said to Gould.

"No. But I think I'm getting the drift of this.''

"Yes.'' Tess shook her head, tried to hand the baby to the woman. The girl called out weakly, and the woman turned to her, speaking softly, reassuringly. She looked at Gould, then went to the door and called to the Nubian.

He came into the room, his eyes locked on the girl on the table. He went to her, picked up her hand gently. He touched her hair. Tess could hear him murmuring to her. She couldn't understand the words, but his tone was unmistakable.

He was a slave, and he loved a woman who belonged to his master. If that were discovered, he would die for it.

The girl whispered to him. A stillness came over him. Then he straightened and looked at Tess. "This woman wishes you to have her child,'' he said flatly.

"That's impossible,'' Tess said. "She's not a stray kitten I can take in. There is no way I can do that.''

"Listen,'' Gould said to him. "Don't be crazy. This is a United States warship. We don't want any babies. You've got to take them all home. She needs rest, the babies need a lot of care. You just get them all off this ship, now.''

"The woman will not take the girl child.''

"Christ!'' Gould looked helplessly from the Nubian to Tess to the girl.

The baby in Tess's arms screwed up her face, made small smacking noises with her mouth. Her tiny rosebud mouth.

Tess touched a finger to her cheek. The skin was petal soft. How could her mother not want her?

Tess pushed the baby into the woman's chest. The woman stood there, arms at her side. She turned and spoke to the Nubian. He listened, then nodded his head. The woman returned to the girl's side. She lifted her hand and held it to her breast.

"I will translate what this woman says," the Nubian said. The woman spoke rapidly and he spoke as she did. "She asks that this man leave." He gestured toward the medic.

"Now wait a minute," Gould said. "This sailor is a member of the crew of the USS *Murphy*. He's not going anywhere."

"The woman wishes to remove her veil, to show that she trusts you. But she cannot do that with this man present. Only the doctor."

"What about you?" Gould said. "You're a man. You're not leaving."

"I am a slave, not a man. I belong to my master. These are women of my master's household."

"Jesus Christ," Gould said softly. "What the hell are we into here? Seaman Hogarth, I think you'd better leave."

"Sir."

As Hogarth pulled the door closed behind him, Gould said, "Ted, wait. You're still on duty, remember. Stay in the sick bay and keep your mouth shut. I'll talk to you in a few minutes."

"Aye-aye, lieutenant." The door closed.

"Okay, mister," Gould said. "Say what you have to say."

The woman unfastened her veil. As her face was revealed, it was clear she and the girl were closely related. She was handsome rather than beautiful, red-haired and green-eyed. She spoke only to Tess.

"I am called Sakeena. I am the mother of this girl, Fateema." The Nubian murmured a translation as she spoke. "The grandmother of these children. I am a concubine, as is my daughter. This is our fate and we accept it. Now she has a son and her place is secure. So Fateema will bear no more children."

Tess threw Gould a look of inquiry—had he told them that?—and he shook his head.

Sakeena caught the exchange and said, "We have ways for this. My daughter will do whatever she must to prevent more children, as I have done. No more daughters for the life that is ours. We are toys, not women. Fateema wants her daughter to be free. Here, the life of a girl child is worthless. When her father decides she is ready to be given away, she will be given to a man as a toy, a gift. Perhaps to an old man. Or to a cruel man. It will not matter."

The girl spoke, her voice weak and the Nubian said, "Fateema pleads with you. Take this child, she says. You saved her. By the law of Allah, she now belongs to you. Bring her up as your child. Do not abandon her."

The Nubian stopped speaking. The smell of blood was heavy in the small room. Tess shook her head. She tried to speak and had to swallow before she could do so.

"This is not possible. I am sorry." Tess took the child to where the girl lay, held the baby up for her to see. Fateema turned her head, refusing to look at her daughter. The bones of the girl's face seemed barely covered by the white skin, her green eyes were huge and sunken, but Tess could see that she was lovely, a more delicate version of her mother.

"Please," Tess said gently. "Please understand how impossible this is." She bent to place the child by the girl's side but Sakeena put out a hand to prevent her. Tess beckoned to the Nubian. "Tell her what I said. And tell her that I am sorry."

The Nubian translated and the girl answered, her voice a whisper. "Then the child will die."

"No, no. She's a strong baby. She needs care, but she'll survive." Tess glanced at Gould for confirmation.

He nodded. "If she gets the attention she needs."

The girl spoke again. "She will die," the Nubian repeated.

"Don't say that—"

"I will let her die." The Nubian's voice was expressionless as he translated the girl's words.

Shocked, Tess turned to Sakeena. "She can't mean that. You cannot allow her—"

"Fateema will not nurse this child." Sakeena's eyes were filled with tears. "It will not see the sun rise."

"I know you don't mean that. You're trying to make me—" Tess tried to keep the wobble out of her voice. "I'm sorry. I cannot do what you ask."

"That baby's going to need a lot of care," Gould said suddenly. "I can't hide her now, but if you can get her on board with you tomorrow, I can see that she gets what she needs until we get her home to the U.S."

Tess looked at him in amazement. "Do you know what you're saying?"

"Yes. Do you?"

"They won't let this baby die. They're just saying that. It's blackmail—"

"I don't think so. Are you ready to take that chance?"

The baby in her arms moved inside the cocoon of white sheet. A sheet that would be her shroud—she could see it in the faces of the two women. Tess tried not to think what Jim would say. She turned to the Nubian. "Tell them I have no way of feeding her—"

Without translating, the Nubian said, "Food for the child will be sent to you."

It was done, Tess thought. "Tell her I cannot bring the child up as a Muslim."

He spoke to Sakeena and the woman kept her eyes on Tess as the Nubian translated her answer. "This is good. We are Circassian, Christian, Muslim only because it is required of us." Sakeena's lips shook as she touched the head of the child. "She is now your daughter."

The baby yawned, showing pink gums, a tiny tongue. Tess held the small form closer. She and Jim had planned to stop using birth control on the ship home, anyway. Jim would have to see that she'd had no choice.

She looked at the Nubian. "What about you? Will you keep this to yourself?"

"You may trust me. I will go to my grave with the secrets of this night."

"I have your secret, also. And my husband has a long reach into this country." She nodded toward Fateema. "You love this woman." Should there be a word, a breath, even a suspicion that such a thing was possible, he was a dead man, and he knew it.

His eyes flickered. "You have my life in your hands."

"As long as we understand each other," Tess said. "Now, you had better take Fateema and her son back to your master. Go with God."

1

Beverly Hills, California
1990

Liz Ryan eased her right foot from her gold sandal and tried not to think of the twenty-seven bones being forced out of alignment by vanity and four inch heels.

The Crystal Room at the Beverly Wilshire Hotel was warm, heady with scent from the immense flower arrangements, women's perfume, the drifts of expensive cigar smoke from the few holdouts still puffing on the cigars they wouldn't allow their patients.

Liz scanned the room and caught sight of Bob Gould pushing his way toward her.

"Lizzie, there you are. I've been looking for you. Did you get my message?"

"Yes, sorry I couldn't be here earlier," she said. "I got hung up at the hospital."

"Well, you're here now, that's the thing. I'm counting on you to help entertain Prince Abdullah. Luckily, he hasn't arrived yet."

Liz looked at Gould's face, alarmed again by the change in him. The pouches under his dark eyes looked bruised, the lines from nose to mouth were noticeably deeper, his hair more gray. In the past six months, Bob had aged five years. Even the chief of surgery at a busy teaching hospital should not have aged that much, that fast. And rumors were circulating, a word here, a word there, sotto voce. She could not bear to think there was any truth in them.

She smiled at him. "You don't need me to entertain your big guns. Where's Melly?" She looked around for Bob's wife of thirty years.

"Backing some poor soul against a political wall, no doubt. I don't want her anywhere near Prince Abdullah. She'd have him into the problems of the Middle East before he could blink."

Liz laughed. "Well, I'm afraid you'll have to count me out for anything serious. I'm operating early in the morning, and I'm not planning a late night."

"A surgeon has to be involved with more than just cut and sew, Liz. Sometimes we have to schmooze with the money—"

"And a beautiful woman can do Saint Luke's a lot of good along those lines," a voice said. "Don't underrate sex when trolling for cash. Right, Bob?"

Liz shook her head. Donald Talbot was a brilliant reconstructive surgeon, she could learn a lot from him. Too bad he was such a pig.

"We are not trolling for cash, as you so elegantly put it, Donald," Bob Gould said. "Tonight is simply for the people on staff at Saint Luke's to meet Prince Abdullah personally."

"A bit of PR for our benefactor, is that it?" Talbot said. "Yeah, well, it's something to celebrate, all right. Where else in these United States are you going to find a pavilion called the Prince Talal bin Abdul Azziz al Sa'ud Surgical Wing attached to a Catholic teaching hospital?" Talbot laughed.

Liz noticed the tightening around Bob's mouth. The minute he got around Donald Talbot, Bob lost his sense of humor. But it really was funny.

"That was a wonderful job you did today," she said to Talbot. "Mr. Cinetti was lucky to have you."

"They're all lucky to have me."

Liz repressed the urge to roll her eyes. Like most great surgeons, Talbot had an ego to match his talent.

Talbot grinned. "Okay, which one was Cinetti?"

"The crushed jaw. I saw his family tonight. They're very grateful."

"Oh, yeah. He'll do okay. He's one of the lucky ones. His insurance will cover most of it." He looked at Bob Gould. "Your protégée here is good. We're going to have to do something for her." He grabbed a glass from the tray of a passing waiter. "Let's talk, Liz. Have your girl call, set something up for next week."

Liz looked down to mask the excitement in her eyes. The great Talbot was going to ask her to become a permanent member of his surgical team. She'd been filling in for the past six months whenever he called, juggling her commitments to be available. Now, if Armin Bodessian at UCLA just fell and broke his leg—just a little bit—it was a done deal.

"Sure. I'll have Ms. Mendoza call first thing Monday." She put a slight emphasis on Pia's name.

Talbot caught her rebuke and laughed. "Okay, have *Ms. Mendoza* call. That suit?" He tapped her shoulder. "You've got to learn to relax, honey. Life's too short." He waved his glass at someone behind her. "Well, there's my bride, looking lost as usual. I'd better go and rescue her." He sauntered off.

Liz stared after him. Could she do it? Could she work with him without killing him?

"Give him his due," Bob Gould said. "He donates time down at County Hospital. There would be a lot more poor kids with cleft palates and God know what else in this town but for him."

"He's impossible. Always touching, slapping the O.R. nurses on the rear."

"No one's complained that I've heard."

"They need their jobs," Liz said. "Can you imagine bringing a sexual harassment suit against a doctor of his international standing?" She gave her eyebrows a quick teasing upward flick. "And a hospital as well-known as Saint Luke's?"

"Liz, please!" Gould clutched his chest. "Not even in jest. Just make sure he keeps his hands off you."

"Mine would be the last ass he ever slapped. I'm pretty fast with a scalpel." Liz squeezed his arm. She had known Bob all her life—he and Melly were her parents' oldest friends. Throughout her decision to go into medicine—and not the diplomatic corps as her parents wanted—the twelve years of training and her choice of specialty, he'd been there to encourage, listen, advise. "Talbot's going to ask me to join his medical team. What do you think?"

"What can I say? He's one of the best in the country. Maybe the world. See what's on his mind but don't commit yourself until we discuss it." Gould tucked her hand into the crook of his arm, guided her through the crowded room toward the door. "Where's Judd tonight?"

"On duty. He might be able to get away later, but you know what an E.R. is like on a Friday night."

A flurry of activity in the motor court attracted their attention, and Gould quickened his step. "Looks as if Prince Abdullah's arriving. Come on, Dr. Ryan. Time to turn on the charm."

Before the black limousine had rolled to a stop, three robed figures were out of the passenger seats, right hands hidden. Hard dark eyes examined the cobbled courtyard between the two wings of the hotel, probing shadowy corners, sweeping over guests entering and leaving, lingering on the ubiquitous paparazzi who staked out the Beverly Wilshire Hotel as a matter of course. Satisfied, one of the men bent to open the rear door.

"What does he think we are?" Liz murmured in Gould's ear. "A bunch of Beverly Hills terrorists?"

"Now, Lizzie, behave yourself," Gould said.

They hovered outside the Crystal Room with half a dozen of the top hierarchy from the hospital. The courtyard was exquisite, tiny lights woven into trees, more cascading over the decorative iron grillwork at either end of the courtyard, which stretched from the glitter of Rodeo Drive on one side, to the quiet of El Camino Drive on the other. Gould moved forward with the rest of the hospital elite. Liz held back, watching.

The man stepping out of the rear door unfolded himself to his full height then paused for a moment. His gold-edged black outer robe billowed in the breeze, his black-and-white checked headdress, held in place by a ring of braided black cords, fluttered.

A nice bit of theater, Liz thought. Only men born to them could manage to look so dashing in those robes—Peter O'Toole excepted, of course. The Saudi was strikingly handsome: long, narrow black eyes under straight, thick brows, prominent nose, heavily mustached as men from that part of the world seemed always to be. Forty, she guessed, maybe older, it was hard to tell. A severe face, unsmiling.

His eyes swept the crowd of people who had stopped to watch his arrival, came back to rest briefly on Liz, then moved on to the welcoming committee.

Inside the Crystal Room, conversation dropped off, a discreet applause greeting Prince Abdullah bin Talal bin Abdul Azziz al Sa'ud as he made his way through the crowd. At his request, there were to be no speeches. This was to be an informal occasion, a chance for him to meet the people who would be working in the new surgical wing named for his father. Two years ago, Prince Talal had suffered an accident at his Bel Air mansion, severing an arm and teams of surgeons at Saint Luke's had reattached it. In gratitude his family had donated a new surgical wing in his name.

The noise level in the room gradually picked up as waiters circulated with trays of champagne. Liz drifted along behind the main group so that she could watch the action, the civilized jockeying for position among her colleagues. She laughed inwardly as Melly Gould engaged the prince in earnest conversation, in spite of Bob's efforts to keep her silent—Melly was a tireless worker in great causes and not easily put off. Liz edged closer so that she could hear the exchange.

"...since Saudi Arabia is just across the Red Sea from the Horn of Africa," Melly was saying, "a short flight, nothing at all, really. Think how easy it would be for your government to ferry food to them. Starving Muslim women and children saved by the protectors of the holy places of the Muslim world. What do you think, Your Highness?"

Abdullah nodded gravely. "As soon as I return, I shall most certainly put the suggestion forward to the correct authority...."

"Liz. Quick." Bob Gould, looking harassed, grabbed Liz's elbow. "Any minute now, Melly will be asking him for a donation to Temple Beth-El's Famine Relief Fund. Come on."

"Melly's making a hell of a good point, though, Bob," she whispered. "Haven't you ever wondered about that? It would be no problem for them, they're so close to the Horn of Africa—"

"Not now, Liz." Gould held her arm in a tight grip and drew her forward. "Your Highness. May I present Dr. Elizabeth Ryan?"

Liz smiled, held out her hand, waited for the prince to

speak first. He gave a slight bow and pressed her fingers gently. A faint, dry scent drifted from him as he moved.

"Dr. Ryan. *Salaam.*"

"Prince Abdullah." Liz wondered if she ought to have used "Your Highness," but it was such a silly form of address, like something out of Gilbert and Sullivan, she couldn't get it past her lips. His robed men stood in a protective half circle behind him, and she caught the intent gaze of one of them, held a touch too long before he lowered his eyes. Momentarily disconcerted, she fumbled for words. "I'd like to add my own thanks for your family's generosity. The new pavilion is a wonderful addition to our hospital."

Kwang Ho Lee, the administrator of Saint Luke's, standing with the president of the hospital, heads of departments and their wives, nodded and smiled his agreement. They all looked as if their smiles were pinned in place by surgical staples.

Prince Abdullah inclined his head. "A small expression of thanks for the life of Prince Talal."

"I trust the prince is still in good health?"

"Thanks be to Allah, he is." A waiter offered a tray and Abdullah took a glass of champagne, handed it to Liz, helped himself to plain sparkling water. "What is your specialty, Dr. Ryan?"

"Reconstructive surgery." Liz looked at him over the rim of the glass, enjoying his surprise. She'd take a bet that he assumed she was a pediatrician. Amazing the number of men who did.

Abdullah met her eyes and laughed. "You have surprised me. But then, I think you knew you would." He glanced at Bob Gould, who was half turned away, speaking to his wife. The Prince moved to separate himself and Liz from the group surrounding them, creating a small island of privacy. "The second time you have surprised me."

"How is that possible? We've never met."

"Your name. Ryan. Irish, is it not?"

"Yes."

"But I think you are not Irish. You are pure Circassian."

"Circassian?" Liz shook her head. Talk about ancestry, anyone's ancestry, made her uncomfortable. "I don't think so."

"Oh, yes. There are many Circassian women in my country. They are much valued for their beauty."

He made them sound like prize horses. Liz sipped the champagne, wondering where this conversation was going.

"You have the classic Circassian coloring. The deep red hair. Eyes the color of fine emeralds."

Whew, Liz thought. "Sorry to disappoint you. Irish. County Mayo." She'd always thought of herself as Irish. Her parents had never said otherwise—they always said they didn't know. But she'd never believed them.

"There are Circassian women in my family. Their skin is their pride. Of course, in my country they are careful to keep out of the sun for fear of darkening that pure ivory tone."

My God, he's coming on to me, Liz thought. She felt the blood creep up her throat, stain her face. Damn. How old would she have to be before she outgrew blushing? Only her mother still thought it cute. She cast around for a way to change the subject without appearing rude, God forbid, to the princely benefactor of Saint Luke's Hospital.

"You must give me a geography lesson, Prince Abdullah. Where is Circassia? I've heard of it, but I'm not quite sure where it is."

"An area of southern Russia famous for the beauty of its women. Red-haired, green-eyed women."

"How do people from southern Russia find their way to Saudi Arabia? I thought yours was a society closed to outsiders."

Dark eyes suddenly hard, brows gathered in a frown, Abdullah looked at her. Then he laughed. "I think you are fencing words with me. Good. That is good." Smiling, he said, "They came along the ancient caravan routes as slaves, the women as concubines. But we Saudis have always been a liberal people. Our slaves came from the four corners, but it was not uncommon for our concubines to become our wives, mingling their bloodlines with ours."

That explained why the three men standing behind him were of such different types, Liz thought. Two of them were clearly Arabic, but the man who had stared at her was black, with strong African features.

What on earth could he have been looking for?

Bob Gould watched the interchange over Melly's shoulder. He had never seen Liz look so beautiful. Green eyes sparkling, a flush to her skin. An instinctual response, blood to blood? Mentally, he shook himself. Utter nonsense, no basis in science. But just the same, suddenly he wished Judd were there. He grabbed the arm closest to him, dragged the surprised doctor toward Abdullah.

"Prince Abdullah, may I introduce," he looked at the owner of the arm, "Dr. Louise Eberhardt. Eminent pediatrician."

"Ah, Dr. Eberhardt," Abdullah said smoothly. "A pleasure."

Louise Eberhardt pumped the prince's hand, her voice boomed a greeting. Liz smiled at Abdullah over Louise's shoulder, then stepped back and turned away, as if glad of the chance to remove herself from his unsettling presence.

Bob noticed that Abdullah kept his eye on her, a tall, slim figure in a white silk suit, as she melted into the crowd.

2

Liz opened the door from the garage, stepped into the service area and heard the phone ringing. Not already, she thought—she was on call this weekend but she'd only left the hospital fifteen minutes ago. Dropping her briefcase and jacket onto a hall chair, she dashed into her study, leaned across the desk and picked up the jangling phone.

"Dr. Ryan."

"Hey, sweets," Judd Cameron's voice said. "Hope you didn't wait for me last night."

"No. I was tired, left early. What happened to you?"

"Nothing. Just the E.R. being its usual nasty Friday night self. How about dinner later? Thought we might run up the coast to Malibu."

"Sounds lovely, but I'm on call. I'll decant Chinese here though if you like. Bring some wine—" The doorbell chimed. Automatically Liz looked at her watch. Four o'clock on a Saturday afternoon. She wasn't expecting anyone. "Got to go, someone's at the door. Come about seven-thirty. And bring a decent bottle. I don't want one of your undrinkable bargains left over to pollute my kitchen."

"Okay, okay." He was laughing as she hung up.

She opened the front door and stared in astonishment at her visitor.

The dark eyes of Abdullah's black bodyguard lingered on hers—a breath too long?—before he bent his head in greeting.

"*Salaam,* madam."

"Hello." Liz was at a loss. She looked at the mass of flowers he held. They were orchids, of a type she had never seen before. "How lovely."

He bowed. "With the compliments of my master, His Highness Prince Abdullah bin Talal bin Abdul Aziz al Sa'ud."

She took the orchids from him. The vase, crammed with blossoms, was surprisingly heavy. "Thank you. They are very beautiful." Small and delicate, creamy white with blushed throats. "Please tell Prince Abdullah…" Tell him what? "Please thank the prince."

"*Salaam,* madam," the bodyguard said again. He bowed, backed up three or four paces, then turned and walked to the street, his sandaled feet silent on the graveled path.

Slowly Liz closed the door. As she passed her study, she glanced out of the window, surprised to see that he was still outside, standing motionless by a black Mercedes, his eyes riveted on the house. Puzzled, she stood watching him for a moment, then the weight of the vase demanded it be put down, and she went into the sitting room.

By seven-thirty a small pitcher of martinis was in the freezer, just enough for Judd—on call tonight, she would not be drinking. The table in the bow window overlooking the garden was set with linen and crystal; thick white candles waited for a match. The food from the little Chinese restaurant on Wilshire was in bowls ready for the microwave—about the extent of her cooking. Each time she passed the open door of her study, Liz glanced through the window facing the street, unnerved to find the bodyguard still there. Still watching. Maybe she ought to invite him to dinner; he certainly gave no indication that he intended to leave.

She lit the fire—it was cool enough, a sea fog had rolled in from the Pacific only a block away—then stood back to survey her handiwork. Not bad. Rather good, in fact. It promised a romantic evening, something she and Judd rarely managed. She selected a CD, listened for a moment to the heartbreak of Billie Holiday fill the room, then went upstairs to change into Judd's favorite, her green velvet caftan.

She took the orchids with her, uncertain about explaining them to Judd, yet strangely unwilling to put them in her study where she could not see them. Finally she chose a table by the window in her bedroom.

Judd banged on the front door fifteen minutes early, and Liz ran down to open it, eager to see him, to be swept up by him.

"Hey, babe." He put his arms around her, juggling yellow roses and the bottle of wine, and nuzzled her neck. "Mmm, you smell good."

"The latest thing. Eau de O.R. Like it?" Liz glanced over his shoulder. Only now was the Mercedes gliding away from the curb. Perturbed, she held Judd closer.

"Very romantic." Judd closed the door with a practiced kick, managing to deposit bottle and roses on the hall table without loosening his hold on her. He ran his hands over her buttocks, pulling her against him.

She opened her mouth to his tongue, dragging his polo shirt free of his belt, loosening the buckle so that she could slip her hands into the tangle of black hair on his belly. He was already hard.

"What do you think?" he murmured. "Now or later?"

"I think both."

"Upstairs?"

"By the fire."

A trail of discarded clothing marked their passage from the hall to the rug in front of the blazing fire in the sitting room.

Judd refilled Liz's glass with Pellegrino, his own from a bottle of Iron Horse Chardonnay. "As usual, my compliments to the chef.''

"Jesus Sung Ling."

"You're kidding."

"What can I tell you?" she said, laughing. "That's his name. Jesus Sung Ling. The cultural mix. His mother's Guatemalan.''

Liz rolled a pellet of melted wax between her fingers and studied him. Even in the soft light of the candles, Judd looked every day his thirty-eight years. A big man, six-two, 220 pounds. Not handsome, but a good face. A typical Celt—gray eyes, dark hair, nose bent in the middle, the result of an encounter with a hockey puck. He still played with a team in the San Fernando Valley, on the other side of the Santa Monica Mountains.

"When are you going to let me fix that nose? A little carving on the inside there. A little bone graft in the middle. No big deal."

"Keep your hands off my nose. It's okay."

Liz laughed. "Big guy like you, scared of a little surgery.''

"When are you going to marry me? Big girl like you, scared of a little commitment."

"Don't start that again." She rose to her feet to clear away the plates.

Judd caught at her hand. "Liz. I love you. You love me—" He stopped. "You do love me. I just wonder when are you going to admit how much."

Liz dropped a kiss onto his forehead. "I'm going to keep you guessing," she said. She dropped her voice a throaty octave and lowered her chin so that she could look at him from beneath fluttering lashes. "Add to my mystery, dahling.''

Judd grinned and pulled her onto his lap. "Yeah? Well, spare me. You're mysterious enough."

Liz leaned back against his encircling arms, linked her fingers behind his neck.

"Donald Talbot is going to ask me to join his team. He as good as told me so last night."

"Liz, that's terrific! You'll be staying in Santa Monica. Let's get married—"

"Sweetheart, I can't even think of marriage. It takes too much effort—"

"What effort? We'll call your folks, see the judge, go on a honeymoon, I pack a suitcase and move in. Simple. Or we can get a larger place. Whatever you want."

Her duplex was large enough: two bedrooms, a den she used as her study. The down payment had been a gift from her parents, a not-too-subtle inducement to stay in California at the end of her residency. She was their only child and they wanted to keep her close.

"That's not the point," she said. "Being married is the effort. I need everything in me to make it in my specialty. It's an all-male club, I can't afford distractions—"

Judd tipped her off his lap and rose to his feet. "Guess this is where I came in." He piled the congealing remains of moo-shoo pork and lemon chicken onto a tray. "Did old Jesus send over some fortune cookies?"

"Oh, Judd, that didn't come out right. I'm sorry. I didn't mean you were only a distraction in my life—"

"It's okay, babe. Let's not spoil the evening with this. You don't want to marry me right now. I'll survive." He leered at her. "Anyway, I have a plan."

"Yeah?"

"Yeah. I'm going to wear you down with my wit and charm."

Liz put her arms around him. "That you've already done. Let's take the cookies to bed for me, the rest of the wine for you, and watch a video—"

"I've got a better idea. It's Saturday night. First we pray

you don't get called out, then we make long, leisurely love all night and sleep in tomorrow.''

"Well, that, too. After. I got that William Hurt movie where he's a doctor who becomes a patient in his own hospital—"

Judd started to laugh.

"What? What?" She looked up into his face, laughing with him. "What did I say?"

"Does it ever occur to you to get a movie not about doctoring? An old John Wayne, or a Monty Python?"

"Yeah, well, smart-ass, I got one of those, too."

The bedroom was calm and inviting, a restful palette of cream and sand, touches of blue and celadon, thanks to her mother's eye for color. Before going into the bathroom, Liz switched on only one of the bedside lamps, hoping the orchids would be lost in the dim light.

Over the sound of running water, she heard Judd moving around in the bedroom, undressing, putting a match to the logs in the fireplace. Then his voice said, "Where did these come from?"

Her toothbrush stopped. She didn't need to ask what he meant. "What?" she called.

"This giant bunch of flowers. Where did they come from?"

She rinsed her mouth, put her head around the door.

"Oh, that's what came to the door when we were talking this afternoon."

"So, who are they from?"

"The Saudi. Prince Abdullah."

Judd didn't answer. Liz threw her caftan over a chair. Wearing only a deep-green silk teddy, she walked to the fire, sat on her heels while she poked at the logs. She stole a glance at Judd, hoping he'd notice the firelight on her bare shoulders and legs and forget the orchids. She didn't want to talk about Abdullah. Particularly not now, and certainly not with Judd.

Why hadn't she left the damn orchids downstairs in her study?

"Pretty lavish," Judd said. "Expensive vase, too, by the look of it."

"Mmm." It was Waterford—hand-cut crystal, highly faceted. Too fancy for her taste.

"What are they, these flowers?" he asked.

Judd couldn't tell a daisy from a sweet pea. Early in their relationship she'd told him she loved yellow roses. So that was what he brought her. Yellow roses. Every time he thought of flowers, he thought of yellow roses. She always found it funny. And rather sweet.

"Orchids."

He bent, put his nose to the delicate blossoms. "They don't smell."

"Maybe if you let me fix your nose, they would." She grinned at him, but he didn't smile back. "Just teasing. Orchids don't have any scent. Come on, Judd. Lighten up. I bet he sent them to everyone."

"Generous guy. Do you think everyone got a little jewelry box, as well?"

"Jewelry box?"

She walked over to him. Deep among the orchids was a small, green velvet box. Liz retrieved the box and an ivory-colored envelope and could have kicked herself for overlooking them. She drew out the card.

"Don't keep me in suspense." Judd waited for her to read it to him. When she didn't, he reached over, took the card from her fingers.

"'To match Circassian eyes,'" he read aloud. No signature. Judd turned the card over. Nothing. He looked at her. "Circassian eyes? What the hell does that mean?"

Liz held out the box. Nestled in the white satin interior

were earrings, large cabochon emeralds of a deep pure green, encircled by diamonds.

The prince had a good memory. The emeralds were the exact color of her eyes.

3

"Who delivered this?" Prince Abdullah turned over the package, looking for a name or a return address.

"A messenger, Abdullah," Nassir said. Free men used only first names to address their princes, and Nassir had served Abdullah's family long and honorably, as slave and now as a free man. "The man awaits your attention. But I, Nassir, have examined the package. It is what it appears to be. Harmless."

Abdullah nodded. He had to be careful. These were treacherous times in Saudi Arabia, with the mad Iraqi Saddam Hussein threatening the oil fields, and fundamentalists—his own brother Bandr among them—maneuvering to gain power with the insane idea they could repel the encroaching twenty-first century, save the country from the influence of the West.

Abdullah picked up a small dagger from the desk and sliced open the brown paper wrapping. A green velvet jeweler's box became visible.

The hot blood of anger rushed to his face. She had returned his gift. He looked up.

"This is all?"

"A letter, Abdullah." Nassir placed the envelope on the desk.

Abdullah swung his swivel chair around to face the window, turning his back to Nassir. Sunlight streamed through the lacework of the palmetto palms outside the mansion he'd bought on a whim, glinting on the distant aquamarine pool, dappling light and shade across the green hills of Bel Air rising beyond. Beautiful, but unlike most of his countrymen, he'd found he could enjoy such depth of color for only a short time before he began to long for the subtle tones of sand, the feel of it beneath his feet, the call of the *muezzin* at dusk.

He opened the envelope, took out the folded note. "Prince Abdullah," he read. "Please accept my thanks for the orchids. They are exquisite, a type I have never seen before.

"The earrings I must return to you, with thanks for your generosity. In our culture, for a woman to accept such a lavish gift from a man she hardly knows is not considered appropriate. I hope you understand.

"Sincerely, Liz Ryan."

He did, indeed, understand. He had been impatient. Abdullah swung his chair back to face Nassir.

"Dismiss the messenger."

Nassir bowed. Abdullah waited while his bodyguard crossed the rich blue of the Naim carpet and silently closed the door behind him, then he reached for the telephone.

The ringing tone went on and on. He was about to hang up and try again when a voice sang in his ear.

"Saint Luke's Hospital."

"Dr. Ryan, please."

"Which Dr. Ryan would that be?"

"Dr. Elizabeth Ryan."

"Dr. Liz Ryan?"

"Yes." Abdullah held back a sharp reply. "Dr. Liz Ryan."

"Transferring you."

He drummed his fingers.

"Dr. Ryan's office. Pia Mendoza speaking."

"Dr. Ryan, please."

"Dr. Ryan is not available. Do you want to leave a message?"

"When is she returning?"

"Hard to say. She's in surgery all day. She'll be calling in for her messages, though."

"This is Prince Abdullah bin Talal bin Abdul Azziz—"

"Can you spell that, please?"

Abdullah held on to his temper. Since birth, his slightest wish had been fulfilled within minutes—not the best training for dealing with a democracy. He spelled out his name, omitting the title.

Still dressed in O.R. greens, Liz switched on the light over her desk, leaving the rest of the office in darkness. Pia was gone, her connecting office dark and silent, the bustle of activity in the corridor outside winding down as the evening progressed. Liz opened the bottom drawer in her desk, rummaged around in her stash of emergency supplies, ripped open a small packet of peanuts—she was ravenous, there had been no time for lunch—and crammed them into her mouth as she riffled through the pile of messages. During the course of the day she had dealt with the more urgent. These were the remainder Pia considered marginal.

The name jumped out at her. "Abdullah bin Talal, etc.," Pia had written.

Liz lowered herself into her chair, leaned her chin into her hands, stared at the name as if she could make it disappear if she stared hard enough. Not that she wanted it to disappear. Not really. She knew he'd call, sooner or later. All day, whenever she'd had a minute to breathe, in spite of herself, she'd thought of him.

"Wouldn't leave a number," Pia had written on the pink telephone slip. "Said he'd call you again at seven, then at eight. Eager beaver."

Liz glanced at her watch. Almost seven. She could wait,

or leave now and let the switchboard take a message. They wouldn't give out her home number, and she wasn't on call tonight.

Her thoughts turned to Judd. He'd astounded her with his jealousy—it was so unlike him. She'd made light of the earrings. A gesture of goodwill, nothing personal, she'd said. A bit clumsy on the prince's part, but no big deal.

"So what's with the Circassian eyes? That sounds plenty personal to me."

"He's got relatives with the same color eyes as mine, that's all. He told me so at the reception. Came from someplace in southern Russia. We had a conversation about it, small talk, you know how these things go." She'd become increasingly irritated at having to defend herself. "Emerald earrings are about as significant to this guy as a book. He probably thought it was cute. He comes from a different culture—"

"I'll say. One that's notorious for the way it treats women. Or doesn't that matter to you?"

She'd shrugged and refused to engage any further. The evening was ruined. They'd made love, but not with the leisurely exploration they'd planned. They'd both been urgent and impatient, eager to finish. She'd slipped the earrings into a drawer out of sight, and on Sunday they were not mentioned. She didn't tell Judd about the bodyguard watching the house, as she had intended. And perversely, she didn't tell him she planned to return the damn earrings first thing Monday morning.

At her elbow, the light on her phone started to flash. It was seven precisely. She could be out of the door before it rang, tell herself she hadn't heard it.

The telephone rang. She picked it up. "Dr. Ryan."

"Dr. Liz Ryan?"

"Yes."

"This is Abdullah bin Talal."

"Oh. Hello. Thank you again for the orchids, and, of course, for the lovely vase."

"But not for the earrings."

"No." She started to relax, secure in the darkness, only her hands visible in the pool of light on her desk. "They're very beautiful, but I couldn't possibly accept such a gift."

"I understand. I will keep them for you."

"No, I think you don't understand. Jewels like that are not a casual gift. They are simply not acceptable."

"You will accept dinner, perhaps?"

"Thank you, but I don't think so."

"You are not married, Liz Ryan, so you must have another reason."

"Prince Abdullah, I really don't think—"

"Abdullah," he said.

"What?"

"Abdullah. Did you notice I did not use a title with your Miss Mendoza? Very discreet, I thought."

"Yes, but completely unnecessary. Your name is well-known at St. Luke's."

He laughed. "I think not to Miss Mendoza. In this city, so many different names from so many countries, they must all run together. Who would remember one more? I will pick you up at nine, we'll talk more over dinner."

"No, I'm sorry. It isn't possible. I have a commitment—"

"Dr. Judd Cameron?"

She was taken aback. "How did you know about Dr. Cameron?"

"I know a great deal, Dr. Ryan. But I am right? He is the commitment?"

For a brief moment, she hesitated, then said, "Yes. He is."

"Ah. Well. Our paths will cross. I will keep the earrings for you. Good night."

The dial tone sounded in her ear. For a moment Liz sat with the receiver in her hand, struggling with a tangle of feelings—excitement, regret, confusion, certainty that this was not the end.

She dropped the phone into its cradle, switched off her light. She still had rounds to make.

In the house in Bel Air, Abdullah tilted his chair and swung around to face the window. For fifteen minutes he stared at the hillside rising behind the swimming pool, oblivious to the ribbon of molten gold where the evening sun touched the water. Then he turned back to his desk, picked up the phone and punched out a number. A voice answered.

Abdullah leaned back. "Dr. Gould, this is Abdullah bin Talal. I have a proposition I think might interest you. Could we meet, perhaps?" He listened, then said, "I am leaving for Washington in the morning. Tonight would be a good time if that suits you? Good. Tonight, then."

4

Liz pulled off the surgical mask and removed the cap covering her hair—both hair and cap were soaked with sweat. She was still keyed up, eager to join the informal postoperative analysis already underway among the rest of the team. She dropped her bloody gloves into the bin and shouldered open the door to the surgeons' lounge, headed for the coffee.

"Jesus." Tom Randall was on her heels. "I thought I was going to lose it."

"Yeah, it was pretty bad." Liz handed him the coffee she had poured for herself. She'd noticed his white face, the staring eyes over the mask when Talbot handed the cancerous jawbone with the partial tongue dangling from it to the nurse. The mutilation had been horrifying, half the patient's face gone, the throat a gaping hole. Donald Talbot had gone on to do a magnificent reconstruction, completing it with a two-foot slab of skin he'd lifted from the shoulder. The patient would be eating solid food in a few weeks. That was why she had chosen to go into reconstructive surgery, to be able to perform miracles like that. "You have to remember what we're doing here, Tom."

"Yeah, I guess."

Liz touched his shoulder as she turned toward the table. Someone should advise Tom to stick to face-lifts, she thought. He'd never have the balls for this line of work.

"Dr. Ryan." Larisha Brown's head appeared around the door. "Dr. Gould wants to see you."

Liz glanced at the clock.

Larisha raised her eyebrows. "Right away, doctor."

"Tell him I just got out of surgery and I've got another case in an hour."

"When you decide to refuse a request from the chief of surgery, you'd better tell him yourself, doctor," Larisha said. "Don't ask me to run interference for you." She withdrew her head and slammed the door.

"Wow! Take that!" Rusty Walsh, still wearing blood-spattered surgical greens, was sprawled at the table drinking coffee. He grinned. "Better get going, Liz. Don't keep the master waiting."

Exasperated, Liz got to her feet and took a last hurried gulp of coffee before moving to the door.

"I hear he's leaving us," Rusty said. "Too bad, what's happening. He was a great surgeon in his day."

"He is still a great surgeon." Liz stopped, swept her eyes over the group of men at the table. "And just what is supposed to be happening?"

Walsh shrugged, glanced at the other young doctors. Embarrassed, they stared into their coffee mugs. Rusty said, "Sorry, Liz. Maybe I'm mistaken. I guess you'd be the first to know if he was going."

Liz paused in the doorway. "Don't believe everything you hear, guys. Especially about a man like Dr. Gould. You'd like to be half as good a surgeon as he is any day."

She punched the elevator button impatiently. Rumors! The hospital was a hotbed of rumors. Who was sleeping with whom. Who had marital problems. Who drank too much. Who was writing their own prescriptions for drugs.

She walked past Larisha's desk in Dr. Gould's outer office and waved a hand.

"What are you doing, Doctor?" Larisha started to her feet. "You can't barge in there—"

"Thanks, I can find my own way in, Larisha." Liz knocked and opened the door to the inner office in one motion.

Bob stood behind his desk, telephone to his ear. He looked at Liz blankly, then turned to face the window behind him. Liz glanced at her watch. She forced herself to browse the medical books on the shelf, trying not to listen to what he was saying.

"I'll have to call you back, I have someone here now. Goddamn it, you'll get it, I told you that, every dime. You always have. Now don't call me here again." He slammed the receiver down, stood for a moment with his hand still on the telephone, shoulders slumped. With an effort, he straightened his back, turned to face Liz, a smile pasted on his face.

"Come in, Liz. How did you get past Larisha?"

Liz wished she hadn't. "Is everything all right?"

"Sure. Of course." He gestured to a chair. His hand was shaking. "Sit down."

Liz shook her head. "I haven't got time. I'm in surgery again in forty minutes." She had to look away from the anguish she saw in his eyes. The rumors were true—she couldn't pretend any longer not to see what was happening to him. It was worse than she thought. So far, he'd been lucky, he hadn't made a massive mistake in the O.R. or killed someone. He would, though, sooner or later, if he didn't stop drinking.

"Have you seen Talbot yet?" Gould asked. "It's been, what, two, three weeks since he asked you to call him?"

"I saw him yesterday. I didn't call you, I've barely had a minute to breathe—"

"Has he offered you anything?"

"Yes, but now is not a good time for me—"

"Did you give him an answer?"

"No, of course not, not without speaking to you." She looked at her watch. "I've really got to go—"

"Well, I've got a proposition for you. You'll find it very interesting—"

"Bob, can we talk about this later? I really do have to go." She opened the door to the outer office to emphasize her words.

"Sure. Of course. You get back to work. Come on over to the house when you're through. Melly would love to see you. We'll have a drink and talk."

Gently, Liz closed the door behind her. He was in deep trouble. It was true—the whispers that assistants did the work he was scheduled to do because his hands were too shaky, that more than once before surgery he'd had a drink to steady them. All of it. True.

Rusty was right. He wasn't the surgeon he had been—he wasn't the man he had been. The booze was catching up with him at last. It had to happen.

Her godfather. Her mentor. It was as if a curtain had suddenly swung back, and she could see the man who'd nurtured her career like a father falling apart before her eyes.

The Goulds' home on Mesa Road above the Santa Monica Bay, an original Craftsman kept in immaculate style, was barely visible behind the giant old Moresby Bay fig trees that lined the street. Liz parked in the driveway, waved at Gould already walking toward the car and guessed he must have been watching for her. Briefly she wondered why, then dismissed the thought as he opened the car door and held out his hand.

"Come on in, honey. Melly's still out, it's her afternoon at Children's Hospital, so we'll have an hour or two by ourselves to talk." Gould put an arm across her shoulder as he walked her into the house.

"I can't stay that long, Bob. Judd'll be over in a while. He's leaving tomorrow for his reserve duty, two months this year—still paying his debt to the Marine Corps for his medical training. He'd like to have a quick drink with you before we go on to dinner."

"Oh."

Liz looked at him. "That's okay, isn't it?" Judd had always been as welcome here as she was.

"Sure, of course. I just hope the two of us have time to talk." He threw open the doors to the wooden deck overlooking the bay, then gestured to one of the chairs around the redwood table. The umbrella was folded, allowing what sun there was to filter through the eucalyptus and sycamore trees and warm the deck. June weather was cool and foggy at the beach. If the sun did finally manage to break through, it was late in the day. "What's your pleasure, madam?"

"A glass of white wine would be good."

Gould went to the outdoor bar, poured the drinks, brought them to the table. Liz found herself noticing that he'd barely splashed his Scotch with water and had used no ice cubes that would dilute the whisky.

"Well, Lizzie, here's to a great future." Gould raised his glass, took a deep drink. "Now, what did Talbot have to say?"

She ignored his question, instead plunged right in to what was on her mind. "Bob, I heard today that you were thinking of leaving Saint Luke's. Is it true?"

He stared at her. "That damned hospital. I swear to God, sometimes I think it's wired for sound."

Wine spilled over her fingers from her tipping glass and Liz slid it onto the table. "Then it is true. You're leaving."

"I've made no decision. That's one of the things I wanted to talk to you about. A lot depends on you." Gould rubbed the palms of his hands with a napkin as if they were sweating, then aimed the crushed paper at the bin. "Bull's-eye."

"On me! What's it to do with me?"

"I've been sitting on something for a couple of weeks, Liz, so you know I've given it a lot of thought." He stared out over the trees, away from her searching eyes. "I've been offered a great position abroad. I want you to go with me."

"Where?"

"Saudi Arabia." He leaned back, looked at her. "For a year. Just a year."

The words took her breath away. "You're crazy. There's a war going on out there—"

"In Kuwait, Liz, not in Saudi Arabia. You know our government will never allow those oil fields to be threatened. Anyway, that's really why this position has opened up." He held up a hand to stop her before she could break in. "Just hear what I have to say. That's all. Just listen. Nothing's going to happen in Saudi Arabia, we know that, but because of the situation the Saudis are reassessing their entire medical infrastructure. They want someone to establish what needs to be done, draw up a blueprint, implement some changes, light a few fires. Quite a challenge, Liz."

At least it meant he wouldn't be operating, she thought. "Good. Sounds like a great offer. Are you going to take it?"

"Haven't made up my mind yet. They're going to create specialized surgical teams, with the mobility to respond to provincial towns if they do come under attack by the Iraqis, which, of course, they won't, but they need to be ready. With a bit of luck, if you're with me, I'll even have enough spare time to do some of the writing I'm too busy to do now. Maybe publish again."

"Sounds terrific. Made for you."

"Yes, that's what I think. But I can't do it alone. I want you with me."

Why was he pressuring her like this? Liz wondered. She said, "Bob, I'm flattered, really I am, but this is not my kind of thing. Anyway, Los Angeles is full of guys who'd jump at the chance to work with you, in Timbuktu, if that's what you offered.''

"Lizzie, this is a great opportunity for you.'' He kept his eyes on the glass in his hand. ''And you're the one I want, not some fly-by-night guy looking for a bit of action.''

"Bob, please. You must be joking. I'm on track with Talbot—''

Gould did not meet her eyes. ''Lizzie honey, I need your help.''

Liz looked over his shoulder. Around the Bay, lights were coming on from Point Dume in the north to Palos Verdes in the south. Her eyes misted and she willed the tears back. How could she have been so blind to what was happening to him? Since she was a young teenager, beginning to think of medicine as a career, he'd been generosity itself. He'd given her years of encouragement, showered the same love on her he'd given to his son Jake. Always generous with time and interest, never holding back.

Her voice gentle, she said, ''You don't need me, Bob. You'll have Melly.''

"Melly won't be going.''

Liz couldn't believe she'd heard correctly. ''What? A year's separation from Melly? Are you sure you want to do this?''

"It's time for me to get out of the rut, same thing, day in day out. It's driving me crazy. I need to stir things up a bit. And the salary is pretty impressive.''

"Yes, but without Melly?''

"Jake's got another year at Dartmouth and he needs to know someone's here at home.''

"He's still clean?'' she asked anxiously. Jake was like her kid brother, they'd been brought up so closely. Until he went to college and everything changed.

"Sure, absolutely. Goes to his NA meetings regularly, they've got groups on campus."

Liz nodded, relieved. Someone should take Bob to AA in Santa Monica, she thought. Hell of a lot easier to get to than Saudi Arabia.

"So, come on, Lizzie, what do you think? I wouldn't ask you to do this if I didn't think it was a great opportunity for you. King Khaled Clinic in Jeddah is world-class—"

She stopped him. "I'm a reconstructive surgeon, Bob. I don't want to organize surgical teams or write guidelines for wartime medical networks. I want hands-on work with an established team in my own field—"

"You could have that, Liz. Your own team. You'd head it up."

She sat stunned for a moment. "Bob, that's crazy at this point in my career." She shook her head, trying to keep a cap on her soaring ego. She was good, maybe better than anyone else in the city except Talbot, but she was not ready for that. Or maybe she was. "Anyway, I can't see myself buried in the third world somewhere."

"You wouldn't be buried, far from it. I'm telling you—no, I'm guaranteeing you—you'll get experience there you'll have to wait years even to see in this country. I'd make sure of that."

She wondered how he thought he could pull that off if he was going simply to inspect, evaluate, suggest change. But she didn't ask—it would only put him on a spot. "I'd rather hone my skills with Talbot. So thanks, but no thanks."

Gould got up to refill his glass. "What's the deal with Talbot?"

She told him. "It's a great offer."

"And the downside?"

"I don't know," she said. "I'd work only on his cases, none of my own. That's the biggest problem. No chance to build a practice. That and his personality. He made a point of telling me that he and his girls—he meant his scrub nurses—understand each other. Made it quite clear that he runs the show, told me point-blank he would entertain no suggestions for change. I'm going to have to watch him slap rear ends, pinch nipples, listen to his sexist jokes.'' She shrugged. ''No problem, as long as he keeps his hands off me.''

''You think he will?''

''He'd better.''

''So you do nothing but his work, then when you feel ready to move on, you struggle for years, waiting for referrals, grateful for the crumbs that fall from the great man's table.''

''Well, that's the way it works, isn't it?''

Gould shook his head. ''Why do it the hard way? With the kind of experience you could get at King Khaled Clinic, I'd see to it that you got an appointment wherever you want. The National Institutes of Health in Baltimore if you like. I've got a lot of strings I can pull.''

''I don't want to go to Saudi Arabia, Bob.'' But she was wavering, unable to bear the look in his eyes. He'd given her so much, never once asked anything of her. ''Thanks for the offer. Who's behind it?'' She grinned. ''Prince Abdullah?'' She'd meant her teasing words as a joke, and was surprised to see Gould's face turn a dangerously mottled red.

''What put that in your head?'' he asked. ''I thought I was offering you a great opportunity.''

''Well, it's all right if he did, Bob. I'm sorry if I said the wrong thing.'' She wanted to ask why he was so defensive, but didn't have the nerve. It was not the way a young doctor spoke to Dr. Robert Gould, no matter how close their families were.

''No, no. The offer came as a complete surprise, that's

all. I'd mentioned casually that I thought everyone should get shaken up in their middle years, keep the blood flowing to the brain, just party chatter. Abdullah called me out of the blue. Said part of the reason he was here in the United States was to recruit someone to do this job. Didn't even dream I'd be interested.''

"Well, good luck, you've got your challenge. It will certainly be an experience.''

Gould got up, poured himself another drink, put it on the table before him without tasting it. "Liz, before you turn this down, I want you to go home and talk to your parents. Tell them about this conversation.''

Liz laughed. "They'll tell me to grab Talbot's offer before he takes it to Armin Bodessian at UCLA.''

"You might be surprised. Ask them what they can tell you about Saudi Arabia. What you learn from them could change your life.''

Her heartbeat suddenly skipped around. "What could they possibly tell me that would make a difference?''

"Did they ever tell you about their time in Saudi Arabia?''

"My parents? In Saudi Arabia? No. They've never told me that. You've got to be kidding!''

"They were there, Liz. In Jeddah, on the Red Sea.''

Her mouth was suddenly dry. How could they have forgotten something so important in their lives? "How do you know?''

"Ask them. Then come talk to me again.''

"No, you tell me now. What are you talking about?'' Her heart was pounding.

The peal of the doorbell floated out to them. Gould shoved back his chair, rose to his feet.

"Bob, Lupe will get it. It's Judd. Please, what's this about?''

Gould patted her arm as he passed.

Liz stared after him. He always left it to their Salvadoran maid to open the door, so obviously he didn't want to answer her questions. Then why had he opened that particular can of worms? Why now?

She rose to her feet, took her drink to the wooden rail at the edge of the deck and looked over the wooded canyon to the ocean beyond. Her father had started his career in the Foreign Service years ago, she knew that. But he and her mother had never breathed a word of Saudi Arabia. Voices drifted from the house. Gould's and another. A male voice. Not Judd's. She turned, almost choked on a quick indrawn breath.

Smiling broadly, Bob was ushering a tall, robed figure through the French doors.

"Prince Abdullah, you've met Dr. Elizabeth Ryan."

"Ah, yes. Not old friends, but certainly we've met. How do you do, Dr. Ryan?"

Liz took the outstretched hand. Thoughts stuttered incoherently. Bob should have told her he was coming, given her a chance to… She looked like hell, it had been a long day…. Goddammit, this was no surprise visit; she'd been maneuvered into this. Quickly, she shifted mental gears.

"How nice to see you again, Prince Abdullah. I hope you are enjoying your stay in Los Angeles."

"I regret I have not had the opportunity to see much of Los Angeles, Dr. Ryan. I have been tied up in Washington since we last met."

"Prince Abdullah, can I get you something?" Gould said. "Sparkling water? A soft drink?"

"Apple juice, perhaps, and a little Pellegrino with it. Thank you."

"Excuse me, then."

Bob left them alone, and Prince Abdullah motioned Liz toward the rail, passing without comment the outdoor bar that held a selection of juices and bottled water among the wine and liquor.

"It was my hope that you could be prevailed upon to show me something of your city, Dr. Ryan. I have a few days before I must return to Riyadh."

"I'm sorry, Prince Abdullah, I can't do that. Nothing has changed since our conversation on the telephone. I have the same commitment that I had then, and I'm a very busy doctor, besides. No time for sight-seeing. But if you ask Dr. Gould, I bet he'd be delighted to free up some time. Disneyland is a lot of fun." She grinned at him. "Knotts Berry Farm?"

Abdullah laughed. "Not exactly what I had in mind."

"You should have nothing in mind concerning me, Prince Abdullah." Her pulse hammered. Her blood felt hot, racing through her veins. "And you really must stop sending me flowers."

Twice a week, a mass of the same orchids he'd sent to her home arrived in her office. No message. Pia didn't know how they got there; she'd never seen them delivered.

"It would please me if you call me Abdullah. And I will call you Liz. You will permit that? It is what your friends call you, is it not?" He raised his eyebrows, waiting for her to agree. He smiled when she nodded. "Flowers are acceptable, I believe. I simply want you to know that I think of you. You are an unusual woman."

"Well, thank you. But, really, you must stop sending them."

"You would not deny me the small pleasure of knowing that in your office you have flowers that tell you I am thinking of you? I do not send them to your home, you notice."

A breeze caught the edge of his headdress—the *ghutra,* she had discovered from the encyclopedia—fluttering it against her hair. She put up a hand to brush it away at the same moment he reached to remove it. His touch burned into her flesh.

She should leave, she thought. She had the sudden feeling this man was dangerous to her. "Dr. Gould tells me that you have offered him a position in Jeddah," she said.

"Yes. I hope he will accept."

"He hasn't given you an answer?"

"No. He is considering it, he says."

"Oh. Well, Bob loves a challenge."

"And you?" He smiled into her eyes.

She shook her head. "I go for familiar territory every time."

Abdullah laughed, and Liz had to laugh with him. God-damn it, she thought. He knows exactly the effect he is having on me.

Where was Judd when she needed him?

"A guy in a nightshirt—"

"It's called a *thobe* not a nightshirt—" Liz said calmly.

Judd slammed the gear into third, then second, jammed a foot on the brake as a jaywalker jumped to safety. "So you're now an expert on exotic male attire. What's the big deal with this guy apart from his billions—"

"What's his money got to do with anything? What's the matter with you? You behaved like a clod—"

"So now I'm some kind of redneck—"

"That's not what I said." Liz fought to keep her voice from rising.

"I was perfectly courteous, I just didn't fawn all over the guy."

Liz lowered the window, looked at the Pacific Ocean through the trees on the bluff. She knew it had been a mistake to drop her own car off at home so they could drive together to the restaurant.

"If that's what you call courteous, I'd hate to see what

you consider rude." He'd arrived at the Gould's, exchanged a few terse words with Prince Abdullah, then pointedly looked at his watch and reminded her they had a dinner reservation. The tension between the two men had sparked the moment Judd had walked onto the deck, an anxious Bob Gould hard on his heels.

"Yeah, well, I guess I caught the looks—"

"Oh, Judd, for God's sake. What looks?" Liz waited for an answer, then glanced at his grim face, realized he was really hurting. And leaving tomorrow at dawn. She softened her tone. "Anyway, I'm hardly responsible for the way a man looks at me—"

"I'm not talking about the way he looked at you, babe. I'm talking about the way you looked at him."

Liz felt the blood rush to her face. "Are you crazy?"

"Babe, I could feel the sex humming between you. You barely even knew I was there."

"Don't keep calling me babe. I'm no one's babe. I certainly knew you were there, an hour late. And obviously with your imagination in overdrive."

"You're lucky I turned up at all. I damn near didn't."

"Not so lucky if you're going to continue in this temper. I don't understand what's going on with you—"

"Then I'll explain. I was early, so I thought I'd pick you up at the hospital, we could drop your car off on the way to the Goulds, save us doing it later. Getting the picture?"

Liz didn't answer.

Judd shot her a glance. "Yes, I thought so. Your office looked like a goddamn funeral parlor, all those flowers. Orchids, right? You know, the ones that come with cute little jewelry boxes tucked in them?"

"Judd, there was no way I could send those flowers back. I didn't know where they came from."

"But you damn well knew *who* they came from." He slammed a hand against the wheel. "It didn't occur to you to send them up to pediatrics? Oh, not the little boxes, of course. What did you do, tell him not to send his expensive offerings to your home?''

"I didn't tell him anything. I haven't spoken to him—''

Judd cut in. "So I drove around. And while I was driving I realized that you just think I don't have the right to know when a man showers you with flowers and jewelry—''

"That's not true. And I wouldn't accept jewelry, you know me better than that.''

"No, I don't. Maybe I just thought I did.''

"What's that supposed to mean?''

"It means, *babe*, the Liz I know doesn't lie and cheat—''

"Turn the car around. I'm not spending another minute with you in this mood—''

"Suits me.'' Judd spun the Blazer into a tight U-turn. Horns blared, cars swerved. A guy in a Porsche flipped them the bird, his mouth wide in a shout of rage they couldn't hear. "And fuck you, too, buddy.'' Judd shoved a foot on the gas, roared onto Georgina, skidded to a stop in front of Liz's duplex.

"When you get ready to behave like a reasonable human being,'' Liz said, "call me.''

Judd reached across her, unlatched the door. "If you want to fuck this guy, now's the time, babe. Get it out of your system while I'm away. When I get back, we'll talk.''

"My God, you can be a prize bastard sometimes, Judd.''

She got out, slammed the door without waiting for him to answer. She heard him peel away from the curb, but didn't turn.

She hadn't had a chance to tell him about Bob Gould's offer, or his strange comments about her parents.

Judd was right. What did he know about her?

What did she know herself?

5

Liz took the Olive Mill Road exit from the 101, through Coast Village, past the Montecito Inn—once owned by Charlie Chaplin as a hideaway for his Hollywood buddies—and turned onto Middle Road, up into the hills above Santa Barbara. The old sycamores lining the creek had their first tender leaves and the afternoon sun penetrated the canopy in shafts of light and shade. The air was sweet with the scent of eucalyptus from the groves covering the hills on the other side of the creek and moist from the water still flowing after the rain.

Then, on her left, the split log fence of the lower paddock appeared, empty now, the horses given long ago to Camp Saint Jude's when her parents finally accepted that she had left home for good. Liz turned onto the graveled tree-lined driveway leading to the house, alert for Charlie. She slowed when she saw the bottom half of her mother's studio door open and the old dog break into an arthritic run toward the car, barking a welcome. Somehow he always knew when she came home.

Liz climbed out of her black Miata and dropped to her knees to bury her face in the dark shiny coat, laughing, avoiding the wet, determined tongue. Ten years ago he'd been starving on the street in Santa Barbara, sick, almost hairless from the fleas sucking his blood. She and Tess had brought him home, nursed him back to health.

"Hi, sweetheart, how was the traffic?" Tess Ryan called.

"Hi, Ma. Good. Just over an hour from Santa Monica."

"Then you drove too fast as usual." Tess put her arms around her daughter, held her briefly, then stepped back and looked at her. "You've been working too hard."

"Why do mothers always say that?"

"Because they're mothers?"

Liz laughed. "Daddy home?"

"No, he's in court today. He'll be home in time for dinner, though."

"Big case?"

"They're all big to your father, you know how he is."

Liz pulled a bag from the trunk. "How are the preparations going for your show?"

"Good. Terrific, in fact. I'll have twenty-four major canvases and some drawings."

"Mmm, not bad!"

"Gallery's very enthusiastic, going all out. Hoping for a lot of sales."

Liz put an arm around her mother's waist as they strolled toward the house. She knew Tess loved it when people remarked how alike they were, but it was only to a casual eye. Tess was several inches shorter, her hair a lighter red—nowadays discreetly maintained by her hairdresser—her eyes a bright blue and round rather than the almond shape of Liz's own eyes set above the high cheekbones she'd hated when she was younger. They made her look too exotic, she'd thought then, although now she rather liked them.

Liz ran her eyes over the garden as she always did when she came home, wriggling back into the safe enclosing warmth of childhood, before the storms of her teenage years—storms that were long behind them now, thank God.

"Roses look good, Ma," she said.

Heavy clusters of white Iceberg roses tangled with ferns close to the rambling single-story house, crimson bougainvillea massed on the roof of the veranda, tendrils drifting downward in a fringe of color.

"I dread to think what we'll do without Mr. Fujihara," her mother said. "He does only our garden now, and that only because Daddy helped his youngest granddaughter with some immigration problems. He's getting pretty old."

"Mr. Fujihara will never retire," Liz said affectionately. "One of these days you'll find a weathered old tree stump you hadn't noticed before, and there he'll be."

Charlie pushed his way ahead of them into the kitchen, his nails clicking on the flagstone floor. For as long as Liz could remember, through a series of animals, that sound was a familiar part of her life.

"Shall we have tea in the garden before Dad gets home?" Tess said. "I made some scones this morning when I knew you were coming."

"Just what the doctor ordered, Ma. Put the kettle on. I'll just dump my things in my room."

A few minutes later, with scones, butter, plum jam and teapot on the tray, they walked across the grass to the old picnic table under the sycamores.

"So, how's Judd?" Tess poured tea, Assam, strong and dark as they both liked it and handed the cup to Liz. "Still pressing to get married?"

"He's away on his reserve duty." Liz busied herself with the milk and sugar. "Be gone a couple of months."

Tess shot her daughter a look. "Nothing wrong is there?"

"No. Everything's fine."

"Then what's up? Something's on your mind. I saw it the moment you arrived."

"My mother, the psychic." How to lead into this? "I am kind of worried about Bob Gould. Have you spoken to Melly lately?"

"Not for a couple of weeks. Why?"

Liz couldn't bring herself to tell Tess about the rumors

flying around the hospital, her own fears for him. Instead, she said, "He's leaving Saint Luke's."

"No!" Tess clattered her cup back into its saucer. "Melly never breathed a word about retirement." She frowned. "He can't be retiring, he's too young. He's only Daddy's age. Melly would have told me."

"No, he's not retiring. He's been offered a position overseas." Liz broke off a corner of her scone, fed it to Charlie. "He wants me to go with him."

"Oh, Liz! Overseas! That sounds exciting. Where?" Over her brilliant smile, Tess touched fingers to her cheek beneath her right eye, then picked up the teapot and started to refill her own cup.

"Saudi Arabia." Liz saw the muscle in her mother's cheek jump, a sure sign of distress. "He said you and Dad were there once, when Dad was with the Foreign Service. You never told me that."

The teapot wobbled dangerously, and Tess put it down before she dropped it. "Surely, I must have."

"Ma, you know you didn't.... Are you all right?"

"What is Bob Gould thinking of?" Tess's voice was sharp with anxiety. "It's madness to even suggest such a thing, war's going to start there any minute. Haven't you seen the pictures of those Kurdish villages wiped out by Saddam? This man gasses his own people, Liz." She reached for her teacup, put it down without drinking. "Anyway, you can't go there. Pointless for Bob to suggest it. Saudi Arabia doesn't recruit women doctors from the West, only from the Muslim states."

"Well, you certainly keep up."

"I just happen to know that Western women are never allowed into Saudi Arabia. Not unless they're wives of men working there, or maybe nurses."

"Bob said you'd have a strong opinion about whether I go with him or not. Guess he was right."

Tess dug a knife viciously into her scone, split it in two. "Goddamn Bob Gould. Still sitting on the right hand of God in case he has to step in when God's too busy to attend to details."

"Ma!" Liz said, laughter in her voice. "What a thing to say!"

"Well, it's true, isn't it?"

"Sure. The best surgeons all have a God complex, Ma." She grinned at her mother, teasing her. "That's what makes us the best."

Tess shot her daughter a look. "Oh my, not another one like him!"

"He steered me through the medical maze. Guess he left his imprint. Anyway, what did he mean?"

"You'd be crazy to go to Saudi Arabia, honey. There's going to be a war there."

"What did Bob mean, Ma?"

"What about Judd? What does he say?"

"I haven't told him. I wanted to talk to you and Daddy first. Ma, look at me. You never told me you and Dad lived in Saudi Arabia. Why not? Is it a secret?"

Tess stared at her. Liz leaned across the table, put a hand to Tess's cheek to still the twitching muscle.

"What, Ma? What is it?"

Tess leaned into the caress, then put her own hand over Liz's. She rose to her feet. "I have something for you, Lizzie. Leave the tray, I'll get it later." She held up a hand, shook her head to Liz's questions.

Liz followed her mother back across the grass to the house, into Jim Ryan's study. Tess switched on the table lamp at the end of the sofa. The sun was going down, and this room, with its book-lined walls, always seemed darker than the rest of the house, particularly with the trees growing so close. Lamplight filled the room with a soft glow, softening sharp edges, leaving the corners shadowed, mysterious.

"Sit down, sweetheart."

Nervous now, wishing she had never asked but knowing she'd had no choice, Liz settled into a corner of the sofa, nudging Charlie off when he attempted to climb up beside her. With a sigh of resignation, the dog stretched across her feet. Liz watched her mother open the glass door of a cabinet containing part of her father's law library and press a hand up inside the dome of the cabinet. The top line of books swung open.

"And I thought I knew every part of this library," Liz said.

"Not everything," Tess said briskly. "You were never allowed to touch the law books."

"Didn't mean I didn't try."

"Well, we were one step ahead of you." Tess opened the door of a safe, reached in and withdrew a large bundle wrapped in white. She swung the door closed, then turned to Liz. She had to use both hands to carry the bundle over to where Liz sat and place it in her lap.

"This is yours, Liz."

Liz stared at the package. It weighed heavily on her thighs, and she felt suddenly immobile, a little sick. As soon as she unwrapped that white silk, Liz Ryan's life as she knew it now would change forever.

The moment stretched. Outside a mockingbird called in the dusk, and at her feet, Charlie whimpered and twitched, a young dog again, chasing rabbits in his dreams. She could even hear the short fluttery pattern of her mother's breath.

"What is this?" she asked at last.

"Your inheritance, I suppose we could call it. From your mother."

Liz heard her own disembodied voice. "Then you've always known about me." She thought of the pain of Tess's refusal to discuss her birth mother, her own insistent search, the letters to agencies, the replies to a post office box. And nothing. No one knew. She'd felt like a nonperson.

"Yes. But I couldn't tell you, Lizzie. Believe me about that. Other people were involved—"

"Oh, Ma." How could that justify so much pain?

Tess put a hand to her eyes, took a moment to gather herself, then looked back at her daughter. "I'm sorry, Liz. You are my heart, and I guess I so needed you to be mine. If I didn't tell you about your mother, she didn't exist."

Liz remembered the miscarriages and Tess's anguish. She could only guess what Tess must be feeling now—her own emotions were in turmoil. "Mom, you are my mother. You should have known nothing could ever change that."

"Yes. I am your mother. I know that. It just took so..." Tess's voice drifted into silence. Then she said, "Well, this is from the brave girl who gave you life. She wanted you to have it. Open it. Then we'll talk."

Tess went over to the window, her back to Liz, and stared out into the garden.

Liz picked away the tape around the bundle. Slowly she unwrapped yards of white silk, old, yellowing in places, apparently undisturbed for years. Then gold spilled out—coins, she thought at first, then realized it was jewelry. She held up what appeared to be a great multistringed necklace, although it was unimaginable that anyone could wear the heavy ten or twelve strands, each of them bearing gold coins too numerous to count at a glance—they would cover the chest like chain mail, reaching to the waist of a tall woman. Liz lifted the mass of gold—belts, necklaces, bangles, cuffs. Soft yellow antique gold of such purity that some of the ornaments were bent from the years of being piled together. A silk kerchief revealed smaller pieces—rings, long intricately worked earrings, strange pins, ornaments for the hair.

"Ma."

Tess turned back to the room.

"Who was she, the girl who gave you all this?"

A Circassian, Liz thought her mother would say. But she didn't.

"Her name was Fateema. They said she was thirteen..."

Darkness had fallen, deepening the shadows in the corners of the room not reached by the lamp on the table at the end of the sofa. Neither woman noticed until the timer turned on the lights under the sycamores outside the study.

"What did Dad say when you brought me home?" Liz asked. "Was he angry?"

"No. Oh, no," Tess said. "It was amazing. Well, first of all, he exploded. You know your father. But while I was telling him what had happened, you started to whimper. You were very tiny, Liz, very weak. He peeked inside the sheet—I'd had to keep you practically smothered to get you back to the house through the *shamal*—and you opened your eyes wide and looked as if you were smiling at him. Of course, you weren't, but he put his finger out and you grabbed it. That was it."

"He didn't want to send me away?"

Tess shook her head. "Never once."

Liz reached down to touch Charlie's ears, the soft fur of the animal comforting. She spoke without looking at her mother.

"Do you think they would have let me die?"

"No. I don't. They applied the most pressure they could, that's all. They wanted you to live."

"Doesn't sound like it."

"Liz, they were very brave women, both of them," Tess said. "They risked their lives to do what they did. If they had been found out, I can't even imagine what would have happened to them. Anyway, a few hours later, the Nubian came to the house. I was worried about feeding you, trying to keep you quiet so that Hassan wouldn't hear you crying, wondering how we'd keep you alive on the way home.''

Liz could see that her mother was lost in the past. She barely breathed, fearing to break the spell that held them both.

Tess continued. ''The Nubian sent a slave to say that he was in the alley outside and would wait there until I came. He had a woman with him, an Egyptian. Her own baby had just died and she wanted to go home.''

Liz caught a note of anguish in her mother's voice and guessed that Tess had spent thirty years wondering about the child's convenient death. She shivered, suddenly cold. So many secrets.

''Next day she came on board the *Murphy* to help me settle in,'' Tess said. ''She was carrying you under her robes. In the chaos of boarding, there were hordes of people—princes, advisors, slaves, God knows who else—and it wasn't difficult to hide her. She was your wet nurse until the *Murphy* reached Alexandria. She went home a rich woman. We got a supply of formula in Alex and from then on it was easy.''

Liz tried to imagine tall, green-eyed women like herself, with the same dark red hair. ''You never saw either of them again, Fateema or Sakeena?'' After all the years of wondering and searching, she couldn't bring herself to use the word *mother* for anyone but the woman sitting across from her in the quiet study filled with law books.

''I saw Sakeena,'' Tess said. ''She was at the dockside when the *Murphy* left. It was very dangerous for her to be there, a woman from what must have been a powerful household, out in broad daylight in a crowd of men. I was at the rail with Daddy, worrying about you hidden in our cabin with the Egyptian, but trying to behave as if everything was normal. I saw a group of Nubians standing separately at the edge of the crowd, surrounding a totally veiled woman. Even her eyes were covered. But I knew her. I waved. She put her fingers to her forehead, then to where her lips would be under that black shroud. Then she put her hand over her heart.'' Tess's voice caught with emotion. That moment in Jeddah in 1958 had obviously never left her. ''I knew what they had done, the risk they'd taken. They'd sent everything they had, all the gold given to them by the men who owned them. The big Nubian brought it when he brought the wet nurse. I wanted to send it back to them, but he refused to take it. Said it would dishonor them. I tried to point Sakeena out to Dad, but we couldn't find her again. She'd gone.''

Liz closed her eyes, leaned her head in her hands. Her mother was silent. Then Charlie rose to his feet, tail wagging, and a moment later came the sound of a car turning in from the road.

''There's Daddy,'' Tess said. She went to the door. ''He'll want to talk to you. Is that all right?''

''Oh, Ma. Of course.'' Liz started to her feet.

''No, stay there. Mix some martinis. You know how Dad likes them.''

The vermouth just a breath in the gin. Liz went over to the small wet bar in the corner of the study, listening to the hum of her parents' voices outside the door.

Then the door opened. Her father came into the room. He held out his arms and Liz went to him, felt his hand on her hair.

''I'm glad you know, Lizzie,'' he murmured. ''We should have told you sooner. Bob Gould always said we should when you were a teenager.''

''It's all right, Dad, I understand what it was all about.''

Tess joined them and Jim's arms encompassed both.

''Okay, now. Sit down, girls.'' Jim passed a thumb over each eye. ''Let's have a drink.'' He poured the martinis, handed a glass to his wife, another to Liz. ''Did your mother tell you that we smuggled you ashore in Newport News, Virginia?''

Liz shook her head.

''I pulled some strings, got your birth registered in Washington, told the family we'd adopted you there.''

''Why didn't you just say I was yours, born in Saudi Arabia?''

''We couldn't. Everyone knew that if your mother had become pregnant in Saudi, she'd have been sent home immediately. In 1958 Jeddah had no care available for Western women, let alone one that was pregnant.''

Liz held the martini without tasting it. She didn't need a drink. ''Did you try to find out what happened to Fateema and Sakeena?''

Jim shook his head. ''Honey, it's hard to believe what a closed, Islamic fundamentalist world is until you've actually lived in one. You don't even get to work in Saudi Arabia unless you're invited. There was no way I could figure to make inquiries about the women of a Saudi household without endangering them, or raising a lot of questions I couldn't answer.''

''So it was because of me you had to leave the diplomatic service,'' Liz said, her voice low.

Jim left his chair, crossed to the sofa where Liz sat and put his arm around her. ''Now, sweet pea, how did you figure that? You had nothing to do with it. Dragging your mother from post to post just didn't seem such a good idea.''

''I wanted more children. It was hard for me—'' Tess broke off.

Jim reached to take Tess's hand. ''Anyway, leaving government service was the best thing I ever did. I've made a pile of money in private practice. Damn sight more than I would working for the State Department.''

Liz looked at her father—handsome black Irish, wide humorous mouth, his dark blue eyes serious now, though they usually snapped with laughter—not really believing him. Not sure, even, that he ever had stopped working for the U.S. government; he still took the mysterious, unexplained trips to Washington, the Middle East, other places in the world, as he had throughout her childhood.

So many questions, she thought.

But her parents would have no answers to the questions she most wanted to ask.

Who were these women who had risked so much?

What had happened to them?

Were they alive? Dead?

And where were they now?

6

Liz watched the steward make his way down the aisle of the 747, bending to murmur in the ears of a number of the male passengers. As soon as the steward passed, the men stood to allow the women with them to leave their seats.

"I think we must be getting into Jeddah," she said to Bob.

"Surely not yet."

"Well, there seems to be quite a dash for the ladies room. I'm wondering whether I'd better join it."

She caught the shy glance of a young girl in the window seat across the aisle. They'd been exchanging smiles since Heathrow, but hadn't spoken. The man in the seat next to her nodded as the steward leaned over him, then he said a few words to the girl, standing to allow her to leave her seat.

"Getting gussied up for Jeddah?" Liz asked her.

She was very pretty, dark eyes and hair, little more than a child. The girl nodded shyly, then glanced at the man with her.

"She speaks little English," the man said pleasantly. He spoke to the girl and she scurried up the aisle toward the toilet. He smiled at Liz, then opened an Arabic language newspaper.

Liz went back to her book, but the words ran together on the page. Since the night her parents had told her about her birth, she'd felt as if she'd been living one step removed from reality. She'd found herself stroking the skin on her arm as if it belonged to someone else, or standing in front of a mirror, staring into her eyes as if she had never seen them before. She'd been grappling with what it was to be Circassian, daughter and granddaughter of slaves, not third generation Irish-American as she had convinced herself she was.

In one hour on a cool spring evening, the Elizabeth Ryan named for her great-grandmother in County Mayo had been wiped out of existence.

Who would take her place?

She and her parents had stayed up talking half the night. Her father knew she had to accept Bob's offer. Tess had taken some convincing—the talk of chemical and biological weapons had terrified them all—but finally, reluctantly, Tess had come around.

Liz did not mention Prince Abdullah and, strangely, the Goulds never did, either.

The man across the aisle jostled her elbow and murmured an apology as he stood to allow a small, black-shrouded figure to slide into the seat against the window. Liz looked around at the rest of the first-class compartment. Veiled anonymous figures were taking the seats once occupied by brightly dressed, fashionable women.

The steward stopped by her side. "Would you like one last drink, madam?"

"Are we landing?"

"Not yet, madam, but we are about to cross the international boundary. No more alcohol will be served as soon as Captain Maguire confirms we are in Saudi airspace."

"Better get me a double Scotch, then," Bob said. "You, Liz?"

She shook her head.

"This is going to be quite an experience," Bob said as the steward left. "Giving up booze."

Liz kept her face carefully neutral. This was the first time Bob had even hinted he had a problem. Not much, but it was a beginning. Maybe he could do it, maybe he could give it up.

The steward brought his drink, at the same time handing them each a landing card. "If you need any help filling them in, please call me. I'll collect them before we land." He gave a bright, professional smile before moving on to the next passengers.

Liz quickly filled in the details. Name, address, country of birth, passport number, religion.

"Religion?" Her eye fell upon what Gould had written in that spot. "Since when have you been Episcopalian? Does Melly know?"

"Well, I can't put Jewish."

"Why not?"

"You know why not. I couldn't get into the country if I said I was a Jew."

"Bob, is this job really that important to you?"

"Yes. To me, it is." Deliberately, he turned to look out of the window. "We should be able to see Jeddah soon."

For a moment she studied what she could see of the face he had turned from her, then picked up her book without comment. Her father had told her that Bob had always stayed in touch with them. He'd decided on Los Angeles when his navy tour ended partly because the Ryans were already in Santa Barbara, and he could stay close to the child he'd helped save. When he and Melly had Jake, they naturally became extended family to each other's kids. Her father had told her, too, of the countless times Bob had urged them to tell her about her birth—yet never passed judgment when they couldn't do it.

She'd already thanked him for sending her to talk to her parents that day, for giving her this chance to find out who she really was, but he'd seemed uncomfortable, so she'd dropped it. A good man, Dr. Robert Gould. The best. She reached over and squeezed his arm.

Bob looked at her, surprised. He smiled, patted her hand, went back to looking out into the darkness.

An hour passed. Captain Maguire's voice informed them that they were approaching the city of Jeddah, the temperature on the ground was a mild seventy-five degrees, no wind, and thank you for flying British Airways.

The man across the aisle stood to allow his daughter to leave her seat. Liz closed her book and shoved it into her carry-on. She rose to her feet and made her way toward the service area for a last cold drink before landing. The young girl was already returning to her seat bearing a glass of juice, and Liz smiled at her. Immediately, the girl lowered her eyes. There was no way of knowing if she had smiled back, her dark eyes had been visible for only an instant. It was as if the veil hiding her face had changed a friendly child into a guarded wraith.

"Makes you cringe, doesn't it?"

Liz looked at the woman who had just spoken. An American, standing by the door, coffee cup in hand. She was shaking her head.

"What does?" Liz asked.

"That." The woman gestured with her head, her eyes on the small figure resuming her seat. "I've got a daughter about that age. I won't even allow her to date yet."

Liz looked at the girl's father, leaning toward her solicitously. "Well, sure, it's too bad she has to wear that Halloween outfit, but her father probably takes the same care with her."

The woman laughed. "That's not her father, honey. That's her husband."

Liz stared at the back of his head—the girl had disappeared, swallowed by the depths of the seat.

There but for the grace of God, she thought. Suddenly, it

was no longer about herself, about finding her own roots. By some fluke, she had been given a year in this alien society. And now it was about finding Fateema to thank her for her courage.

She owed her that.

The ride across the tarmac in the darkened shuttle bus was no preparation for the cacophony of the airport building. Enormous, marble-lined and elegant, it seethed with humanity in every shade of color and dress. The flowing robes of North Africa and Egypt; the voluminous baggy pants and overshirts of Afghanistan and the Indian subcontinent in various soft tones of white, green, pale blue; skinny, fine-boned dark men wearing enormously wide bell-bottomed pants last seen in the U.S. in the seventies; the men of Saudi Arabia dashing in white *thobes,* the color of their *ghutras*—red-and-white check, black-and-white check, plain white—seeming to constitute the entire range of their sartorial choice.

A few women—sari clad or shrouded from head to toe in black, veiled or with faces covered by leather masks that left nothing visible but dark eyes—hunkered silently on the floor, babies clutched to their chests, countless older children huddled close, wide-eyed and anxious.

Liz found herself looking for a tall, regal figure among the crowd, knowing it was foolish to expect him. A prince did not meet airplanes, although his presence had been felt during their preparations to leave. Visas that usually took months of exhaustive inquiry and bureaucratic paperwork had arrived within hours. Plane reservations had been made, tickets hand delivered, luggage picked up. She found herself saying her goodbyes before she had time to catch her breath.

"Dr. Gould?" A skinny Saudi stepped forward. "I am Selim. I am here to help you through the formalities."

Bob shook the limp hand held out to him. "Ah, thank you."

"Follow me, please."

Liz glanced at Selim, ready with a smile as she waited to be acknowledged, but he flipped the corner of his black-and-white *ghutra* over his shoulder and ushered Gould toward the baggage carousels. Two bearded men shuffled behind, their bare feet thrust into sandals, heads covered by the untidy flat turbans of Afghanistan.

Liz picked up her hand luggage and followed. This was going to have to be remedied, she thought. No matter what the customs of Saudi Arabia, she was an American doctor as well as a woman. She strode briskly to Selim's side.

"I am Dr. Ryan." She held out her hand.

Bob stopped in midstride. "Oh, Liz. My God. Sorry. The excitement...forgive me. This is Selim. Dr. Ryan, my associate."

The Saudi stared at her hand as if he'd never seen such a thing before. Then, without looking at her face, he murmured a greeting, touched her hand briefly with the tips of his fingers before turning once more toward the first-class luggage.

Too keyed up to be irritated, Liz left it to Bob to deal with the bags and turned to study the crowd.

Unfamiliar languages created a seamless buzz of background noise. The cheap perfumes assaulting her nostrils simply added to the exotic strangeness of the scene. In front of the uniformed customs officials, noisy, chaotic lines of robed men formed and reformed. Skinny soldiers in khaki, assault weapons hanging over one shoulder, bullied them roughly into place as if they were errant cattle.

Clumps of American oilmen stood out, tight Levi's low on the hips, belts with fancy buckles, tooled boots and cowboy hats, towering over the men around them. The difference in their attitudes was striking—the Americans laughing and relaxed, the men from the East watching the Saudi officials anxiously while nudging forward the largest suitcases Liz had ever seen in her life.

Luggage retrieved, Selim led them directly to the front of one of the lines. Liz looked apologetically at the men they were displacing, expecting to see the annoyance an American crowd would show, but the eyes of the waiting men slid away from hers.

An immigration officer stamped their passports, the customs man marked their bags without comment. Then he gestured sharply to the magazine in Liz's hand.

She looked at him blankly. He reached over to grab the magazine.

"It's *Vogue,*" she said. "A fashion magazine."

He flipped through it, then dropped it into a bin at his side.

"What's wrong with *Vogue*?" Liz looked from the Saudi official to Selim. "It's fashion. Clothes. Nothing subversive."

"If you have more newspapers and magazines, you must surrender them now," Selim said.

"Why?"

"It is required."

"Lizzie, don't argue," Bob said. "It's late, I'm tired. We're both tired. Just do it."

Liz surrendered *Newsweek* and the *New England Journal of Medicine.* The journal was handed back to her, *Newsweek* followed *Vogue* into the bin.

In the next aisle the woman Liz had spoken to on the plane was arguing with an official. She looked over at Liz.

"Can you believe this," she called. "He thinks my bag's made of pigskin. As if I'd be stupid enough to try to bring pigskin into Saudi Arabia."

She turned back to the fray.

* * *

Outside, the air was balmy. Selim ushered them to a Mercedes limousine parked alone directly in front of the building, the driver, a dark-skinned man with fine Nilotic features, Ethiopian, perhaps, or Somali, waiting by its side. Behind the Mercedes was a station wagon for the luggage, and Liz was relieved when Selim climbed into that, leaving her alone with Bob for the journey into Jeddah. Making conversation with a reluctant Saudi was more than she wanted to deal with during her first glimpse of the city in which she had been born.

Liz kept her eyes glued to the passing scene, half expecting to see the torchlit biblical town Tess had described. Instead the road leading from the airport was brilliant with overhead lights and heavily planted with palm trees and giant aloes, the median massed with oleander and decorated with stylistic metal sculptures vaguely reminiscent of human figures engaged in a variety of sports.

The modern Jeddah proved to be a city of paved streets and fluorescent streetlights, although gradually it became clear that beneath the modern veneer it was also a city in transition, elegant buildings juxtaposed against rows of flimsy windowless shops blotched with peeling stucco in pink and green and yellow. Broken sidewalks with crumbling edges four feet above the road—Liz could only assume that hapless pedestrians had somehow to vault on and off. Bamboo scaffolding lashed together with frayed rope held up buildings either under construction or in the process of demolition, it was hard to tell, and gaudy, marble-faced commercial buildings alive with Arabic signs in neon were lonely outposts in the middle of acres of raw desert.

Gould drew her attention to a freeway entrance signed in green and white, English and Arabic. *Makkah. Medina.*

"I don't think we're in Kansas anymore, Toto," he said.

Liz felt a thrill of excitement. "It is kind of exotic, isn't it?"

The Mercedes turned into a residential neighborhood of high, blank stucco walls, passing crews of Afghani workmen with water trucks carefully hand watering young street trees, then hosing the leaves clean of fine dusty sand.

The Mercedes slowed. A gate opened and they drove through. A short driveway lined with trees ended in front of what appeared to be a two-story hotel—ocher stucco, surrounded by palms and crimson canna lilies and giant scheffleras. Selim and the station wagon waited beneath a portico. Selim ushered Bob through high double front doors, across a beige marble foyer, through an arch, and Liz trailed after them.

She paused in the archway, met Bob's eye. For a moment, neither spoke. Then Bob said, "Very handsome."

The room was cavernous, harshly lit by a row of fixtures suspended from a high ceiling. Overstuffed sofas and armchairs lined the walls, leaving the center of the room completely empty except for oriental rugs. Landscapes in heavy gold frames hung haphazardly.

Certainly not the stuff of *The Arabian Nights.*

"This is the *majlis,*" Selim said.

Bob advanced into the room, looking stunned, like an actor who'd somehow missed his cue.

Liz smothered a grin. "A home away from home. I'm sure we'll be very comfortable, Selim. Thank you."

"Men only here," Selim said without looking at her. "This is an official guest house—"

"It's not a hotel?" Gould asked.

"It is an official guest house. His Excellency Idi Amin lived here while his own house was being built. Women are not allowed in these rooms. Not allowed," he repeated.

"Oh." At least she wasn't going to share the former digs of the Butcher of Uganda. Liz waited, nonplussed. "Then where are my quarters? In the harem?" She meant it as a joke and hoped Selim realized that.

"This is Dr. Gould's house," Selim said. "I will take you now to your house."

Not the harem, then. She threw Bob a glance. He was going to rattle around alone in a house large enough for a dozen people to live in without ever bumping into each other, and down the road, she would be doing the same. Well, when in Rome...

"Do you want me to come with you, see you settled in?" Bob asked. He sounded too tired to move.

"No, of course not. I'll be fine." She nodded to a hovering servant dressed in narrow white cotton leggings, long white overshirt, short dark waistcoat. "I think he's waiting to show you to your bed. I'll see you tomorrow."

Her luggage had already been transferred from the station wagon, and Liz sat alone in the back of the Mercedes. After carefully closing the courtesy window between front and back, and drawing together a pair of lined, white lace curtains, Selim settled himself next to the driver.

The neighborhood seemed to grow progressively older, streets more dimly lit and narrower, no room now for sidewalks or Afghani workmen with their water trucks, although flowering oleanders and bougainvillea hung over the high stucco walls. At last, they turned into a lane without lights and halfway down the car stopped. Selim climbed out, knocked on a small Judas gate in heavy wooden doors. Along the street, nothing moved, nothing was visible except the flower-draped walls and sets of plain metal-bound double doors like those in front of them.

The silence was unnerving.

This was the Jeddah her mother had described, Liz thought. She felt her heart thumping heavily, as if she were about to enter a world she would recognize. Then the double gates swung open and Selim waved the Mercedes through.

Liz looked for old Mansour the doorkeeper smiling a *salaam*, but it was Selim who opened the car door. The

Saudi standing behind him was stocky and bearded, with a red-and-white checked *ghutra,* his *arghal* set at an angle.

Liz climbed out and looked around the courtyard.

Wait until Bob sees this, she thought. He'll be green.

The blank walls facing the street hid a tree-filled garden that would grace Palm Springs. Tamarisk and white oleander, orange and pink lantana, and somewhere frangipani bloomed—the air was filled with its sweetness and with the sound of trickling water from a tiled fountain. A deep colonnaded verandah promised shaded windows on the hottest day, and half a dozen shallow steps led up to the front door of a house.

A house—human-size, not a hotel.

"This is really lovely, Selim."

He smiled back at her, the first time he'd actually looked at her since the airport. Then his eyes slid down her body to her breasts.

Restraining a desire to smack him, Liz turned to the Saudi who had opened the gates.

"I'm Dr. Ryan."

"This is Yousef," Selim said. "He is in charge of this house. He will be your driver also."

Not Mansour. Of course not. "How do you do, Yousef."

"Madam."

"Hello, madam. Welcome." Two slight female figures came down the steps from the house, half bowing, heads bobbing as if to assure Liz of their desire to please. "Welcome, madam."

"Thank you." Liz smiled. They seemed little more than children, fragile immature forms hidden beneath knee-length tunics over baggy trousers.

"Get the luggage," Selim said.

Both girls hurried to the car. Liz waited for the Saudis to help. When they didn't, Liz joined the struggling girls, brushing aside their protests. She followed the girls up the steps.

"Thank you, gentlemen," she said pleasantly. "Good night."

Selim started up behind her. "I will show you the house."

"Oh, I think we women can manage that by ourselves, too. Selim is leaving, Yousef. Please close the gates behind him." Smiling to herself, Liz closed the front door.

She turned to view what would be her home for the next year.

Across an expanse of pale limestone floor, three steps led down into a large living room facing a garden. White silk sofas strewn with pastel pillows, pink, green, blue; armchairs and small tables; scattered oriental carpets glowing like jewels on the honey-colored floor.

And everywhere, vases of familiar white orchids.

Liz fumbled for the bedside clock. It was 5:00 a.m. That couldn't be right. Someone was half singing, half shouting a strange plaintive song right outside her bedroom window. She sat up and brought the clock closer to her face: 5:00 a.m. The sun was just beginning to stain the eastern sky a delicate washed pink.

The call rose and fell with a descant from farther away, and then another and another as if the sound were being picked up all over the city. Liz pulled on her robe, stumbled to the door. The smell of coffee drifted in from the recesses of the house, and she followed her nose, passing the living room—the orchids a pale disembodied glow in the early morning light—then the dining room with its eighteen chairs around an enormous table; the television room with an equal number of chairs in rows in front of the screen, and finally the kitchen.

The taller of the two girls, Siti, was busy at a counter.

"Good morning," said Liz. "What is that?"

Siti looked at her, an anxious smile hovering around her mouth. "Madam?"

"That! Listen!"

"Oh. Prayer call. That is prayer call, madam."

"Prayer call!" Liz picked up the coffeepot and opened a cupboard door, looking for a mug. "Hope that doesn't happen too often."

"Five times every day, madam." Siti produced a china cup and saucer, took the coffeepot from Liz's hand and started to pour.

"Five times a day?" she said incredulously. "Not every morning. Not at five o'clock every morning."

"Oh, yes, madam." Siti nodded her head vigorously. "Every morning, prayer call is at dawn." She handed Liz the cup of coffee. "And at noon, and midafternoon, and evening prayer and at night."

"My God!" Liz sipped the coffee and felt new life pouring through her. Three hours of sleep on top of a long journey and jet lag, and who knew how many hours of work were ahead of her today. "It sounds as if it's coming from the garden."

"The mosque is at the end of the street." Siti set a tray with milk and sugar. "Many mosques, all over, so men can walk to them and not miss prayer." She picked up the tray. "Please, madam, I will bring your breakfast to the dining room."

"Oh, no, thanks, I'll eat here in the kitchen." The haunting call fell away. "Just some cereal."

Siti put the tray on the table. "There is bread and *labneh* and yogurt," she said softly. "And fruit. Mangoes and melon."

Liz noted the frightened voice and realized Siti was terrified of making a mistake. She smiled and nodded. "Well, that sounds very good."

Siti uncovered a napkin-wrapped basket revealing an

enormous round of flat bread. It smelled wonderful and Liz tore off a fragment. It was fragrant, thick and delicious, still warm from the oven. Someone had been out very early to fetch it. On the table was a bowl of yogurt, platters of sliced fruit. Liz spooned yogurt liberally over the mango, then took a mouthful. It was wonderful. Rich. Full of fat.

"Perhaps we can add some cereal for tomorrow," she said. "And some nonfat milk."

"Yes, madam. Please, you must tell Yousef what you want."

"You take care of it, Siti. You run the kitchen, don't you?"

"I cannot tell Yousef."

"Then just have him drive you to the supermarket."

"He would not do that, madam. It is not allowed for us to leave the house."

Liz stopped eating. "You mean you never go out?"

Siti shook her head. "No, madam."

"Not even on your day off?"

The girl looked puzzled. Liz put down her spoon. "You do have a day off."

Eyes lowered, Siti shook her head.

"You mean you work seven days a week?"

The girl nodded.

"How many hours a day?"

"Madam?" Siti whispered uncertainly.

Liz could see her hands trembling, and she realized the girl was scared to death by her questions. She wondered how old Siti was. Seventeen, eighteen at the most.

"Don't be frightened, Siti. You and Megawati have no time off for yourselves?"

Siti shook her head.

"Well, I haven't got time for shopping lists. From now on, you are going to do that for me."

"Madam, you must give Yousef instructions to go to the market."

Liz refilled her cup, tore off another piece of the bread and helped herself to more mango. "Does Yousef live in the house?"

"Oh, no, madam! He cannot be here with women. He lives in his own apartment, by the garage with the car."

Liz wondered how he could be in charge of the household as Selim had said. Maybe by remote control. "Well, I can't keep track of such a large establishment as this." She tried not to think of Judd, laughing as he looked into her empty refrigerator at home. "It looks as if you girls are going to have to take over."

"But we cannot tell Yousef to go to the market." Siti sounded shocked. "He is a man!"

"Well, Yousef will do as I say, and today I will instruct him to drive you. You and Megawati together."

"To the supermarket? Oh, madam!" Siti's eyes sparkled as if she'd been offered a ride on a magic carpet. Then her face clouded.

"There is something wrong with that?" Liz asked.

"The *mutawain*, madam. They look for us."

"And who are they, the *mutawain?*" Liz expected to hear of demons, exportable from Indonesia.

"The religious men, madam. *Mutawain* are always looking for girls who are here for working and should not be out of the houses."

Liz held her cup out for a refill. "If you have on that black outfit from head to toe, how would the *mutawain* know whether you were Saudi or Malaysian or Filipina, or American for that matter?"

"They'd know, madam. *Mutawain* know everything."

Liz laughed. "I doubt that."

"Oh, yes, madam—"

"Siti, please, call me Dr. Ryan, and tell Megawati that

from now on, you are both going out to do the shopping at the supermarket. You will ride in the back of the car and you will be completely covered from head to toe. Okay?''

"Yes, madam, Dr. Ryan.''

So this was the society from which she sprang, Liz thought as she walked back to her room. Where slavery had been abolished, but not really; where thought police dictated what people could read and young girls were terrorized in the name of religion.

How was she ever going to find Fateema in such a world?

7

"Perhaps we should wait for the director of the hospital," Gould said. "Our appointment was for ten. Something must have delayed him."

Dr. Lars Thorensen hesitated, then said carefully, "The Saudi concept of time is somewhat different from what we in the West understand. You may be in for a long wait."

Liz glanced at her watch. They'd already been waiting forty-five minutes. "How do you manage an operating schedule if some of your doctors don't turn up on time?" she asked.

"The medical staff has no problem with time, Dr. Ryan. What makes you think they don't turn up?"

"Didn't you just say that Saudis have a different concept of time than we do in the West?"

"Ah. Well, as you know, the contract at King Khaled Clinic is held by Johannesen Medical Corporation of Copenhagen. The medical staff here is almost entirely Scandinavian, plus a few other Europeans. No trouble with time."

"No Saudi doctors?" Bob asked.

"Dr. al-Turki, our esteemed Saudi director." Lars Thorensen leaned back in his chair, the tips of his fingers resting against each other, his pale blue eyes amused, his face bland. "This kingdom is run by contract, doctor. There is a joke here. If they ever have a war, the Saudis would put it out to bid, and the Koreans would get the contract." Thorensen laughed, showing large white teeth. "But now, of course, it looks as if the Americans have beaten them out."

Bob looked at the grinning blonde with obvious dislike. "And the nursing staff?"

"All Muslim, Filipina, mostly. The male nurses from Pakistan. We maintain a good standard."

Gould made a production of looking at his watch, then stood. "Well, Dr. Thorensen, it's good of you to make time for us in your busy day. I think we'll take you up on your kind offer of a tour."

The hospital, noisy with musical tones and disembodied voices broadcasting messages in Arabic and English, bustled with activity like any in the United States, except that it was a picture in black and white. Men in *thobes* and *ghutras* shepherded veiled, black-clad women, held children by the hand, leaned over nurses' stations to speak for the anonymous figures standing silently behind them.

"Women are not allowed to visit the hospital alone," Thorensen said in reply to Gould's question. "Some male member of the family, husband, brother, father, son, is always present, and he speaks for them."

"Doesn't that make diagnosis difficult?" Liz asked.

"Well, once inside an examination room, they are allowed to answer questions. But, of course, the male escort is always present and sometimes it's a struggle to keep them quiet so that the women can answer for themselves."

Thorensen led the way through corridors and wards, into elevators and down stairs, through kitchens staffed by Singhalese, and laundries where Pakistani workmen tended huge washing machines. The operating rooms were on the third floor.

"We don't do autopsies here," Thorensen said. "Koranic law does not allow it, bodies must be buried before sundown on the day of death. And it's not unknown for the family of a patient to demand blood money from the doctor in charge of the case if he dies while in our care.''

Liz smothered a grin at the look on Bob's face. Thorensen ushered them along the corridor toward the ICU, stopping to speak to a tiny Filipina nurse bending over a monitor.

Then the loud, plaintive chant Liz had heard at five that morning sounded and resounded. Thorensen clicked his tongue against his teeth impatiently. ''Noon prayer. We'll have to wait now until it's over. Time got away from me this morning.''

Every man in sight, orderlies and nurses, visitors and clerks, started toward the open space in front of the elevator. Rugs were produced from a closet and spread over the marble floor. The men organized themselves quickly into rows, a white-bearded man took his place in front. Each man placed his hands upon knees, bowed, then prostrated himself upon the rug. The bearded elder led the chanted prayers.

''Everything stops?'' Bob asked.

''You'll get used to it. Let's sit.'' Thorensen pointed to a row of chairs. ''They are praying toward the northwest, you see? That is toward Mecca.''

''What about the women?'' Liz whispered as if she were suddenly in church. The nurses had continued with whatever they were doing, the others, presumably patients, sat silently waiting. ''Don't they pray?''

Thorensen shook his head. ''Maybe in their homes, I don't know, but in public, only the men.''

Twenty minutes later, the rugs were rolled up, replaced in the closet, the men returning to whatever occupied them before prayer call. Thorensen punched the button on the elevator. Back on the ground floor, the director's door was still closed. Thorensen tapped softly.

''Come in,'' a deep male voice called.

Thorensen opened the door, motioned them inside. The office was twice the size of Thorensen's, richly carpeted, lined with bookcases, sofas and chairs grouped for conversation. A tall, stout Saudi in white *thobe,* black *arghal* keeping a red-and-white checked *ghutra* in place, came from behind an enormous, bare mahogany desk, hand outstretched in welcome, wide smile on his large handsome face.

"Dr. al-Turki, may I present Dr. Robert Gould and his associate, Dr. Elizabeth Ryan?" Thorensen said.

"Dr. Gould. Dr. Ryan. Welcome. Welcome, indeed. Sit. Sit. We'll have coffee."

He got them settled on sofas, then picked up his phone and ordered coffee. No reference was made to the missed appointment. Dr. al-Turki chatted about the flight, asking how they found London, one of his favorite cities.

"But I also spent a number of years in your country."

"You trained in the United States?" Liz looked at the wall behind him, trying to read the lettering on the certificates hanging there, then realized they were in Arabic.

"No. I was educated in Mecca, then Cairo for medicine. Very good, Cairo."

The three Western-trained doctors carefully avoided each other's eyes and nodded without comment. The coffee arrived—tiny cups that Dr. al-Turki filled with a green brew unlike anything Liz had tasted, herbal and nasty. Politely she gulped it down, and Dr. al-Turki nodded his approval and refilled her cup, waiting, smiling, until she sipped.

"Prince Abdullah bin Talal has the interests of the Saudi people close to his heart," Dr. al-Turki said. "And of course, we at King Khaled Clinic will give you all the help you need to accomplish what he has asked of you. This is a time of great testing for the people of Saudi Arabia. With the help of Allah, we will be equal to the task before us." He glanced at Thorensen.

Thorensen finished his coffee, replaced his cup, then rose

to his feet. The two Americans followed suit. Goodbyes were brief, and they were outside the door.

Thorensen said, "He's a good man. Not much of a doctor, but a decent guy. How about lunch?"

The lobby of the Red Sea Palace Hotel overlooking the Manaquaba Lagoon was three stories of pink marble and pink smoked mirrors. Groves of green-and-gold enamel palm trees sheltered deep upholstered armchairs and glass-topped tables, banks of machines clacked continuously, the reams of market reports spilling out checked constantly by the mostly Saudi guests. Thorensen passed the European restaurant and American-style coffee shop, led them through a wide arched doorway.

Liz wanted to laugh. This was more like it, a bit of Arabia by way of Hollywood. She grinned at Bob, who was taking in the billowing blue canopy held up by decorated golden poles, the pillows piled on oriental rugs, the camel saddles set around smooth stone hearths with brass coffeepots resting on beds of charcoal, a wall of carved, wooden screens at the rear to give a sense of intimacy.

The smiling Egyptian maître d' led them through the almost empty restaurant, past tables set with white linen and silver, past a dazzling buffet table decorated with flowers and ice sculptures. To Liz's astonishment, he ushered them behind the screens, and with a smile in her direction, pulled out a chair at a table well hidden from the rest of the room.

Not a billowing canopy in sight.

Liz waited for Thorensen to protest. In Beverly Hills, or anywhere else for that matter, a table in the far Siberia of an empty restaurant would be reason for loud complaint.

Busily unfolding his napkin, Thorensen caught her look. "This is the family section," he explained. "In the rest of the country, a woman would not even get this far. Women must never be in the company of men outside their immediate family so they certainly do not eat in restaurants. We three took a chance driving here together. Fortunately, Jeddah is a bit more progressive than the eastern provinces, probably because it's a port city."

"Are women allowed to do anything in this country?" Liz asked.

Thorensen shook his head. "Not much, I'm afraid."

He wasn't joking. Liz picked up the menu. "This is going to be a long year."

"It's not as bad as it sounds. We find ways around it."

"That's nice. How, exactly?"

Thorensen leaned his long body toward her. "You must let me take you under my wing. Introduce you to the expat life here in Jeddah." He looked deep into her eyes, then smiled quickly to include Gould. "A bit of a bore for us old bachelors with so few women, but we manage a fair social life. Swimming, tennis, that sort of thing."

Bob nodded. "Sounds good. Don't you think so, Liz?"

"Yes. I'd love to pick up on my tennis game." Her mind turned to Judd and his determined assaults on the tennis ball whenever she enticed him out on a court. He'd telephoned in response to her letter telling him that she had accepted an offer to work out of the country, asking him to call her as soon as he could. He'd been icy, refusing to listen as soon as she mentioned Saudi Arabia, told her to give his best to Abdullah when she got to Jeddah, then hung up before she could explain about Fateema. She'd been furious. Everything had moved along so fast after that. Before leaving, she'd tried to reach him at the Marine base in Pendleton, but he hadn't called back. She'd left another letter for him with her parents. If he cared enough for her, he'd call them. If not... It hurt to go further with that thought.

They passed on the buffet and Thorensen ordered for them, starting with *mezze,* a selection of appetizers—*bourek, samboosik, dolma,* tasty little pizzas called *lahmajoun, tab-*

bouleh, humus; then the main dish, *salek,* an Arabian specialty of chicken and rice fragrant with mint and cardamom.

Over dessert of rich Lebanese pastries, Thorensen said, "So, Dr. Ryan, I will call you for tennis, yes?"

"I thought you said fraternization between unmarried people was frowned upon," Liz said.

"Forbidden, in fact, and even more so lately. The fundamentalists are becoming more militant every day. Outside of work, we never see our Muslim women colleagues any more. The knee-jerk response to any problems here is always a crackdown on women, they're easy to control." Thorensen waved a hand, indicating the bleak room, empty of guests. "Right now it is the fear of pollution by a foreign military presence that has the Saudis spooked. But ex-pat wives invite what few single Western women there are, a couple of private duty nurses, stewardesses on layover." He grinned, showing the large, white teeth. "If bachelors are also present in their houses, who is to know? As long as unmarried people are careful not to be alone together in public."

"What happens if they are?" Liz asked. "Out in public, I mean?"

"Then they risk the ire of the *mutawain.* The Committee for the Protection of Virtue and the Prevention of Vice."

Liz caught Bob's eye and they both laughed.

"You're joking, right?" Liz said. "That's what they're called? The Committee for the Protection of Virtue and the Prevention of Vice?" She let the words roll off her tongue. "And what, exactly, do they do?"

"Don't laugh, my friends," Thorensen said. "They can be very dangerous. It doesn't do to cross them."

"So what can they do?" Liz was still amused. "Issue an illegal fraternizing citation?"

Thorensen filled small cups with thick Turkish coffee. "Let me tell you a little story. Two weeks ago, a British nurse was caught leaving the Inter-Continental Hotel with a member of the aircrew from a BA flight. Both, of course, were taken off to jail. The nurse was given 180 lashes, not enough for blood—the Holy Koran was held under the arm using the whip—but enough to cause a great deal of discomfort. The next night, she was taken onto a Saudia flight to London in handcuffs, dragged the entire length of the aisle just as she was, straight out of a Saudi jail, stinking, old mascara streaking her face. She was shackled into her seat. The message was rammed home to every ex-pat on that plane. Later it turned out the man she'd been with was her brother, but they didn't speak Arabic, and the *mutawain* didn't speak English, or said they didn't. Who knows really? They made their point.''

"And the brother?'' Bob asked. "What happened to him?''

"Also 180 lashes, but for him, a warning. He was spared the humiliation.''

"My God!'' Liz said.

Thorensen lowered his voice. "You must understand something very basic about Saudi Arabia. This is an absolute monarchy. There is no free press, no political parties, no right of assembly, no vote. In fact, nothing we take for granted in the West. It is a country of *shari'ah,* the law of the Koran. The Saudis are their religion. Believe me, the two cannot be separated. The *mutawain* are men of great piety, much respected, and more than anything else they fear the contamination of their society by ideas from the West. They literally keep watch over public morals, and they administer the punishment for infractions. They are not...'' Thorensen searched for the right English word "...merciful.''

"You make them sound pretty damn ominous,'' Bob said.

"Just do not take them lightly,'' Thorensen warned.

"Keep an eye open for men whose beards are stained with henna and who carry camel whips. And—" he touched a finger to Liz's bare arm "—wear long sleeves."

"Yes. Thank you," she said. "I certainly will."

Talk turned to the possibility of war. One hundred thousand Iraqi troops were massed on the Kuwaiti border, and Jeddah was preparing for delegations from both countries to discuss the crisis. Iraqi and Kuwaiti flags decorated the city, and everywhere streets were barricaded to allow passage of motorcades.

"Of course, the Iraqis have a case," Thorensen said. "The Kuwaitis have been drilling diagonal shafts into their oil fields for years, stealing their oil. It's a way of life here, but Saddam has a lot of internal problems, so what better than an external threat to unify the country?" Thorensen picked up the check left by the Filipino waiter, smiled at the two Americans. "But, like the rest of Saudi Arabia, I sleep easier at night knowing the American Air Force is on the side of Saudi oil."

While they waited for the credit card slip, Bob rose, excused himself to visit the men's room. As soon as he left, Thorensen leaned toward Liz. "What about Thursday? Are you free?"

"Well, I hadn't really thought about it," she said, "but I'm sure on a Thursday we'll be working, probably quite late. We haven't even started to look at the job, yet."

"Surely you won't be working on the weekend? Here that's Thursday noon until Saturday morning. We could play tennis at the Aramco compound as soon as it cools off, stay for their barbecue afterward and a swim in their pool." Thorensen leaned closer, and Liz leaned away, half expecting to see henna bearded men descending upon them. "Then Friday a few of my colleagues and their wives are driving up the coast for windsurfing and some diving. The Red Sea is magical for tropical fish.'' He pulled out a small leather notebook. ''What is your telephone number? I'll call.''

''I don't know it, I'm afraid. We only arrived yesterday, and I haven't had reason to use it yet.''

''No matter. I'll get it from one of the nurses. They'll know. You'll be in one of the women's residences attached to the hospital.''

''No, I have a lovely house, fountain in the garden, high walls. Total privacy. You must come and see it. With a friend and his wife, of course, to maintain the proprieties.''

Lars Thorensen stopped writing and looked up from beneath his brows. ''You have a house, alone?''

''Yes. Silly, isn't it?'' Liz said, laughing. ''Bob's rattling around in some barn of a palace, and I'm alone in a house that looks as if it should be in Moorish Spain or Palm Springs. Really, you must come and see it.''

Thorensen closed the notebook, slipped it back into the inner pocket of his jacket. He kept his face lowered, not meeting her eyes. ''What a memory I have. Of course, I am on duty this weekend.'' He rose and waited while Liz picked up her bag. ''But I'll be in touch.''

She'd said something, Liz thought. Something that really upset him. But what?

8

Jeddah General Hospital seemed to lack damn near every facility available to patients—and staff—that the cool, world-class King Khaled Clinic had. Every day since she had started at Jeddah General—pinch-hitting until its medical director, Hisham Badawi, could recruit female doctors from the Muslim world—Liz had complained, and every day Dr. Badawi had assured her that the air-conditioning in the surgical suite was the top priority on that day's list of repairs to be done. Not much more than that seemed to happen.

Liz turned her head, keeping her eyes steady on the pads of bloody flesh on which she was working, and leaned toward the Filipina nurse. Swiftly, the nurse dabbed a square of gauze on the beads of sweat on Liz's forehead, catching them before they could drip into her eyes, or into the open wound of the woman lying under the draped surgical sheets. The fixtures over the operating table threw a clear white light, but with the unreliable air-conditioning, the heat they produced was relentless.

Liz placed the diseased breast into the receptacle one of the scrub nurses held ready, then started to close up, the silence in the operating room broken only by the soft voice of the nurse-anesthetist at the patient's head murmuring verses from the Koran in Arabic. Liz never dreamed that one of the things she would miss most would be Talbot's tuneless humming while he worked to the big band music he loved, or the sound of Rusty Welch's baritone singing along with the Delta blues. If her own patients had expressed no preference, her taste in the operating room had run more to Mozart. No longer. Now it was verses from the Koran. Even without understanding them, she found the cadence of the verses as soothing as the patient probably did.

Liz glanced at the nurse-anesthetist. The patient's vital signs were steady—with luck she had another thirty hard years of herding goats in the desert ahead of her—and Liz stepped back to allow the nurses to prepare her for the recovery room.

Exhausted—her day had started as soon as the dawn prayer was over—Liz made her way to the changing room she shared with the nurses to strip off her greens before speaking to the family.

Alone in the silence, Liz thought of the surgeons' lounge at Saint Luke's, the discussions of the day's work with her colleagues, the exchange of gossip. And Pia—blessed Pia, always on top of the details. Tonight she still had a couple of hours work ahead of her, dictating notes that the Pakistani clerks might or might not get around to transcribing the next day.

Occasionally, when she had the energy to spare, she wondered how she'd got so deeply involved here in five short weeks. She and Bob had met Badawi when they had toured Jeddah General to assess its readiness in case of Iraqi attack. A few days later Badawi had called her. The *mutawain* had issued an edict stating that it was an abomination for male doctors to treat women and girls over the age of seven. Jeddah General, with a patient population of tribal Bedouins, urban poor and foreign contract laborers, had suddenly found itself with no surgeons to treat its female patients. Badawi had asked for one day a week, maybe, very occasionally, a few more hours, no more. He'd called her directly, not Gould, which was amazing in itself, and she'd heard the anxiety underlying his words. With Gould's blessing, she'd agreed to help until a female surgeon arrived—a week, not more than two, he'd assured her; Muslim doctors were eager to work in Saudi Arabia, all he had to do was pick up the phone. Now most of her time was spent here and, like the air-conditioning, recruitment of the female Muslim doctor was always top of his list.

In the crowded waiting room, her patient's Bedouin family had staked out a corner, the old man surrounded by five sons, one of whom spoke some English. Liz had been amazed to find how full waiting rooms in Saudi hospitals could be, whole families camping for days rather than leaving a loved one alone. In the far corner she noticed Dr. Badawi in earnest conversation with another anxious group.

The Bedouins stood as she stopped in front of them.

Liz addressed the old man. "Everything went well. Mrs. Lateef will sleep now for several hours, but there is no reason she should not make a complete recovery."

The son translated. The initial consultations had been with these two men while her patient had remained silent behind her veil. Later, when Liz had asked her through a nurse if she was interested in breast reconstruction, the woman had been shyly pleased. If her husband gave his permission, she said. But he had dismissed the suggestion; such a thing was not the will of Allah. Liz had tried to change his mind, but found it beyond her linguistic ability to argue the religious implications of reconstructive breast surgery.

"We will take her back to her place now," the younger Bedouin said.

"That is not possible," Liz said. "She is in the recovery room. The nurse will let you know when you can see her for a few minutes."

The young man repeated her words to his father. Without looking at Liz, the old man waved a dismissive hand.

"We will take her to her place," the young man repeated.

"I'm sorry," Liz said patiently. "Your mother will be in the hospital for at least another week." Not this man's mother, she thought. She knew from her patient's file that she was a third wife, maybe the same age as the interpreter, maybe less.

"Dr. Ryan. Perhaps I can be of assistance?"

Gratefully, Liz turned toward Dr. Badawi. "Oh, thanks. Will you explain that Mrs. Lateef will be in the recovery room until the morning and will definitely not be discharged from this hospital for at least another week? I want to give her the rest. She's just had a breast removed and they want to take her back to the desert. Now, tonight. And I'm not sure they understand it is imperative that she return to the hospital on a regular basis for chemotherapy. Will you please impress that upon them?"

Dr. Badawi nodded, then spoke in Arabic to the group of Bedouin. Liz kept her eyes on him as he spoke, trying to follow his words. He was heavily mustached; his red-and-white checked *ghutra* framed a round face with skin pitted with old acne scars. He listened respectfully to the old man, nodding at his words, and his own voice was patient when answering.

Silently the old man gestured to his sons, and they resumed their seats without a glance in Liz's direction.

"They are grateful, Dr. Ryan, please don't think they are not," Dr. Badawi said. He waved a hand, indicating their surroundings. "But this is a different world for them, a different century even."

"Thanks for your help. I had visions of that poor woman in the back of a pickup, heading out to the desert." Liz fell in beside him as they left the waiting room. "You're late tonight."

Badawi shrugged. "As usual. Let me give you a cup of coffee. You look as if you could use it."

Liz hesitated only a minute, thinking of the pile of charts awaiting her. "You're right, I could. Thanks."

Badawi left the door of his office open. "It's stupid, but we have to be careful. Assholes are everywhere."

"Hisham, you are going to get into trouble, talking like that."

"Fuck 'em," he said.

"Dr. Badawi, I think you spent too many dissolute years in the U.S," she teased. He'd done both his training and his residency at Massachusetts General.

"Sit." He motioned to the chair in front of his desk, then turned to pick up the carafe of coffee from the automatic coffeemaker almost hidden among stacks of papers and files and filled two mugs. Jeddah General Hospital was one of the only two hospitals in the city not operated under Western contract, and here, nothing was remotely reminiscent of the lavish quarters occupied by Dr. al-Turki at King Khaled Clinic.

"Liz, I still don't know how to thank you," Badawi said. "I don't know what we would do without you. You are a gift from the Prophet, blessings be upon him."

Liz shook her head, smiling at him, and he raised his eyebrows and grinned back at her, enjoying the knowledge that she was on to him. Hisham Badawi was a master manipulator—he'd got her there, managing daily to involve her deeper and deeper with his patients. Her salary was still paid through Dr. Gould, and every week Badawi failed to recruit the promised Muslim surgeon, he could apply the funds he saved to a thousand and one other needs of his hospital. He was the only hands-on Saudi physician Liz knew, dedicated to the community he served. And in no rush to change the status quo. Nor, she found, was she.

Liz sipped the strong American coffee. "Were you able to get CNN today?" CNN was their only reliable source of news, that and the BBC World Service on shortwave radio, but reception was iffy, blocked by the government whenever they felt like it.

"No, nor the BBC. The Aramco people might be getting them, but we can't. They've been blocked since the king invited U.S. forces into the kingdom. Rumors are flying around the mosques, though. There's a lot of trouble in Mecca."

"In Mecca? What kind of trouble?" Liz asked.

"Fundamentalists with guns. Speeches about the corruption of the Al Sa'ud, rioting because the king has brought infidels into the kingdom desecrating sacred Islamic soil." Badawi picked up a circlet of blue stone worry beads from his desk, ran them through his fingers. "I don't know who's worse, the fundamentalists or the Al Sa'ud. There's no place in today's world for an absolute monarchy, no free press, no voice in the affairs of the country."

"Hisham, please." Liz looked nervously at the open door.

Badawi shrugged. "Something in this kingdom has got to change, or the fundamentalists are going to take over. And things will get a thousand times worse if that happens."

"Hisham, at least lower your voice."

He didn't. "This country is headed for trouble, Liz. Too many princes use our resources as their own private funds, and the only alternative is people who want to take us back to the fourteenth century, when what we need are leaders who will help us get ready to join the rest of the world in the twenty-first."

Liz got up, went to the door and looked along the corridor outside his office. It was empty. She left the door open, returned to her seat.

"Okay, okay." Badawi reached behind him for his coffeepot, gestured to Liz to hold out her mug for a refill. "So, how are you doing in our desert paradise? Missing L.A., I bet."

"Sometimes. It's different, that's for sure."

"You're doing a lot of good work here, Liz."

"I'm grateful for the chance to do it." As Bob had promised, she was working on cases she'd never get to see in the United States.

She hesitated. She'd been looking for an opportunity to talk to Badawi. There would never be a better time than this. "Hisham, if I wanted to find a woman in a Saudi household, how would I go about it?"

He looked puzzled. "Find a woman? What woman? A patient?"

"No, not a patient. Someone my mother knew thirty years ago."

"Your mother was here in 1960?"

"1958. My father was with the American legation in Jeddah."

"And your mother had a Saudi friend? In 1958? Wonders never cease. What was her name?"

"Fateema."

He raised his eyebrows. "That's it? Fateema?"

Liz nodded. "That's all I know."

"Liz. Can you imagine my going to Boston and asking if someone at Mass General knew my old friend, Rashid? Good old Rashid, lived in Boston thirty years ago?"

"Boston is not exactly the Jeddah of thirty years ago. Anyway, I didn't ask if you knew Fateema. I asked how I could go about finding her."

Hisham leaned back in his chair and laced his fingers across his small paunch. "I don't know. What else do you know about her?"

"Well, she was, still is if she's alive, Circassian, not Arab."

"A relation of yours?"

"What makes you say that?"

"I don't know. Your green eyes, I suppose. Red hair. A

lot of Circassian women have that coloring. Is she a relation?''

''I don't know. Maybe. A branch of the family went to the United States. Another branch could have leafed out in Jeddah.''

''Who was she married to?''

''She was a concubine.'' The words were out. A mistake. She put her mug down. ''Not important.

''Dr. Ryan, you are full of surprises. Your mother had a friend who was a concubine in a Saudi household? In 1958?'' His eyebrows had almost disappeared into his *ghutra.* ''How old would this Fateema be now?''

''I don't know.'' Liz couldn't say forty-five. How could she explain a friendship between an American woman and a thirteen-year-old Circassian concubine? She rose to her feet. ''It's not important, just a thought. My mother suggested I look her up. Thanks for the coffee, Hisham. Don't work too late. Good night.'' She crossed his office, went out, then poked her head back around the door before leaving. He had turned on his desk light and was pulling a stack of files toward him. ''And for heaven's sake, get that air-conditioning in the surgical suite fixed.''

Hisham grinned at her. ''It's at the top of the priority list for tomorrow.''

Two hours later, paperwork finished, Liz emerged from the hospital into the parking lot and breathed in the soft night air. During the day, the moisture that came off the Red Sea was a nightmare of humidity, but at night it cooled the air, brought out the green scent from the seven million trees and shrubs planted in Jeddah since the oil boom started.

Yousef was hunkered down beside the black Mercedes. As she approached, he closed the book he was reading and rose to his feet, carefully nipping the glowing coal from his ever present cigarette before stowing the remainder in a pocket of his *thobe*.

"Evening, Yousef. Sorry to have kept you waiting." Liz smiled brightly, convinced that one of these days, he would have to smile in return.

"It is not waiting when I study the word of the Prophet, blessings be upon him."

"Amen." Liz climbed into the back seat. She had insisted that the curtains between front and back be left open so that her vision was not restricted to the side view. Easing out of the parking lot, Yousef turned right onto Al Matar Road, passing the building that housed the female medical staff. When she'd first arrived, she had been surprised at the sight of armed guards in front of the gates. To safeguard the women, she'd been told—from what had never been made clear. Now she no longer noticed them. Tonight, though, her attention was caught by a different group of men. Long henna-dyed beards. Unkempt.

"Yousef, slow down. What's happening?"

"The holy men, madam. They make sure the women are inside. There are rumors of unrest in Mecca."

"And the nurses are doing a bit of illegal gun running in their spare time, no doubt." Liz expelled a disgusted breath. She leaned back. "Okay, go on."

All across the city, knots of men hung around the mosques, deep in heated discussion. They looked jumpy, groups forming, reforming, arms waving. Even the fear of Saddam Hussein and his SCUDs had not produced this degree of tension.

Her own neighborhood was quiet. A few men lingered by the tiny mosque at the end of the street. In the narrow lanes leading to her house on Al Fatayah Street, the rising moon silvered the ghostly blossoms of white oleanders hanging over the walls, and halfway down she picked out the drift of purple bougainvillea that marked her own garden.

Robed figures waited outside her gates.

"I will go on, madam," Yousef said. "This is not good, I think."

"Who are they?"

"Holy men from the mosque. I drive on."

"No. Go to the gate as usual."

"This is not wise, I think—"

"Yousef, these men have no business attempting to terrorize me, if that's what they intend. I'm tired and I want to go home. I will not give in to this."

As Yousef slowed the car, one of the men broke free of another's grasp. He rushed forward, thrust his face against the window of the Mercedes—a foot from her own face, close enough for her to see the straggling henna-stained beard, the wild eyes, the gaping, shouting mouth, the gobs of spittle bursting against the glass—horrifying even though she knew he could not see her. A hand on the door, he paced at a half run with the slowly moving car, wrenching at the handle. Yousef stopped in front of the gates, and half turned to speak to Liz.

"Open the gate, Yousef," she said before he could argue. "Open them."

"Madam—" Yousef stopped as a man, tall, heavily built, detached himself from the cluster of *mutawain* and rushed forward.

Yousef got out of the car—to run, Liz thought, leaving her alone. She grabbed the back of the front seat—if they wanted her they were going to have to drag her out, and she didn't think they would do that. But instead of ripping open the door, the man seized the *mutawa*, thrust him away from the Mercedes, then positioned himself between the car and the angry *mutawain*. In the confusion of struggling bodies, Liz caught a shocked glimpse of a gun in his right hand—no one owned guns in Saudi Arabia.

Then Yousef was back in the car, slamming on the gas,

and they were through the gates. Liz turned to look out of the rear window. Their rescuer was struggling alone to close the gates while keeping the *mutawain* at bay, until Yousef got there and dropped the wooden bar in place.

It was over.

His features had been hidden by the black-and-white checked *ghutra* wound around his face, only a slit left for eyes that were impossible to see in the dark. But Liz knew she had seen that tall, solid figure before.

Yousef opened the car door, peering in when she did not move. "Madam?"

Liz gathered her bag and briefcase. Her heartbeat was slow to return to normal and it didn't help that she could still hear raised voices outside the walls. "Well, what was that all about?" she asked. "What is he shouting, that madman?"

Yousef hesitated, then said, "He thinks bad foreign women live here."

"Ah. Of course. I should have guessed. But why here particularly?"

Yousef shrugged.

"Who was the other man? The one who held them off?"

Yousef kept his eyes on a point somewhere over her left shoulder. "An emissary of the Prophet, blessings be upon him."

"A pretty solid angel, Yousef."

"Who are we to question the Divine, madam?"

Liz waited for a moment, but knew he would tell her nothing. He'd known the man, she was sure of it. He'd shown no surprise, just accepted his help without question.

"Well, thank you for getting us through. Usual time in the morning. Good night."

Yousef slid behind the wheel, and Liz watched until the car disappeared around the back of the house toward the garage. Not for the first time, she wondered how it was that he was here, a Saudi in a household of women not of his family. Where was his own family, his wives and children?

"Good evening, madam, Dr. Ryan." The front door opened, flooding the courtyard with light. "Fresh coffee is ready. American coffee."

"Hi, Siti." Liz relinquished her briefcase to the young maid and walked into the peaceful living room. "I'm about coffeed out. Do we have any Pepsi?"

A Coke was out of the question. Only Pepsi-Cola was available in the kingdom. Lars Thorensen had volunteered that bit of information when she'd attempted to order a Coke at The Red Sea Palace when they'd first arrived. Something about investment in Israel. Coca-Cola did, Pepsi-Cola didn't. They'd settled for nonalcoholic beer that day, and she'd watched Bob struggle to believe it had some sort of kick, his eyes closing as he savored the maltiness on his tongue. But there was no buzz from .005 percent alcohol. Since then he'd connected—a bunch of Scandinavian doctors would certainly have a line on some booze, even if they had to make it themselves. Some mornings, Bob looked like hell, shaky and sick. But at least he didn't get into an operating room anymore.

"We've had another delivery, I see."

"Yes, madam, Dr. Ryan," Siti answered.

The orchids were fresh and glowing. She hadn't heard from Abdullah, but twice a week the orchids arrived, as they had at Saint Luke's. She had stopped asking Bob about Abdullah—he'd heard nothing from him, either. Not surprising as Saudi Arabia was deep in crisis and Abdullah was close to the king. What did surprise her, though, was the depth of her disappointment at his silence.

Liz dropped into the corner of a sofa, stretched her legs in front of her. So much she didn't understand.

"Dr. Ryan, madam."

Liz opened her eyes and sat up. Siti held out a tray bearing a moisture-beaded glass of Pepsi, and the three newspapers Yousef picked up every day, the *Saudi Gazette*, the *Times* from London, and the *Herald Tribune* from Paris. Liz unfolded the *Times*.

"Well, quite a lot missing today, Siti. Look." She held it up. The front page looked like misshapen origami, whole columns cut out. Any mention of Israel, any reference to members of the Royal House of Sa'ud, any war news not passed by censors were all forbidden. On the inside pages, ads for lingerie had been blacked out, and the legs of the dancers for that night's performance of the Royal Ballet Company's Swan Lake at Covent Garden had been covered with a black grease pencil. The man-hours involved to censor every single piece of foreign newsprint entering the country boggled the mind. Liz looked up at Siti, ready to laugh.

The girl's eyes were red, puffy from tears. Liz noticed her shaking hands and put aside the decimated paper.

"What is it, Siti?" she asked. "What's the matter?"

"Don't send us away, madam, Dr. Ryan," Siti whispered. "We did not do wrong. We just went to the supermarket, as you said."

"What happened?"

Siti held the tray to her thin chest. "He hit Megawati."

"Who did? Who hit her?"

"The *mutawa*. Her legs, madam, Dr. Ryan. He said they will send her away, and send me away. Take our wages, not let us work anymore here. And our fathers need the money we send to them."

Liz knew that everything they earned was sent back to their parents, after the cut taken by the labor broker. Liz had been giving them a few extra *riyals* each week, insisting they use it to buy bits and pieces for themselves, hair ribbons, lipstick, a magazine. She felt as much to blame for this as anyone.

"No one's going to send you away, Siti." Liz spoke with more conviction than she felt. These girls were in her care, and she hadn't thought it through, made the connections she should have. The Saudi newspapers had been running articles lately condemning the un-Islamic behavior of girls shopping in the newly built air-conditioned malls, fluttering their *abayas* so the young Saudis hanging around could catch a fleeting glimpse of forbidden skirts, or worse, have their lusts aroused by the sight of a female foot, decorated with intricate patterns in henna, clad in a sexy high-heeled sandal.

Liz got to her feet, went to the kitchen, Siti following her. Megawati was standing in the middle of the room, her face pale and tearstained. She seemed even younger, certainly smaller and more frail than Siti.

"Megawati, it's all right," Liz said soothingly. "Let me see where you are hurt."

The girl hesitated, looking at Siti for reassurance.

"It's all right, Megawati," Liz repeated. "No one will send you away. Let me see."

Megawati turned, loosened her baggy pants, stepped out of them and lifted her long tunic. Liz tightened her lips. The backs of the girl's thighs were a mass of welts. To make marks like that, through her clothes, the *mutawa* must really have laid in. Liz wondered how much was religious fanaticism, and how much was sexual psychosis fed by these legal beatings of young girls.

"The marks will fade, Megawati. They are not permanent," she said. "I'll get you some salve to soothe the discomfort. How did it happen?"

"We were coming out of the supermarket," Siti said.

"Both of you? You were together?"

"Yes, madam, Dr. Ryan."

"You were both veiled?"

"Oh, yes, madam, Dr. Ryan." Siti sounded shocked.

''What sort of shoes were you wearing?''

''The Reeboks you bought for us, madam, Dr. Ryan.''

''Then there's nothing to worry about,'' Liz said firmly. ''Nothing's going to happen to you. You'll be working here long after I am gone. The welts will go down with the salve, and I'll give you something to help you sleep.'' She patted Megawati's shoulder and was glad to see an answering, wavery smile. They were good kids, quiet and innocent. What the hell could their parents be thinking of, allowing them to be in servitude so far from the protection of home and family?

She caught herself. What did she know of the conditions of their world? These girls, for all she knew, were the sole support of a whole network of people—parents, siblings, elderly grandparents. And she herself probably had roots in the same sort of tribal society, peopled with blood kin she would never know.

It was in her bloodstream, too, that world.

9

Liz jerked awake. The pounding was at the bedroom door, not inside her head.

"What is it?" She switched on her bedside light, peered at the clock. It was 2:00 a.m.

"Liz, are you awake?" Bob Gould's voice called. "We have an emergency."

"Coming." She grabbed a robe, pulling it on as she crossed the room. Gould was on the threshold as she opened her bedroom door. Behind him Siti and Megawati looked frightened.

"Have the Iraqis attacked?" She could hear no explosions, no sirens.

"No, no." Bob turned to the two girls. "There is nothing for you to worry about. Why don't you both go and make some coffee? Wake us all up." He turned back to Liz. "I've sent Yousef back to bed. You'd better get dressed, Liz."

"Right." She didn't waste time asking questions. She closed her bedroom door, crossed to the bathroom and quickly brushed her teeth, splashed water onto her face. She dressed in loose, comfortable trousers, a shirt and jacket. On the way out she picked up her medical bag—out of habit she had it always ready on a chair by the door—and made her way to the kitchen.

Bob had sent the two girls back to bed. He poured a mug of coffee and handed it to her. His hands were shaking. "Drink it quickly," he said. "We have to leave."

Liz gulped the strong black coffee. "What's happening?"

"We're going to Mecca."

She smacked the coffee mug down, slopping coffee onto the table. "We can't do that! We're infidels!" Mecca was protected. Enormous signs in English and Arabic warned infidels not to approach the roads leading to Islam's most holy city, and armed checkpoints made sure they didn't.

"Infidels or not, that's where we're going."

"That's crazy. Crazy!" Liz said. "There's an uprising there, Jeddah's seething with rumors. Haven't you heard? If we're caught in Mecca in the middle of all that trouble, it wouldn't be jail, Bob. It would be execution, on the spot. No infidel has ever been in Mecca—"

"Yes, they have—"

"Okay, who?"

"Sir Richard Burton was there in 1853 and wrote about it, and we don't really know how many others," he said. "Anything's possible here, Liz, you know that. With a controlled press, nothing leaks unless the Al Sa'ud says so. Who knows who gets in and out? It's never reported, that's all. Who's going to ask questions, some investigative reporter? I don't think so. Liz, we're doctors and we're needed—"

"If surgeons are needed, let them send Muslims—" She stopped at the sound of a male voice, becoming louder as the speaker came down the hall from the front of the house. "Who's here?"

"Dr. Gould? Dr. Gould?" A young Saudi came into the kitchen. At the sight of Liz, he stopped, looked at Gould, then back at Liz. "Good morning," he said politely. He turned to Gould. "Please, we must go. Where is Dr. Ryan?"

"This is Dr. Ryan," Gould said.

The young man looked at Liz silently, the expression on his face speaking volumes. He turned his eyes back to Gould. "A Western woman cannot be taken into Mecca."

"If I'm to go, Dr. Ryan goes, too. She is a surgeon, and

a very good one. This is Prince Samir, Liz. Dr. Elizabeth Ryan.''

"How do you do?" Liz said.

To her surprise, Prince Samir reached out a hand, and she took it. The handshake was firm and brief. He did not smile.

"I am sorry," he said. "This is not possible. Please, we must go now. A helicopter is waiting—"

"If I'm to operate," Bob insisted, "I must have Dr. Ryan with me. I need her."

Liz looked at Gould's hands, and then at his eyes, bloodshot and moist. Goddamn it, he was hungover. That's why he had insisted on strong coffee. Not to make sure she was awake, but to steady his nerves.

"Liz, the king's cousin, Prince Bandr, is in the Grand Mosque in Mecca." Gould held up a hand to silence the protest from Samir. "She has to know what she's being asked to do. There is fighting there," he said to Liz, "and the prince has taken a wound to the head. No one knows the extent of the injury. I have been instructed to ascertain this, and if necessary, perform whatever procedure is indicated to save his life. I'll need your help for that."

She couldn't bear to look at Gould, at the silent plea in his eyes. "Perhaps it would be better if someone else from King Khaled went instead of you, Dr. Gould. Or Dr. Badawi from Jeddah General. He's an excellent surgeon."

"We are wasting time," Samir said. "Dr. Ryan, Prince Bandr is an important man in Saudi Arabia, the king's cousin and a close adviser. You may have heard of him, your press refers to him as the fundamentalist prince. Prince Abdullah has sent for Dr. Gould. He wants Dr. Gould to attend Prince Bandr. Had he wanted a Muslim surgeon, he would have sent one—"

"Then why didn't he?" Liz asked.

"Prince Abdullah has given his instructions. I do not

question them." Prince Samir looked at Gould. "Prince Abdullah said nothing about Dr. Ryan."

"Well, if Prince Abdullah needs me in Mecca, I need Dr. Ryan. Liz?"

The note in his voice cut to her heart. Liz picked up her medical bag. "All right. Of course. Let's go."

Prince Samir did not move.

Liz put down her medical bag. Bob sat in one of the kitchen chairs. They waited.

Finally Samir said, "You must be covered. *Abayah* and *gutwah.*"

Liz stood. "I can get that. Just a minute."

She ran through the service pantry and the laundry room, banged on the door of the room shared by the two maids. A small face appeared through a crack in the door.

"Siti, I need to borrow an *abayah* and *gutwah.* Quickly."

The girl scurried into the room, then thrust a bundle of black cloth into Liz's hands. Liz slipped into the *abayah*— it smelled of Attar of Roses, the supermarket brand from India—and draped the *gutwah* over her head, fighting the fabric.

"God, how can you see through this?"

"Be still, madam, Dr. Ryan. I will do it." Siti adjusted the folds of the veil so that a rectangular mesh "window" settled over Liz's eyes, marginally improving her field of vision.

"Siti, both of you, stay inside the house until I return," Liz said. "Tomorrow, the day after. I'm not sure. Don't speak to anyone, not even Yousef." Especially not Yousef. Suddenly her suspicions leapt onto center stage. Who did he work for? Who commanded his loyalty? Paranoia was catching, she was getting as bad as the rest of the country.

So be it. After the run-in with the *mutawain,* her own and theirs, she needed to know the girls were safe, locked inside the house until she got back. "Shut the gates when we leave," she instructed Siti. "Keep the front door closed and don't answer the phone."

When she returned to the kitchen, now an anonymous black figure, Samir nodded. "Good. Dr. Gould, you could pass for an Arab but only as long as you don't speak. Please remember that."

Twenty minutes later, Samir turned onto the military road that led to the airport. He called out a few words at a checkpoint and guards stepped back hurriedly. The car picked up speed across empty runways. In the distance, giant C-5s of the U.S. Air Force were bathed in fierce white light, men and machinery unloading their cargoes.

Another five minutes and they were in a remote part of the airport, no buildings, no lights. Just one helicopter painted in desert camouflage parked on the rocky sand.

Samir climbed aboard, turned and held out his hand. Liz took it, hiked up the *abayah*, and scrambled up beside him, Gould close behind her. Samir slammed the door, then settled into the pilot's seat.

"Hope you've got some hours on this thing," Bob said.

"I was trained at the air force academy in Colorado Springs," Samir said. "Now, sit please. The journey will not be long."

The engine whined, the helicopter shuddered, then rose into the star-filled night.

Liz struggled to free herself from the unfamiliar *abayah*, and its stale scent. Impatiently she pulled off the *gutwah* that covered her head and body and fell into folds that seemed to tangle with the *abayah* at every movement she made. Finally free, she buckled up.

Samir turned, pointed to the earphones hanging above the passenger seats. Gould unhooked them, handed a set to Liz. "You must stay covered." Samir's voice was close in her ear.

"Don't push your luck," Liz said. "Are there nurses in Mecca?"

"Of course, nurses."

"She means at the Mosque, waiting for us," Gould said. Prince Samir shrugged.

"No nurses," Gould said to Liz. He took off his earphones, motioning to Liz to remove hers. He rose from his seat, put his mouth against her ear. "I'm going to check the equipment he said was onboard. I want to make sure we're not expected to dig around in Prince Bandr's brain with a screwdriver."

Beneath them the desert was black and interminable. In California, deserts were dotted with light from clusters of ranch buildings, the occasional spill of a small town. Here the density of the emptiness was frightening. She'd hate to have to travel across those sands; the deserts of Arabia had to be among the most unforgiving places on earth.

The terrain below started to change, mountains rising suddenly from the desert floor. Samir pointed to a fold in the hills. "The road to Mecca."

Liz nodded, fighting an urge to laugh. The prince would not be amused to know that it sounded like a movie title from the forties, the old *Road* films of Bob Hope and Bing Crosby, with Dorothy Lamour in a sarong. She and Judd both loved them, waiting for the familiar old gags and laughing every time. She wondered where Judd was now. Certainly somewhere in the Gulf already, maybe within a few miles. Liz wished he would write to her, but until he decided to respond to her last letter, she wouldn't write again. His silence made his feelings clear. But she missed him, more than she thought possible. More than he would believe.

Samir uttered a sharp word in Arabic. To the west, the night sky was glowing.

"What is it?" she yelled at him. He didn't answer.

"Fires in Mecca," Bob said. He had settled himself back in his seat, replaced his earphones. "Supplies are okay. Adequate." He buckled himself in as the helicopter tilted, swinging toward the fires.

The pitch of the engine changed as the chopper descended. Below them city lights glittered like diamonds across the hills. The great jewel of the Grand Mosque was unmistakable—floodlit colonnaded buildings and minarets surrounding an immense courtyard.

And there was the *Kaa'ba,* the true center of Islam.

Awestruck, Liz gazed at the gigantic black-and-gold shrouded structure, the place that God commanded Abraham and Ishmael to build over four thousand years ago, the most holy place of Islam, the center to which every devout Muslim turned to pray five times each day. She might be the only female infidel who had ever seen it, or ever would.

Along one edge of the courtyard, tongues of flame reached skyward.

The craft shuddered. Samir slipped the chopper sideways. Liz looked straight down, out of the window. Her stomach tilted.

"Oh, my God! He's not going to try to put us down in that courtyard," she shouted. She could hear the wobble of fear in her voice.

"Won't be easy if he is." Bob pointed. "See those flashes? Grenade launchers."

The chopper dropped, bouncing in the shock waves of an explosion. Liz could hear snatches of Samir's voice. Verses from the Koran. She tried to think of a prayer, but the only words that came were, *Now I lay me down to sleep.*

The noise was deafening: exploding rockets, the whine of the engine, the whomp of the rotors. Liz hung on to the frame of her seat. She tried to swallow, but had no saliva.

Gould reached over, patted a hand. "Don't worry. These jokers couldn't hit the USS *New Jersey* at fifty paces."

She shot him a look. He was grinning. He looked better than he had in her kitchen in Jeddah. The young naval lieutenant who had saved her life when she was born was struggling to repossess his own life. Men, she thought. Who could understand them?

He leaned over her to get a better look at the ground. Fifty feet below, the robes of what seemed to be an army of gunmen were pinned against their bodies by the wind kicked up by the hovering craft, their *ghutras* fluttering wildly in the chop. The courtyard was bright with orange-and-red flames from the fires, a paler reflection thrown across white paving stones. Automatic weapons pointed upward. No sound of gunfire could be heard over the noise of the rotors, but Liz could see the shuddering arms and shoulders of the gunmen taking the recoil.

A ribbon of bullets opened a seam just above Gould's head, smashed across the cabin.

"Bull's-eye," he yelled. "Their aim's improving."

Suddenly, painfully aware that the metal skin of the craft was no protection, Liz unbuckled, ripped off her earphones, got to her feet with some confused notion that movement would make it harder for a bullet to find her soft, vulnerable flesh. She stumbled toward Samir.

"You're not landing in the courtyard?" she yelled.

"We have to."

"But it's filled with gunmen—"

"When we get lower, they will scatter."

Beads of moisture trickled into his dark beard and his fine white cotton *thobe* was damp beneath his arms, stuck to his skin between his shoulders. The smell of male sweat hung heavy in the close confines of the cabin.

"Can't you find another landing spot, a hospital or office building?"

"This isn't New York," he shouted. "We don't know what the situation is in the rest of Mecca, but we do know for certain that my father is somewhere beneath the mosque. We have to land now, without delay. Men are waiting for us.''

''Prince Bandr's your father?''

''Put on the veil,'' he shouted. ''I'm putting down.''

''I can't see anything in it! How am I going to get from this helicopter into that building without getting shot if I can't see anything?''

''Get the *abayah*,'' Samir shouted. ''Get it!''

The chopper was only a few feet above the ground. As Samir predicted, the rotors had driven the gunmen back. The helicopter settled. Samir turned off the engine. He grabbed the *abayah* from the back of Liz's seat, draped it over her shoulders, then threw the veil over her hair. Liz fumbled her arms into the slits in the seams of the *abayah*, struggled to find the mesh rectangle in the *gutwah*. She picked up her medical bag.

Gould was already wrestling with the door.

''Wait!'' Samir yelled. He grabbed a weapon from a rack beside the door, then nodded. Gould slammed the door back, Samir sprayed an arcing burst across the courtyard, then jumped to the ground. Liz could see his mouth moving, but could hear nothing but the chatter of automatic weapons firing. Along one edge of the courtyard, she could see flames shooting from several buildings. Gould's hand in the middle of her back urged her forward. Adrenaline kicked in. She jumped, felt Bob on her heels.

The air was hot, filled with smoke and the stink of explosives. Bodies were everywhere. Automatically she bent low, providing as small a target as possible. Samir was running, and she followed, medical bag clutched in one hand, *abayah* gathered in the other, peering through the mesh to keep Samir in view.

Samir gained the cover of a colonnaded gallery, Liz a step behind him. She threw the veil back from her face and leaned against the wall, panting, still high on the adrenaline rush. From the ground, the great square was even more immense, the enclosing buildings multistoried, arched, colonnaded, domed, ornate.

As soon as she could think, she realized that not all the bullets were coming their way—some of the gunmen were firing out toward the perimeter, laying down protective fire—and in the same instant saw that Bob was not crouched against the sheltering wall with them. He was yards away still, in the open courtyard. He staggered and without thinking, Liz jumped toward him. Samir grabbed her arm, jerking her back.

She struggled. "He's been hit!"

Samir's answer was a tightening of his fingers around her arm. Gould steadied, covered the last few yards, then hurled himself into the shelter of the gallery, slumped against the wall behind her.

"Goddamn medical bags weigh a ton," he panted. "I'm getting old."

"Age has nothing to do with it. You smoke too much and you drink too much," Liz yelled at him, furious.

Gould started to laugh. "Not now, Liz. Now is not a good time for that particular lecture."

An explosion battered their ears. Shock waves threatened to rip the air from fragile lungs. Instinctively they flung their arms over their heads and ears, curving their bodies to protect vulnerable organs. Heat seared unprotected skin as arcs of fiery aviation fuel spewed like napalm.

When they were able to look, scattered heaps of burning rubble was all that remained of the helicopter—and the medical supplies it carried.

They had managed to get into Mecca. Now they had no equipment beyond what they carried in two medical bags.

And no way out.

Liz's thoughts flashed to Judd, wishing he was with her,

glad that he was not. He'd be face-to-face with his own mortality soon enough.

Samir pointed at a door set into the wall where it intersected with another, and she nodded, glancing at Bob to see that he was ready. Crouching low, Samir started forward along the gallery, and Liz followed, Bob behind her.

The crump and whine of heavier weapons overlaid the din of automatic weapons fire. Bullets pulverized the stones at their feet, laced across the protective columns and the walls above their heads. A gunman, clad in a khaki *thobe,* was running toward them, and Samir raised his weapon. The man yelled. Samir shouted back, and the man waved the weapon in his hand, screaming orders to the men following him. Several more khaki-clad men raced to join him, turning as they ran, fanning out to protect the prince, firing blindly at the men pursuing them. Samir wrenched the door open. In the instant before hurling herself into the safety of the doorway, Liz snatched another glimpse of the courtyard. Several of their protectors were down, their blood leaking across the stones. Bob crashed into her. She staggered forward. The heavy door slammed, sealing them into the musty blackness.

Outside they could hear the fight still raging, but the door was old and heavy and the sounds were muted, like the soundtrack from a movie showing in the next theater.

"There is light here," Samir's voice said from the blackness. A switch clicked uselessly. "The electricity has been cut—"

"Good God!" Bob said. "We can't do anything without electricity."

And precious little with it, Liz thought. With no equipment beyond what they carried, even Bob Gould at his best wouldn't risk brain surgery, if that was what was required. And Bob was way past his best. How could they carry a man with a head injury through that maelstrom of gunfire? What they needed was a medevac team.

She kept silent. Nothing would be gained by pointing out the obvious.

Slowly the darkness became less impenetrable, Samir's white *thobe* clearer. They were in a corridor, the walls stretching into a black interior.

"Come," said Samir. "I know this building. I studied the Holy Koran here."

Samir put a hand on the wall, feeling his way. The two Americans followed, inching deeper into the Grand Mosque. Twice the building was shaken by explosions, plaster flaking from the ceiling like a snow shower.

Then light wavered at the end of the corridor. Samir stopped and they heard voices. Samir stretched an arm across the two Americans, urging silence.

Liz pulled the veil across her face, pressed herself against the wall. A group of white *thobe*-clad men came into view, their way lit by the lanterns in their hands, running along a corridor that crossed their own. An image from a biblical past, she thought, until the ugly snub-nosed assault weapons they carried jerked them back into the twentieth century. Liz tried not to think of hostages imprisoned by fundamentalists in Iraq and Lebanon.

The moment dragged, but the light faded and the men disappeared, the sound of their sandaled feet slapping against the tiled floor falling away into darkness.

"Now," Samir whispered. "Hurry."

Catching the last of the light as it receded, they moved more rapidly. Before they reached the end of the corridor, Samir opened a door.

"Be careful. The stairs are steep."

He took Liz's hand. She put out a tentative foot, sliding it over the edge of a steep stone step. Behind her Bob was breathing heavily, and she could feel the heat from his body, infinitely comforting.

Then the bottom of the stair became dimly visible. A man waited, lantern raised. His face was obscured by a heavy beard. His khaki *thobe* was loosely belted at the hips, his *ghutra* red-and-white checks. Bandoliers of bullets crossed his chest. He, too, was a figure out of history, a warrior who rode with the young Abdul Azziz ibn Sa'ud, father of his country. Samir spoke to him in a rapid undertone. The man answered and Samir turned to the Americans.

"This is Naif, Prince Bandr's bodyguard. He will take us to him. I told him you were Turkish doctors, volunteers for this, father and daughter, devout Muslims. He will not know the difference between English and Turkish, but it will be best if you speak little."

The area beneath the mosque was a labyrinth of passages. Liz lost count of the turns, the stone stairs, the doors through which they passed. Several times groups of armed, robed men passed them. Following a wavering lantern carried by a man who looked as if he belonged in another century, she felt she was in dreamtime, and knew from the glances they exchanged that Bob felt the same. In a whisper she asked Samir how Naif had managed to find them.

"Men have been posted at entry points all over the mosque looking for us. If it hadn't been Naif, it would have been someone else. The situation is not clear." Samir's voice shook. "Iraqis are here—they came as pilgrims and hid in the city, then joined with some of our own fundamentalists. Opponents of the Al Sa'ud. They have taken control of part of the Grand Mosque."

Bob put his mouth against Liz's ear. "Prince Bandr is the leader of the most rigid Muslim sect in Saudi Arabia, the *Wahhabis.* He's tight with these fundamentalists. So what the hell is going on here?"

Liz shook her head. She was frightened, deep in the bowels of an ancient building forbidden to non-Muslims, in the middle of a shooting war between fanatics. She didn't know anything except this wasn't the way to find Fateema, and that was the only reason she had come to Saudi Arabia in the first place. She wished she had never gone to that damned reception at the Beverly Wilshire, never met Abdullah bin Talal....

Naif had opened a door and Samir stood immobile on the threshold. In the light of the lantern, his normally olive-skinned face looked as if it had gone gray with shock.

Gould pushed past him, Liz close on his heels, into a room, dimly lit. Their patient lay on a table in the center. His *ghutra* and *arghal* had been removed, revealing gray hair matted with blood. Blood had run down the sides of his face, stained the white beard and pooled on the metal table.

Bob put a hand to Prince Bandr's face, then raised each eyelid. Delicately he lifted a strand of sticky hair, looking for the wound, careful not to move the head. "Prince Samir, bring a lantern, please."

Gently Liz felt for the pulse in the prince's left wrist. Thready. She slid her fingers down to grasp his hand, holding it firmly. It helped to let an unconscious person feel the presence of another human being.

Gould was impatient. "Bring a lantern. I can't see what I'm doing—"

Light flooded the room, flickered, then brightened and held steady as the hum of a generator came from behind a wall. The air cooled. Liz glanced around the room, then caught Bob's eye.

"This is an emergency field hospital, rough but adequate," he said softly. "They were preparing for trouble."

Prince Samir made sure the door was secure, motioning Naif to stand guard in front of it, then crossed to stand at Liz's elbow, facing Gould on the other side of Prince

Bandr's body. He made no attempt to touch his father, to replace Liz's reassuring hand with his own.

"What is Prince Bandr's condition?" he demanded.

Gould slid his hand beneath Bandr's head and turned it carefully. Clumsy attempts had been made to clean up the blood, a good portion of his hair hacked away in the process.

"How long has he been like this?" Gould asked.

Samir addressed a few words to the bodyguard. The man answered and Samir said, "About four hours."

Gould said, "His skull is intact, but there may be subdural hematoma. He's certainly in shock."

Samir's mouth tightened. "What does this mean?"

Gently Gould slipped his hands from beneath the unconscious man's head. "It means that blood may be leaking into the skull cavity and pressing on his brain. The blood you see is from a laceration in the scalp, not important, it can be repaired. It is my guess that Prince Bandr was struck from behind."

Samir placed both hands on the edge of the table, steadying himself.

Gould spoke softly. "Can you trust this man? Prince Bandr's bodyguard?" Samir did not answer and Gould looked up. The prince's eyes were unnaturally bright, burning in his head.

"I would have staked my life on it," Samir said, "but now I... You must do something, release the blood."

"I am not sure what is needed, and under these conditions, it's too risky to get in there to explore. Besides, everything we needed was in that helicopter. We must get him to a hospital. Can you call in another chopper?"

"Yes. But I must gather men I know to be loyal if we are to evacuate Prince Bandr through that courtyard."

"I think you had better tell us what is going on here."

"Nothing that need concern you—"

"Prince Samir, Dr. Ryan and I are infidels in Mecca.

Armed Iraqis are swarming all over the place. If we are captured—''

"You will not be," Samir said curtly. "The National Guard is drawn mostly from the *Wahhabis,* simple men, loyal to the Al Sa'ud. You saw them up there."

"Could they have been infiltrated?"

Samir hesitated. "It's possible. We have information that Afghani fundamentalists are here, also. The worst kind of fanatics. They could have inflamed some of the more extreme—''

His words were cut off by noise outside, a muffled confusion of voices coming closer, then the banging of fists on the door.

Quickly Liz pushed at the end of the gurney. Gould grabbed the other end, between them they maneuvered the injured man away from the direct line of fire from the door. The brass doorknob rattled.

My mother will never know how I died. The thought raced through Liz's mind. *My mother will never know how I lived.* I wanted her to know that she had given me a good life in the West.

She stood in front of Prince Bandr's body, and felt Bob's shoulder pressed against hers.

10

The door burst open with the weight of the bodies behind it, slamming Naif back against the wall. Liz turned to throw herself across Prince Bandr and felt Bob trying to cover them both with his own body. Liz could hear Naif shouting, *"La, la, la,"*—"No, no, no,"—as he jumped at Samir, pushing the barrel of his weapon down. The smell of blood mingled with the stink of explosives and burning oil clinging to stained and torn *thobes*. Liz waited for shots, for the feel of rough hands grabbing her. Instead, there seemed to be a sudden silence in which she could hear men groaning.

Samir's voice penetrated the distance that separated her from what was happening. His face was inches from hers.

"They're from the courtyard," he shouted. "The wounded."

The world came back into place. Liz tested her legs, found they could hold her. She stepped over a man across the doorway—a glance told her there was nothing she could do for him, his comrade had brought down a dead man—and went to a huddle of men against the outside wall. Beside her, Bob touched her shoulder, and she nodded to let him know she was all right. Between them they started to drag bleeding bodies into the room.

The sound of voices came from the end of the corridor. Both Americans looked up. Armed men—white *thobes,* not the khaki of the National Guard—running toward them. Liz felt beyond speech.

Gould lifted one man in his arms and tried to drag him. "Samir! We need help here!" He shouted in English—there was no time for concern about language. With luck the men around them could be convinced later it was Turkish. "These men are still alive. We've got to get them inside. Hurry!"

"No, it's all right." Samir shoved his way into the corridor, feet slipping in the blood. He shouted, bringing the running men to a halt.

"Christ, what a mess," Bob muttered to Liz. "Who the hell is loyal, who isn't? Let's get these people inside, anyway."

With Bob at the shoulders of the groaning man, Naif at his feet, they started the job of clearing the doorway.

"I'll get to the rest." Liz turned to the men milling about outside the door, shouting questions at each other that no one could answer. Most were bloody, a number half-conscious, supported by the less wounded away from the fighting in the courtyard. They needed a triage nurse, Liz thought. They needed Judd. This was his line of work, not hers. She caught Samir's sleeve.

"We have to get these men sorted out, who can wait, who must get immediate treatment. Tell Naif and whoever else is mobile to get as many blankets here as they can find. Now. Get going. Hurry."

An hour later, she knelt by the side of a dying man lying on the floor of the corridor. He was heavily sedated, but she kept a hand on his forehead.

"Prince Bandr needs attention," a voice said above her.

She glanced up at Samir, keeping a spurt of anger under control. Bandr was his father; she had to cut him some slack.

"We've repaired the scalp wound," she said, "and we'll keep checking on him. That's all we can do right now. These men are more urgent." She nodded toward the wounded. "What would they have done if we had not been here?"

Samir shrugged. "All men live or die at the will of Allah."

"Tabeeb!" Gould used the Arabic word for doctor. He beckoned from the doorway.

Liz took the hand of the dying man in hers, gestured to Samir to kneel by her. "Stay with him," she said. "It won't be long." Samir took the man's hand, and Liz got to her feet.

"There's a lot of surgery to be done," Bob said when she reached him. "We'll start with this leg. It has to come off."

"Right." Liz moved toward the sinks in the corner of the room to scrub. The lights flickered. "Where are their own doctors? Why aren't they here?"

"Probably they can't get in for the same reason we can't get out. Control of the courtyard. The Saudis were caught with their *thobes* down on this. They didn't expect it."

"Then why the field hospital?"

"This kind of thing has happened before, Liz, in the early eighties. I remember reading about it. They must have kept this place going, in case it happened again."

"Do you think this was an assassination attempt on Bandr?"

"A crime of opportunity, maybe, some asshole making a point. Didn't start this fight, though. Got a bunch of holy fanatics to thank for that."

She wanted to ask him why Abdullah had sent him to care for Bandr instead of a Muslim doctor, but he turned off the water with his elbow and went toward the man whose leg they were about to remove. Later, she thought, when there was more time.

An unceasing stream of men were brought down from the fighting going on over their heads. Each time Naif opened the door to wheel a man out to wait—for recovery or death—in the corridor, they could hear the crump of weapons. Twice the generator coughed. They held their breath while the lights flickered, breathed again when they brightened. They were still operating when a broadcast voice reverberated through the room.

"Prayer call." Gould kept his eyes on the arm on which he was working. He could feel the fractured ends of the ulna and radius grating on each other and carefully fit them together. "Must be dawn. Samir, what exactly do those words mean? I've been meaning to ask someone."

"'*Allah akhbar,* God is most great.'" Samir replied. "It is repeated several times. 'There is no god except God,' several times, then 'Mohammed is the Messenger of God. Come to prayer.' Something along those lines."

"And will they?" Gould asked. "Stop fighting and come to prayer?"

Samir shrugged.

"They probably can't even hear the call," Gould said.

"Probably not." Samir stood staring down at his father. All night, he'd been dividing his time between the courtyard and his father's side. Neither Liz nor Bob made a protest at the constant comings and goings. They'd lost control of the primitive O.R. before they'd even started, with bacteria flooding in from the air-conditioning vents, from the door opening and closing to admit wounded men and Naif disposing of bloody detritus.

The *muezzin's* call fell away and Liz glanced up as Naif followed Samir into the corridor. She motioned Gould to look through the open door.

Wounded men struggled to their feet, lined themselves up in ragged lines. Prince Samir took his place in the middle of the front line, flanked by members of the rank and file of the National Guard. A gray-bearded man, his khaki *thobe* torn and bloodstained, adjusted his *ghutra* and moved forward to stand alone in front. In unison, the lines of men placed their hands on their knees, bowed, and started the first of the five times they would pray that day.

* * *

The day wore on, the passing hours marked off only by the *muezzin* calling the faithful to prayer, his recorded voice thrown throughout the Grand Mosque by loudspeakers.

The number of men requiring attention came now in spurts, and whenever they could, the two Americans took turns to rest. While Bob catnapped, sitting upright in a chair, legs stretched in front of him, head resting against the wall, Liz checked on Prince Bandr. They had taken turns monitoring his condition as often as they could during the course of that long night, and even longer day. Liz held her fingers to the pulse in Prince Bandr's neck. It was stronger, and his skin no longer had a sheen of sweat, the unhealthy gray yielding to a normal olive tone. As she bent over him, prayer call again blasted into the room. His eyes flickered open at the sound. The pupils showed no sign of dilation. For a moment they stared at each other.

Then, "You're awake," she said softly. "Good. How do you feel?"

The prince stared at her without comprehension, then closed his eyes. He took a deep breath and turned his head.

"Please, no English." Prince Samir had entered the room and was at her side. He took her arm, drew her away from the gurney and beckoned to Gould. "Come now, quickly," he said softly. "The army is here. Prince Bandr will be taken out and this thing will soon be over. But you must both remain hidden until it is safe to get you out of Mecca, and you, Dr. Ryan, you must now stay veiled. This is important."

"How are you going to explain the disappearance of the Turkish father and daughter?" she asked.

"The fighting is not yet over," Samir answered. "Many casualties will still occur. Now, please, hurry."

Liz stared at him, suddenly frightened, wondering what he planned. She looked around for Bob, saw him already outside in the corridor. Samir opened a cupboard door, grabbed the bundle of black fabric she had stowed there earlier and pushed it into her arms. She slipped the *abayah* on over her scrubs, held the veil in her hand in case she and Bob had to make a run for it, then followed Samir. She had to trust him if only because right now there was no other choice.

The whomp of helicopter rotors filtered down from the courtyard, but after the chaos of the night, the bloodstained corridor was eerily silent. Only the dead remained, lying close to the walls, their heads wrapped in their checked *ghutras*. The living had been taken to rest in emptied storerooms.

Within minutes, they had left the friendly light created by the generator. Samir led them without hesitation through the maze of passages, keeping the flashlight beam shaded with one hand, until only the sound of their feet disturbed the silence, and the air had the still and deadened cold of a tomb. They met no one. Finally, he stopped, opened a door. A musty smell greeted them.

"You will be safe here," he said. "These are old storerooms, never used now." A rustle of sound stopped as he spoke.

"I hope that's only mice," Gould said.

Prince Samir handed the flashlight to him. "I will come for you as soon as it's safe."

"Does Prince Abdullah know we are here?" Liz said.

"He knows. Don't worry, please. I will be back as soon as I can."

Samir pulled the heavy door into place, and the sound of the old lock turning, sealing them in, terrified Liz. Samir's footsteps receded and the silence closed in, as solid as rock. She fumbled at the door, opening it to reassure herself that they had not been entombed, then closing it again with the same ominous tumble of the ancient mechanism.

"Do you think he plans to get us out of here?"

"Liz, for God's sake, don't let your imagination run riot.

Prince Abdullah knows we're here, you heard what Samir said.''

Gould played the beam of light over bulging sacks piled against every wall, then went to investigate their contents. His feet crunched over a littered floor.

"Beans. Rice." The bottoms of the sacks had been gnawed by sharp rodent teeth, their contents spilled across the rough wood-planked floor.

Liz, her back glued to the door, decided not to move.

"That wasn't done by mice, Bob."

"Sure it was—"

"Have you seen the rats in the veggie *suq* on Masra Road in Jeddah? They hunt the cats who live there."

"Yes, but Saudi cats are very small, Liz."

"What you mean is that Saudi rats are very large. I have seen with my own eyes rats that were almost three feet long."

"Yes, but you're counting the tail."

"True." Liz tried a small laugh.

"That's better. We won't be here long," Bob said cheerfully. "I'll keep the light on, and if we keep talking, anything fancying a bean-and-rice dinner will be scared off."

Liz looked down at the bloodstained scrubs she wore over her own clothes. She took off the *abayah*, stripped off the pants and tunic.

"I'd get out of those bloody greens, if I were you, in case whatever calls this place home decides on a change of diet."

"Oh, Jesus!" Swiftly, Bob stripped down to sweater and slacks, bundled the scrubs together, then threw them into the farthest corner.

Liz leaned against the door, becoming more and more exhausted as the sudden inactivity drained her body of the adrenaline that had kept her going at full-tilt for the past twenty-four hours. She felt her head droop and hadn't the strength to raise it.

"Here, hold this." Bob handed her the flashlight and started to tug at the sacks.

"What are you doing?"

"Well, it might be a while and we can't stand up the whole time." He dragged the sacks apart, examining each one to make sure it was intact, leaving no trail of food. He leaned one with several others to form a backrest. "Come on, Liz. Sit down. We have to rest."

Too tired to resist, she said, "Only if we take it in turns with the flashlight."

She eased herself to the floor and encircled her raised knees with her arms, letting her head drop onto them. Gould kept the flashlight beam moving.

The night wore on. Nothing penetrated the room—no sound of fighting, no voices, nothing to tell them what was happening above their heads. Without prayer call marking off the hours, it was impossible to keep track of time. In the rush to leave, neither had thought to retrieve the watches they'd removed before starting to operate.

In the dark silence, the rustles became louder. Squeaking fights broke out.

"They're getting used to us," Liz said. The hair on the back of her neck rippled.

"They won't come any closer, not with the light."

"You promise?"

The squeaks increased. Bob kept the beam dancing around the room, catching the glow of small eyes.

The movement of a furry body crossing her feet jerked Liz into full consciousness. It was her turn with the flashlight, and she'd dozed, allowing it to droop in her hand and point uselessly at one spot on the floor. Rats were all around them. Shuddering with horror, she drew her feet beneath her, scooting back to make herself small, cowering against the sacks. She waved the beam frantically around the room.

"Bob, wake up! They're all over the place—"

As an arrow of light stabbed from the door, enormous brown rats scurried for cover.

"Come, it is time," a voice behind the light said.

Blinded, the two Americans struggled to their feet.

"Samir?" Gould said. "Is that you?"

"Yes." The robed figure raised the light so that they could see his face. "A helicopter is waiting. You must hurry."

"Oh, thank God." Liz, dizzy with relief to be getting away from the rats, would have welcomed Saddam Hussein himself. "Has the fighting stopped?"

"It is over."

"What about Prince Bandr?" Liz asked.

"Already in Jeddah."

Samir closed the door behind them, then led the way through the labyrinth of narrow passages. This part of the building was older, the floor crumbling and sandy, the air cold and still. Samir shone the flashlight onto a stone stairway opening out of the passage and started to climb, carefully holding the beam so that the Americans could see each step. Several times the stairs turned at a landing, finally emerging into a wide, windowless hallway.

For the first time they could hear the sound of activity outside the building. A rumble of engines, the sound of shots, penetrated the thick walls. Samir played the flashlight over a heavily barred outer door.

"Dr. Ryan, please, the *gutwah.*"

Liz slipped it over her head while the two men lifted the wooden crossbar, leaned it against the wall and opened the door. Air flowed into the stuffy hallway. Liz closed her eyes, breathing deep, but all she could feel was a slight coolness through the mesh window of the veil, the movement of a breeze on her hands. She had a rush of sympathy for the women who spent their lives muffled in black, barred from the touch of what meager amount of cool air there was in a desert land.

It was very dark. The air reeked of ash from burned buildings, of sodden wood, the indescribable stink of charred flesh, mingled with the fading scent of Siti's attar of roses still clinging to the veil.

"Hurry. Keep close," Samir urged. "Dr. Gould, keep Dr. Ryan close between us and don't linger. I don't want to be challenged and men are jumpy."

Liz kept her head down, taking in as much as she could through the mesh over her eyes. Bodies were laid out in tidy rows against the wall of the mosque. Buildings smoldered, wisps of smoke still rising. Armed troops lined the roofs of the structures that were still intact. An occasional shot rang out, and Liz guessed that mortally wounded insurrectionists were being dispatched.

Samir reached the end of the wall and turned into a quadrangle untouched by the fighting. A small helicopter waited. Within minutes they were airborne.

As they swung southeast over the city, Gould pointed. "Poor bastards."

A square just beyond the courtyard of the Grand Mosque was filled with rows of men, hunkered down, hands on bare heads. Personnel carriers lined the square, their weapons trained on the captives.

"What do you think will happen to them?" Liz asked.

"Hate to think. This is Saudi Arabia, Lizzie. There's no one here to worry about their civil rights, that's for sure."

They kept watching until the doomed men receded into the distance, and the black of the desert was everywhere.

11

Liz turned her head toward the sound that must have awakened her. A hoopoe, singing in the tamarisk tree outside her bedroom. A golden evening light filtered through the branches, pooling on the pale, sandy gravel of the raised planter. She'd slept like the dead all day.

The door cracked open and Siti peered into the room.

"Madam, Dr. Ryan. Are you awake?"

"Only if you've brought coffee."

Siti giggled, entered with a tray in her hands. "A man is here, madam, Dr. Ryan. He asks for you."

"Dr. Gould?"

"No, madam, Dr. Ryan. A Saudi."

Liz sipped the coffee, toying with the idea of having Siti send whoever it was away. She had nothing to say about the events of the past couple of days. If he—whoever he was—wanted conversation, let him talk to Bob. Then she remembered the gates opening the instant Samir had slowed in front of them when they'd returned early this morning. Someone must have given Yousef instructions.

Who else but Abdullah knew they were on their way?

She threw back the light blanket. "Tell him I'll be a few minutes." She padded into the bathroom and turned on the shower.

Ten minutes later, she entered the living room. She had taken time only for a touch of mascara and a swift pass with a lipstick. She wore tailored black trousers and a white silk shirt, gold in her ears, damp hair twisted into a knot. She looked better than she had early this morning, which wasn't saying much. But every inch, she thought, a cool, dedicated professional.

The effect of her entry was wasted. The room was empty.

She crossed the room, noticing that the orchids were fresh, then took the three wide marble steps that led into the entry.

And smothered a jab of disappointment. The tall figure standing just inside the front door was imposing, even familiar. But he was not Prince Abdullah.

"I am Dr. Ryan. You wanted to see me?"

He turned. Dark eyes held hers. For a breath of time, Liz had the strange impression of a great swirl of emotion emanating from him, enclosing them both, drawing them together. Then he bowed, and said, "Madam."

He seemed to find pleasure in the word, spoken like a caress, yet completely devoid of sexuality. Liz stood still, sensing that something significant was happening, content to allow the moment to linger, then pass as it would.

"I am Nassir," the man said.

"Yes, I remember. You came to my house in Santa Monica, and then you waited outside for several hours. Why did you do that?"

"I regret that I am not at liberty to tell you."

Liz nodded. The moment had passed, leaving an echo that allowed her to accept his answer without question. If this man had his reasons, they were good reasons.

"Won't you come in?" she asked.

Nassir put a hand over his heart and inclined his head.

"Thank you, no. I bring you a message from my master, Prince Abdullah bin Talal bin Abdul Azziz al Sa'ud."

"Yes?"

"My master wishes me to inform you that he will take

the liberty of calling upon you this night, immediately following the evening prayer.''

A command performance, not a request. ''Thank you, Nassir. Please convey my regrets to Prince Abdullah. I have evening rounds tonight at Jeddah General Hospital and will not be available for visitors.''

Nassir's eyebrows shot up, his eyes widened. Then he looked down, but not before Liz had caught a flicker of amusement, and his full dark lips tightened as if smothering a smile. He gave his graceful half bow in acknowledgment, then opened the front door and was gone.

While Yousef drove her to the hospital, Liz searched the *Arab News* and *Saudi Gazette* for reports on the trouble in Mecca. Both newspapers were filled with the Arab League's condemnation of Iraq's aggression, and the promise by its members to send troops to Saudi Arabia.

Nothing about Mecca.

The *Trib* was mere shreds, more holes than newsprint, as was the *Times*. CNN had been clear when she'd tuned in before leaving Al Fatayah street, reporting that troops from Great Britain, Egypt and Morocco were now arriving in Saudi Arabia. At that moment, the picture and the sound had been lost. Censorship or atmospherics, who knew?

Liz lingered over evening rounds. In the public ward for female surgical patients, five beds on each side, she caught the anxious eyes of a small figure midway down and waved. The child waved back. Her mother, shrouded in black even in this place of women, stood as Liz approached. Liz nodded a greeting, then carefully removed the light dressing covering the child's face. Smiling, she stood back so that the mother could see the results of her daughter's surgery. There were fine scars where there had been a large, ugly cleft lip, a separation of nose and mouth that had exposed the child's gums and the teeth that had never been aligned. In the

United States, such damage would have been repaired at birth. This child had spent eight years with a ruined face, and the knowledge that a bleak future awaited her, without a husband, or at best, as the workhorse fourth wife of an old man who would marry her as a *chatwah,* a good deed that would bring him favor in the eyes of Allah.

"Your daughter is beautiful," Liz said to the mother. "She will find a handsome husband."

The smiling nurse-interpreter murmured a translation, and the mother looked at Liz with tear-filled eyes.

"Insh'allah," she said.

God willing. Liz patted her arm. She smiled at the child and turned to her final patient. Mrs. Lateef was making a good recovery and her prognosis was good. Liz made a mental note to ask Hisham Badawi to keep after the Bedouin family to bring her back for her chemo and to press for reconstruction of her breast. Replacing Mrs. Lateef's chart, she smiled reassuringly at her, wishing she could speak Arabic as she met the woman's timid smile in response.

"Tell her she's doing well," she said to the nurse.

She left the ward, used the stairs rather than wait for the elevator, and ran into Dr. Badawi as she opened the door into the corridor.

"Ah, Dr. Ryan," he said. "Good evening. How was Riyadh?"

Liz looked at him blankly, then remembered the note she had left for Yousef to deliver to his home before he left for the hospital on Thursday morning, asking him to take over her patients until she returned. Badawi wouldn't think twice about ignoring the *mutawain's* edict regarding male physicians and female patients, at least for a couple of days. She had to travel to Riyadh with Dr. Gould, she'd said, to meet with the Minister of Public Health.

"Good. It was a productive meeting."

They walked companionably along the corridor toward Badawi's office.

"Did you manage to get CNN while you were there?" he asked.

"Not more than here in Jeddah."

"Then you heard nothing about the insurrection in Mecca?"

Several orderlies were within a few feet, men Liz recognized, devout Pakistanis always first to prayer. She didn't speak until they were well past, then said, "Dr. Badawi, you really must be more careful. No one mentions insurrection."

"Oh, what are they going to do? Report the director of Jeddah General Hospital to the thought police?" He opened the door to his office. "Coffee?"

Liz glanced at her watch. It was 9:00 p.m. The evening prayer was long over, but she did not want to go home, not just yet, and she wouldn't call on Bob as she sometimes did. He needed a little peace and quiet after the chaos of the past two days and nights. So did she.

"Thanks."

Liz pushed the door wide and left it that way as Badawi went to the coffeemaker on the cabinet behind his desk, filled a mug and handed it to her. He sat back in his chair and grinned at her.

"There was a small report in the Arab papers about a demonstration in that place you don't want to talk about. Shi'ites, agitators, Sunnis. Take your pick. But everything is now back to normal."

"So it's all over."

"If you believe it."

"And you don't?"

"Of course I do. Would our government lie to us?" He raised his eyebrows. "I just wondered if you had heard anything more from your sources."

"I don't have any sources, Hisham. What do you think, I'm in contact with the CIA?"

He laughed. "It's my devious Arab mind. So, any further along in your search for your mother's friend, Fateema?"

"No, afraid I've not had too much time to think about it. I see I'm on the operating schedule for tomorrow. I'm warning you, if that damned air-conditioning hasn't been fixed, I'll be exercising my God-given right to strike."

Badawi looked at her blandly. "I gave the order for it to be done by the weekend crew. Priority list. But should they have been too busy praying to carry out the duties for which they are paid, you might be interested to know that in our great benevolent absolute monarchy, striking is illegal."

"Hisham, do you talk like this to everyone, or just to me?"

Badawi laughed. "Go home, Liz. I've got work to do."

The lane outside the house was empty of cars. Not that she really expected him to be there, not after the message she'd sent. But she'd had some crazy idea that if he really wanted to see her, especially after Mecca, Abdullah would come anyway and wait for her.

She dismissed Yousef and entered the house, surprised to find no lights, no Siti waiting to greet her. Even more surprised to find the doors from the living room to the garden standing open. Liz crossed the darkened room to close them before putting on the lights—the huge suicidal moths outside were just waiting for their chance to commit auto-dafé the minute the lamps went on.

She reached out to close the door. A tall figure was standing beneath the tamarisk tree.

He turned toward her. "Liz."

It had been months since she'd last seen him. It felt like yesterday. It felt like forever.

"Abdullah. I didn't see your car outside." She didn't ask

how he got in. His *bisht,* the black outer cloak worn over the white *thobe,* was richly edged with gold embroidery, his bearing regal. His very appearance would terrify Siti into throwing open the house for him.

He looked up at the sky. "The night is beautiful, don't you think? One day I will take you to the desert, far from the lights of the city. Only there can the heavens be seen as Allah intended them to be seen."

"I'm kept pretty busy at the hospital," she said. "Not much time for forays deep into the desert, I'm afraid."

"Come. Join me." Abdullah held out a hand. "It is pleasant out here in the cool air. Now is the best time of the day."

Liz stayed where she was, in the doorway. "Can I offer you something? Coffee, iced tea?"

"Your maid brought juices and ice." He let his hand drop and went over to the white wicker serving table against the wall. "I will pour something for you. Sparkling apple juice, is that all right?"

"Thank you." She left the security of the doorway, feeling as if she were venturing into uncharted waters, and sat in one of the four wicker armchairs set around a glass-topped table at the edge of the terrace. The air was soft and fragrant with the scent of frangipani, and a slight warm breeze rustled through the leaves of the tamarisks. She found it difficult to breathe, suddenly. He was so close. Her body remembered him, handsome, exotic in *thobe* and *ghutra.*

"You have come to talk about Mecca, I take it," Liz said.

Abdullah handed her a glass, then took a seat on the other side of the table. "I have come to thank you for what you did. And to ask your pardon for putting you in such peril."

"That was my choice, not yours. I could have refused to go." She paused then said, "What I would like to understand is why you sent Dr. Gould in the first place. An American, an infidel, in Mecca.''

''What does he say about that?''

''He doesn't. I haven't been able to talk to him about it. I haven't seen him since we returned.''

''Isn't it enough to say that I sent Dr. Gould because I know I can trust him to keep his own counsel about what he found in Mecca?''

Liz felt an undercurrent to his words. Something other than what was being said. ''What makes you so absolutely certain? You asked him to risk more than his life.''

''You mean your life, too?''

''No, Prince Abdullah, I don't. I mean capture by fanatics not inclined to show mercy toward infidels.''

''Are you saying that you think my confidence in Dr. Gould is misplaced?''

''Of course not. Dr. Gould is a brave and loyal man.'' As she had every reason to know. Liz held the glass between both hands, resting on her lap, and felt the chill of the ice against her thighs. ''You're not going to tell me, are you?''

Abdullah was silent, considering her words. Then he said, ''Dr. Gould had considerable gambling debts. They were paid upon arrival in the kingdom. When his contract here is completed, a substantial sum will be put in trust for his wife and son. That, I think, answers your question.''

Liz sat back in her chair as if she'd been pinned there, trying to process what he had said. The conversation she had tried so hard not to overhear that day at Saint Luke's fell into place. Someone had called to threaten him. Of course. And, of course, Bob would risk anything to secure his family's future. His private business was not hers. No reason to feel betrayed. She had been given the chance to search for her mother, to practice the sort of medicine he'd promised. But she felt as if she'd been looking through a kaleidoscope and someone had just nudged her arm. Suddenly everything had changed.

Abdullah's voice came through the tumult of emotion as she tried to order her thoughts.

"Had I thought Dr. Gould would ask you to accompany him to Mecca, I would have forbidden it."

"How did I get into this? Was I part of this deal in some way?"

"Deal? I don't understand, what deal?"

"The arrangement you had with Dr. Gould. Was I part of that?"

"Why would that be? He needed you here. Why should I question that? You are a good doctor, we need doctors."

She had to believe him, let it drop. No way could she pursue this without sounding foolish. "You should have sent a Muslim team, anyway."

"Liz, let me explain something to you," Abdullah said. "This kingdom is the seat of Islam. Because of that, a delicate balance must be kept here between many devout men, each of whom knows with utter certainty that his particular understanding of the teachings of the Prophet, blessings be upon him, is the only way to serve Allah." He spoke slowly, considering each word. "I have many responsibilities in our government, and one of them is to make certain that the country, and the Islamic world, are not alarmed unnecessarily. I could not risk sending to Mecca someone who might talk of the measures that sometimes have to be taken to ensure that balance."

"And whatever he saw, Dr. Gould would keep silent," Liz said. Or was it that Bob Gould would never have been allowed to fall into the hands of fanatics, to be paraded before the world, an infidel sent into Mecca by the Al Sa'ud? That orders had been given to kill him first? She could only imagine Abdullah's consternation when he was told she, too, was in Mecca. "You are the head of some kind of secret police? Is that what you are saying?"

Abdullah leaned forward. "I am of the Al Sa'ud," he said sharply. "I do not direct cadres of secret policemen. Even if we had such a thing. Which we do not. Mine are political responsibilities."

She'd pressed a hot button. "I'm sorry. That was impertinent."

He shook his head, dismissing the need for apology and relaxed in his seat. "So, I have come not only to thank you, but to ask for your cooperation also. It is imperative that no word slip out about the extent of the situation in Mecca. Of course, such events cannot be kept totally secret—we have no intention of even trying. But we must put our own spin on them." He smiled. "Politics, you see. No different from Washington."

"How is Prince Bandr?"

"He has recovered from the concussion, thanks be to Allah. The stitches you put into his head show a fine hand."

"That was an assassination attempt, Abdullah."

"Maybe. Officially, no such thing happened. I wish to talk to you about that also. My brother—"

"Prince Bandr is your brother?" Liz asked. "I didn't know that. He's so unlike you. He hates the West."

"It is true that Prince Bandr is a deeply religious opponent of the West, but he is a close adviser to the king. That is his special value, his gift to balance in the kingdom."

For a moment she had difficulty concentrating on his words. What she had just learned about Bob was almost more than she could absorb, that and the chilling thought they both might have been killed to ensure silence.

"You understand I am speaking of matters never discussed with outsiders. I am trusting you."

Abdullah's dark eyes demanded her attention. Liz nodded. "Yes, I understand."

"My brother is an important elder of the Al Sa'ud. It is understood that, through him, the king gives great weight to the views of the devout." Abdullah rose to his feet, turned toward the garden. A few seconds passed.

This was hard for him, Liz realized. She should tell him it didn't matter, she didn't need to know any more. But she did. She had risked her life. He owed her this explanation.

"His assassination in the Grand Mosque would send quite a message to the Islamic world, do you see?" he continued. "The Al Sa'ud cannot protect their own, they cannot protect the holy places of Islam, they are careless with the most holy of holies, the Grand Mosque in Mecca. While you were in Mecca, broadcasts were made calling for the overthrow of the Al Sa'ud." Abdullah reached into a pocket in his *thobe*, retrieved a string of amber beads and ran them through his fingers as he spoke. "Our grandfather, King Abdul Azziz ibn Sa'ud, united the Arabian peninsula with the sword, gathering the tribes under his leadership. And now, in the middle of all that is happening here—"

He turned to look at her. "The threat to our oil fields, Western troops on our soil, the billions it will cost, negotiations you cannot imagine—in the middle of this—the king had to summon the *ulema*, the religious council, to ask for a ruling on whether he could send in the army to clear the Grand Mosque. Muslims were shedding the blood of Muslims in Islam's most holy place, but his hands were tied while we waited for the *ulema* to reach a decision."

He kept his eyes on hers. Liz wondered what he wanted from her. Understanding? Absolution? She nodded, to let him know she was listening.

"That is why I could not get you out the minute I knew you were there. That was very difficult for men, Liz. I think you must know that. And I am aware just how deeply I am in your debt. Well," he returned to the table, refilled her glass and his own. "Enough. We will never talk of this again. Agreed?"

"One more question," she said. "What will happen to the men taken prisoner?"

Abdullah shrugged. "As in your country, they will be tried. I cannot say what the verdicts will be, that is up to the judges. But I can say that justice will be swift. No appeals that will drag on for years." He leaned back in his chair, regarding her. "You know, this is the first time I have had a conversation like this with a woman. Our women do not take an interest in such things."

"What can you expect? You refuse to educate them, treat them as objects on which to hang expensive clothes and jewelry, take them out of the country to display them, bring them back and throw black bags over them—"

Abdullah held up a hand, laughing. "Peace, Liz. I just wanted you to know how novel this is for me, talking to a woman. Now, tell me how you are."

"What can I say? Busy. I came to work with Bob Gould, as you undoubtedly know, but since the ruling that women and girls must be treated only by female doctors, I spend most of my time at Jeddah General Hospital. Not much energy left for anything else." And no invitations, anyway, a puzzle she had given up trying to solve.

"I have been aware that you were here in my country since the moment you arrived," he said softly.

"But you've been too busy to pick up the phone."

"I think you are chastising me."

Liz smiled at him. "Who would chastise a prince?"

"You would, I think. But you must forgive me. I am in Riyadh, Liz, rarely in Jeddah. My time does not belong to me. But you must know that you are much on my mind. I send you the flowers, the same flowers I sent you in Santa Monica. Did you notice that they were the same?"

"Now, really, how could I miss it? Of course I noticed."

She smiled. "Thank you. You must have them flown in every day."

"Yes."

"With the flowers for your own household? Households? Wife? Wives?"

He laughed. "I am between wives, Liz."

"Oh." Divorced? Widowed?

"But I am glad of your interest." He rose, held out a hand.

Liz placed her hand in his, allowing him to draw her to her feet. He towered over her, red-and-white checked *ghutra* flowing over his shoulders, the gold-edged *bisht* billowing slightly, his complete otherness exciting. Her heart pounded.

"I have something of yours," he said.

"Of mine?"

He curled her fingers around a small smooth box. Liz stiffened. The touch of the velvet was like a dash of cold water. She pressed the box back into his hand and drew away from him.

"I'm disappointed in you, Prince Abdullah. I thought you understood in California that expensive gifts from you are not acceptable to me. What makes you think that has changed because I am here?"

"Liz, it is nothing," he said. "Not a gift. If you like, a small acknowledgment of your courage and help in a difficult situation."

"You mean payment for my silence about Mecca? You don't have to buy that. You have my word."

He raised his hands in confusion.

Liz glanced at her watch. "I'm in surgery early in the morning. Do you need to call for your car?"

"I drove myself."

Liz reentered the house, crossed the living room and took the steps to the front door, waiting for him to join her.

"Next time you plan a visit, it would be wise to call first.

I am often delayed at the hospital.'' She opened the door. ''Good night, Prince Abdullah.''

For a moment he stood close to her. ''My apologies. I have offended you.''

''Not at all. It's late, and I work.''

Liz closed the door behind him. No doubt Yousef was around somewhere, watching, waiting to open the gates. Not much escaped Yousef.

12

Liz skimmed the *Saudi Gazette*. The situation in Kuwait was grim. In the five weeks since Iraq invaded, thousands had fled into Saudi Arabia, and the kingdom was becoming hard put to house them all. The *Herald Tribune* had a story on the influx of men and matériel into the kingdom, planes from the U.S. landing every ten minutes. A couple of days ago, the *Times* of London reported that Saudi Arabia had agreed to cover virtually all of the monthly operating costs of the U.S. forces in the kingdom. She wondered how the fundamentalists would react to that—not only were infidels on their sacred soil, the kingdom was paying them to be there.

The rest of the newspapers were scattered over the back seat of the Mercedes. She had taken to reading them on her way home from the hospital. She had more work than ever, lately, and had to take her paperwork home with her. A lot of refugees were turning up at Jeddah General. She'd have to start putting some serious pressure on Hisham to get the promised surgical help. Maybe there was a woman surgeon among the Kuwaitis. Liz rummaged in her briefcase for her Daytimer, made a note to speak to Hisham.

She threw the papers aside, stared out of the window. The city was quieter, the panic that had infected the streets when Iraq marched into Kuwait had subsided. She loved this part of Jeddah, full of verdant traffic islands, each decorated with an amusing sculpture. A giant bicycle; a freeform something or other made of enormous shiny air-conditioning compressors; the moon in all its phases, coming and going; a boat riding metal waves; a sixteen-foot tall Carrara marble sculpture of a prince's thumb; and her favorite, a stupendous treasure chest with jewels cascading from a mysterious interior. They always raised her spirits.

It was five weeks now since Mecca. Abdullah had not called, although the orchids still arrived. He was in her debt, he'd said, and then she'd promptly sent him away. Smart move, sweetie, she thought. Why hadn't she made up a story to engage his help in finding Fateema, something that wouldn't have endangered her?

Yousef turned onto Al Madinah Road and passed the Rhida Amin Mosque on the edge of one of the empty patches of desert that peppered the city. A cluster of boys were playing. A second glance showed they were stockpiling stones, throwing them at a target. Something about them drew her attention.

She leaned forward. "Yousef, what are those boys doing? Slow down."

The determined aim of the rocks they were throwing was frightening, their feverish search for more ammunition spelled mischief.

"Boys, madam?"

"Those kids— Stop! Stop the car!" She had seen their target. "Back up. Hurry! Back up!"

She was out of the car before it stopped, running toward the boys. Five kids, a sixth hurrying across the rocky sand to join them.

"What the hell are you doing?" Shouting at the boys, she dropped to her knees by the side of a dog lying against a large boulder. "Yousef! Get my bag. Hurry!"

Three newborn puppies were lying in a small hollow where several rocks came together, the only den the mother had found in which to give birth. One glance told her the pups were already dead, their tiny bodies smashed by the stones the boys had thrown. Their mother was still alive. She had just given birth and she was bleeding from several gashes, but she was alive.

"It all right, girl." Liz ran a hand down the animal's flank and found nothing broken. She was the common, semiwild saluki type creature that eked out a bare survival on the edges of human habitation, handsome, yet treated with loathing by the Saudis. Except for the periodic sweeps for extermination, cats were ignored—the Prophet was known to have tolerated cats—but dogs were regarded as filthy creatures, unfit to live among the refuse that littered Saudi villages.

The dog raised her head, tried to struggle to her feet. Gently, Liz pushed her down. The animal lifted her lip, showing her teeth, growling in her throat, but hadn't the strength to bite.

A rock hit Liz in the back. Still kneeling, she turned.

"Get away from here, you disgusting brutes," she yelled.

A large boy in a plain white *ghutra,* his cheeks and upper lip already shadowed with beard and mustache, shouted back. He picked up a stone and threw it at the dog. The others bent, searching for more rocks. Liz looked around for a stick, found a splintered plank of building lumber and grabbed it. Standing astride the dog, she brandished the weapon toward the boys.

"Stop it!" They wouldn't understand English, but they'd certainly catch her drift. "Yousef! Get over here! Bring my bag!"

She snatched a glance at the car. Yousef had her medical bag in hand but hadn't moved. She beckoned with the plank as a rain of stones fell around her. She turned, jumped at the big ringleader. The boys gave ground, shouting, careful to stay out of reach, enjoying the game. Stones struck her chest and stomach.

Yousef ran toward her. "Madam, please! Come away. This is not good."

"Tell them to get the hell away from here," she shouted. She grabbed the bag, sank to her knees to tend the dog. She could hear Yousef trying to placate the boys and their defiant responses. Another stone thudded against her shoulder and Yousef shouted. Heavy male voices answered him.

Liz looked up. Three men, *mutawain* from the nearby mosque, had joined the group of boys. Jesus, she thought. This was serious. She stood.

"I don't want any trouble here," she said firmly. "Yousef, tell them that if these boys leave now, I won't press charges for assault." She felt Yousef's astonishment.

A *mutawa*, heavy henna-stained gray beard covering his chest, shouted at her in Arabic, and Liz turned to meet Yousef's eyes. Her usually impassive driver looked nervous. "Tell him what I said, please, Yousef."

Yousef spoke a few rapid sentences and was cut off by the combined voices of the three men facing him. They gestured to the boys, and one of the men bent and picked up a stone, throwing it halfheartedly at the dog. The heavily bearded elder continued to shout directly at Liz, brandishing a camel whip under her nose.

"Yousef, tell these men that this brutality to a helpless creature brings discredit upon them and upon the Prophet, whose mercy is well-known."

Yousef looked aghast. "Madam, I cannot—"

"All right. All right," she said. "Just tell them to get out of my way. I am taking the dog away from here."

"Madam, this is a filthy animal. What are you doing? This creature is nothing—"

She cut him off. "Do as I say. Tell them I'm taking it away. Then get the blanket from the trunk." She bent to put a reassuring hand on the frightened dog.

The *mutawain* were still shouting, louder by the minute,

whipping themselves into a frenzy, waving their camel whips at her. The graybeard stepped closer, yelling directly into her face. Involuntarily she stepped back to avoid the spray of saliva, unbuttoning the lab coat she still wore over her shirt and trousers. She pushed it aside to feel in a trouser pocket for a tissue to wipe her face. Her action enraged the holy man. He shrieked louder, threw back his arm, then brought it forward. Liz felt the sting of the camel whip across her pubis.

The shock made her cry out. Rage coursed through her veins. She waved the plank of wood in his face, losing all thought of the trouble that could ensue. "How dare you touch me?" she shouted.

"What is happening here? Liz, what's the matter?"

A familiar voice penetrated her rage. She turned to see Hisham Badawi hurrying across the hard rocky sand. His car was half on the road, half on the sand, where he had hurriedly slammed to a stop behind her Mercedes.

"Hisham, this madman hit me with a goddamn camel whip. Tell him I'm going to sue him for bodily assault."

Dr. Badawi raised a hand to placate her, turned to the *mutawa*, spoke in Arabic. The graybeard shouted, pointing the whip at Liz's crotch. It was clear he was calling her a whore.

"Liz, listen, just leave," Badawi said. "Let me straighten this out. I can do that better if you go."

"Hisham, these are madmen. You can't deal with them—"

"Yes, I can. But not if you stay here. Get in your car and leave."

Encouraged by the presence of the *mutawain*, a couple of the boys picked up stones and started to throw them at the dog.

"Stop it! You goddamn savages," Liz shouted.

The *mutawa* struck her again. Badawi grabbed his arm.

The *mutawa* struggled to free himself. The two others screamed at Badawi.

Dr. Badawi said loudly, "Liz, get in your car. Leave. You are making this situation worse. Go."

Without waiting for the blanket, Liz started to lift the bleeding dog.

"Leave the dog where it is," Hisham said. "If you want a dog, pick one up somewhere else, they're everywhere. It will make them worse if you take this one. They cannot afford to let these boys see their authority challenged, especially by a woman."

"Tell them to go fuck themselves," Liz said.

Badawi stared at her, then laughed.

A mistake.

The *mutawa* lunged at Liz with the whip. Badawi stepped in front of him, blocking the blow with his own body.

"Take the dog, Liz. Go on, take it but get out of here. Hurry. I can handle these people better without you here."

Liz picked up the dog—the skinny creature weighed practically nothing—and ran toward the Mercedes. Yousef kept up with her carrying her medical bag, the group of boys trotting half a dozen paces behind. A few stones struck her, then the boys turned back to the arguing men.

"Open the door." She leaned against the car, both arms supporting the saluki. "Yousef, open the door."

"It is bleeding—"

"I know that! Open the goddamn door."

She struggled into the back seat, the dog draped over her knees. As they left, Hisham Badawi was still arguing. But he waved, and she waved back.

It was the image of him she would always carry with her.

After the last prayer of the day on Saturday, Liz rapped "shave and a haircut, two bits" on Badawi's door, to let him know who was knocking. It wasn't unknown for him to refuse to open to people he didn't want to see. They'd fallen into the habit of sharing a cup of coffee at the end of the day, taking pleasure in each other's company, talking about work and the war news, but eventually getting around to Hisham's years of training in the United States and his affectionate memories of the city of Boston, Mass General in particular.

"Dr. Badawi is not here," a voice behind her said. "Can I do anything for you, Dr. Ryan?"

She turned to see Dr. Mohammed Mukarek, the hospital's Egyptian assistant director. Unlike the Saudis, whose *thobes* and *ghutras* gave the meanest of them a certain dash, Dr. Mukarek wore a Western suit that had the unmistakable cut of local Indian tailoring, hugging his plump body like an ill-fitting skin.

"I don't think so, Dr. Mukarek, thank you," she said. "I wanted to check with Dr. Badawi about a patient. He promised to see that her family brought her in regularly for chemo." The explanation tripped from her tongue. There was no reason why she, a surgeon, had to explain why she wanted to see the head of the hospital. But he was male and she was female, and the separation of the sexes made sex an issue in the most ordinary exchanges in Saudi Arabia.

"We have not seen him all day," Dr. Mukarek said. "Most unusual."

"Did he call you?"

"No. Nothing. He did not visit the hospital at all since Thursday when he left here." Dr. Mukarek's round face sagged. "Most unusual."

"Perhaps he had an appointment out of town," Liz said.

"No. No. Nothing like that. I would have been told. As the assistant director, I am responsible when he is away."

The end-of-day quiet in the hospital seemed suddenly touched with menace.

"Did you call his home, Dr. Mukarek?"

"Oh, yes, of course," he said. "This morning. Then again, after the afternoon prayer. There is no answer at his house."

Liz realized how little she knew about Hisham Badawi. He was certainly married, he'd mentioned having a wife with him in Boston. Regretfully, she'd thought at the time. It had amused her.

"Mrs. Badawi wasn't at home?"

"No answer." Dr. Mukarek looked at his watch. "Well, it is late. I must go home myself. If you are sure I can do nothing for you, Dr. Ryan?"

"No, thank you, Dr. Mukarek."

The minute she reached her own home, she phoned Bob. She had never told him of Abdullah's late-night visit, nothing of their conversation. Instead, she struggled to come to terms with the truth of what Bob was—a good man with flaws, conflicted loyalties, struggling to do the best he could. He just wasn't who she thought he was, and that was okay.

"How's the mutt?" Bob asked.

Liz let out a breath. He was sober. "Doing great."

As soon as she'd got home on Thursday she had called him for help, telling him only that she'd found an injured dog, none of the details about the confrontation with the *mutawain*. He'd made some calls and discovered there was a Scottish vet in Jeddah, one of only two in the entire country, the other was an American in Riyadh. Dr. Mackay had met her at his office, given Belle an injection to suppress lactation and assured Liz she would survive.

"Feed her up, give her some love and attention, that's all she needs," he'd told her. "Does wonders for these dogs, they're lovely creatures. I've got half a dozen of them myself."

He'd given her antibiotics and the special food his wife prepared for the sick and injured dogs rescued by ex-pats, and sent her home, with the silently resistant Yousef at the wheel of the Mercedes.

"Hisham Badawi wasn't at the hospital today," she said to Bob. "No one's heard from him."

"Well, he's the director. He doesn't have to ask permission to take a day off."

"No, I guess not. Bob, can you come over here? I want to talk to you, but not on the telephone."

"What's up?" he asked. "Something wrong?"

"I don't know. I've got a bad feeling, though. I'll tell you about it."

Twenty minutes later she opened the door to him herself. She'd alerted Yousef at the gate, then sent the two girls off to their room to watch an Indian video she had bought for them.

"Let's have a look at this mutt first," Bob said after he'd hugged her. "Where do you keep it?"

"Her name's Belle," Liz said. "Right now she's in my bedroom, but as soon as the girls get used to having a dog around, she's going into the kitchen. She's very smart. She's never been inside a house before, but she goes out into the garden when she has to, then comes straight back to her blanket." At the sound of Liz's voice, the dog got to her feet, long feathered tail swinging gently. Liz had made some inroad into the matted coat with a brush.

"And who cleans up the garden? Yousef?" Bob grinned.

"Are you kidding? A Muslim, a Saudi, a man, cleaning up after a dog? No, I do it. I don't mind, I'm used to cleanup duty. Mom didn't think her beloved Mr. Fujihara should have to clean up after our dogs."

Bob held out a hand. Belle flattened her ears. Her upper lip rose, exposing white teeth. She held Gould with an unwavering stare.

"She doesn't seem to like men," Liz said. "She's tried

to bite Dr. Mackay and Yousef. She's all right with me and the girls.''

''She'll be a bit of a problem for Judd if you decide to take her home with you.''

Liz closed the bedroom door and led the way back to the living room. ''Of course I'm taking her home with me.''

''Have you heard from Judd yet?'' Bob asked.

''Not since we left. He didn't answer either of my letters.''

''I heard from Melly—she said he dropped by before he left. He's been recalled, of course, must be somewhere here in the Gulf already.''

''He went to see my folks, too.'' He took the letter she left him, her mother wrote, but she'd heard nothing from him herself. Which said everything that needed to be said.

Bob glanced at her face and put a comforting arm across her shoulders. ''Don't worry, Lizzie. The military has the best defenses possible against chemical weapons, full-body suits, the most advanced, effective antidotes. Wish we had as much.''

''Yes. Anyway, that's not what I wanted to talk about.'' Liz poured coffee from the pot Siti had left for them. She told him about the confrontation with the *mutawain*. ''When he hit me with his camel whip, Hisham was furious, stepped in to take the blows instead. In front of those boys. I don't like it that no one has heard from him. I think someone ought to check at his home.''

''Well, if he doesn't show up tomorrow, maybe you're right,'' Bob said. ''The guy to do that, of course, is what's his name. Mukarek.''

''Yes, but how can I insist without telling him why I'm concerned? Mukarek is extremely devout, all our doctors are, that's why they're here. Well, that and the cash, of course.'' She paused, then continued. ''But friendship between a man and a woman? And I sure can't tell him about

Hisham confronting the *mutawain* over a woman and a dog. Can you imagine?'' Suddenly she felt close to tears and realized how tense she was. Heartsick about Judd, worried about Hisham. Filled with turmoil over Abdullah and grief over the realization she had no hope of ever finding Fateema, the reason she'd come to this goddamn country in the first place.

''Well, if he doesn't turn up tomorrow, let me know.'' Bob didn't sound concerned. ''Maybe I can do a bit of pushing. But it's probably some family matter. You know how Saudis are over family.''

Liz nodded. A male member of the family had to be there if a repairman called, or if any other emergency came up that might require the presence of a strange male—and a stranger was any man not husband, father, son or brother.

But Liz didn't think Hisham Badawi was sitting at home waiting for the Maytag man.

Sunday morning Liz checked Hisham's office as soon as she arrived at the hospital. No one answered. No cause for alarm, she told herself. It was early yet, just past seven.

She knocked again immediately after noon prayer. There was no reply. A group of Filipina nurses smiled at her as they passed, then lingered chatting at the end of the hall. Liz left without opening the door.

During the afternoon prayer, about 4:00 p.m. she rapped ''shave and a haircut,'' waited in vain for Badawi's voice to call to her to enter. She glanced both ways along the corridor, found it empty, quietly opened the door and slipped inside the office.

The blinds were still drawn, the room dingy in the half light, no feeling of recent occupancy. Quickly she crossed to put a hand on Hisham's beloved coffeemaker. It was cold. In the bottom of the glass carafe dregs of coffee had crusted to the color of old blood.

Get a hold on yourself, Liz, she thought. The dregs were ordinary, dried out, dark-brown coffee dregs, several days old. Nothing sinister in that.

She crossed the room and opened the door. After checking the corridor and hearing the chanting responses of the men still praying in the lobby, she slipped out unseen.

Before evening prayer call, she dialed Hisham's internal number from her office, listened to the ringing tone, automatically counting, seven, eight, nine. She hung up after ten, then dialed Dr. Mukarek.

"Dr. Mukarek, this is Dr. Ryan."

"Ah, yes?"

"I was wondering if you had heard from Dr. Badawi. I haven't seen him all day."

"No. He has forgotten to keep us in touch with his movements. But, of course, I am well in charge, so all is smooth. Yes, smooth, I think." Mukarek's voice was wary. "Do you have a problem, Dr. Ryan?"

"No, no. Everything is fine." Or would be if the damned air-conditioning in the surgical suite ever got fixed and she got the help Hisham had promised. No point in going into that with Mukarek. "I just wondered if you heard from him, that's all."

"Probably tomorrow."

"Yes. Well, when he arrives, perhaps you would tell him I wish to talk to him about Mrs. Lateef?" Who had already been discharged after promising to come back for her chemo.

"Most certainly, Dr. Ryan. That is all?"

"Yes. Good night, Dr. Mukarek."

She dialed the number of King Khaled Clinic, Jeddah's sparkling monument to Western medicine that made Jeddah General look even more like the dump it was, and waited to be transferred to Dr. Gould's office.

"Bob," she said when he answered. "Hisham Badawi

didn't turn up again today. He hasn't been here since Thursday. I had Yousef drive to work this morning by way of the place where I found Belle, and his car is gone. Someone's picked it up. I think you should start exerting some pressure."

"Mukarek's stonewalling," Gould said. "Can't say I blame him. Hear no evil, see no evil, and don't ever mess with the authorities. No one's got a job in Egypt, he needs to hang on to his." He drank, grimaced at the taste of the nonalcoholic beer Siti had brought him. "Anyway, I told him I had to see Badawi immediately regarding joint preparations for civilian casualties should Iraq start sending SCUDS our way. He blustered a bit, said I could talk to him, he was in charge. So I dropped Prince Abdullah's name. That got his attention." Gould took a handful of peanuts from a bowl on the wicker garden table and offered one to Belle lying at Liz's feet. The dog gave him her unwavering, malevolent stare, so he tossed the peanut gently toward her. She flinched, but didn't move from her place, nor take her eyes off him. "Mukarek is worried, Liz. He finally told me he'd called Dr. Badawi's home early this morning and got his wife. She's a traditional type, apparently, wouldn't talk to a strange man even by remote, and turned the telephone over to the fourteen-year-old son, Sami. The boy says his father hasn't been home since Thursday morning when he left for the hospital, and they haven't heard from him."

"My God! Bob...my God!" Liz put a hand to her mouth. "This is Monday night. Have they been to the police?"

"Mukarek didn't seem too sure."

"Then we must. We've got to do something."

"Wait a minute, Liz. Mukarek has to be the one to do that. I suggested he report Dr. Badawi as missing, but he's not going to do it. He's not a Saudi. His *iqama* is his lifeline.

He certainly doesn't want to get involved with the Ministry of the Interior Security Forces.''

"Interior Security Forces? Oh, my God. This is getting worse by the minute.''

Dealings with the Security Forces were chancy for anyone, but especially for foreigners. Interior Security men had a tendency to throw everyone—complainant, accused, innocent or guilty, or even just interested parties—into jail, confiscate precious *iqamas,* the work permits without which no one could stay in Saudi Arabia, and sort everything out at their leisure. Which could, and often did, take months. Logic had no part in police proceedings, conducted as they were at the whim of whoever was in charge at any given time.

"I don't know what else we can do, Liz. It seems to me it's out of our hands if Mukarek won't move on it.''

"You could get hold of Prince Abdullah," Liz said, "see if he could help.''

"For God's sake, Lizzie, Abdullah is in the middle of negotiations to pay for a war, who knows what else. I can't just go waltzing in with a story about a man not turning up at work for a couple of days.''

"Okay, I'll go to see Mrs. Badawi tomorrow, find out what she knows.'' Liz stroked Belle's head. "Do you know where to reach Abdullah? You can't just look a prince up in the phone book.''

"I can reach him.'' Bob drained the last of the nonalcoholic beer, and stood up. "You see what Mrs. Badawi has to say. Then we'll talk about the next step.''

Liz shaded her eyes and squinted along the bare, sunscorched street. Nothing moved. The area was new, without a twig of green, houses built on haphazard stretches of desert, then surrounded by high stucco walls. She banged on the wooden gates again. The silence was overwhelming.

She looked over at Yousef waiting in the Mercedes, ostentatiously studying his Koran. He'd made no attempt to mask his curiosity when she'd called to tell him to pick her up at the hospital in the middle of the morning and take her to the same address to which he'd delivered her note before Mecca. When she refused to be drawn out, he'd relapsed into sulky silence.

She turned back at the sound of the gate creaking open. A boy's face, half hidden by the white *ghutra* he wore low over his forehead, looked out at her.

"Hello," she said. "I'm Dr. Ryan. Are you Sami, Dr. Badawi's son?"

The boy stared at her. She tried again, enunciating each word carefully, not sure whether or not he understood her.

"I am sorry I do not speak Arabic," she said and pointed to herself. "I am Dr. Ryan. Are you Sami Badawi?"

The boy was too young to have the lines of strain that showed on his face, the dark rings under his eyes. He looked as if he hadn't slept for days. Liz motioned the boy to wait, then went to the car to get Yousef to translate. The car window was rolled up, the motor running to keep the air-conditioning going. She rapped on the glass, then heard the creak of unoiled hinges behind her. She turned to see the boy disappearing behind the closing gate.

"Wait a minute. Don't go, please." She ran back, but it was too late. The gate was closed. Swearing under her breath, Liz pounded on the blank wooden door.

Inside she heard a woman's voice raised in question, the answering voice of the boy, half broken, neither man nor child, then the woman pouring out a torrent of words, high and shrill.

The gate swung wide, the boy motioned her inside. Liz threw Yousef a glance, then the gate closed behind her. For the first time, she was inside a Saudi family compound.

Apart from the nondescript saplings struggling to survive

on each side of the front door, the entire enclosed area was bare, sandy, untouched desert, relieved only by the surprising presence of a classic black goat-hair Bedouin tent against the far perimeter wall.

Small wonder Hisham thought so fondly of leafy Boston.

Liz followed the boy across the sand to the flat-roofed house, two stories topped with the huge spherical ball of a water tower, common on the roofs of Saudi houses. He slipped off his sandals before entering the house, and Liz did the same.

The hall was cool, with tile floors and ringed by closed doors. The boy pointed to the far side, then opened the door closest to him and disappeared.

The silence was heavy. She crossed the hall, opened the door he'd indicated and poked her head inside.

A dozen pairs of eyes stared at her.

The room was filled with women, sitting on divans and chairs and large pillows set against the walls. The center was bare of furniture.

"Mrs. Badawi?" Liz said to the room at large, wondering briefly how many women would respond. She didn't know how many wives Hisham had. By Koranic law, he was allowed four.

A small, round woman stood. "I am Mura Badawi," she said in heavily accented English. "These are my mother and my sisters and my cousins. Please, come in."

Liz entered, heard the door close behind her, and waited to see what would happen next. What she had envisioned was a private talk with Mrs. Badawi. She had not planned to speak to a Mrs. Badawi surrounded by a dozen female relatives, none of whom smiled when they caught her eye.

A small figure, struggling to keep aloft a large brass tray laden with bottles and glasses, entered the room. The women watched the girl, hardly more than a child, without moving, and Liz quelled an impulse to rush forward to help.

Eyes carefully guarded, the Malaysian maid lowered the tray onto a small table and scurried out.

"You will refresh yourself with a cold drink?" Mrs. Badawi asked. "The dates are from my husband's family grove." Her hands trembled as she poured Pepsi into a glass, then placed dates on a plate.

Liz murmured her thanks, accepting the glass and the small plate. The Saudi custom of hospitality to the stranger was inviolate, honored on every level of society before any business could be transacted.

The women watched her sip the cold drink and nibble on a date. Liz looked around the room, careful to smile and nod as she caught each set of dark eyes. No one responded. The women were dressed in a variety of bright, even garish, colors, mostly dresses to midcalf that did nothing to flatter thickened bodies. All were unveiled. Obviously, this was the women's quarter, and it looked nothing like the West imagined a *harem* would look. No dancing girls, no music, no trickling water, chattering monkeys, exotic twittering birds. The only luxury was the Persian rugs on the floor. The walls were bare.

"Mrs. Badawi," Liz said. "I am a colleague of your husband's at Jeddah General Hospital—"

"I know who you are," Mrs. Badawi said. "You are the American woman who helps the faces of children."

Liz was amazed at her words. Amazed and pleased. Maybe this was going to be easier than she'd thought. "Yes. That's right. I haven't seen Dr. Badawi for a couple of days, and I need to talk to him about a patient I have, Mrs. Lateef." Thank God for Mrs. Lateef, Liz thought. "Do you know where I can find him?"

An old woman spoke in a loud voice and Mrs. Badawi replied, obviously translating what Liz said. The old woman stared at Liz with unfriendly eyes.

"We know nothing," Mrs. Badawi said. "He has been taken away."

"How do you know that?" Liz asked. "Have you been to the police?"

"My brother is coming from Amarqur. He will find my husband."

"Then you don't know where he is?"

Tears filled Mrs. Badawi's eyes. "He has been taken from us."

"But who would do that?"

"I don't know. He is gone."

Liz was at a loss. They were getting no further. What else could she ask? She looked at the date in her hand, sticky, unappetizing, unable to replace it on the plate for fear of offending the women watching her.

"He wanted to change things," Mrs. Badawi said suddenly. "He wanted to make our country like Boston. My husband is a good man, but the West has poisoned him. He does not go to the mosque regularly any more. People see. They know. My husband was devout, then Boston took him away from us."

"Mrs. Badawi," Liz said evenly, "your husband is highly regarded by everyone. He is a man of great education. But you know that, of course. You were with him in Boston."

"Every day in that cold, dark place was terror for me." Mrs. Badawi's lips were shaking. "I could not leave the apartment, the streets were crowded with people, women who drank, smoked, showed their legs, their bodies to strangers. But I had to be there. His father would not allow him to study in the West. Then he said, yes, if he took with him a wife. To keep him safe from the evils that lurk in the West to entrap good men."

"I am sorry you were so unhappy in the United States."

At least one other woman understood English. Liz heard

a low rapid undertone as she translated and the murmurs of response.

"I do not understand your ways, Dr. Ryan," Mrs. Badawi said. "Some of your women in Boston said that I was a prisoner, that I had to break free of Islam, from the *gutwah* and *abayah*. But I do not wish to break free." She gestured to her relations. "We are not prisoners. Saudi women are respected, according to our customs. Do we try to force you to our ways?"

Mrs. Badawi held Liz's eyes until Liz shook her head. "No."

"Why are you here?" Mrs. Badawi asked.

"Your husband is my colleague. My boss if you like. The director of the hospital. I need his help for my patient—"

"Why are you here?" Mrs. Badawi asked again. "You are a woman. You should be among your own people. A woman needs her family around her. It is her place. You think I do not know what the West is. You despise us, but you are whores. Yes. I know that word and that is what you are. You think we hate our lives, the *gutwah,* the *abayah,* but you are wrong. They are our protection, our security. We have our place. We are respected. *We* are not whores."

As Mrs. Badawi spoke, her voice rising, becoming impassioned, the old woman started to wail, her hands waving, body swaying back and forth, gold bangles clanging on her skinny wrists. Mrs. Badawi buried her face in her own hands, swaying, wailing in Arabic. The hysteria spread, and the rest of the women raised their own voices, swaying in the anguished tumult of grieving women.

Liz spoke sharply. "Mrs. Badawi, please. Perhaps I can help."

The woman lowered her hands and looked at Liz with wet, kohl-smudged eyes. "How can you help? It is you who are the poison. I told Hisham but he wouldn't listen. I told him he should not go to Boston. I asked him to go to Cairo, to our own kind of people. And now he has gone. The West has taken him.''

''Well, it is here,'' Liz said, ''in the Islamic city of Jeddah that he has disappeared, Mrs. Badawi, not in the city of Boston.''

''You must go now. Go away.''

Liz got to her feet. ''I am sorry, Mrs. Badawi. I will ask one of the men at the hospital to try to find your husband. I'll send word if I find out anything.''

She closed the door behind her, slipped into her shoes outside the front door and crossed the bare, sun-scorched enclosure toward the gate. Before leaving, she looked back.

The boy, Sami, was sitting in the recesses of the goat-hair tent, a small, lone figure.

13

Liz walked into the calm order of King Khaled Clinic's shining lobby, a world away from Jeddah General with its mass of humanity jostling for the attention of indifferent Sudanese clerks. She walked purposefully, eyes down, hoping she wouldn't run into Thorensen and have to listen one more time to his stumbling assurances whenever their paths crossed, that he would indeed call her—as if she gave a damn. She made her way to Bob's office, rapped on the door, entered at his invitation. She refused coffee, then sat on the edge of the chair.

"I saw Hisham's wife," she said, "he's only got one. She says she doesn't know anything, and she's made no attempt to find him. She's waiting for her brother to come up from some small town in the south. I'm going to have to go to the police myself. It's unlikely that they'll detain me."

"You can't do that, Liz! A woman? A Western woman? You'll make the situation a damn sight worse if what you believe is true."

"I don't know what I believe."

"Well, it seems to me you think he might have been snatched by the *mutawain*."

For the first time Liz heard her fears put into words. She felt cold.

"Yes, I guess that's what I think."

"Then don't mess with them."

"Bob, someone's got to go to take this further." She stared at him, waiting for him to offer.

Gould picked up a pen from his desk, fiddled with it. "I'll go," he said finally.

"Thanks. Do you think you can do it today?"

"Well—"

"Bob, we can't let it go. He's already been missing for almost a week."

"All right," he said. "Okay, I'll see what I can do. Can you stay for lunch?"

Liz looked at her watch, shook her head and stood. "Sorry, I'd love to, but I've got a full afternoon. I'll call you later, see what you found out. If you're not at home, don't worry, I'll institute a search party."

"Very funny."

She left Jeddah General in time to get to the Safeway— a chore she undertook more often since the episode the girls had had with the whip-wielding *mutawa*—before it closed for the *al-maghreb* prayer at six-thirty. Fifteen minutes before prayer call, clerks patrolled the aisles alerting customers to the time. At the first rising note of *"Allah akbar,"* the *mutawain* made their own sweep, making sure the place was empty and the doors closed. Strange how quickly one got used to it, she mused. The first time she had been hustled out of the smartest department store in Jeddah, she had been astounded, stepping over clerks prostrating themselves among the luxury-laden counters. Now, like everyone else, she planned her days around prayer call without thinking about it.

In the Safeway parking lot whole families, men and women, were pushing heavily laden market baskets. Liz stared, suddenly frightened. Normally women emerged only at night, at the women's *suq* shopping for veils and *abayahs,* kohl, henna for hair and skin, or at the gold *suq,* the rows upon rows of small, open-fronted shops casually festooned with a king's ransom in gold.

"Yousef, something's happened," Liz said urgently. "Get the news on the radio."

Yousef twiddled the knobs, shaking his head as he tuned in the wailing music stations. Impatiently, Liz left him to it. If she didn't hurry, she thought, there would be nothing left. And she was right. Inside, the Safeway looked as if it had been attacked by locusts. Very little remained on the shelves. Not a bag of sugar or flour, no rice or salt. No breakfast cereal, no dried fruit, no cooking fat or oil. The meat counter was empty. Liz stopped a harried Egyptian clerk.

"What's happening?" she asked.

"The Iraqis, madam." His eyes bulged with fear. "People say they are coming."

Liz raced along the aisles, grabbing what little remained: a few packages of Ritz crackers, pasta, all the remaining boxes of tampons—unavailable at the hospital, although how the Koran managed to get into that question wasn't clear—lightbulbs and toilet paper, whatever else was still available.

All she could think of was Judd. He'd be in a field hospital, maybe under attack from poison gas or biological weapons. If only he would write to her.

In the parking lot, Yousef left the radio on as he loaded her meager purchases into the Mercedes, the excited voice broadcasting in Arabic. The parking lot was a madhouse of sound with every car radio tuned to a different broadcast playing its loudest.

"What are they saying, Yousef?" Liz asked. "Yousef! What are they saying?"

"Saddam has threatened to attack us," Yousef said. "He wants the Americans to lift the embargoes or he will attack us and the Zionist state."

Liz tightened her lips in irritation but didn't speak. Yousef would choke on the word *Israel.*

"And many more Kuwaitis are driving across the border. Many women are driving. They are driving cars and trucks. I heard it myself." Yousef sounded as if he'd just heard the entire female population of Kuwait was dancing naked in the streets.

"Well, good for them. Better than staying there, waiting to be raped by foreign troops," Liz said brutally. "The Holy Koran certainly doesn't recommend that."

Yousef drove silently, his shoulders rigid with disapproval. Liz stared out the window. The wide main streets were empty, her own residential neighborhood eerie in its silence. As they passed Bob's guest house, on impulse she leaned forward.

"Turn in, please. I want to see Dr. Gould."

Bob opened the door himself.

"I just came from the Safeway," she said in greeting. "Nothing's left. No one's on the streets. Are the Iraqis invading?"

"Well, they're certainly threatening to," he said. "But they won't, they're blustering. They know the Sixth Fleet is out there and that's a hell of a lot of firepower. Come on in, I was just putting on the TV. Maybe we can get CNN."

She followed him into the depths of the enormous house. Most of the rooms were as cheerless as ever, but Bob had had the furniture rearranged in a few of them, making himself more comfortable.

"What did the police say about Hisham?" she asked.

"They'd never even heard of him."

"Do you believe them?"

"Well, the guys I spoke to seemed sincere enough. Who the hell knows?"

Bob gestured to one of the enormous armchairs arranged in front of the television screen, poured a glass of wine from an unlabelled bottle on the table by the side of his own chair and handed it to her. She took a sip.

"Not bad for homemade."

"Last Tuesday was a good vintage," he said with a grin. "An amusing little wine, doesn't take itself too seriously. Wouldn't trust it to age too well, though."

Liz laughed. It was the sort of thing Judd used to say to send up their pompous friends. Bob turned on the television set. CNN was blank. He turned to the local Saudi station, muted the sound until the endless report on the king's day, always the top of the news, was finished. The newsman then read a report about another influx of refugees coming across the desert, referring to a map behind him.

"I wonder why they don't have film," Liz said. "They must have cameras out there covering this story."

"They can't show women driving," Bob said. "Their own oppressed class might get ideas above their station."

There was no mention of Saddam Hussein's threat to invade Saudi Arabia. Liz watched the newsreader silently for a moment, then said, "I can't let this thing with Hisham go on, not knowing. I can't sleep, worrying about him."

"Do you want me to talk to Abdullah?"

"Well, I think that's the next step." War or no war, he was the only resource they had.

"Okay. I'll call you when I have something to report."

She refused to stay for dinner. The television news had depressed her. And she was tired. Tired and frightened. An early night, a book, her dog asleep on the floor beside her. And her mom bringing cookies and milk. If only.

"Dammit." Liz opened her eyes and groped for the ringing phone. "Dr. Ryan."

"If it is convenient, I should like to call upon you."

Liz sat up. "At this hour?"

"What hour is it?" Abdullah's voice said. "You said I should call you first."

Liz peered at the clock. "But not at 3:00 a.m."

"A good hour. The cool of the night."

"The middle of the night when everyone who has to work should be sleeping."

"But I have the time now. Shall we say five minutes?"

"Shall we say tomorrow, at noon?" she countered.

"Tomorrow is Friday. I shall be in the mosque at noon. I shall be at your house in five minutes."

The dial tone buzzed in her ear.

"Oh, dammit!" Liz stumbled into the bathroom, brushed her teeth, splashed water on her face, then ran a brush through her hair. She threw on a caftan that covered her completely, from neck to ankles.

Belle's nails clicked on the marble floor behind her as the dog followed her as close as her shadow through the darkened house. A murmur of male voices came from the entry hall, then Liz heard the front door close.

Abdullah was alone in the living room.

"Prince Abdullah. Good morning." She looked over his shoulder. "I thought I heard voices."

He gave a dismissive wave. "Nassir. He will wait outside with the gatekeeper." He gestured to the corner of a sofa. "Please. Sit."

Liz switched on the table lamps then settled into a large overstuffed armchair.

Abdullah remained where he was, watching her as she tried to brighten the room, turning on lamps.

He nodded at Belle lying at Liz's feet. "That is the animal who has caused the trouble?"

"No. How could she? Belle is just a dog. If there is any trouble here, the *mutawain* have caused it."

He shook his head. "What do you want of me, Liz?"

"Bob Gould didn't tell you what happened?"

"I want to know what it is that you want of me," he repeated.

So he was going to make it personal. "I need help to find Dr. Badawi."

"Who is he, this Badawi?"

"The director of Jeddah General Hospital—"

"I know that," Abdullah said impatiently. "What else is he?"

Frowning, Liz shook her head. "A damned good doctor. What else could he be?"

"All right. Tell me what happened."

Quickly she ran through the events of the past few days—Hisham's intervention with the *mutawain,* her visit to his home, Gould's inquiries at police headquarters. Abdullah listened without interruption until she finished. A minute passed in silence.

"So," he said finally. "You think a respected, innocent Saudi doctor has been snatched off the streets of Jeddah and is being held against his will by sinister men of religion. Is that a fair summation?"

"No." Irritated, Liz rose to her feet. Immediately, Belle stood and paced at Liz's heels as she prowled the room. "I don't know. Maybe there is another explanation. If there is, we can't find it. His wife is..." She groped for the right word. *Resigned,* she thought. Mrs. Badawi was grief-stricken, but without hope. "...frantic with worry. Badawi has disappeared. No one can find him."

She stopped speaking. For a minute there was silence in the room.

She said, "Will you help find him?"

"Come." Abdullah held out a hand. "Come." He beckoned gently.

The room felt suddenly as if the air had been drawn from it, leaving it heavy and still. Liz stared at him, a tall figure robed in black and white, dark, bearded face framed by *ghutra* and *arghal*. Exotic. Unknown.

As if drawn by an invisible thread, Liz felt herself move toward him. The same strange dry scent she had smelled on him before seemed to work in her blood like an aphrodisiac. Abdullah kept his eyes on her as she came toward him. He placed his hands on her shoulders, drawing her closer. He slipped his hands beneath the heavy red hair on her neck, cupping the curve of her skull. He tipped her head back, lowered his face to hers.

A rattling growl broke the silence. A long slender body hit his shoulder. Abdullah staggered against the wall, the dog at his throat.

Liz grabbed the saluki and wrestled her to the floor.

"Abdullah! Are you hurt? Did she get you? I'm so sorry—"

"No. No. It's all right." Abdullah straightened at the same moment Nassir burst into the house, a pistol in his hand. Quickly Abdullah called, "Do not shoot the animal."

Nassir lowered the weapon, looking from one to the other.

"Leave us," Abdullah said.

Nassir holstered the gun and turned to leave. As always his sandaled feet were silent, strange for such a large, solid man.

"I'll lock her up," Liz said. She was shaking. "Wait. Just a minute."

She kept a light hand on Belle's neck until she could push the dog into her bedroom, closing the door firmly. She took a moment to steady her breath. Her head whirled. Was he making a sexual relationship his price for finding Badawi? No. He had not crowded her. He had merely beckoned and she had gone to him. Without even a thought.

She must be mad.

"Will you help find Badawi?" she asked briskly as she reentered the living room.

"Yes, of course. I'll have someone look into it."

"Thank you. I knew I could count on you. Is it too late for coffee? I'm sorry, I should have offered earlier—"

"Stop. Liz, stop talking."

He crossed to where she stood hovering in the hallway that led to the kitchen.

"When I have news, I will bring it to you myself. When I come, keep the dog locked up." He put a palm against her cheek, running his thumb gently over her lips. "Good night."

"Good night," Liz said to his retreating back. As he passed out of the room into the entry hall, she saw him reach up, press a recessed light switch. Every lamp was extinguished, the room plunged into darkness. She heard the front door open and close, the sound of voices outside, the wooden outer gate swing to. Then silence.

How had he known about a light switch on that wall? She had certainly never noticed it before.

14

The gold dome of the small exquisite white marble Mosque of the Prophet suddenly caught the sun and blazed with glory. Liz kept her eyes on the view—the mosque, the green-and-white ribbon of the road stretching for ten miles around the bay, the silver-gilt streaks of sunlight arrowing across the azure water of the Red Sea, the creamy waves breaking gently on the arc of pale sand—careful to avoid the eyes of the men passing her on their way to the mosque. They muttered among themselves, the glances sliding her way more overt than usual, even hostile. A strange air of excitement hovered over them. War fever, she thought. It was infecting everyone.

Liz picked up her pace, remembering Sunday morning walks at home, an ecstatic Charlie chasing gulls, dashing around palm trees along the beach in Santa Barbara. The Corniche at Jeddah, a replica of the Corniche on the Riviera, was perfect for walking a dog. But this was not the South of France. Belle was safely locked up at home.

"'Morning. Beautiful, isn't it?" a female voice called.

Surprised, Liz turned her gaze from the sea. A woman in gray sweats leaned against one of the priceless marbles that decorated miles of the Corniche—this one a Henry Moore—while she dug around in her running shoe.

Liz slowed. "Good morning. Yes, it's fabulous."

"Ah. Here's the little sucker." The woman tossed a small pebble, replaced the shoe, then bent to lace it. "Too bad people don't enjoy it more. The women particularly, do them a world of good, a bit of exercise. Still, some of them do at least get to come down here with their families at night, so that's something, poor things." She lowered her foot to the path, wriggled her toes. "There. That's better."

Liz eyed her. She was blond, blue-eyed, tanned, somehow familiar. "You run?" Liz asked.

"Yeah. Most mornings. Go crazy otherwise. I've seen you down here a couple of times, always in the distance though. You don't run?"

"At home I do, but here," Liz glanced down at her bosom and grinned. "Afraid I'll bob around, attract the *mutawain's* attention. Doesn't bother you, obviously."

"Honey, you let those nasty-minded little men rule your life, they've got you in the same hammerlock they got on their own womenfolk." The accent was East Texas. She fell into step beside Liz. "Besides, my Johnny's got a bit of clout here, they'd never get to me. Do you know, you sure look familiar...."

"Yes, I was thinking the same thing."

They looked at each other, then laughed and said in unison, "British Airways."

Liz said, "Did you convince the customs man your bag wasn't pigskin?"

"No. Little bastard confiscated it, gave me a plastic trash bag for my stuff. That's life in Saudi. Sure envied the way you got through. You must have friends in high places."

Liz smiled, held out one hand. "I'm Liz Ryan. Glad to meet you." In fact, she was delighted. This was the first easygoing conversation she'd had with a Western woman since she had arrived. Everyone else, the few wives who'd issued invitations, seemed nervous around her, watching every word.

"Mary Lou Tibbets. You must be the Dr. Ryan I've heard

about. The surgeon who's doing marvelous things for kids at Jeddah General.''

"Well…" Liz laughed, a little embarrassed at the praise. "I've repaired a few faces, I guess."

"Oh, don't be so modest, honey. You did some work on the daughter of one of my husband's drivers at the port. Guy was so proud, he took the kid's *gutwah* off to show Johnny what you'd done. Even with her daddy there, Johnny said he damn near had a fit, young girl with a bare face in his office. That child's whole life has changed because of you. Now at least she won't end up as the slave of some clapped out old man doing her a favor in marrying her.''

They walked on, chatting. John Tibbets oversaw loading operations at the port for oil companies in Jeddah and Yanbu, three hundred kilometers north on the Red Sea coast. In twenty years of marriage, they'd lived all over the world, Iran under the Shah, in the Yemen, Venezuela, Hong Kong, Singapore, Aberdeen.

"Sounds glamorous, honey, and it's been a good life. Still, I miss my kids. My thirteen-year-old's in school in Texas, lives with my parents. She comes to stay with us every holiday, but my boys are over sixteen now. Twins. They're not allowed into Saudi anymore."

"Why on earth not?"

"You know the Saudis, honey. Paranoid. Rock and roll. Tight jeans. Drugs. The usual bullshit. Half the male population takes off for the whorehouses in Bangkok every couple of months to get loaded and screw their brains out, and the other half does the same thing in London and the States. The princes bring in any kind of booze they want, no questions asked, and if the rest want dope, *qat* can be found in every veggie *suq* in town. It's a joke.''

Mary Lou caught sight of Liz's puzzled face. "*Qat*. You know. You've seen it. Looks like a load of limp lettuce leaves. They chew it. Down in the Yemen, the men spend their entire lives loaded on the stuff. What the hell. My boys are in a wonderful school in Switzerland. Company pays. Not bad.''

"Hard on you, though, I would think.''

"Yeah. Well. Want a cup of coffee?'' Mary Lou pointed to the large ornate building on the other side of the road. The Hotel Bel Aire.

"What, the two of us? I don't think they'll serve a couple of women alone.''

"Yeah, they will. Not in the coffee shop, of course. Johnny made an arrangement with the manager to give me a cup of coffee out of the kitchen. Isn't that a goddamn laugh?''

Liz grinned and shook her head. "I've got to do rounds, Mary Lou, otherwise I'd love it.''

"But it's Friday. You work on Friday?''

"Just hospital rounds. A few patients.'' And she wanted to check Hisham's office again. The hospital would be quiet. Liz glanced at her watch. "My God, I must go. There's my driver.'' Yousef was standing by the Mercedes thirty yards away, making a production of looking at his watch. "He goes to the big *Juma* mosque on Fridays for noon prayers. This morning he made a point that he couldn't be late. They probably have a firebrand preacher.''

"Oh, shoot, honey. Send him off to say his prayers, and come and have a cup of coffee. Johnny comes by the hotel to get me. He'll drop you off at the hospital on the way home. Your man can pick you up there.''

Liz hesitated only a minute. She hadn't had an hour with another woman over a cup of coffee since she arrived.

"Okay. Thanks. Hold on a minute, I'll tell him.''

She left Mary Lou by the low white seawall while she went to tell Yousef to go on to the mosque. "Pick me up at the hospital this afternoon, about one.''

Yousef shook his head. "Madam, you come with me

now. I take you to the hospital now, come back to the hospital for you after prayers—''

"Yousef. Please. Don't give me an argument. Just be at the hospital at one."

Yousef stared over Liz's shoulder at Mary Lou. "Not then, Madam. Too early."

"Okay. Get there when you can and page me."

"Madam, you come with me now. I will take you to the hospital, come back after prayers. It is not good for you—''

Suddenly irritated at the constant barrage of words he threw against her every time she asked him to do something, Liz cut him off him in midsentence. "Yousef, go on to the mosque, please. You said you didn't want to be late today."

"Madam, you must come now. It is not good for you in the streets. Not safe—''

"Oh, sure it is. This is Saudi Arabia. Women are safe on the streets. I'll be at the hospital when you get there. Page me."

She heard him muttering behind her, then the door of the car slammed hard.

"I swear to God," she said when she reached Mary Lou, "that man does nothing but argue with me, and he's getting worse."

"It's odd that he even works for you. I've never heard of a Saudi deigning to drive anything but those long-distance haulage trucks. They won't touch private work. All the family drivers I know are Sudanese. Wish we could drive ourselves. I feel a damn fool sitting behind a chauffeur."

Liz made a mental note to ask Bob to find out who exactly paid Yousef's salary—something she should have looked into before.

They crossed the wide boulevard, pausing on the landscaped median to allow a convoy of vehicles to pass. The Pakistani laborers crowding the backs of the trucks waved at them excitedly, a few bolder spirits calling out in an un-familiar language.

"From the labor camps on their way to Friday prayers. They're sure fired up over something," Mary Lou said.

They crossed to the other side of the road, and Mary Lou led the way around the hotel to the rear, past a parking lot with a few old cars, then to the loading areas. At the garbage cans, a dozen skinny stray cats sprang away, running for cover. Mary Lou caught Liz's eyes following them.

"Honey, the East will kill you if you don't grow calluses on your heart. No point in bleeding over these critters." She pushed open a door. The sounds of a busy hotel kitchen blasted them, pans clattering, voices raised, the wail of Egyptian belly dancing music. Mary Lou wove through the activity, calling greetings and waving a friendly hand. The men working smiled back at her.

"Madam!" A plump Sri Lankan, small paunch straining the bottom buttons of his white linen jacket, hurried toward them. "I did not think you would be here today."

"Why not? I'm here every Friday." She turned to Liz. "Liz, this is James, the maître d' of this fine establishment. This is Dr. Ryan, James."

He bowed, and Liz murmured a greeting.

"Please." The maître d' swept them toward a swinging door at the rear of the kitchen and ushered them into a secluded corner of the coffee shop. He clicked his fingers, and two Afghanis hurried forward to arrange a screen around the table. "Coffee, yes?"

"And Danish," Mary Lou said. "Liz?"

"Sounds good, yes, thanks."

James bowed again, bustled away.

"I thought you had to drink your coffee in the kitchen," Liz said, smiling.

"Well, I'm usually never this late. They probably want

us out of the kitchen during prayer call. Or maybe it's your heavy-duty medical presence."

Liz looked down at her old sweats. "Oh, right."

The coffee arrived, and with it a plate of tiny Danish pastries. They helped themselves, gossiped through prayer call, then talk turned to Kuwait.

"Our company wants women and children out," Mary Lou said.

"Are you leaving?"

"I don't have a choice, but without my Johnny—"

"Who's this taking my name in vain?"

A short stocky figure came around the screen. Liz smothered a grin. Johnny Tibbets was hardly the quintessential lanky Texas oilman. She could give him a couple of inches, and he could give her fifty pounds. His blue eyes were bloodshot from too much sun, his thatch of sandy hair buzz cut. Liz hoped he used a good sunscreen on that fair, freckled skin.

"Hi, honey," Mary Lou said. "Meet Dr. Liz Ryan. She's the miracle worker who fixed young Ilima's face. This is my Johnny, Liz." She gazed at him, smiling.

Liz found her hand swallowed by a hard-callused palm, then John Tibbets pinched his wife's cheek. "I'd give her a kiss but I don't want to frighten the natives," he said to Liz. "You did some job on that kid's face. Her daddy's a different man since you came to town."

"Well, that kind of cleft lip does show a dramatic improvement when it's repaired."

"You girls about finished here?" he asked. "I'm ready for my afternoon nap."

Mary Lou laughed, sliding him a glance. Liz looked down, smothering another grin. In the ex-pat community more heart attacks occurred on Friday afternoons than at any other time of the week. It seemed a fair number of married people spent Friday afternoons in bed, but not in rest.

"I told Liz we'd drop her off at Jeddah General. Is that okay, honey?" Mary Lou said.

"Sure. Glad to."

John Tibbets dropped a pile of crumpled Saudi *riyals* on the table to settle the bill, waving away Liz's polite attempt to pay. The lobby was deserted, a couple of Pakistani clerks dozing behind the reception counter the only sign of life.

Outside, the dryness slammed against their skin. All moisture seemed drawn from the air. The sun was just past its zenith, and Liz retrieved her sunglasses from her fanny pack and slipped them on. The sea was a silvery pewter, the sky drained of color. Nothing stirred in the heat. John Tibbets backed his Mercedes station wagon out of the parking lot onto the Corniche, then turned east on Palestine Street. The streets were strangely empty and he put his foot down.

"You're here with Dr. Gould, right? Y'all must come visit. Mary Lou, did you set a day for this lady to come eat dinner with us?"

"Not yet, sugar, but I plan to. I'll call you, Liz, if that's okay?"

"I'd like that," Liz said. "Call me at Jeddah General and I'll give you my home phone number."

John had turned onto Al Sahrudda Street. Cars were parked haphazardly on both sides as they drove closer to the enormous King Sa'ud Mosque, the *Juma* mosque, the equivalent of a cathedral in a Christian city. The large busses that brought the Koreans into town from the construction camps lined the perimeter of the square in front of the building, the trucks that brought the other laborers parked among them.

"I've never seen Koreans here on Fridays before," John said. "They're not usually Muslims."

A mixed throng of men milled about the square—Pakistani, Afghani, Filipino, Sudanese, Ethiopian, a mix of races. More Saudis joined from the side streets as the smaller mosques around disgorged their congregations.

Liz pointed. "John, stop! There's my car. I can save you a trip to the hospital. It looks as if prayers are over, people are coming out. Yousef will be here in a minute— Wait, there he is. Stop!"

John had already been forced to slow the car. The crowds in the street were becoming too dense for any speed.

"I don't want to let you out here," he said. "I think it would be better if I take you on to the hospital—"

"No, no, it's silly for you to take me all the way to Jeddah General when Yousef is right there. Look, see him?" Liz pointed into the crowd. "He'll just have to get in the Mercedes and follow us, anyway."

The Tibbets' car was stationary now. Yousef had the door of her own car open just a few yards away and was reaching inside. Liz pushed open the door against the flow of the crowd.

"Give me a call, Mary Lou. Thanks for the coffee and chat." She jumped out, slamming the door behind her. She bent to smile at the Tibbets, smacked the top of their car in farewell, then started to weave through the press of men toward Yousef.

He straightened, a pack of cigarettes in his hand, then looked up as he closed the door of the Mercedes and caught sight of her. Liz waved. His eyes widened. Liz could have sworn he went pale.

"Excuse me," she said to the men around her. "Let me through here, please."

She tried to push through, but found herself being swept along. No one gave way. She was being forced away from her car, toward the *Juma* mosque. The Tibbets were already out of sight and so was Yousef.

She was hemmed in on all sides. The smell of the unbathed bodies of sweating men was heavy and sickening, the heat intense. She had to struggle to retain her footing.

"Let me through here." She raised her voice and kept repeating the words. "Let me through." Vainly she tried to fight her way back to where she had last seen Yousef but couldn't find him.

The sea of humanity bore her forward until a barrier slammed against her back. She managed to turn and found herself facing the empty paved forecourt of the King Sa'ud Mosque. The broad front steps were empty, the entire front of the mosque cordoned off.

Somehow she had got herself into Chop Square. On a Friday after the noon prayer.

Her head was pounding and she had lost her sunglasses in the melee. She felt sick, from the sun, from the horror stories she had heard over the dinner table at Gould's—the legal sentences that were always carried out in front of the *Juma* mosque after noon prayers on Friday, the warnings from ex-pats to avoid the place like the plague. She couldn't let herself think of what might be about to happen here, she had to keep her focus narrow, concentrate on getting away. Otherwise panic would rise, escape her control.

She turned to try to inch along the barriers. If she could reach the far edge of the square, she could probably manage to force a path through the crowd there, using the buildings along one side of the square as protection, and find her way back to the car.

She managed a few yards, but was forced to stop when a procession of vehicles barred her way, slowly entering the forecourt from the side of the mosque: an unmarked car, several black vans, two buses. The vehicles stopped, the doors of the busses opened and a stream of uniformed Saudis armed with submachine guns jumped to the ground, fanning out along the three sides formed by the crowd control barriers. She was trapped.

The eyes of the men around her blazed with an excitement that was almost sexual.

A uniformed army officer emerged from the unmarked car, assumed a place in the middle of the empty forecourt. He took a document handed to him by an underling, started to read, his voice booming through the microphone in his hand. The deliberate words in Arabic rolled slowly over the crowd. He was still speaking when the doors of the mosque swung open. A massive black man stepped forward. He paused, then slowly walked down the steps, white *ghutra* fluttering, the embroidered black cloak that covered him from head to toe billowing with each step. Across his chest was strapped a broadsword sheathed in a heavy, gold-ornamented scabbard.

The doors of the black vans opened. Men stumbled out. They were dressed in fatigues, their arms pinioned behind them, their heads bare. Most moved as if dazed; a couple kept their heads up, still defiant.

The insurrectionists from Mecca. Eight or ten—

Liz's eyes went back to the front of the line. Her breath stopped, choked off in her throat. The pit of her stomach felt as if it had left her body.

The third man out of the van was Hisham Badawi.

Liz grabbed the barrier in front of her. Her legs felt as if they could not support her weight. Only the press of men around her kept her upright. For a moment she was too stunned to react. Then panic gave her a false strength, and she leaned over the barrier, reaching her arms toward him.

"Hisham," she screamed. "Hisham Badawi."

He looked up, searching the crowd. His face lightened as he found her. He seemed to accept her presence among the crush of men without surprise. He made no attempt to speak, moving his shoulders to show her that he was bound and unable to respond in any other way. A skinny khaki-clad guard prodded him and he stumbled forward.

A uniformed Saudi jabbed the butt of his submachine gun at Liz's face, forcing her back.

Liz grabbed at the gun like a lifeline. "That man," she said, her voice panicked. "The third in line. He's a doctor. He's not an insurrectionist. Let me through. I have to speak to someone in charge."

The soldier wrenched the weapon from her grasp, thrust at her shoulder with the butt. His eyes showed no comprehension. He did not speak English.

She leaned around the soldier, shouted at the officer. "Please, speak to me. This is a mistake. You are making a mistake."

The officer glanced her way, then stared at her, seeming stunned at the sight of a lone Western woman hemmed in by turbaned men. With studied indifference, he flipped the end of his red-and-white checked *ghutra* over his shoulder, turned back to the document in his hand.

"It's a mistake," Liz screamed. "You've got to listen to me. He's a doctor. You're making a mistake."

The men around her laughed, mimicked her woman's voice without understanding her words. The soldier in front of the barrier put the butt of the gun against her mouth and pushed. Liz jerked her head away and shoved at the gun. The soldier moved back a pace.

The officer's voice stopped. The executioner stepped forward. The first of the insurrectionists was forced to his knees. Silence descended on the crowd. The officer struck the back of the man's neck with a small black club. His chin dropped toward his chest.

The executioner withdrew the blade from the scabbard. Both hands gripping the hilt, he held up the sword for the crowd to see. Then with a small graceful dancing step, he moved back, raised the sword to its apex. Sun glinted on the metal. The executioner swung the sword down in a wide arc. The severed head hit the ground with a fleshy thud, bounced, rolled to a stop. Spurting blood, the headless body fell forward.

A sigh ran through the crowd. From the first touch of the club to the final blow, only seconds had passed.

The executioner moved to the next rebel. As he held up the sword for the crowd to see, blood flowed down the runnel, dripping crimson onto the gray flagstones of the mosque's forecourt. Sunlight flashed on metal. The head thudded to the ground.

Liz was dumb with grief. Nothing could stop this. She could only watch as the massive executioner moved on.

Hisham Badawi was forced to his knees. He did not resist. He was a casually observant Muslim, but even so, Liz knew he would be resigned, believing his death to be the will of Allah, inscrutable and unknowable, not to be questioned.

The executioner raised the sword.

Liz wanted to pray, for Hisham's soul, for the comfort of this brave, good man, but her mind wouldn't work. She didn't close her eyes as she wanted to, but kept them fixed on him, willing him to know he was not alone in his last moments, that a friend was close.

Badawi's head bounced obscenely onto the flagstones, then rolled. His body fell. Liz heard only the air roaring around her, in her ears, in the empty place in her heart. There was no fight in her. Just a great void.

Ten men were executed. As each head fell, the same heavy sigh ran through the crowd. Then it was over. Each head was placed onto the body from which it had been struck, the corpse lifted to a stretcher, then placed in the back of the vans that had brought them to meet their executioner.

The crowd control barriers were removed and men surged forward like a football crowd running onto the field after a game. But these *thobe*-clad men ran toward the blood pooled on the stones, eager to see and touch. Liz moved her legs automatically. Her mind was a blank, but her body remembered that she had planned to force her way to the edge of the square before this horror started, and she started to push her way through, oblivious to the buffeting, the noise, the smell of unwashed bodies and garlic-laden breath.

Then she felt a hand on her arm, a voice speaking to her.

"Madam. What are you doing here?" The ebony face framed by a white *ghutra* was creased with concern.

Liz looked at him dumbly, without recognition.

"Madam, it is I, Nassir. How did you get here? Come. Come. You must get away from this place."

"Hisham Badawi was just executed." Her voice sounded hollow to her ears, like a distant echo. "He didn't do anything. All he did was help me save a dog."

A clot of henna-bearded men strode past, deliberately bumping hard against her. She lurched forward. Nassir barked a few words in Arabic and put up an arm to shield her. The men melted into the crowd, and Nassir glared around him, forcing the mob by the strength of his will to leave space for her to move forward.

"Dr. Ryan. Yousef is here. I have seen him. He will come soon to your car. Do you know where it is, your car?"

"It's on Al Sahrudda Street, couple of blocks down."

"Come then, I will take you there."

Nassir hovered over her like a giant black-and-white bird, one arm stretched behind her, using his body as a barrier to protect her without actually touching her, steering her from the square. On Al Sahrudda Street, the crowds thinned, and Nassir dropped his protective arm.

"Yousef should not have allowed you to come here," he said. "He should have stopped you. It is dangerous, particularly now."

"It wasn't his fault. He didn't bring me." Her throat was almost too dry for speech. "I was at the Corniche, walking. I sent him for prayers, then I saw him at the car and a friend dropped me off. I got caught up in the crowd and couldn't get away."

The Mercedes was still where she had seen it, but there was no sign of Yousef. Nassir opened the door—never locked since car theft was unknown.

"Do you have a key?" he asked. "I will drive you myself."

Liz shook her head. "I don't carry a car key, there's no point. I can't drive here."

"Then we will wait. Please."

He gestured her into the hot car and Liz shook her head. The sense of being violated by the primitive savagery of what she had seen was beginning to recede, although she knew it would gather force, return later when she was alone.

"What will happen to them now?" Liz asked. "Their bodies?"

"They will be buried before nightfall. Their graves will not be marked."

"What about their families?"

Nassir shrugged. "They will be told where."

"They made a mistake with Dr. Badawi." She scanned the noisy crowd making their way to parked cars. They looked as if they had just come from a winning football game. "He was the medical director of Jeddah General Hospital. A good doctor."

Nassir shook his head. "Mistakes are not made."

"Well, one just has been."

Nassir did not answer and Liz didn't pursue it. Nassir probably had never heard of Hisham Badawi before his name was read out by the officer in charge of his execution.

"What happened to the other men captured in Mecca?"

"Today is the day of their execution."

"More than those ten were captured." She wondered if Nassir knew she had been in Mecca during the fighting. "I heard there were more, anyway."

"Many more. Today they died in Riyadh, Tabuk, Dammam in the Eastern Province. Buraydah in the north. It is the will of Allah."

"It wasn't reported in the English language papers."

Nassir shrugged.

"Well, today your swordsman took the life of an innocent man." She couldn't let it go. His head rolling...

"The sword is our way, Dr. Ryan. You are not part of our world. You do not understand us."

Before she could answer, Yousef materialized out of the crowd. He cast a nervous glance at Nassir, then addressed Liz, breaking into hurried speech.

"Madam, I saw you and tried to get to help you. But you were lost in the crowd—"

Nassir broke in, speaking angrily in Arabic. Yousef answered heatedly in the same language.

Liz wanted to scream as their voices scraped her nerves raw. "Stop yelling at each other. If you want to quarrel, do it later. Nassir, thank you for coming to my rescue. I am in your debt. Yousef. Please. Let's go."

She waited until Yousef slid behind the wheel, then got into the back seat. The car was hot and airless, filled with the stale smell of the scented oil Yousef used on his beard. Exhaustion swept over her. Nassir slammed the door and she waved to him, then leaned back against the burning leather. She closed her eyes. She thought of her mother, tea in the old stable studio, Charlie asleep across her feet, the clean smell of Tess's oil paints and unfinished canvasses.

"Why don't you think it over for a while?" Bob said. "You've had a shock. It must have been terrible, even for you."

"What do you mean, even for me?" Liz said.

"I mean an experienced surgeon—"

"Being an experienced surgeon does nothing to prepare

you for witnessing the beheading of a friend. An innocent man. To say nothing of the other prisoners. There's nothing to think over. I want to leave this country. Now. Today. I want to go home.''

Somehow she had managed a couple of hours of hospital rounds. Enough time for her to know what she wanted to do. On the way back to Al Fatayah Street, she'd had Yousef detour to Gould's house.

''I wish you'd wait before you make that decision, Liz,'' he said. ''The war may well spill over into this country. If that happens, these people are going to need your skill—''

''Sorry. They're not my people. I'm going home.''

''What about your mother? You'll never have a chance like this—''

''My mother is in Santa Barbara and in a few days I'll be right there with her. There is no way to find the woman who gave birth to me, you know that, and now so do I. I was a fool to ever think there would be. Just get me my passport, and I'll be on the next plane out.''

''All right, if that's what you want, I'll start the paperwork. It will take some time to get an exit visa, our passports are held by the Ministry of Health in Riyadh. I'll call them tomorrow morning—''

''Bob, I don't want this done on Saudi time. Pull some strings. Call Abdullah. He couldn't find Hisham Badawi, but maybe he can find my passport. I mean it. I want to go home.''

She got to her feet. She was still dressed in her sweats, a lab coat over them. Her head was bursting, the same thoughts spinning around and around. If only she hadn't stopped…if only she had listened to him, left the dog where it was…

''Stay for dinner,'' Bob said. ''I've got some people coming over.''

''No, thanks,'' she replied. ''You spend too long over

drinks and I like to eat before midnight. The last thing I want is to rehash the death of a friend with a bunch of half-ripped doctors." News of the beheadings must be all over Jeddah by now. "I'm going home to a long soak in a warm, scented tub."

"I've cut down on the booze."

Liz glanced at him, walking by her side to the front of the house, a trek over what seemed like miles of marble floor. His color was good, the bloat gone, and she'd noticed his hands no longer shook.

"Well, you're looking a lot better. What you should do is cut it out entirely. It's going to kill you."

"Yes. I know. I plan to."

Yousef was waiting in the courtyard. Bob saw her to the car, then called good-night.

Back at her own house, she said to Yousef, "Wait, please. I'm going out again."

Siti was waiting to welcome her home, as usual. Liz greeted her, told her to hold dinner and went straight to her bedroom. Belle rose to her feet, her tail swinging rapidly from side to side. The dog was stronger, had a little more substance. Liz tousled her ears, murmured softly to her.

Hisham's life had not been taken because of a dog. Hisham Badawi had been destroyed because narrow, bigoted, frightened men wanted to keep even the smallest window on the world closed, a window Hisham Badawi had tried to pry open.

The thought did nothing to ease her guilt.

The room was peaceful in the rich evening sun, silent except for tentative sounds from the hoopoe gearing up for its nightly concert.

Only six hours before, she had stood in the forecourt of the King Sa'ud Mosque and watched ten men die by the sword, and she still could not believe such a thing had happened. Since then, she had moved through the day as if watching life from outside herself. Distanced and numb. But if she couldn't feel, she could still think. She could still act.

Foregoing the long scented bath she had promised herself, she showered quickly, ran the dryer over her hair and opened the door of the vast dressing room off her bedroom. Her clothes hung in a tiny clump at the back, and it took seconds to pull out the only black outfit she had brought with her, a long-sleeved silk tunic she usually wore belted over narrow pants. This evening, she dispensed with the belt, allowing the tunic to fall loosely. She covered her hair in a black silk chiffon scarf, winding it around her head as the Palestinian women did.

She looked at herself in the three-way mirror. No hair showing. No pubis. Face and hands only. Satisfied, she tossed down a couple of aspirin, patted Belle again and left the house.

Yousef was waiting. He opened the door of the Mercedes, and she got in.

"Take me to Dr. Badawi's house."

"Madam. Dr. Ryan." He sounded appalled. "You cannot go—"

"Do you remember how to get there?"

"Yes, but—"

"Take me there," she repeated.

"I cannot, madam, Dr. Ryan."

"What do you mean, you cannot? Of course you can."

"No. I cannot," Yousef said firmly.

"Yousef, do you know who Prince Abdullah bin Talal al Sa'ud is?"

Yousef half glanced over his shoulder. His face, framed by his white *ghutra*, was strained.

"Yes. I know of him."

"Prince Abdullah is a powerful man, Yousef?"

"Yes. He is very powerful."

"Do you work for him?" As good a time as any to ask.

"No, madam. Not for Prince Abdullah."

He could be lying but she didn't think so. He sounded too nervous. "Well, I do. You know this to be true, you have seen Prince Abdullah at this house. Now, if you want Prince Abdullah to know that you refuse to do what I ask of you, or to take me where I wish to go, I will be happy to tell him. Do you understand?"

"Yes."

"Please take me to Dr. Badawi's house."

"I do not know the way."

"Yes, you do." She kept her voice calm. "Now, take me there please. Or, if you prefer, you can take me to Prince Abdullah's house."

Yousef turned the key in the ignition. She leaned back and closed her eyes. It would be an intrusion, and Mrs. Badawi would probably refuse to see her, but she had to start somewhere. Hisham Badawi couldn't be allowed to die without someone finding out why.

The city was quiet, traffic lighter than it would be to-morrow, the first day of the Muslim week. In less than twenty minutes Yousef turned onto the unnamed street where Hisham Badawi had once lived.

It looked almost exactly as it did the first time she had seen it, a week ago. The sun was low today, throwing long, dark shadows of the walls across the sand-blown road. Be-tween the houses a few scrawny camels grazed on sparse desert bush, but as before, no one was about, no children, no *thobe*-clad men, or women covered from head to toe in black.

Liz rapped on the wooden gates of Badawi's house. Noth-ing. She pressed her ear against the door. From far off she could hear female voices rising and falling in that timeless wail of grief common to the East.

This was going to be worse than she thought.

She rapped again, harder, and waited. Finally she heard

shuffling footsteps from the other side of the gate, a fumbling with the lock. The wooden gate opened. The same boy's face peered at her as before. Hisham's son. The same, but thinner, more frightened. The boy's eyes were enormous, the dark rings beneath more pronounced. He looked as if he hadn't slept since his father disappeared.

"Hello, Sami," she said. "I have come to pay my respects. To your mother, and to your family."

He stared at her without speaking. His dark eyes seemed filled with pain, a mirror of her own anguish. Because of her...her self-righteousness, her stubbornness...his father was lost to him. The thought was insupportable.

"And to you, Sami. I am so sorry about your father."

Maybe he didn't understand what she was saying, but perhaps he understood that what she wanted to convey came from her heart, beyond words. But the black depths of his eyes reflected nothing.

From behind him, a male voice called in Arabic. Without taking his eyes from her, Sami replied. A brown hand appeared on the boy's shoulder, then a short, squarely built Saudi stood beside him. He looked at Liz from beneath a *ghutra* that he wore unusually long, almost touching the rims of his spectacles, and waited.

"My name is Dr. Elizabeth Ryan," she said. "I worked with Dr. Badawi at Jeddah General Hospital. I would like to see Mrs. Badawi if it is not too great an intrusion."

The man opened the gates a fraction wider and Liz took it as an invitation to enter. She squeezed through. To her surprise the man beckoned her to follow him to the Bedouin tent against the wall of the compound. He sat, indicated that Liz should do the same. She lowered herself uncomfortably to the carpet, legs bent sideways, tucked beneath the tunic. He spoke to Sami, and the boy went toward the house.

Liz started to speak, and the man held up a hand. They sat in silence. Minutes ticked by. Then Sami returned bearing a tray. On it were dates and a carafe, two tiny porcelain cups. The boy put down the tray, filled the cups and served Liz, then the man. Silently, the man motioned Liz to drink first, and she sipped. Sweet peppermint tea. Sami offered a plate of dates, and Liz took one, held it to her lips to be polite. If she ate, she would vomit.

"You have no place here," the man said when she lowered the date. His English was heavily accented, difficult to understand. But his intent was clear. Hostility flowed from him.

"I came to pay my respects to Mrs. Badawi. She knows who I am."

"She does not wish to see you."

"Perhaps she would if she knew I was here."

"She will say go away. She will say you have brought enough misery to our family."

"You must be her brother." The man nodded. "She said you were coming, she was waiting for you. Did you find out why Dr. Badawi was arrested?"

"He was dealing in drugs."

Liz could only stare, the breath knocked out of her. "But that's impossible. He was a good...a dedicated doctor."

"He sold drugs from the hospital for money."

"Dr. Badawi did not deal in drugs," Liz insisted. "It's impossible. I would have known."

"Yes. You would know."

The accusation hung there. The man stared at her, then he said, "No poison touched this family before you came here. You are a Western woman. My sister knows your kind. She was in Boston. She knows about drugs, about the sickness of the West. Hisham Badawi was a good man before you came here."

"He remained a good man." Liz looked at Sami, then back at his mother's brother. "For this boy's sake, you must believe that. His father was an honorable man. A good doctor. He would never deal in drugs.''

''Allah sees all. Your punishment will come, as Hisham Badawi's punishment has come for sniffing after the evils of the West. Allah knows all.''

He rose to his feet, stood waiting. Liz put down the cup, uncertain what she should do with the date. Finally, she put it on the tray, and rose. The man turned, went back to the gate and she had no choice but to follow him. He opened the gate as he had before, reluctantly, a mere crack, enough for her to slip through. She turned to ask him at least to give Mrs. Badawi her condolences, but she was too late. The gap narrowed, closing off the two white-clad Saudis, the round, fleshy figure standing behind the dark, skinny boy. Then the gate slammed shut.

Liz stood there for a moment, her hand still on the gate where she had tried to hold it open, too stunned to move.

Whoever had brought those charges against Hisham Badawi had done so knowing the outcome. There was only one punishment in Saudi Arabia for drug dealing.

But Hisham was no drug dealer. His crime was that he had challenged the power of the *mutawain.*

The journey back to Al Fatayah Street passed in a blur. Evening prayers were over. The streets hummed with life, colorful neon signs throwing patterns of red, green, blue across white *thobes,* giving color even to the clots of black-shrouded women that moved among them. It was a scene that usually had the power to enthrall her with its utter foreignness. Tonight, though, she saw nothing.

She shook her head at Siti's offer of dinner, told her to go to bed. The living room was quiet and she didn't turn on the lamps. The only light came from beneath the trees outside, and she sat in the half dark, watching the graceful sway of the leaves in the breeze, too tired to get up, too tired take the long bath she had promised herself, the grief and guilt of the past terrible twelve hours too deep for tears.

15

Liz awoke with a start, the space of a breath was still caught in the half waking nightmare from which she had been struggling to free herself—the faceless men, the swords dripping blood.

She heard again what had released her from sleep. The scrape of a key in a lock. She sat up, staring at the moving shadows made by the whispery fronds of an acacia in the garden outside the living room. She had fallen asleep on the sofa.

The house was silent. She must have been mistaken.

Then came the small metallic click of a lock turning. The soft sibilance of an opening door.

The front door, behind her.

Her mouth was like sandpaper, dry, rough. She felt sick from the lurching, uneven beat of her heart. She thought to scream for help but stopped in time. She was alone but for the two young maids, asleep in their room. A scream would bring them running, endangering them, too.

But Yousef was in his quarters behind the garage. Maybe she could get to him through the garden.

Quickly, she rose to her feet, turned. A dark figure stood at the top of the marble steps to the foyer.

"You have no right to be here," Liz said. Her voice was steady, surprising her. "I am not alone."

"Dr. Ryan. It is I, Nassir. Please, do not fear."

He pressed the switch Prince Abdullah had used. Soft light illuminated the room.

Liz put a hand on the back of the sofa.

"Nassir! What are you doing here? It's the middle of the night! How did you get in?"

"I have brought someone."

A smaller figure moved from behind him. Smaller only compared to Nassir's bulk.

Liz knew instantly.

She was tall, slender under the black *abayah*. Only her eyes were visible above her *gutwah*. The same eyes that looked back at Liz every time she looked in the mirror.

The woman unfastened the veil, revealing her face.

Liz was speechless. She could only stare. Then she said, "Fateema." And again, "Fateema."

"Yes. I am Fateema," the woman said in English. "Fateema, who gave you to your Western mother. But I have thought of you every day since."

Liz tried to find words, but nothing came to her.

"Thank you," she said finally. Her voice was a croak. The ache in her throat spread down to her chest. She swallowed, trying to clear it before she risked speech again. She stepped back, gestured to the living room. "Please."

Fateema turned to Nassir, spoke to him in Arabic. Nassir had not taken his eyes from her face, as if drinking in every detail, imprinting them in his memory. He answered her softly, then looked at Liz. "For a short while only. I will wait outside the door."

His words sharpened Liz's awareness of the danger. In the United States, nothing could be more innocent than a visit such as this. But this was Saudi Arabia, and Nassir had brought a woman not his wife to a house that was not in the possession of her family. They both had risked their lives to come here tonight. After today, the executions, the sword, such a thought was no longer as bizarre as it once would have been.

Fateema came down the marble steps. She removed her *abayah* and *gutwah,* uncovering her hair. Liz was not surprised to see that it was the same deep red as her own. She wore dark-green, a gold-embroidered velvet vest over lace, and a full heavy silk skirt. There was gold around her neck and in her ears, more on her arms.

"Tess Ryan, your mother. She is well?"

"Yes. I speak to her on the telephone every week. Maybe you would like to talk to her—"

Fateema shook her head quickly. "It is better not."

There was a small, awkward silence. Then Liz said, "I don't know what to say first. I feel a bit overwhelmed."

"Tess Ryan told you of me?"

"Yes," Liz answered. "She told me how brave you were, even as a young girl. When I was grown, she gave me the gold you sent her to keep for me." She could not tell Fateema that Tess had revealed the story of her birth only months ago—that she had grown up knowing nothing of the woman who twice had given her life, once in birth, again when she had relinquished her to the freedom of the West. "How did you know I was here?"

"Nassir," Fateema said. "He was there when you were born, and then in the United States, first he saw Dr. Gould... He thought he was the doctor from the ship. Then he saw you. So he knew." Fateema smiled for the first time. "You look like me."

Liz nodded. Tess had told her that Nassir had risked his life then, loving the young girl Fateema had been—the thirteen-year-old who gave birth to twins thirty-two years ago. "Your son...my brother. Is he well?"

"He is well."

"I'd like to meet him."

Fateema shook her head again. "No. This would not be good."

"And my father?"

She hesitated, then said, "He is well."

"Who is he?" Liz asked.

"I can tell you nothing. It is better this way. We have a secret that we must carry to our graves. At the very least, Nassir would die for what he did so many years ago."

"Why did he decide to bring us together, now, tonight?"

"Nassir has known that my life has a place that grieved for the daughter I would never see. Today, he saw you, he saw that you were in need. He sent word to me."

"He loves you a great deal."

Fateema shrugged. "He is a slave."

Liz looked at her, shocked at her casual dismissal of Nassir's love and loyalty. The difference in their worlds, the East and West, jumped into focus.

"Not any longer, surely."

"No. Not for many years."

Officially, slavery had ended in 1966, but the rumor was that here, as in other Middle Eastern states, the trade in human beings still flourished.

They sat for a moment, strangers who had yet to learn how to communicate with each other. Then Liz said, "My...Tess said that back then, Nassir had to translate for you. But you have learned English."

"The language my daughter would use in her new life." Fateema smiled, then her tone changed. "My master was kind, he allowed me to pass the time in learning."

Liz caught the note of bitterness, but did not know how to pursue it, or whether she should. Instead, she said, "My grandmother, she is also a brave woman. Will it be possible to meet her?"

"Perhaps." Fateema smiled again. "She will be so proud that you have been educated."

The front door opened and closed softly. Nassir appeared in the entry to the living room. "We must leave now. It is late."

Without thinking, Liz said, "Oh, no. Not yet, surely. You have only just come. There is so much to say—"

"No longer. It is too dangerous," Nassir said.

"Oh. Of course. What have you told them?" Liz asked Fateema, wondering who "them" could be.

"Nothing. If I am questioned when I return, a visit to my mother. She is visiting here, in Jeddah with her own household. She will be told what she needs to know."

"There is so much I want to know about your life."

"Yes, I, too, wish to know much. So I will find a way for us to meet again." Fateema stood and reached for her *abayah*.

They were the same height, the same build, the same coloring, Liz thought. They looked like sisters, or cousins, ten years, perhaps, separating them. She realized that neither had made an attempt to touch the other, and ached that the chasm between them, mother and daughter, women of such different cultures, was perhaps too wide to be bridged.

"Next time, please, we must spend time," Liz said. "There is so much we have to learn of each other's lives. I want to know everything."

Fateema, eyes huge, brilliant with unshed tears, placed a hand against Liz's face. Liz sighed. Her arms went around her mother, and she felt the strength in Fateema's answering embrace.

"Thank you." The words came naturally. Liz pressed her cheek against her mother's. "Thank you for giving me a chance. You are very brave."

"No. Your freedom was all I had to give you. You have not wasted my gift. I am very proud of my daughter."

Liz signed her name to the last of her surgical notes and leaned back, hooked open the bottom drawer of her desk

and propped her feet. Her eyes felt raw, her nerves jangled
with caffeine. After Fateema and Nassir had left, she'd tried
to call home, a more complicated operation lately—all over
the kingdom, it was suspected, phones were tapped. She'd
waited what seemed like forever, listening to echoes and
clicks on the line, then as soon as she'd heard the first ring
in Santa Barbara, she'd hung up, the events of the day suddenly too overwhelming to encode in small talk indecipherable to unwanted listeners. She'd lain sleepless until dawn,
then got up and wandered through the garden with Belle,
drinking coffee, listening to the hoopoe, watching the sky
lighten until it was time to leave for the hospital.

The damp fabric of her surgical greens rasped against her
skin, sticking to her back, clinging to her armpits. She'd
been exhausted from the heat in the operating room and
hadn't bothered to change before sitting at her desk. Once,
only days ago, she would have been able to march into
Hisham's office, repeat her demand that the air-conditioning
in the surgical unit be fixed, replaced, demolished, something, anything. Hisham would have laughed, given her
more coffee and promised the moon, and she would have
felt better even knowing that nothing, probably, would be
done.

But she had no rapport with Dr. Mukarek, frightened of
losing his job and more concerned with seeing that everyone
prayed on time than in running the hospital. Stray cats had
invaded the corridors and this morning, she had found a
skinny animal with a litter of sickly kittens in a linen room
on the surgical floor. She had instructed the Afghani orderly
to deposit them carefully outside, and clean the room, aware
that her instructions would be ignored and all six destroyed.
But at least the room had been cleaned to her satisfaction,
and she had managed to procure clean linens for her patients
by "stealing" from the basement laundry.

Wearily, she got up, turned out the lights.

Outside the hospital Yousef had the Mercedes at the front steps. On the way home they were held up at an intersection while a Bedouin herded a flock of goats across the road before disappearing into an alley between mud-brick houses, a scene out of the Bible. She watched four anonymous black-shrouded figures, each carrying an infant, scurrying after a portly *thobe*-clad Saudi; a group of boys kicking a soccer ball on a patch of sand, their *thobes* held high, *ghutras* flying as they ran, skinny brown legs and sandaled feet flashing. Several henna-bearded *mutawain* lingered in front of the mosque.

No girls played, no women chatted, laughing, going about their day.

Liz ate the food Siti put in front of her without tasting it, then stood under the shower until her skin started to pucker. She rubbed her body hard with a towel, smoothed on a sweet-smelling oil she had bought at the women's *suq* and felt marginally better.

Before her first surgery of the day that morning at seven, she had called Bob at King Khaled. He hadn't arrived yet, and she left word for him to call her, but he hadn't done so. All day the nightmare of Hisham Badawi's death had hovered, mingling with the amazement and confusion, the flashes of joy at meeting Fateema.

She pulled on a robe, then went into the television room to call Bob. Her hand was on the telephone when it rang. She picked it up.

"Liz Ryan."

"I have news for you," Abdullah's voice said.

She could barely bring herself to reply. "I know. Hisham Badawi is dead. I already know."

A moment's silence.

"I will be at Al Fatayah Street in ten minutes. Put the animal away."

She thought of telling him not to come, then realized that if anyone could get to the bottom of what had happened to Hisham Badawi, it would be Prince Abdullah bin Talal al Sa'ud.

She dropped the phone into the cradle, took Belle back to her bedroom and closed her outside in the garden. She threw on a pair of trousers, a shirt and slipped her feet into sandals. She was waiting at the front door when Yousef opened the gates and a black Jaguar entered the courtyard. Abdullah was at the wheel, and he was alone. He got out of the car, spoke a few words in Arabic to Yousef, then came toward her.

He took her hand. "I am sorry about your colleague,"

Liz nodded. The sobs that had never been far for the last few days lumped painfully in her chest. "How could such a thing have happened?"

"Come." He touched his fingers to her elbow. "We will talk."

Siti had left a selection of bottled water and fruit juices as she always did, and a thermos jug of coffee. Liz busied herself for a moment pouring Pellegrino for Abdullah and yet another cup of coffee she didn't want for herself. What she really wanted was a stiff drink.

"Have you seen his wife?" she asked.

"Liz, how would I be able to do such a thing? This is not California." Abdullah took the glass of water from her, waited until she seated herself in the corner of the sofa, then took an armchair across from her.

"Well, I tried, but Mrs. Badawi refused to see me," Liz said. "Her brother told me what had happened."

"And what did this brother tell you?"

"He said that Hisham Badawi was executed for drug dealing. That's completely mad. Anyone who knew him would know what a ridiculous charge this is. Hisham Badawi was an honorable man. A very good doctor. He cared about that awful hospital, always fighting for more money to run it properly. He cared about the poor he treated, the laborers and Bedouins. No. That accusation was chosen because the penalty is death. He was killed as a lesson to others."

"Oh, Liz. Come. That's a...what would you call it? A paranoid fantasy. Who would do that?"

"The Islamic fundamentalists? The *Wahhabis*? I don't know. The men who believe the earth is flat? Hisham laughed when the president of the Islamic University in Medina wrote a paper insisting that that was the case, but he was embarrassed by it, all the same. Sometimes he wasn't discreet. Hisham Badawi wanted to take what was good from the West. So he was snatched off the street and framed and killed. You tell me. Who would do that?" She met his gaze.

"Liz, you must be careful with such words."

"Do you think I don't know that? Mrs. Badawi's brother as much as accused me of knowing about Hisham's supposed drug dealing, maybe even being complicit in it. Believe me, I am very discreet, Abdullah. I know I could find myself slapped into a Saudi jail."

"You have a vivid imagination. That is not going to happen. This is a civilized country. Such things—"

She interrupted him. "Abdullah, I was there. I saw Hisham Badawi beheaded outside the King Sa'ud Mosque on Al Sahrudda Street on Friday after prayers."

He looked at her, appalled. "How did you come to be there at that time? Did no one warn you to stay away?"

"You certainly didn't. You must have known."

"Why would I think to warn you? I have responsibilities in government that you know nothing about. This was a significant event for all Islam, not only this kingdom. How was I to even suspect that you would be anywhere near that mosque, the *Juma* mosque, on a Friday? You must know to stay away at that time. All Westerners know that if executions take place it is after prayers on Friday—''

"Well, I didn't."

"Such things are published in the newspapers—"

"You know that's not true. Afterward they are, not before. No newspaper carried the information that last Friday the insurrectionists from Mecca would be executed in different locations all over the country."

Abdullah looked into his glass. He had been party to the decision to present a fait accompli to the world. A fine line—a dangerous line—was being walked by the House of Sa'ud. The strict Islamists, his own brother Bandr who was close to the King's ear, had to be placated in spite of the fact that invasion by Iraq could come at any time. Americans wouldn't understand execution by the sword, and this was not the time for the endless discussions about human rights that they loved so much.

"I am sorry you witnessed that," Abdullah said. "Judgment is swift in this country and sentences are carried out immediately. Murderers are not allowed to spend years on death row finding obscure ways to cheat justice."

"Our system at least gives the innocent every chance to prove that innocence before he forfeits his life."

"Liz, you are not discreet—"

"What will happen to them now? Hisham's son, Sami. Mrs. Badawi?"

"They will go back to her father's household, or if he is no longer living, she will go to her eldest brother. The boy will be brought up there."

"So she loses all autonomy. What little she had."

Abdullah shrugged. He didn't understand this Western passion for independence. Where else would a woman go?

"And Sami Badawi will grow up believing his father was a criminal. A good man, an honorable man, will be killed in the memories of the people who loved him, over and over again." Liz knew she was on the edge, and she slowed her rushing speech. "If I give you my word that Hisham Badawi was innocent, will you find out who brought these charges? How such a thing could be allowed to happen to an innocent, decent man—"

Suddenly, the pain in her chest shattered into sobs. She leaned forward to put her coffee cup down, but couldn't seem to find the table. Her hand tipped and hot coffee slopped onto her skin, dripping onto the floor.

Quickly, Abdullah rose, sat beside her. He took the coffee cup from her hand and placed it on the table, then put an arm around her and drew her toward him.

Liz turned her face into his shoulder, her body shaking in a ferocity of grief, her tears unstoppable. The horror of all she had witnessed, the sound of the sword striking flesh, the thud of skulls on stone, eyes bulging in heads without bodies, jerking limbs of decapitated torsos, the sighing breath of the crowds of men, the flies, the heat and mingling stink of blood and garlic and sweat and cheap-scented oil— all came welling out of the depths of her being. She wanted to wail, to throw herself on the floor and beat her head on the cold marble—to turn back the clock.

Abdullah put a hand on her head, stroking as he would to quiet a child.

"Shh," he murmured. "Shh. I'll find out what happened. I promise you. I will find out."

Gradually, her sobs subsided, becoming merely a catch in her chest each time she filled her lungs. She lay quietly against Abdullah, listening to him murmur to her, feeling the touch of his hand on her hair, too exhausted with the torrent of emotion to push him away. He was warm and present, the faint dry scent of him familiar as if she had known it forever. She took a corner of his *ghutra,* wiped her eyes with it.

Abdullah laughed. The soft ordinary sound lifted Liz's

heart—for the past few days her life had been filled with fear and confusion and tragedy. He transferred her weight to his left arm, pulling her back as she tried to sit up. He reached into a pocket in his *thobe* and produced a linen handkerchief. He tipped her face up toward him. Obediently, Liz closed her eyes, allowing him to mop her tears. She felt the touch of his lips on hers, the roughness of his beard and mustache against her face.

Abdullah put his hand against her throat, allowing his fingers to trace its length, over the fine skin, the bone structure of her chest, the soft swell of her breasts.

Liz slipped a hand beneath his black-and-white checked *ghutra*, caressing his neck, the short crisp hairline. She opened her mouth to take his tongue, exploring him with her own.

Abdullah rose to his feet, bringing her with him. He held her to the length of his body, one hand spread against the small of her back. Liz found herself fumbling with the voluminous robes of the desert, trying to slip her arms beneath the *bisht*, to hold him, to feel the outline of him, the soft wool, the cotton *thobe*, strange and exciting.

Abdullah took her hand and led her toward the bedroom. For a nanosecond, she wondered how he knew where she slept, then the thought drifted, dissipated.

The room was cool, the air-conditioning low. Belle was outside, the windows closed against her, against the night. Abdullah reached up, stripped off his *ghutra* and *arghal*, threw the *bisht* across a slipper chair, then reached for her.

Liz moved into his arms. He felt hard and warm and sure, a stable center in a world that had been spinning out of control. She felt the cool air on her skin as he unbuttoned her shirt, slipping it from her to bare her shoulders. She pushed him away and reached behind her to unclasp her bra. Her nipples brushed against his bare chest, and she had a momentary flash of surprise that his body was smooth, free of hair.

He bore her toward the bed. Judd's face flashed in front of her and she drew in a sharp, shaky breath. But it was too late to turn back. Her body was screaming out for the man touching her now, exploring her. She pulled him onto her, opened her legs to receive him. Then in a small pocket of clarity Mary Lou Tibbet's words came into her mind, "...every capital in Europe..."

"No." With a strength born of sudden terror, she shoved at his shoulders. "Abdullah, no. We can't do this." Liz threw herself sideways, pulling her knees to her chest, denying him. "This isn't safe for either of us."

Abdullah grabbed her legs, tried to open them. She fought him, her fists doubled, legs flailing.

"No. No. Listen to me. We have no protection. Do you hear me? It is not safe for either of us."

His body was heavy on her, but he was still. "What are you saying?" he said against her ear.

"I'm saying we cannot make love. Not unless you brought condoms with you." Her own body was trembling, with the ferocity of the moment, with wanting him.

"A... You are asking me..." Words failed him. He tried again. "You are telling me, Prince Abdullah bin Talal ibn Sa'ud to use...to use..." He sat up.

Now that she could look at him, it was as if for the first time. His hair was short, threaded with silver and cut close against his head, hard and crisp as if it would curl if worn longer. Even with the familiar beard and mustache, he looked like a stranger who had taken Abdullah's place.

"I'm sorry," she said. "I should have thought—"

He made a rough gesture to shut her up. "Stop! I cannot even speak of such matters with you."

Liz swung her legs to the floor, careful not to touch him— her own resolve was uncertain. Her body was good, she had no reason to feel embarrassed by her nudity, but she had to force herself to move freely rather than inch her way to the bathroom on the other side of the room. She closed the door behind her, leaned against it briefly before crossing to the mirror.

The eyes staring back at her were heavy, almost bruised. Her mouth was slack and she put up her fingers to rub at it, still feeling the heat of his lips. Her face burned, and she ran cold water, splashing until her skin cooled. She picked up a towel, dabbed, lingering in the opulent marble-and-gold room. Finally, she removed her terry cloth robe from its hanger, half wishing it was the more glamorous black satin tailored affair Judd had bought her. She slipped her arms into its sleeves, tied the sash. Then she took a breath and opened the door.

The bedroom was empty. Abdullah was gone.

16

Bob Gould swerved to avoid the donkey who'd taken a sudden impulse to amble across the sand-covered road directly in front of the car.

"Why does the donkey cross the road?" Liz asked, laughing.

"To get, you should pardon the pun, an ass full of fender so that the poor ex-pat who kills it has to pay an exorbitant amount of blood money to its owner. Why else?" Bob looked in the rearview mirror to see the donkey fading into the distance and shoved his foot down on the gas.

Liz glanced at the speedometer as the needle reached one hundred. "Well, Saudi Arabia certainly agrees with you, Bob. You're at least twenty years younger than you were when we arrived."

"I feel pretty good."

"You must be cutting down on the sauce."

"Haven't had a drink in a couple of weeks, as a matter of fact."

"Mmm. Melly will be pleased."

Liz looked out of the window. The desert was stony, dotted with sparse, dry bushes festooned with trashed plastic bags. Villages hadn't yet found a way to dispose of twentieth-century garbage, so most of it ended up blown about the landscape by the strong desert winds. Abandoned cars were everywhere, two or three every kilometer, some with crumpled body work, others totaled. It made no difference;

their owners had just walked away and left them there. A herd of skinny camels grazed on both sides of the road, somehow finding sustenance in the dehydrated bushes. Liz let her eyes drift over them, her mind busy with Abdullah.

It had been two weeks now since she'd seen him and he'd rarely been out of her thoughts, except when she was working. She had a feeling she would never see him again, had tried to convince herself it didn't matter, and in the next breath knew it mattered too much.

They passed a minute mosque, smaller than a garden shed, built by hand to serve passing truckers. The tiny dome was a sun-faded blue, topped by the crescent of Islam, the whole whitewashed mud building lopsided and windowless, its little minaret leaning out of plumb.

"Melly would be fascinated by all this, a fourteenth-century culture being shoved willy-nilly into the computer age," Liz said. "Too bad she's not here."

"Can you see my Melly keeping her mouth shut about women's issues here, or the way they treat their animals? Can you see her saying she's a Catholic or some other alien denomination?"

Liz laughed. "Well, not now that you mention it. But she could be a help keeping you on this new straight and narrow."

Bob snorted. "She couldn't do it in L.A., so what makes you think she could here? Anyway, I'm doing all right on the straight and narrow by myself, thank you very much, so don't start a lecture." He glanced at her. "We're supposed to be out for a little recreation, a picnic, a little dip in the Red Sea. You look as if you could use some R and R." He slowed the car, studying the landscape. "I think this must be it. Kilometer 78. We turn off, drive eight clicks until we run into the Red Sea."

The car bounced off the road onto an unmarked goat track that wound across the empty desert. Then the sea glinted in front of them, a rose-tinted silver in the afternoon sun, lapping only inches deep over miles of rippled golden sand. Except for a group of men windsurfing in deeper water about a half a mile distant, the beach was empty. Bob stopped in the sparse shade of a scrubby tree close to the water and unloaded the umbrella and mats.

Liz opened the basket Siti and Megawati had packed—cold chicken, stuffed grape leaves, tiny wrinkled black olives, tomatoes, *khubis*—the flat round Arab bread—enough fruit and feta cheese for a platoon of hungry men.

Bob popped a can of nonalcoholic beer and handed it to Liz, then took a deep swallow of his own while he studied her.

"You're too pale, Liz," he said. "Some pretty good smudges under the eyes, too. You're working too hard."

"You sound just like my mother. She says that to me every time I go home to Santa Barbara."

"Well, why don't you ease up until your exit visa comes through?"

"I've been wanting to talk to you about that," Liz said. "I'd like to put it on hold for a while."

"I thought you couldn't wait to get away from here."

"Yes. Well, since then I've met Fateema."

"What?"

Liz laughed, pleased at the effect of her bombshell.

"Bob, your mouth is open and I think a fly just went in to investigate."

"What do you mean, you've met your mother? How? When? How did you find her?"

"I didn't. She found me. She just knocked on my door, late one night. The night Hisham was killed. You remember the slave who took her to the *Murphy*? He brought her."

"The slave? The black slave? How could... My God, it's been, what, thirty-two years? You were a newborn, how could you know him?"

"He's the bodyguard who goes everywhere with Prince Abdullah. You know who I mean?"

"The big black guy. Yes, sure, I've seen him. Is that him? Yeah." He slapped his forehead with his hand. "Yeah, of course. Why didn't I see it? How did you know him? Okay, Liz, come on! You've made your impression. How did all this come about?"

Liz told him everything she knew, from the moment Nassir had brought the orchids to her house in Santa Monica, how he lingered outside her door until Judd arrived, how she ran into him in the crowd after Hisham had been executed, then the midnight visit by Fateema.

"That's some story, Lizzie," he said when she'd finished. "How is she, Fateema? What's she like now?"

"Remarkable." Liz smiled. "Strong, bright, beautiful. Mom told me she was."

"For a kid who'd almost died in childbirth, she was amazing even then. I'd like to meet her now that she's a woman."

"No, I don't think that's possible." Liz shook her head. "I don't know where she lives, I don't know anything about her, not even her family's name. My only contact with her is through Nassir, and I can't just pick up a phone and call him, either. There's no way I can reach them. I just have to wait until they get in touch with me. That's why I want to put the exit visa on hold."

"What about Yousef?" he asked. "From what you say, it sounds as if he and Nassir know each other."

"Yes, I spoke to him, but I had to be very careful. He says that he sees Nassir sometimes at a coffeehouse, but I couldn't press it or ask him to have Nassir call me. I'm so scared after Hisham. I think Nassir could lose his life over this. But what if Fateema can't get a message to him? She's not a free agent, Saudi women can't just come and go as they please and it's been a couple of weeks now. I'm beginning to think I may never see her again...."

"Lizzie, if she said she'd see you, she will."

"But supposing she can't? She could be taken away by this guy—she calls him her master as if she's still a slave."

"Wait a minute." Gould reached into his shirt pocket. "I think there may be a way you can get a message to Nassir, see what's going on. Look at this." He handed her an envelope. "Hand delivered for you at King Khaled Clinic yesterday. I got one, too."

"What is it?"

"Open it," he said.

She did so. "It's an invitation."

"Yes. Prince Abdullah bin Talal al Sa'ud is giving a reception for some American military people. If Nassir is there, and I'm sure he will be, you might be able to get close enough to get a message to him. What do you think?"

"I think I'll buy a new dress."

The enormous two-story building, a row of columns fronting cream-colored marble and glass, blazed with light. Cars drew up beneath a porte cochere, and a parade of young Saudis with red-checked *ghutras* flowing over their white-clad shoulders opened each car door, escorted the guests into the palace and returned to greet others.

"Very impressive," Bob said.

The line of cars waiting to pull up beneath the porte cochere inched forward between an avenue of triple rows of palms, each lit from below. Beyond them on each side, Liz glimpsed heavily landscaped gardens, flowers and trees, illuminated fountains splashing into pools, other buildings somewhat smaller than the palace itself. A palatial compound rather than a single palace.

Behind the wheel, Yousef straightened his shoulders. Liz had noted that he had taken special pains with his appearance for the occasion, beard freshly shampooed and oiled, *thobe* and *ghutra* both snowy. As they'd driven along the Corniche, he had pointed with pride to the blaze of lights visible from miles away, although the palace itself was hidden. Elaborate iron gates were open to the tree-lined private road. How strange to think she'd admired them, always closed, on her walks along the Corniche with no idea that Abdullah lived behind them. Tonight, armed soldiers stopped each car as it entered, checking invitations and identities.

Their turn came at last. Yousef drew up under the porte cochere, and a Saudi escort stepped forward, opened the door.

"Welcome, sir." He smiled at Liz. "And madam."

He started to usher them into the palace. A voice penetrated the hum of conversation rising from the arriving guests.

"Dr. Gould. Dr. Ryan. Welcome." Dashing in a Saudi Air Force uniform, *arghal* tilted to a rakish angle, Prince Samir walked toward them, a hand outstretched. He murmured to the Saudi greeter in Arabic, and the young man turned to the next waiting car.

"Prince Samir." Bob pumped the outstretched hand. "Good to see you. How are you?"

"Eager, Dr. Gould. For the coming battle, I mean. Saddam will be sorry he challenged us." Samir looked over Gould's shoulder at Liz. "You are looking very beautiful tonight, Dr. Ryan."

She'd spent two months salary on an Oscar de la Renta dress from the French designer boutique in Jeddah—owned by a princess, so it was said—midnight-blue, long sleeved and ankle length, but formfitting beneath layers of silk chiffon that swirled at each movement, giving only a hint of her body.

"Thank you. We both look a little different from the last

time we met." The words were out, and she could have kicked herself. Not the most tactful thing to say, reminding him of an infidel's presence in Mecca, a woman at that.

"Come, please," Samir said. "You must have a drink, meet some of our other guests. We have many Americans here tonight."

He ushered them into the palace, across a marble-floored entry hall. Liz stared around her, dazzled. Behind Samir's back, she caught Bob's eye, and raised her eyebrows. The entry was a gallery of impressionist paintings: Monet and Matisse, Bonnard, Cézanne, Van Gogh, Manet, Sisley, Roualt, too many to absorb.

Samir led them through an arch and into a reception hall where a dozen chandeliers shimmered above pink marble floors inlaid with white. Overstuffed chairs and sofas lined the walls in the Arab style, leaving empty the vast open space in the center. More masterpieces decorated the walls.

"Can these be copies?" Liz whispered to Gould.

"No way," Bob murmured back. "You're looking at millions of bucks worth of art. Hope he's insured."

"Do you think they're all Abdullah's?"

"It's his palace."

The emerald earrings really had been a bauble, Liz thought. She remembered the night she had first seen Abdullah, the subtle light in the Crystal Room in Beverly Hills carefully designed to flatter. She glanced around the room. They did not have to bother about that here. She looked to be the only woman in the crush of males of every shape and color and dress, from Saudi *thobe* and tribal African, to military dress uniforms and civilian black tie.

"Your Excellency," Prince Samir was saying. "May I introduce two American doctors who are working with our own doctors to prepare our civilian population in case of attack by our enemies. Dr. Gould. Dr. Ryan."

Liz found her hand pressed between two cushioned

palms, and she caught a whiff of a heavy scent. She smiled, murmured a few words, then stood back to allow Bob Gould to carry the conversation so that she could discreetly search the room. She'd missed His Excellency's titles and had no idea to whom she had just been presented. But whoever he was, he was a heart attack waiting to happen unless he lost at least eighty pounds and stopped smoking. She let her gaze wander, looking for Abdullah, and Nassir who would be at his elbow.

Everywhere great vases were filled with flowers. Cigar and cigarette smoke drifted in blue clouds around the chandeliers, voices rose and fell. Yet the gathering was strangely bland, without the undercurrent of vivacity usually present in a crowd of this size.

No women. No feminine laughter. No leavening.

Samir lifted a couple of glasses from a tray offered by one of an army of circulating Filipino waiters. He held one of the glasses out to her.

"Saudi champagne." He grinned. "Lots of fizz, no bang."

They drifted away from Gould, deep now in conversation with His Excellency and the group of men surrounding him.

Liz took a sip. "It's good." She smiled over the rim of the glass. "Well, okay."

Samir laughed. "The real thing isn't for public consumption, but I can send a case of Veuve Clicquot over to you if you like." He grinned at her, a flirtatious sparkle in his eyes.

"Thanks, but no thanks, Samir," she said. "It's safer to wait until I get home."

"Probably wise. I can hardly wait to get back to the States myself."

"I thought it was the war with Iraq you were waiting for so eagerly."

"That, too. I'll get a couple of medals, then spend a few

years at our embassy in Washington. Maybe you and I can meet there. Washington is a beautiful city."

She smiled at him. "You know Washington?"

"Certainly. The Pentagon. Langley. I'm the military prince, remember?"

"Oh, of course." She looked around. "I don't see Prince Abdullah, so I haven't had a chance to thank him for inviting a lowly female. I seem to be the only one here."

"Almost. But I wouldn't call you a lowly female, Dr. Ryan. Liz. On the contrary."

He was smiling down at her, standing a little too close.

Liz said, "Is that General Readhead? I met him once, several years ago and would love to say hello. Would you mind introducing me again?"

Samir's smile lost a few degrees of warmth, but obediently he nodded. "It will be my pleasure."

Several of the Americans, resplendent in dress uniforms, turned as they approached, smiling a welcome. Liz barely saw them, her eyes riveted on Abdullah at the center of the group.

A sudden shortness of breath caught her unaware, and the pounding in her chest seemed so loud she was sure it could be heard. He was elegant in stark black and white: tailored *thobe* and black-and-white *ghutra,* black *bisht* deeply edged with gold.

How stupid, she thought. How stupid of her to feel this way.

Three feet behind him, Nassir stared impassively at an empty space above her head.

Abdullah held her gaze for a second before inclining his head. He didn't speak, turning instead to resume his conversation with the general.

A dismissal. Liz felt the tingle of blood rushing to her face. Why had he asked her here? She smiled quickly at the colonel beside her, glancing at the name pinned to his tunic.

"Colonel Brand. Welcome to Saudi Arabia," she said.

"Thank you." He looked uncertainly at Samir then back at Liz. "You're an American?"

"From California. Santa Barbara."

The colonel seemed uncomfortable, his eyes darting toward Samir, talking now to Abdullah and General Readhead, and back again to Liz. Suddenly she understood the reason for his discomfort and laughed.

"I work here, Colonel. I'm a surgeon at a hospital here in Jeddah." She glanced at Nassir. How could she possibly speak to him?

Colonel Brand laughed with her. "I didn't want to tread on any toes here. I thought maybe you were married to Prince Samir."

At the sound of his name, Samir turned. "Forgive me. This is Colonel Michael Brand. Dr. Elizabeth Ryan, Mike."

General Readhead turned at the mention of a female name. He reached a hand across his aide. "Charlie Readhead, Dr. Ryan."

Liz took his hand. "It's nice to see you again, General." She flashed a smile. "Good evening, Prince Abdullah."

"Dr. Ryan. I am glad you came tonight."

Liz noticed his stillness, as if he had to make an effort to control his breathing. A sudden jolt lifted her heart. He felt as she did.

"You know, I thought we'd met," the general was saying. "I never forget a beautiful woman. Jog my memory."

"Three years ago. A dinner in Los Angeles for reserve medical officers. I was there with Dr. Judd Cameron. You made a wonderful speech."

"Yes, right." He smiled broadly. "I remember."

The officers around her were introduced, and she smiled and nodded to each in turn. The conversation turned easily from military hardware to falcons, Samir using his hands to illustrate the swoop of the hunting birds dropping on prey.

Liz could feel the impact of Abdullah's presence and knew from the careful way he kept his eyes from her that he felt her just as strongly. How could the men, laughing and talking, not feel the tension humming between them like a taut wire?

"So, you were with Major Cameron that night." General Readhead had managed to detach himself from the conversation. "A fine officer. A credit to his country. Marine, right?"

Liz turned to him in relief. The general was said to prefer women's company to that of men when he had a choice. Tonight he seemed in particularly high spirits. The Saudis must have given him everything he'd asked for. She flicked a look at Nassir, willing him to acknowledge her presence, but he stared resolutely at the same empty spot above her head.

"Yes, general." She returned her gaze to him. "How kind of you to remember. Judd got his medical training in the Marine Corps."

"So, you two must be planning to meet here on the exotic Red Sea coast, eh?"

"I don't know. Maybe that depends upon you. I imagine Judd is with your army, wherever that is."

"Ah. Well. I'll have him call you. Maybe he can arrange something. These marines are a resourceful bunch. Okay if I call you Liz?"

"Please, General."

"I'll have him call you, Liz. What do you think about that?"

She was taken aback. "Will you know where to find him?"

General Readhead looked down at her, a quizzical look on his face. "I'm the general, Liz. I know everything."

Liz laughed. "Thank you. Nothing would please me more than to speak with Judd."

"Good. The modern army wants to be sensitive to the needs of the citizen soldier."

Was he serious? Liz looked at him and caught the sparkle of amusement in his bright blue eyes. She grinned at him.

"You're very sensitive, General. I'm sure your troops appreciate that."

The general laughed. The cluster of men was breaking up as more Saudis joined them. Prince Abdullah, with General Readhead and his aide Colonel Brand on either side of him, made his way through the room, speaking to his guests, introducing the American general and his staff. Nassir followed, never more than a pace or two behind his prince. Prince Samir showed no desire to join them, staying close to Liz's side, obviously planning a little flirtation, so daring in his world.

The evening drifted on. Liz managed to stay close enough to catch Nassir's glance should he look her way, yet distant enough to be discreet. Samir was attractive, fun and glued to her side, and she wondered, if Abdullah noticed, how he felt about Samir's attention to her.

About ten, Abdullah and General Readhead and their aides, Nassir among them, left through a door that was closed firmly behind them.

The reception was over.

17

A couple of days later Liz handed her briefcase to Siti, waiting as usual at the front door, and took the glass of fresh mango juice the maid offered and picked up the mail. As she went down the steps into the living room, her eyes sought the vase of orchids as they always did. The flowers were fresh.

She riffled through the envelopes, smiling as she saw a letter from her father, and another from Rusty Walsh in Santa Monica.

She put them aside and looked at a large, pale gray envelope. Scented. She turned it over. On the back was the Saudi crest: crossed swords beneath a palm tree, symbolic of the settling of the oases by the sword of King Abdul Azziz, and beneath them the Arabic calligraphy which she knew said, "There is no God but God, and Mohammed is the messenger of God." Puzzled, Liz ripped open the envelope and extracted a handwritten card.

"Dear Dr. Ryan: Her Highness, Princess Iffat bint Mohammed bin Wahhab, requests that you attend her for tea. 4:00 p.m. Wednesday." The signature was indecipherable. Considerately, a map was enclosed.

Liz had never heard of Princess Iffat bint Mohammed. Not surprising. No one heard about the princesses. No one even knew how many there were, although every one of the 4,200 princes was documented—their parentage, age and place of birth.

Mentally, she ran through her operating schedule for Wednesday. She'd have to make arrangements to leave the hospital early, easier now than when Hisham Badawi was alive. He'd kept every hour of her day occupied. The whole hospital seemed to be winding down since he'd been killed, with fewer and fewer female patients being admitted.

On Wednesday, Liz left the hospital at two, cutting it close since she had to bathe and change and leave the house in plenty of time for Yousef to find the address shown on the map. She knew it would not be easy; there were still large areas of Jeddah whose street names were known only to the people who lived on them.

After a good deal of backing and turning, and muttering in Arabic, Yousef managed to follow the map. He drove into the oldest part of Jeddah, with mud-brick walls, bare, narrow streets—what Liz thought of as Mansour country, in memory of Tess's old gatekeeper. Finally they stopped in front of a pair of closed, featureless wooden gates. The ancient gateman, an ex-slave from the look of his wrinkled black face, dozed inside a small mud-brick gatehouse.

"This is the place, madam."

"Are you sure?" Liz asked, skeptical.

Yousef shrugged. "It is the place."

"Then you'd better wake him up."

Yousef tapped the horn. The old man started as if not quite sure where he was, then smiled, showing a few brown stubs of teeth. He hobbled to the gates, laboriously opened them by hand, then waved the Mercedes through.

The driveway was gravel and lined with dusty pink oleander bushes being washed down by half a dozen Afghani gardeners. To her astonishment, Liz glimpsed a small herd of tiny deer among the date palms, then several donkeys peacefully nuzzling flakes of hay. The princess must be an eccentric. Saudis had no regard for animals. Liz had been told they had killed off most of their wildlife years ago, hunting with machine guns from the backs of specially fitted automobiles, slaughtering entire herds of gazelle in a matter of minutes. Much like the buffalo of the Western plains.

The driveway ended in a bare, circular courtyard in front of a long, single-storey house that, except for a pair of old wooden doors, presented a blank, silent face to the visitor.

Liz got out of the car. Somewhere a peacock shrieked, the only sound she could hear.

Then the doors opened, and a veiled figure stood in the arched entrance. At the sight of Liz, she opened her arms.

Fateema.

Liz stepped into the waiting arms. Through her veil, Fateema kissed each side of Liz's face, then repeated the caress twice more. Above the black cloth, her green eyes were bright.

"Nassir told me you were eager to see me." Fateema laughed at Liz's surprise. "He has found a way of contacting me. It is dangerous, but he does it. He said he saw you at the reception for the Americans and from your eyes he knew that you wondered why you had not seen me. You are not careful, he says." Fateema squeezed Liz's arm, offered no explanation for her silence. "Now, you must come. Princess Iffat is eager to meet you."

She drew Liz into the house. Inside the temperature dropped dramatically as the thick mud-brick walls absorbed the heat of the sun. No air-conditioning here. No priceless pictures displayed on these whitewashed walls. No marble floors. Just simple clay tiles the color of the desert. "She knows you are here," Fateema said.

"Why did she invite me?"

"She's an old friend. She likes to keep up with what is going on in Jeddah."

"What does she know of me?" Liz asked.

"She heard of your work on children's faces. She knows you are an educated woman. A doctor. An American." Liz had the sense Fateema was smiling behind her veil. "You must tell her whatever else she wants to know."

A male servant approached on sandaled feet, and Liz understood why Fateema had kept her face covered. The man was turbaned, clad in baggy white cotton pants and long overshirt. He stood silently, framed by a Moorish archway leading to the main house, waiting for them to leave. Fateema ignored him. She took Liz's arm and led her through a lattice-worked door that allowed air to circulate. She closed it behind her, then crossed a garden enclosed on all sides by the house.

As she walked, Fateema undid her veil, took off her *abayah*. Beneath it she wore a silk dress, dark-green and intricately draped. In the West it would be considered far too elaborate for tea in the afternoon.

"This is the women's part of the house," Fateema said.

"The *harem*," Liz said, laughing, using the American pronunciation—hairem.

"The *hareem*." Hahreem. "Yes. This is a very old house. Women can sit in this garden without fear of men's eyes. A man from outside the family would lose his life for intruding here."

The sound of female laughter drifted through an open archway. Fateema flashed Liz a smile and ushered her into a room filled with women. The laughter dwindled. Liz felt herself studied by dozens of eyes.

A different room entirely from Hisham Badawi's home. For one thing, these women were expensively dressed. For another, they regarded her with curiosity, not ill will. But it was the room itself that was amazing.

It was large and whitewashed, without windows. But just below the level of the ceiling, wooden shutters, open now to allow light, pierced thick walls. The usual massive overstuffed chairs and sofas were ranged against the walls, as well as a number of small tables and brass trays on carved legs.

But it was the end of the room that astonished her. It was entirely filled by a great black Bedouin tent in front of which an old lady, dressed in voluminous layers of colorful fabric, half reclined on a pile of rugs and pillows. Gold—coins, beads, large filigree balls—covered her chest, hung from her ears and ringed her arms.

In a thin voice, she called out in Arabic and beckoned. Fateema led Liz forward. The old woman took Liz's hand, pulled her down beside her onto the rugs. Around them conversation picked up. A servant brought a tray, and Liz took a small glass in a silver filigree holder. The old princess spoke to Fateema.

"Princess Iffat says you are beautiful," Fateema said. She sipped her own glass of tea, and Liz followed suit. The usual mint tea, cloyingly sweet.

"Thank you," Liz said. She smiled at the old lady.

The princess spoke again, keeping her hold on Liz's hand.

"Princess Iffat wishes to know where you were schooled," Fateema said.

"At Georgetown University in Washington, D.C." Liz spoke directly to the old lady. "Then medical training at Harvard, and I did my surgical residency at Saint Luke's Hospital in Santa Monica, California."

She looked over at Fateema, remembering what Tess had said about feeling Fateema's presence when Liz received her degree. Thank you, Liz wanted to say now. Thank you for giving me my chance. Fateema met her eyes and nodded as if she knew what Liz was thinking. Liz turned back to the old princess. She was asleep.

Fateema leaned forward and took the glass from the gnarled old fingers. "You can get up now, Liz. Lying on a pile of rugs is not very comfortable. Princess Iffat was born in the desert—for her it is easy. Not so easy for us."

Gratefully Liz rose to her feet. A woman in an elegant blue silk suit was circulating the room, swinging a large intricately worked incense burner on a chain. She stopped in front of each woman long enough to allow her to lean forward and fan the sweet billowing smoke into hair and clothes.

When she came to Liz, she smiled. "Try it," she said. "It's really very nice." Her English was exquisite.

"This is Dr. Elizabeth Ryan, Nura," Fateema said. "Princess Nura, Liz."

"Just Nura." She waved the incense in front of Liz. "Fateema, do it for her."

Fateema wafted the incense into Liz's hair and clothes with graceful circular movements of her hands. Princess Nura smiled. She handed the incense burner to the servant who had followed her around the room. "You're an American," she said. "Fateema told us you were coming today."

"It was kind of Princess Iffat to invite me."

"She's a dear old thing. One of our last links with the distant past. Her father rode with King Abdul Azziz," Nura said. "She has never been outside this house since she married. Can you imagine such a prison?"

Liz glanced uneasily at Fateema, but Fateema's face told her nothing. "Not a prison for her if she was used to it, I'm sure."

"You don't have to be so discreet. Tell her, Fateema. We are all in prison here."

Liz took a breath, sipped the sticky tea. It seemed safer to say nothing.

"I haven't been out of the country for two years," Nura said. "Sometimes I think I'm going to go mad, cooped up here." She waved a hand around her at the women, chatting now, drinking tea, eating the tiny cakes handed around by the Indonesian serving maids. "They don't seem to care. I'm the only one who does."

"You know that's not true, Nura," Fateema said. "But what's the use of struggling?"

"I was educated at Roedean, the famous girl's school in England. My father was progressive, believed in education for women. I went to Cambridge. Can you believe that?" She gave a laugh. "Cambridge. Now my daughter has to stay in the kingdom to be educated. She will learn nothing."

"The day he became king, Fahd recalled all the women being educated out of kingdom," Fateema said to Liz. "It is said that girls educated in the West are no longer fit to be Muslim wives. Now it is not allowed for women to leave Saudi Arabia to be educated."

"If my daughter wants an education she has to go to King Abdul Azziz University," Nura said. "She'll be taught by a man on television because a man cannot be in the same room with women. Such madness—"

To Liz's horror, Princess Nura's face crumpled. Tears poured down her cheeks. In seconds, she looked twenty years older.

Fateema murmured to her in Arabic. Nura flapped a hand at her, then turned to walk away. Immediately she was surrounded by women and Liz caught the sympathetic looks exchanged over her head.

"She is very upset," Liz said. "Does her daughter want to go away to school somewhere?"

"No. Her daughter will not go to the university, not here, not anywhere. Nura knows that. Her father has arranged a marriage for her."

Liz wondered why such a drama had been made about an education that would never take place. Politely, she said, "Nura doesn't like the young man?"

"Oh, yes, she does. But she is frightened. Dania has been out of kingdom, many times to Marbella in Spain, with Nura. They have a house there."

Liz looked at Fateema, puzzled.

"She is not virgin," Fateema said in a low voice. "You understand? That will be discovered on her wedding night. Nura will be blamed."

"Oh. But if he's well traveled, a sophisticated man—"

"What difference does that make? When it is discovered that she has already known a man, Dania will be sent back to her father. Nura will be divorced."

Liz was aghast. "You mean Nura's husband will divorce her because their daughter is no longer a virgin?"

"Oh, yes, of course. And Dania will be sent back to her father, and he will kill her."

"What did you say?" Liz couldn't believe what she'd heard.

"I said that Dania will be killed."

Liz stared at her, speechless.

Fateema shrugged. "Her father must protect his *sharaf,* his honor, the honor of his family. It is our way."

"My God. That can't be true."

"It is true. It will break his heart. He loves her. He loves Nura, too. But he will do it."

Liz glanced at Nura, laughing now, an hysterical edge to her laughter.

"You do know that the hymen can be repaired?" Liz said softly to Fateema.

"It is not unknown here, Liz. If girls have been foolish they have been taken by their mothers to Jordan for shopping before the wedding. But that is not possible now. King Hussein supports Iraq, so that travel has been stopped."

"She could go to London, Switzerland. She must need a trousseau—"

"No time. The young man is with the army, much is being made of that now, the young warriors need to leave pregnant wives behind them. We are brood mares, you understand. The marriage will go ahead as planned."

"I can't believe this will happen," Liz said. "A loving father surely wouldn't do such a thing."

"But you do believe that a man's head can be taken by the sword because that you have seen with your own eyes. Well. Nura should have watched her daughter more closely. She has to pay the price for her carelessness." Fateema took her hand. "Do not think about it anymore. Your life is not here."

No one could have nurtured a daughter with more care than Tess had. But Tess had been no match for the young god surfing the waves at Rincon Beach who'd dazzled the sixteen-year-old Liz Ryan.

"Have the girl come to King Khaled Clinic for a check up a few days before the wedding," Liz said softly. "I can perform a hymenorrhaphy, but the procedure will not hold the tissue together for longer than three or four days, maybe a week. I'll make the arrangements."

Fateema touched Liz's hand. "Thank you. You will be discreet?"

"Bob Gould will have to be told, but I think you know he can be trusted. What about these women?" She looked around the room. "They all seem to be aware of what's going on."

"The secrets of the *hareem* are famous, are they not?" Fateema's tone was ironic. "Look at them. Fashionable and educated, some of them. All of them living with the same fears as Nura. Divorce. A second, younger wife. Or a third or fourth. No. Dania's life is not threatened by anyone here." She took Liz's arm, gently drew her into the room. "They're eager to meet you. We don't get much chance to speak with anyone from America."

Liz smiled as she was introduced, murmured words of greeting, answered questions, laughed, chatted, listened. But for the rest of the afternoon, her thoughts kept turning to Hisham Badawi, and to the disaster and grief their friendship had brought to so many. And now she was being drawn into these women's lives, deeper than she wanted to go.

Where, she wondered, would this take her? Where would it take them?

18

"**I** want to know what you're up to," Bob Gould said curtly. "The Scandinavians are sending me memos about your use of this clinic. Now I can cover, no problem, but I want to know what the hell is going on." He leaned back, steepled his fingers. "How is it that you've been occupying examining rooms, using the equipment and supplies of this facility when you have been seconded to Jeddah General Hospital and are no longer based here?"

He had not asked her to sit, and Liz stood in front of his desk feeling as if she'd been summoned to the principal's office. "I'm sorry you got involved," she said. "Why don't they talk to me about it?"

"Because my signature is on the authorization for your use of King Khaled." He glanced at the papers in the folder. "They want to know what you're doing, for their records. And so do I."

"You know what I've been doing, Bob. It wasn't meant to, but the word got out." She put a hand on the back of a chair, waited for his nod, then sat. "Look, I don't know if these girls are really in danger, but they think they are, and so do their mothers. They're terrified. Marriages are being moved up because of the war—for some reason it's become fashionable, a sort of patriotic statement. Anyway, the point is they can't just slip out of the country for a couple of days, no one the wiser." Liz could herself hardly believe the words she was saying, although she knew them to be true.

"To travel anywhere, for shopping or medical care or a vacation, whatever, women have to get the written permission of their male guardian, their father, husband, or a brother or son, and even then they are not allowed to go anywhere without a *mahram,* a male chaperon. There's no time to arrange all that with these rushed weddings, even if they could get written permission from the government, which they also need. They're trapped. So I've repaired the hymens of a few young women, and I've saved them some grief."

And maybe even some lives. Princess Dania's terror hadn't been an act. She'd arrived with Princess Nura, both using false names. She'd merely nodded when Liz told her that the procedure would be done without an anesthetic but that the needle was extremely fine and the pain would be less than an injection of a painkiller. She'd whimpered, held on to her mother, even managed a weak smile when it was over. Now she was safely married, a virgin on her wedding night. But why did a girl of twenty have to go through that?

"It seemed to me a good cause," she said. "It still does."

"How do they know where to reach you, these girls? Are you in the yellow pages? Hymenorrhaphy by Dr. Ryan. Satisfaction guaranteed?"

Liz tightened her lips in anger, but replied without heat. She was on shaky ground here, and she knew it. "Hardly these girls. Just four. I know their mothers from Princess Iffat's house. I've been visiting fairly often, it's where I see Fateema. The women trust me and they talk to me." She leaned forward, wanting him to understand. "Bob, you wouldn't believe their lives. They've got nothing to do, in houses filled with servants who spy on them. They live in fear their husbands will put them aside as they grow older, take another wife. Most of them have no education to speak of, and it's even worse for those who have been educated abroad. Some of these women sleep their lives away. They don't wake until afternoon, then they put on elaborate dresses to see the same women they saw yesterday, have the same conversations—"

"Liz," Bob interrupted, "you can't alter this culture."

"I'm not trying to. I'm just trying to alleviate a little of the pain I see. Isn't that what a doctor is supposed to do?"

"And what happens if word of what you're doing gets to the wrong ears? Even a suspicion of it." Bob shook his head. "Do you have any idea what could happen?"

"I don't think about it."

"Then maybe you'd better start. These people are nuts when it comes to their women. Nuts! Jesus Christ, Liz! I want you to stop this, right now." Gould tapped the file on his desk with his pen. It sounded to Liz as if he would like to be tapping her, hard. "If the *mutawain* discover what you're doing... This is very dangerous, Lizzie."

Liz knew he was right. Neither of them could guess the consequences of what she was doing. If she allowed herself to think, she'd probably refuse help to young women whose only crime was to fall in love with a Westerner. Or maybe not in love. Maybe they'd just been rebellious. Or curious. Or simply had raging hormones. What difference did it make?

"Liz, are you listening to me?"

She nodded.

"Good. Put a stop to it, for both our sakes." Gould turned, riffled through a pile of folders on the cabinet behind him until he found the one he was looking for. "I've got to go to Riyadh tomorrow, another meeting at the Ministry of Health, these guys love their meetings. I'm also expected in Yanbu, up the coast. I want you to go to Yanbu for me, get out of Jeddah for a few days."

"I can't just pick up and go out of town, I've got a full schedule—"

Gould raised a hand to silence her protests. "I'll explain

to Mukarek. Hell, I'll even get him another female surgeon for his urgent cases—a Bosnian just arrived here at King Khaled, a Muslim. I'll talk to Dr. Al-Turki, see if I can get her seconded until you get back." He slid the file across the desk. "They've got a small modern hospital under foreign contract in Yanbu al Sinaiyah, the new town, and another for contract labor under local control in the old town. Yanbu will be a prime Iraqi target—it's the major Red Sea oil terminal at the end of the pipeline from the Gulf. If they're attacked, the hospitals need to be up for it. See whether they've made preparations to fit into the general plan I've made up for the west coast. You know the drill."

Liz picked up the file. "Not very demanding." Clearly he wasn't giving her a choice, and she realized she was relieved. She'd been working hard, and it would be good to get a few days away. Away from frightened women; away from Jeddah General and its rapid decline into primitive third-world practices, away from the pervading concern for prayer instead of decent hospital care. Away from the deafening silence from Abdullah.

"Well, I guess it will give me a chance to see Mary Lou Tibbets before she leaves," she said. "John's company suddenly decided to evacuate all dependents before Thanksgiving. She'll be gone in a week, so she's going up to Yanbu on the early plane tomorrow with John to say goodbye to a friend who lives there."

"Good. Take an extra few days, get Mary Lou and her friend to take you to look at the old town. I'm told it's quite interesting, the headquarters of Lawrence of Arabia. His house is still there. I'll call Amundson at Al Nawa Hospital, let them know you're coming in my place."

The 727 made a wobbling turn over the tiny air terminal.

"Oh, God, hang on to your seat," Mary Lou said from across the aisle.

John Tibbets grinned at Liz. "Seems like we got ourselves a trainee in the cockpit."

Liz laughed. Most ex-pats believed, erroneously she was sure, that Saudia had their inexperienced Saudi pilots practice on the domestic runs, saving their seasoned pilots for the international flights. She looked out of the window, and wished she hadn't. The ground was coming up very fast as the wings dipped alarmingly. Maybe the ex-pats were right.

Mary Lou gave voice to a sound midway between a laugh and a scream. The powerful engines surged, and the plane lifted as the pilot decided to go around again. And again. Finally, the wheels hit hard, the plane bounced, then settled. The engines reversed and the Boeing slowed and stopped. Relieved passengers stood, grabbing baggage from the overhead lockers.

"Allah be praised," Mary Lou said in Liz's ear. "Do you want a ride to Yanbu?"

"Thanks, but the hospital is sending a car for me."

Outside the aircraft the air was moist, cooler than in Jeddah, 350 kilometers to the south. People milled around in the tiny airport building, meeting the morning flight and getting ready to board for the return to Jeddah. A number of men wore Western suit jackets over dark flannel *thobes*. *Thobes* and Western jackets shouldn't work together, Liz thought, but on these guys they did. Somehow they managed to look terrific.

"Dr. Ryan?"

"Yes?" She turned to see a short stout blonde thrusting a hand at her.

"I am Gunnar Amundson." He pumped Liz's hand once, then dropped it, as if willing to extend Western courtesy, but not too much. "A pleasure. Good flight?" He reached for her bag.

"A bit shaky coming in."

"I saw. A trainee. But here you are, in one piece."

"Don't forget our date tonight," a voice called.

Liz waved and smiled at Mary Lou being hustled out of the door by John, already deep in conversation with one of his engineers. Mary Lou waved back. "You've got my number, honey. Call me if you get lonely."

Liz nodded, waved again. Dr. Amundson ushered her to a Saab station wagon. He opened the passenger door for her, then went around the car, slid his stout frame behind the wheel and turned west out of the parking lot.

They talked about conditions at the local hospitals.

"Johannsen Medical Corporation has the contract to run the hospital in Yanbu Al Sinaiyah, the new town," Amundson said. "Naturally, it operates to the same standard as King Khaled Clinic in Jeddah but it's a very small hospital, and we will be unable to handle a catastrophic attack. And if the Iraqis use chemical or biological weapons—" Amundson shrugged, shook his head.

"What about the hospital in the old town?" Liz asked.

He kept his eyes ahead. "That I know nothing about."

"Doctor," she pressed, "we have to know what's available to the civilian population. You can give me an idea what to expect."

Amundson slowed to navigate a large tree-shaded traffic island marking the beginning of the old town. "I wouldn't take my cat there, to be honest."

"Oh, God. Another Jeddah General." Liz looked out of the window. Below the trees the traffic island sported a large sign in both Arabic and English. My Brother the Driver, the English translation said. Please Drive Slow to Be Alive for Your Loved Ones. The incredible mortality rate for Saudi drivers was a never-ending source of speculation among expats. Theories ran from a supposed lack of depth perception to the Saudi belief in the immutability of the will of Allah. One's time comes when Allah wills. Caution was unnecessary.

The small town was busy, streets full of cars, sidewalks crowded with men navigating broken paving, huge holes, steep drops in elevation as pavements suddenly ended.

"If this were the United States," Liz said, "litigation would be the main industry. Seems to be a lot of activity. Something going on?" Crews of workmen wearing the untidy flat turbans, baggy pants and tunics of Afghanistan, were busy slapping paint on a series of spindly ceremonial arches that graced, or despoiled, depending on the point of view, most Saudi towns.

"They're sprucing up for the king's visit," Amundson said. "He wants to see for himself what's being done to protect the oil refineries and storage facilities."

"The king's coming here?" Her heartbeat picked up speed.

"This afternoon. Mainly to the port, but he'll pay a swift visit to Yanbu Al Sinaiyah, also. We'll have to take a few hours off to greet him, just part of the crowd, of course, he won't be inspecting the hospital. His visit was supposed to be a secret, but nothing is here."

Would Abdullah be with the king? she wondered. And what difference did it make if he was? Here or Jeddah, his silence was the message. Or had he told Bob that he would be here?

Once clear of the town, Amundson turned onto a four-lane divided highway leading for miles across the empty desert. The only green in sight was the mature palm trees in the median, each with the black pipe of its watering system visible in the basin of earth at its base. An army of Afghani workmen trimmed palm fronds and carefully hosed each tree.

"That's a lot of palm trees," Liz said.

"By special order of the king, one every fifty feet for ten miles. This is his showplace on the Red Sea. If a tree dies, it's replaced immediately. Today each tree is being washed in honor of his visit.''

''Guess it keeps a lot of foreign labor working, sending cash back to the home folks. One way of spreading the wealth.''

''Good way of looking at it.''

They passed a black-veiled Bedouin woman, her flock of goats grazing around her. It was a miracle these women didn't drop like flies from sunstroke, Liz thought, under all that black fabric.

Amundson slowed the Saab. Ahead of them several army personnel vehicles painted in desert camouflage blocked the road.

''Do you have your *iqama?*'' Amundson asked. ''Better give it to me. I took a chance picking you up myself. I don't think the *mutawain* will be hanging about out here today with the king expected.''

A group of Saudis in fatigues, M-16s slung over their shoulders, waved them to a halt. Amundson lowered the window. A soldier bent to peer in.

''I am Dr. Amundson. This is Dr. Ryan. We are medical doctors from Al Nawa Hospital, Yanbu al Sinaiyah.'' He held up their documents.

The young soldier couldn't seem to drag his eyes from Liz's bare face. She smiled at him. His eyes widened even further. Amundson pushed the documents at him and the boy looked down, then seemed to remember his orders and took them to the personnel carrier.

The Saudis took their time, lighting cigarettes, talking among themselves, glancing at the Saab. Then a different young man returned and leaned down to look at Liz. She smiled. He stared impassively in response and waved them through. Twice more in the next six miles, they were stopped by armored vehicles, their *iqamas* examined, their faces studied before being waved on.

"Things are pretty tense," Amundson said. "They've always been security conscious around here with the pipeline and the million-barrel storage tanks. Now that the Iraqi army's poised on the border, they're as jumpy as hell."

The new town appeared on the horizon, hovering for miles like a mirage in the desert, only taking shape as they got closer. Amundson swung a hard right into an avenue of poinciana trees, the red blossoms brilliant against dark leaves. Small houses appeared, the grid patterns of the urban layout softened by flowering shrubs, the green of young jacaranda and coral trees, tamarisk misty with yellow blossom. The desert had disappeared. Both sides of the road were filled with color, oleander and lantana, beds of canna lilies in red and yellow in front of airy administration buildings. Men, Western and Saudi, strolled along shady colonnades. Most surprising were the Western women on bicycles, their caftans hiked carelessly to their knees, baskets piled with groceries.

"Everything is so green," Liz said. "You don't realize how much you miss that."

"The prince overseeing the development of Yanbu, and Jubail on the Gulf, loves Palm Springs," Amundson said with a grin. "He had plants and soil brought over from California by the planeload. A desalinization plant was one of the first things built so we have plenty of water to keep it this way."

Amundson turned into a circular driveway at the edge of a tangle of mangroves. The Red Sea glinted in the near distance. White egrets were poised in the branches of the trees and a flock of green parrots rose shrieking at the intrusion of the car.

"Is this the hotel?" Liz asked.

"You can't stay at the hotel, a woman alone. This is the official guest house of the Royal Commission for Yanbu and Jubail."

"It won't be needed for the king's visit?"

"No. The king will not stay over."

A dark-eyed Sri Lankan dressed entirely in white opened her door. "Welcome, madam." He bowed. "I am Andrew."

"Good morning. My bag's in the trunk." She smiled at the servant. "I won't stay now, but I'll be back late this afternoon."

The hours ripped by. Liz met the medical staff and listened as they explained contingency plans, working out with them how they would cooperate with the hospital in the old town. She called the Egyptian director there to set up an appointment for the following day and made notes for Dr. Gould. Lunch was a quick sandwich in the doctors' lounge, and at three, Dr. Amundson looked at his watch. "I think we should adjourn now and walk over to the administration building," he said. "The king's due in about half an hour. Everybody who can will be there. It might be noted by our local sheikh if we are not." He flicked blond eyebrows, smiled at Liz. "Our contract is coming up for renewal."

The weather had cooled with clouds that had moved in from the Red Sea, and the walk was pleasant, the air soft and fresh. Amundson pointed out landmarks—mosques and schools both Arab and Western, women's centers, the gymnasium for the men, the soccer fields and tennis courts, all rising from the raw desert in less than five years.

Outside the main administration building, *thobe*-clad men waited to greet their king. Liz caught sight of Mary Lou under a poinciana tree on the other side of the road and excused herself from the group of Scandinavians to join her.

"If this is the thin brown line standing between us and the Iraqis, I'm glad I'm leaving," Mary Lou said in greeting. "These guys look as if they rode with Lawrence."

Liz eyed the line of National Guards awaiting the king's

arrival, all shapes and sizes, a lot of white beards. Bandoliers of ammunition crisscrossed chests, hung loosely around
solid hips. They wore khaki *thobes*, red-and-white check
ghutras, leather sandals on bare callused feet, ancient rifles
slung over shoulders.

Wahhabis, Liz thought, the strict fundamentalists loyal to
Prince Bandr. She'd been told they were posted every few
feet along the route the king would travel from the airport.
These were a ceremonial force, mostly elders, but in a tribal
society ruled by old men, a force that illustrated Prince
Bandr's political power.

The wail of sirens and half a dozen army vehicles came
into view, then a convoy of black Mercedes and a giant bus.
The National Guardsmen straightened and a murmur of anticipation ran through the crowd. The cars swept up to the
administration building, the bus stopped. Children, Saudi
and Western, waved their tiny white-and-green Saudi flags.
A portly figure descended from the bus and waved to the
schoolchildren. The waiting Saudis formed themselves into
a fluid line, stepping forward to kiss the king, first on each
cheek, then on his left shoulder.

In spite of herself Liz searched the crowd of men who
had arrived with the king, going back to examine each face
again, her disappointment deepening. She hadn't really expected him. It would have been too great a coincidence.

The king, followed by his retinue, walked into the administration building. The crowd started to disperse.

Mary Lou was saying something about that evening, and
Liz nodded, not hearing.

He wasn't there. And it wasn't until that moment Liz
realized how much she had hoped he would be.

What a fool.

The presentation tent next to the administration building
glowed from inside, golden against the deep-blue desert sky,

outlined by thousands of bulbs. Liz's driver found a place among the confusion of cars disgorging their female passengers, then opened her door.

"What time shall I return, madam?"

Liz looked at her watch. Arab affairs never started until late and it was already past ten. A long night was ahead after an already long day. She caught sight of the Tibbets, Mary Lou elegant in black lace, waiting for her in front of the tent.

"Thank you, I'll get a ride back."

"Can you beat this?" Mary Lou called. "Honey, anything this size belongs in Texas."

"A gift from the Queen of England," John Tibbets said. "You could get the Astrodome inside that tent, easy. Well, have fun, girls. It's all in a good cause." He waved and got into his car.

"He's got himself a dull ole poker game lined up," Mary Lou said, "but we're going to have ourselves quite an evening, I promise you." The two women joined the stream of humanity, Western women in silks mingling with anonymous black-shrouded figures, making their way into the tent. "I've never heard of Saudi women doing this kind of thing," she continued. "The wife of the governor of the province somehow got them organized to raise money for the refugee women and children of Kuwait. It's just what these Saudi gals need, a cause to get them out of their damn houses. Find out there is something in the world they can do for themselves other than have a baby every year."

"Mary Lou! A lot of these women speak English—"

"Good, give them something to think about."

Inside, the floor of the tent was covered by Oriental carpets, thrown down haphazardly, overlapping, rich with color. Tables along the back were crisp with white damask and piled with matching napkins and gold-rimmed plates. Everywhere, anonymous black figures tossed off veils and *abayas,* revealing dresses that spanned a range of taste, from creations out of the great Paris fashion houses to ruched tie-dyed polyester massed with artificial flowers and sequined ribbons. The air was heady with the fragrance of French perfumes and oils from the women's *suq,* the scent of incense from intricate burners carried by young girls. Women bent over the incense, fanning the sweet smoke into hair and bosoms. Liz smothered a grin at the sight of women, old enough to have been part of Abdul Azziz's personal *hareem,* lifting their skirts, directing the smoke upward into their underwear with gentle undulations of their hands.

Mary Lou nudged Liz, sliding her eyes toward a hoop-skirted purple satin dress, garlanded with a sequined pink net fastened with large yellow silk roses. "I saw that in a store in Jeddah."

"You didn't!"

"Swear to God. Cost $3,500.00. Made in Paris by the House of Dior, for their Saudi store." Mary Lou looked around the huge interior, milling with women. "We're meeting Joan Fayad, the girl I came to say goodbye to. She got us the tickets for this affair. We used to be neighbors in Jeddah before her husband transferred to be near his family. Lovely girl, long blonde hair, stunning— Ah, there she is!" Mary Lou waved, steering Liz toward seats at the edge of a stage. Then, "Oh, Jesus," she muttered. "What the hell's he done to her this time?"

Joan Fayad pointed to the two chairs flanking her own, Chanel evening bag on one, *abayah* on another. She wore black silk, full sleeves falling to her wrists. Diamonds sparkled in her ears and around her throat.

"I'm glad you're here, I've been guarding these chairs with my life," she said. "How are you, Mary Lou?" Her voice wobbled. "It's so good to see you."

"I'm a damn sight better than you look, babe." Mary

Lou bent to kiss her. "What happened? You run into another door?"

"Yes. Well." Joan shrugged. Skillfully applied, her makeup did little to disguise the purple bruises along her cheekbone, the swollen and split lips. She attempted a painful smile for Liz. "You must be Liz Ryan. Mary Lou tells me you're her jogging mate. I did the Boston Marathon twice. In a former life."

"I've never been that ambitious," Liz said. She took the chair Joan indicated, nodded at Joan's left arm. "Hope you didn't break that running."

Joan touched the cast supported by a black silk sling that matched her dress. "No, I don't run any more."

"She's into full tackle football these days. As you can see," Mary Lou said.

Joan's blue eyes filled. She tried to laugh but couldn't pull it off, and the corners of her mouth deepened, her throat jerking as she swallowed.

"Oh, honey," Mary Lou said. "You've got to leave him."

Joan shook her head, unable to speak. She glanced quickly at Liz, then at the laughing, colorful crowd of women, keeping her eyes wide so that tears wouldn't spill. She pressed her shaking right hand against her chin, as if to stop its trembling.

"It's okay, Joanie," Mary Lou said gently. "Liz is a doctor. She's heard it all before. Doctors are hard to shock."

Joan Fayad hesitated, then said in a low voice, "There's nothing to say, Mary Lou. He won't let the kids go. End of story."

The tent was filling rapidly, the noise level rising, the air warm and heavy. No one seemed inclined to sit, to wait for whatever was to come next and no one seemed to care. The scene was filled with movement and the flash of diamonds, rubies, emeralds, sequins, gleaming satins and silks in blue, green, yellow, red. Every gradation of skin color from blue-black to pale ivory—skin that had been carefully protected from any touch of sun.

A happy chaos reigned.

"My husband drinks," Joan said softly to Liz. "It's illegal, of course, but you can get anything if you have the money, and he has plenty. Then he gets violent—" She stopped, tried again to laugh. "Boring old story. We've all heard it a thousand times."

Over Joan's bent head, Liz caught Mary Lou's eye. "The police?" she mouthed.

Mary Lou shrugged and said aloud, "The Koran allows a man to beat his wife."

"But surely not put her in a hospital!" Liz said.

"No, of course not. It's supposed to be physical punishment just to keep her in line," Joan said. "It could be worse, I guess. Even his mother thinks Mahmoud overdoes it. She's pretty nice to me, and she adores the kids."

"Have you spoken to the Embassy in Riyadh?" Liz asked.

"Oh, sure," Joan said wearily. "They can't help. I've still got an American passport, but he's got it locked up somewhere. Anyway, I'd need his written permission to travel, and my children can only leave the country on their father's passport." She looked at Liz. "It's the law. I've got a boy and a girl. Six and eight. So even if I could, by some stroke of luck, get my own passport back, I'd have to leave them behind. I'll never do that."

My God, Liz thought. She's really trapped. "How long have you been married?"

"Ten years. We got married when we were students at Boston College. He was gorgeous then. Charmed everyone, even my dad. Mahmoud loved it that I ran the marathon, that kind of thing. But that was ten years ago."

As they talked, Saudi women stopped to speak to Joan in

Arabic or English. No one mentioned the cast and bruises. Joan murmured introductions, and gave no encouragement for the visitors to linger.

"I'm going to be selfish tonight," she said to Mary Lou. "Now that you're going…" Her voice trailed away and Mary Lou took her hand. They sat silently, hands clasped.

Finally a blond Westerner and a beautiful dark Saudi climbed onto the stage. They picked up hand microphones, taking turns to shout for order in both languages.

"Come on, girls, take your seats," the blonde called and it was immediately apparent she was Australian. "Princess Latiyah has asked my friend Tahani Nazar and me to welcome you to this fabulous event. I would add that I hope you will show your appreciation when the baskets are passed later. Cash, checks, pledges. And remember, it's in a good cause, as we all know, to raise some money for the women and children fleeing for their lives from Kuwait. So, dig deep."

"You'd think their own ruling family would pony up for them," Mary Lou muttered. "God knows they're about as rich as the Al Sa'ud."

Joan Fayad shushed her, laughing a little, and Mary Lou grinned back.

"Now, the Saudi ladies have got a great fashion show for us tonight," the blonde was saying. "And we're going to have some terrific food. So let's get started."

Tahani took her turn. No one was listening. The blonde took back the mike, pleading again for order. Finally, she waved to the Western women in the lighting booth. The tent plunged into darkness. Women shrieked playfully. The lights flashed back on. Off, on. Off, on. Gradually, everyone found their seats and the lights dimmed. Strains of "A Pretty Girl Is Like a Melody," floated through the tent. The music changed, and the spotlight picked up two women, Western and Arab, imitating the pelvic thrust of the Paris runway strut, circling the stage. They wore matching cat suits, hugging their bodies like second skins.

Liz glanced at Joan Fayad. Her face seemed carved in pale marble. Her eyes appeared intent on the stage, but somehow Liz knew that Joan was staring at a scene no one else could see—the years stretching ahead, filled with violence and far from the safety of her childhood home in Boston.

The evening wore on. Negligees, play clothes, swimwear, luncheon suits, afternoon dresses, ball gowns. A variety of women, all shapes and sizes, strutted to the techno rap, rock and pop spun by the Western women in the sound booth. Tahani Nazar and the Australian took turns to explain the outfits and the audience was generous with their applause.

"Poor things never get any entertainment," Mary Lou whispered at one point. "They'll talk about this for the rest of their lives." Joan Fayad nudged her to hush.

The show ended with the enthusiastic reception of a bride and a dozen attendants. Then a belly dancer, full fleshed, voluptuous, took the stage to the sound of Arabic music. From the back of the tent, the smell of cooked meat started to fight with the perfumes.

"Liz, honey." Mary Lou leaned forward to speak over Joan's head. "I think Joanie and I are going to leave. You stay on—"

"No, I'll come with you. I'm ready to go." She looked at her watch. "God, it's after one."

"No, stay," urged Mary Lou. "Believe me, the evening's just starting to heat up. These girls won't break up until three at the earliest. You'll never get a chance to see anything like this in the States. You'll be glad you stayed. I'll call you tomorrow."

"It was nice to meet you, Liz," Joan Fayad said, deciding the issue. She stood up, and Liz realized she wanted Mary Lou to herself, perhaps for the last time.

Liz said, "I'd like to stay in touch when Mary Lou's gone, if that's okay. I'll be here in kingdom for a while, yet." And maybe Fateema could help somehow. Or Princess Nura.

"Oh, yes. Thanks. I'd like that." She touched Liz's arm. "Really," she said.

Liz waited until the two women left, Mary Lou weaving through the crowd, Joan behind her, holding Mary Lou's hand as if frightened to let it go. Depressed, Liz made her own way toward the tables ranged along the back of the tent.

She stopped to stare, amazed. She had never before seen so much food in one place. Tables bore entire roasted sheep, truncated limbs stretched across a mountain of saffron-colored rice edged with wholebodied roast chickens. Giant platters of vegetables, raw and cooked; *rooz bouhari; saliq; sambousik; mujadara; bulgur; couscous;* salads—green and leafy, eggplant and tomatoes, sliced cucumbers in minted yogurt, *tabbouleh.* Fruit in bowls the size of a child's bathtub. Piles of *khubis,* hot from the oven. Not an inch of space had been left unfilled by food of some kind.

Desserts, equally lavish, were displayed on tables down the side of the tent. *Halvah, baklava* dripping with nuts and honey. Lebanese pastries mounded with cream. Intricate structures of whole candied tangerines. Western pies and cakes.

The Middle Eastern women jostled and reached, happily calling back and forth, helping each other to choice items. They pulled apart chickens with their hands, tossing dismembered pieces back onto the spilling rice. Western women stood back, seemingly overwhelmed by the choice and by the uninhibited enthusiasm of their neighbors.

Liz took a plate, spotted an untouched chicken, wrenched free a leg and helped herself to a spoonful of *tabbouleh.* An old woman at her side looked at her plate, spoke to her in

Arabic. Liz smiled an apologetic ignorance of the language. The old lady took the plate from Liz's hand, chatting amiably in Arabic as she piled it high with roast sheep, chicken, a sample from every dish she could reach, cruising the table with Liz in tow. Liz murmured *"shakrun,"* thank you, one of her few Arabic phrases, as her smiling benefactress triumphantly handed the laden plate back to her.

Liz stared down at the food. Never in your life, she thought, and looked for a spot to hide it, then realized she had no need to worry about being discreet. Discarded plates were everywhere. Maids scurried around cleaning up rice and meat which had spilled onto priceless carpets, bits of fruit, bread fallen from plates. Liz handed her plate to a young Indonesian, then helped herself to a Napoleon, added some baklava, a candied tangerine—death by sugar—a cup of minted tea, grabbed a fork and napkin, and made her way back to her seat.

Onstage, open braziers flamed. Women dressed in dark flowing skirts and shirts, their foreheads bound with bands of gold coins, held drums close to the fire, warming them and tapping the skin surfaces, adjusting the tension. Then from the back of the tent came the high-pitched ululation of Arabic women, resonant, exciting. An electric thrill ran through Liz's body. It was a sound like nothing she had ever heard—no movie, no television program, nothing had captured its primitive power.

The sound rose and fell, then was taken up from all sides. Lights dimmed. The drummers started a fast rhythmic beat, the heels of their hands banging against the drums, their fingers tapping a counterpoint. Voices rose in wailing song and stringed instruments joined in. A woman from the audience leapt onto the stage, her shoes discarded, launched into a swaying, stamping dance. Other women followed, shoes kicked off, circling, whirling, arms writhing above their heads, hands clapping in rhythm.

The flames from the braziers burned higher, scented smoke billowed. They could have been in a desert, far from civilization, with long years yet to the twentieth century.

Exhausted women left the stage and others took their place. Confining hairpins flew as women swung their heads, dark curtains of long hair fanning wilder and wilder around them. Ululations rose from a hundred throats, fell away, rose higher.

All this on peppermint tea, Liz thought, not a drop of alcohol in the place. Her own blood raced. She felt dizzy from the sounds of the drums, the incense, the scent of fragrant oils from unbound hair, the heavy smell of roasted meat. All sense of time had gone. A few of the bolder Western women had joined the Arabs onstage, and a laughing dark-eyed girl pulled at Liz's hair until it tumbled around her shoulders, then swayed in front of her, hands held out in invitation.

Liz held up her own hands in refusal, laughing, shaking her head. The girl jumped onstage, long brown arms moving gracefully above her, bare feet stamping, eyes closed, lost to the rhythm.

From outside, Liz heard the wail of police sirens rising above the sound of the drums. She glanced at her watch. Past three. No one else seemed to be paying attention to the police sirens. Liz got to her feet, reluctant to leave, but an accident might have occurred and perhaps she was needed.

Outside, the air was fresh and soft, welcome after the heaviness inside. She took a deep breath and looked up. The sky was dark, stars brushing the night with silver. There seemed to be no accident, just cars lined up, a few men hurrying black figures into them as they emerged from the tent. Other men stood in small agitated clumps. At their urging, a uniformed Saudi policeman raised a bullhorn to his lips.

"Mrs. Hitershi," he called. "Mrs. Sarina Hitershi. Come

out. Your husband is waiting.'' Several times he repeated the message, in English and in Arabic, trying the names of other women. Then he turned to the waiting men and shrugged. They gestured angrily, and the policemen got into his police car, drove over the curb and lined the vehicle up as close as he could to the side of the tent. He turned on the revolving lights and sounded the siren.

Liz started to laugh as she realized what was happening. The Saudis couldn't get their wives out of the tent. They couldn't get in because they were men, and the women were partying and refusing to come out.

Checkmate.

Still smiling, she started to walk. The guest house was a mile or two distant, but it was a lovely night. Balmy, scented with jasmine, a hint of the sea.

Then she saw him.

In the shadows, Abdullah leaned against a black car. Waiting for her.

Liz walked toward him.

Without speaking, he opened the door of the Mercedes. Liz got in and he slammed it closed, then went around to the driver's seat.

"They'll never get those women to come out," she said. "They're having far too good a time in there."

"Yes, we could hear them," Abdullah said.

Liz turned her head and looked out of the window at the passing buildings, dark now. Trees flashed by, and canna lilies, drained of color by the night, seemed unreal.

No more words passed between them.

At the guest house, Liz waited until Abdullah opened the door for her. It was the most natural thing in the world to put her hand in his, allowing him to lead her into the dark building.

The door closed behind them, and Liz turned into his

arms, lifting her lips to his. She felt the roughness of his beard against her skin, the demand of his tongue. And there was no reality beyond the man pressed against her, the heat of her own body.

19

Abdullah's lips moved against her mouth, his breath hot, smelling of cardamom. "You must answer him."

"What?" Then through the throb of blood in her ears, Liz heard the sound of a male voice, insistent, coming closer. "What is it?" she called.

"Ah, madam, you have returned. I have waited for you."

The houseman. "Oh, Andrew, thank you, but you shouldn't have done that. Please, go to bed now. Good night."

"May I get you something, madam? Some tea, perhaps?"

In another second, he would be around the corner leading from the main salon. Liz took Abdullah's hand, pulled him behind her across the foyer, toward her suite. Andrew's voice followed them. Caught like a schoolgirl smuggling her lover into the dorm. Liz opened her door, pushed Abdullah ahead of her.

"No, thank you, Andrew," she called. "Good night."

"Good night, Dr. Ryan."

She was laughing, breathless, when she turned to Abdullah. He caught her, trying to draw her back into his arms. She resisted and dropped into an armchair, waving to its mate on the other side of a glass coffee table.

"Saved by the bell," she said, still laughing. "Come and sit down. We can talk until Andrew's safely in bed. Then you must leave."

"I'm not going to leave, Liz. Not tonight."

"Abdullah, you have to. Nothing has changed—"

Abdullah tossed an envelope into her lap.

"What's this?" she asked.

"Read it."

Liz removed a sheet of paper, unfolded it. It was a report on blood taken from Prince Abdullah bin Talal bin Abdul Azziz Al Sa'ud. Dated four days ago and signed by Dr. Peter Andersen, King Khaled Clinic, Jeddah.

"Abdullah!" Astounded, she looked up at him.

Abdullah reached down and pulled her to her feet and into his arms. For a second she hesitated—she still had a choice, she could draw back. Then his mouth was seeking hers. His hand spread across the small of her back, holding her hard against him. Liz slid her hands down his flanks, over the tight muscles of his buttocks.

And the choice was gone.

Abdullah stirred, reached for his watch, saw that it was 5:00 a.m. Liz murmured a sleepy protest as he tried to slide his arm from beneath her head, and he felt his heart soften.

"I must leave," he whispered. His plane would be waiting at Yanbu airport, but even so, he was cutting it close. "I must be back in Jeddah for the dawn prayer."

"Can't you miss it for once?"

"And what should I say to the king?"

"Oh. The king." Liz turned her face into his shoulder, threw an arm across him. "How about telling him you have a new infidel lover who needs a lot of attention?"

"Oh, of course. He will be very understanding." He kissed her, and Liz slid her leg across his thighs, moving damply against him.

Abdullah rose on one elbow and pushed her onto her back, shifting his weight onto her. She opened her legs, taking him deep, closing her eyes so that she could turn inward to his every movement, every nuance of feeling in her body. Completion came fast, sweet, satisfying.

Abdullah emerged from the shower, towel around his waist. He put on form-fitting white cotton trousers, slipped his feet into leather sandals, slipped the *thobe* over his head, settled the *kafiyah* onto his crown, then the *ghutra* and *arghal.* Liz leaned back against the pillows, watching him transform himself from lover to prince. He picked up his *bisht.*

"Abdullah, did you find out anything about Hisham Badawi's execution?" she asked.

Badawi. Abdullah frowned. Then he remembered. The doctor.

"Now is not the time to be talking about this matter. I must leave, there is no time for talk."

"Yes or no? A simple answer—"

"Nothing is that simple, Liz. We'll talk about it another time."

Liz tossed aside the light blanket, got out of bed. Naked, she walked across the room, stood in front of him.

"Did you find out anything?" she demanded.

"It seems a mistake was made. Paperwork misplaced. These things happen—"

"Paperwork? *Paperwork?* A man, a good man, died because of lost *paperwork?*"

Abdullah grabbed her arms. "Quiet! Do you want to bring the household running? Not exactly paperwork." He was trying to placate her, he thought, astonished. Something he'd never done before. "There was much turmoil. Politically, it was essential to act fast. A lot of men were tried and condemned. Dr. Badawi got caught up in the confusion—"

"The *mutawain* accused him of dealing drugs!" Liz interrupted. "That's what happened! Are the *mutawain* so powerful they're beyond the reach even of a prince?"

Abdullah stiffened. "Liz, you must not meddle in these matters. Now, put it to rest. It is done."

"It is not done as you say. Hisham had a wife, a son—"

"Blood money will be paid." Abdullah made a mental note to tell Nassir to look into it. "It will be generous—"

"What about Hisham's reputation, the accusation that he was a drug dealer."

"Liz, stop!" How could he get through to this Western woman? And why was it so important to him that he should? "The Iraqis are on our borders. An attack could come any day. I cannot concern myself with the fate of one man. Our way is to pay blood money, then it is finished."

"That is not enough," she said. "Hisham Badawi must be exonerated. That is everything now. His son has to grow up believing in his father's honor."

He stared at her, amazed. She understood more than he thought. She knew what the loss of his family's honor would mean to this boy. He softened.

"All right. I will see into it. I promise you."

"When?"

"It will be done," Abdullah said with finality. "But this must be the end of the matter. I want no more talk of it." He put his hands into the mane of hair tumbling over her shoulders, tipped her head back. He kissed her lips, but found them unresponsive. With any other woman, he would be irritated, but with Liz, it was part of who she was. Independent, exciting. "I have to leave Jeddah with the king later this morning for Riyadh, but I will see to it that this man's name is cleared." He put his lips to her ear. "It was a wonderful night, but too short. I will call you."

He opened the door, slipped through. A sliver of moon was fading, and stars, that last night had been full and brilliant, had dimmed in the dawn sky. From the mosque, the *muezzin* raised his voice, calling the faithful to the first prayer of the day. Abdullah realized he would be too late to take his place with the king. At least he'd have plenty of time to work on a good story to give him.

Liz paused in the foyer of the house on Al Fatayah street. She dropped to one knee to allow the saluki to nuzzle her, rubbing the dog's ears.

"Was she a good girl?" The beaming maids picked up her overnight bag. It looked as if they were getting used to having a dog around the house.

"Yes, a good dog, madam, Dr. Ryan."

Laughing at the joyful animal, Liz handed her briefcase to Megawati. "Anything exciting happen since I've been gone?"

Trading glances, suppressing giggles, the two maids stood back as she turned toward the living room.

Liz stopped. The room was a bower. Roses, lilies, pale-yellow spider chrysanthemums. Masses of tulips from Holland in every color and variety. Bowls of freesias. Great branches of apple blossom. And everywhere, orchids. The air was sweet with the scent of green, growing things.

"And more in the bedroom, madam, Dr. Ryan. And a note," Siti said, her excitement barely restrained. "Look." She pointed to a vase filled with orchids in the middle of the coffee table.

Liz looked into the depths of the flowers. Buried among the blossoms was an envelope propped against the familiar velvet box. She opened the envelope. A black scrawl slashed across the white card.

"These still match your lovely Circassian eyes. Please."

It was signed, "Abdullah."

A little after nine, the telephone rang. Liz clicked off the English police drama she was trying to follow on television—virtually impossible because of the crude cuts in the action every time a character even looked as if he might pick up a glass or touch a woman—and grabbed the phone, knowing who was there.

"Dr. Ryan," she said.

"I miss you." Abdullah's voice was low. "I cannot go through the night without you."

"Yes. I know. Where are you?"

"In Riyadh. Lock up that dog."

Liz laughed, breathless. "I'll put her outside."

"I'll be in Jeddah in just over an hour. Think of me."

"I already do. Too much."

"Never that. An hour then." He hung up.

She had Yousef open the gate, and over his protests dismissed him for the night. The open courtyard would be considered strange, but not an invitation to burglary, not in this country.

As before, Abdullah was alone at the wheel of the black Jaguar. He parked in the deepest shade, and Liz moved into his arms almost before the front door closed behind him.

For a heartbeat of time, she remembered another man, another place—Judd, the house in Santa Monica the night Abdullah had first sent her the emerald earrings. Then the thought was gone, lost in the passion for the man holding her.

"Are we going to continue to do this?" Abdullah asked. His gaze drifted down her length, enjoying the pale ivory of her body against his own brown skin.

"Mmm. I hope so," Liz murmured. She butted her head against the side of his neck, breathing in the male sweat, the dry scent that was part of him. "You smell so good. What is that stuff you use?"

"It's a secret aphrodisiac, made by the Bedouin from

flowers of the desert that bloom only once every hundred years, guaranteed to put beautiful infidels at my mercy.''

"Aah. So there have been a lot of beautiful infidels in your life."

"Shall I lie?"

Liz laughed. "Yes. Just make me happy."

"You are the only infidel I have ever loved."

Liz was still. "Well. Maybe not that happy."

"The word *love* frightens you?" he asked.

"No. But I don't think it should be used casually."

"I am not using the word casually, Liz."

"Abdullah, you don't have to say that. In the West, we have affairs. We enjoy them. No strings."

"Liz, I am not new to the customs of the West. I was educated at Princeton, remember. At first, I was shocked at the easy ways of men and women." He laughed. "Horrified, in fact. But I soon adjusted."

Liz poked him. "I bet you did. I bet you cut one hell of a swath through the coed population."

"Well, I was not lonely." He grinned, his teeth white against his heavy black mustache and beard. "The years passed too quickly."

She wanted to ask if he, like Hisham Badawi, had been forced to have a wife with him. But she didn't want to know. That was a part of his life that had nothing to do with her. Here, now, was what they had. It was enough.

"I love you, Liz." She was silent. He thought she must hear his heart pounding. He stroked her shoulder. "Do you hear me? Or are you sleeping?"

"I heard you, Abdullah."

"Well. What do you answer?"

"I don't know." Liz put a hand up to his face, let her fingers drift across his lips, tracing their outline. He grabbed her hand gently with his teeth, mouthing her fingers. "We haven't known each other very long."

"For me, time enough. I want you to marry me. I knew from the first moment that you were to be my infidel wife."

Silence. Then, "How many wives do you have, Abdullah?"

"By the law of the Holy Koran, I am allowed four, but you know that. If you marry me, I will have only one. You." He smiled down at her.

"You mean you will put the others away?"

Divorce, she knew from Fateema's friends, would be easy for him. He would say "I divorce thee," three times in front of a male witness. His wife—wives—would retain their dowries. They would return to the homes of their fathers, or closest male relatives, leaving any children with their father. And Abdullah would be free.

Even if it broke her heart, she could never be party to that kind of cruelty inflicted upon powerless women.

"There are no others to put away," he said. "I have been without a wife for three years."

"You're divorced?"

"No. There was a plane crash on the way to Cairo. No one survived."

"Oh, Abdullah. I'm so sorry."

Abdullah shrugged. "It was the will of Allah."

Could I ever find comfort in that kind of submission to the will of God? she wondered. And knew it was not likely.

"Have you been alone ever since?"

"Yes." If Liz agreed to marry him, he decided, he would send Mahraba back to her village in Syria. She was lovely still, undemanding, with the ample flesh of Syrian women, but, at 19, for not too much longer. And he was tired of her. Concubines came and went, and she would have her pick of husbands with the rich dowry he would send with her.

"And before you ask," he continued, "I have two sons,

both twenty, and no, they are not twins. They are from different mothers.''

"Oh. Do they live with you in Jeddah?"

"They are at Sandhurst Military College, in England. They are not yet married, but marriages have been arranged for them. They will not live in your house." He shifted her weight on his arm. "Do these questions mean that you will marry me?"

"No," Liz answered. "They mean that I want to love you." A great rush of joy coursed through her as she said the words. "And I want to know all about you. I want to know the man I am going to love."

"I don't understand. You love or you don't love."

"It's not that simple. You are asking me to give up my life. My work. I've studied long and hard to be a surgeon. I cannot give that up."

"I have much to offer you—"

Liz put her hand again across his mouth. "Don't. I know what you are offering. But I am just starting my career—"

Abdullah slid his arm from beneath her head and swung his feet to the floor. "I must be back in Riyadh before morning prayer."

"You're angry."

"I have duties, Liz."

"You're flying back now? Tonight?"

"I am expected to be at morning prayer with the king." And with his brother, Bandr. Abdullah thought of how his brother's face would look when he announced he was taking an infidel wife. No matter. Liz would have to convert to Islam. But that was not something to tell her now.

Liz knelt, her naked body pressing against his back, her arms twined across his chest. "One thing," she whispered. "If we do marry, you will have to change your secret aphrodisiac. You won't be able to manage more than one beautiful infidel."

Abdullah turned and grabbed her, pushing her back onto the bed, laughing. "All right. Any sacrifice for my Circassian bride."

Dawn was close when he left. Abdullah raced the Jaguar through the empty streets of Jeddah toward the airport and the jet waiting to take him back to Riyadh. He had surprised himself when he asked Liz to marry him. An American wife. It would take time to get used to the idea. She had promised to think about it and that meant only that she wanted him to long for her a little more. She would agree.

She could perhaps be a political asset when dealing with the Americans. He would press that point with Bandr.

The future looked more exciting than it had for a long time. After her marriage, Liz would not be able to practice medicine—that would be pushing Bandr too far—but it would be a novel experience to have an educated Western wife.

Yes, he thought. It was good that he asked her.

20

Liz looked around the walled garden for Fateema, needing her to interpret. The garden was cool—Christmas was only a week away—and gentled by the sound of water rising in the center of a small decorative pool, splashing onto old blue-and-green tiles. On the other side of the fountain, Princess Iffat half reclined among her rugs and cushions in the mouth of another of her Bedouin tents, puffing serenely on a hookah.

Conversation was animated, voices rising in argument, although there were fewer women than usual drinking peppermint tea and wafting scented incense into their hair and clothes. For weeks, the main topic had been the rebellion of the women in Riyadh, who had dared to drive their own cars downtown, their husbands at their sides, for all of twenty minutes before being arrested. Most of the women had been professors at the university—their students all female—but no longer. They had been dismissed, put under house arrest, their husbands disgraced. The crackdown on women since then had been severe. A group of Canadian women had been beaten by fundamentalists in Buraydah in the northwest, and fewer women than ever left their houses. The arguments raged whenever women were together. Should the Riyadh women have waited to stage their demonstration until after the Americans had left? Should they have staged it at all? Was the price every woman in the kingdom now paid worth it?

The tiny woman whose words Liz had been trying to understand drew her down so that she could put her lips to Liz's ear, pouring out a soft stream of Arabic, clearly uninterested in the questions occupying everyone else.

Another daughter, another repair job, Liz thought. Bob would be thrilled. "I'm sorry I don't speak Arabic," she said to the woman. But as Abdullah's wife, she would learn. If she said yes. The thought was exciting, terrifying, seductive. "We need an interpreter."

She caught sight of Fateema in animated conversation with Princess Nura. Her daughter safely married, Nura looked relaxed, years younger than she had that first day they'd met. Liz had already spoken to her about Joan Fayad in Yanbu, but there was little anyone could do, Nura said, especially now, after "the rebellion."

Fateema glanced her way and Liz beckoned. Fateema nodded, held up a hand for a moment's patience. She finished speaking with Nura, then crossed the garden and planted a kiss on Liz's cheek, although they'd already exchanged embraces when Fateema had greeted her earlier at the front door.

Fateema turned to speak to the woman trying to communicate with Liz in Arabic. Soft words answered her. Fateema shook her head, refusing to interpret. The woman insisted. Fateema turned to Liz.

"This is Butheina Hamsa. What she asks is impossible."

"How do you know that? Are you a doctor, now?" Liz smiled at Fateema, enjoying their increasingly easy relationship. "What is it? Tell me."

"Butheina is uneducated, you understand?" Fateema said. "Very traditional. I am surprised to see her here today. She never left her house even before the rebellion in Riyadh."

Liz turned her smile toward Mrs. Hamsa. She was dressed in layers of black, and had refused to relinquish her *abayah* even here among other women, merely throwing it back on her shoulders. At least she had unfastened her *gutwah* so that it hung to one side, maybe to show off the diamond necklace around her throat that would not have been out of place on opening night at the opera in Washington D.C. Earrings of the same opulent design dangled from her ears, a matching bracelet encircled her left wrist.

"Yes. So? Come on, Fateema," Liz urged. "You're stalling. What does she want?"

Fateema took a breath. She looked down at her hands. "Her husband's third wife has a daughter. Butheina lost her own child some years ago, now she fears the same thing will happen. She loves this girl like her own."

Butheina cut in with a torrent of words, looking from face to face. Fateema nodded, held up her hand to stop the flow.

"She wishes to know if you will perform a circumcision."

"She doesn't need me for that. How old is the child?"

"Thirteen."

Something had gone wrong with Fateema's translation, Liz thought. They had started out talking about a girl, now it seemed they were talking about a boy.

"Well, the circumcision should have been done at birth, but it's still a simple procedure, nothing to worry about." She smiled reassuringly at Mrs. Hamsa. "Tell her to take him to King Khaled Clinic. A male doctor will see him there, that would be better for the boy. I can make a recommendation if she wishes—"

"We are not talking about a boy, Liz," Fateema said gently.

Liz looked from one face to the other. She was dumbfounded.

"You are talking about a girl?"

Fateema nodded.

Liz repeated, to make sure she had understood. "She is asking me to perform a circumcision on a girl?"

"A girl, yes."

Liz made no attempt to hide her horror. "A clitorectomy?"

Fateema refused to meet her eyes. She didn't answer.

Liz said coldly, "I thought mutilation of that kind was carried out only in primitive societies in Africa."

"No, it's done here, too. Even more than clitorectomy." Fateema fumbled for a suitable explanation. "In very religious families, everything is cut."

With difficulty Liz held her temper in check.

"Tell Mrs. Hamsa that she is asking me to commit a crime against God and against this child. Tell her that I refuse to be a party to such barbarity."

"Liz, please." Fateema took her hand. "Do not be angry with Butheina. She knows nothing of the world beyond her family. She has never been out of the country, she cannot read or write, her father believes education for women is an offense against Allah. Her husband is very rich, very successful, but a man like her father, traditional." Fateema touched Butheina's arm sympathetically. "All of his daughters have been cut this way."

Butheina's eyes went from face to face as she tried to understand what was being said.

"And Mrs. Hamsa?"

Fateema shrugged. "When she was a child. Of course."

Liz took a breath, aware that Butheina was a victim of barbarity, not a perpetrator. That sin lay elsewhere.

"I'm sorry," Liz said to Butheina gently. "Would you ask your husband to call me at my office at the hospital? We'll make an appointment to talk. Maybe I can persuade him that this procedure must not be done."

"Oh, Liz," Fateema said. "Liz." She laughed, a sad little

sound. "He wouldn't make an appointment with you. Very likely he thinks you are a whore."

"What?"

Fateema shrugged. "Of course. You work with men, your face uncovered—"

"Oh. Right, of course. Then ask him to call Dr. Robert Gould at King Khaled Clinic. Bob will explain to him that this barbaric practice must stop. His daughters could die." She thought of the shock and the massive infection that could occur unless the procedure was done by a doctor—but what modern doctor would be a party to such a practice?

"Butheina's daughter did die, Liz. That is why she is asking that you, a doctor, do this for the child."

Liz shook her head. "No. I'm sorry, I can't. Tell her, please, Fateema. This is not something a Western doctor would do."

Fateema told Butheina what she had said. Eyes fixed on Liz, Butheina removed her earrings, fumbled with the clasp of her diamond bracelet. Shocked, embarrassed, Liz held up both hands to stop her, but Butheina was persistent. She grabbed Liz's hands, trying to force the jewelry into them. Liz backed up a couple of paces, her hands held away from her, feeling under attack by the woman's desperation.

"Fateema, please explain—"

Fateema took Butheina Hamsa's arm, led her away, talking urgently to her. The tiny woman was shaking with sobs, looking back at Liz, her face a mask of tragedy.

As soon as Liz reached home, she called Bob Gould to explain what had happened.

"Can you see this man, Hamsa?" she asked.

"Lizzie, when are you going to get the message? We cannot change this society. And it is not our business to get involved—"

"Don't talk to me about what is or is not our business in this society, Bob," she said angrily. "I'm not asking you to man the barricades for major social change. I'm talking about preventing the mutilation of one kid, one young girl, that's all.''

"Well, if he calls, I'll talk to him. That's all I can promise.''

"Call him, Bob. Hamsa—''

"Okay, supposing I could find him, which I doubt. What do I say? This is Dr. Robert Gould at King Khaled Clinic and I want to talk to you about your daughter's circumcision? What do you think his response would be to that?''

She didn't answer.

"Lizzie, if he calls, I'll talk to him. Be glad to.''

Reluctantly, she put down the phone. There was nothing more she could do. She was powerless.

For days the image of the weeping woman shrouded in black, wearing a fortune in diamonds, haunted her. Several times she found herself picking up the telephone, only to replace it. There was no one to call.

Maybe if she was married to a man powerful in the kingdom she could help bring about some changes. There were women in the kingdom who were ready, the rebellion in Riyadh could be the tip of the iceberg.

It had to start somewhere.

Christmas Day was a day like any other. The usual discreet celebrations held by ex-pats had been canceled—no one had the heart for it with all the children evacuated and most of the wives. On the twenty-third, Saddam had threatened Israel, and the U.S. warned him not to use chemical weapons, ''The U.S. response would be absolutely overwhelming, and it would be devastating.'' Every social occasion turned into a depressing discussion of the morality of using weapons of mass destruction against a country ruled by a madman who threatened to use weapons of mass destruction.

But, as usual, Aramco had brought in priests in the guise of engineers and whoever wanted was able to attend one of the religious services held in private houses, the time and place spreading by word of mouth.

After a chaotic day spent in evacuation drills at the hospital, a marginal success at best, Liz got home late. The phone rang when she was stepping out of the shower, and she wrapped herself in a towel and ran to grab it. Abdullah called most evenings, whenever he could get a few minutes to himself—the king was notorious for conducting business late into the night.

"This is Dr. Ryan." Very businesslike. It always amused him.

"Hey. Merry Christmas, sweetheart."

"What?"

"I said, 'Hey. Merry Christmas.' Then I said, 'sweetheart.' What I really want to say is that I miss you."

"Judd?" She felt for the edge of the bed and sank onto it.

"Who else?" he asked playfully.

"Do you always answer a question with a question?" An old joke.

"You tell me, do I?" A pause. "Liz, it's so good to hear your voice. It feels like years."

"Where are you?"

"Floating around. If you get my drift."

"Oh, Judd." Gladness and guilt mingled, and she wanted to cry and laugh. "Are you still mad at me?"

"No. I miss you too much for that. I went to see your folks before I left, they told me a few things I didn't know. Why you decided to go to Saudi Arabia. Details like that. I read your letter."

"I would have told you everything myself if you'd given me a chance," she said.

"I know. But all I could see was that guy Abdullah giving

you the rush. All that oil money. Jewelry. I couldn't compete with that—''

"You didn't have to compete."

"Yeah, I know, I know. What can I say? I screwed up, Liz."

"Oh, Judd, don't!"

"Did you find her?" he asked. "The lady in question?"

"Yes. In fact she's coming for dinner. I can't tell you too much right now. Not on the phone. You understand what I mean?"

"Sure do."

There was a small silence, bridged by Judd saying, "You've got some influential friends, sweetheart. I got a special dispensation to make this call from a general's aide, no less. A guy called Brand. Know him?"

Liz laughed. "I met him. And the general. Remember, we met him before, at that dinner for reserve officers in Los Angeles? It was several years ago, but he remembered you. Or said he did, anyway. He promised to have you call me, but I thought he'd forget."

"That general doesn't forget a damn thing, and if he does he's got Mike to C.H.A."

"C.H.A.? What?"

"Cover his ass. Essential expertise in the military."

She laughed, then heard some background noise and Judd saying, "I've got to go, Liz. Listen, I'll write. I don't want to lose you because of some guy in a nightshirt. I love you."

"Let me know your address and I'll write and tell you everything that's happened. Merry Christmas, Judd. I'm so glad you called."

"Bye, sweetheart."

He seemed reluctant to hang up, and she heard the pounding of heavy feet in the background.

Suddenly frightened, she said, "Judd. Are you there?"

"Yes."

"What's happening?"

"Gotta go, babe."

No one but Judd called her babe. She said, "Judd, please. Stay out of trouble."

He laughed. "Don't worry. Everyone loves their medics, we get the best care and protection. I love you, Liz."

"Yes. I know."

She hung up. She should have given him the response he wanted. In spite of his lighthearted reassurance, anything could happen in the coming weeks and months. She thought of all they shared, the friends, their passion for the practice of medicine. She remembered the game he played with the cheap wines. The long wonderful nights making love. His steady gray eyes. The broken nose he wouldn't have fixed. His fearlessness. His heart.

What the hell was she doing? she thought with despair.

Falling in love with another man. That was what she was doing. How could she stop that?

But as she dressed, her own heart was heavy, and the magic had gone from the day.

At 9:00 p.m. a silver Mercedes glided into the courtyard.

"Fateema. Welcome." Liz ran down the steps from the front door and opened the passenger door before the Sudanese driver had a chance to do so.

Fateema climbed out. Above her veil, Liz could see that her eyes were smiling. "Dr. Elizabeth Ryan," she said, softly. "Today, there is a surprise. It is the time for it, Christmas, is it not?"

She stood back so that Liz could see that another woman was with her. Then she, too, got out of the car.

For a moment, Liz could only stare. Taller, heavier than Fateema. Green eyes above the veil.

The woman who had risked so much to say goodbye to Tess at the harbor in Jeddah thirty-two years ago.

Sakeena.

Tears sprang to Liz's eyes. Sakeena opened her arms and Liz walked into them. Both laughing and crying, Fateema put her arms around them. The Sudanese driver stared impassively, then lit a cigarette and took a package from the passenger seat, placing it just inside the front door of the house.

Somehow, they got inside. Sakeena did not speak English, and Fateema stumbled over her languages, mixing English and Arabic, unable in her excitement to keep them separated.

Liz poured coffee and offered the canapés Siti had left ready, her eyes constantly returning to her grandmother. She was hardly able to take in that this was the woman who had pressed her as a newborn into Tess's arms. Sakeena had to be sixty, and the years had not been kind. Both Circassian women had shed their veils and *abayahs*, revealing full velvet skirts, Fateema's green, Sakeena's purple, wide-sleeved blouses and vests heavily encrusted with gold thread. They both had gold in their ears and around their necks. Sakeena drew Liz down beside her on the sofa, Fateema sat in one of the white silk arm chairs opposite. She stared first at her mother, then at Liz, a look of shock on her face.

"What?" Liz said to Fateema, laughing. She felt slightly giddy. "What is it?"

"It is good no one is here to see us together," she said. "How would we explain ourselves? Look at us." She pointed to a mirror on the opposite wall.

A sudden chill touched Liz's blood. The two women were unmistakably mother and daughter. And just as unmistakably, Liz herself was a younger version.

"It's a miracle no one has ever noticed the two of us," she said to Fateema. "We must make sure no one sees all three of us together."

"I think that is no problem. Sakeena lives in Taif. She is

here because I begged for her presence as a favor. And soon, my daughter, you will be going back to your country.''

''Perhaps not.''

''Not?'' Fateema smiled, puzzled. ''What does that mean?''

''I have met a man. He has asked me to marry him.''

''An American?''

''A Saudi.''

Fateema's face became very still. She turned to Sakeena, murmuring softly. Sakeena lifted Liz's hand to her cheek. For a moment no one spoke.

Two pairs of green eyes were studying her. ''I know what you're thinking, but you're wrong,'' Liz said hurriedly. ''Your courage was not wasted, don't think that for a moment. I can bring so much to this country, to the women here, that I would never have been able to bring had you not been brave enough to send me away as you did.''

''Who is this man who has captured your heart?'' Fateema asked.

Liz stood to refill their coffee cups. She longed to tell them, to say Abdullah's name. They would be so happy for her. But she had no illusions—Saudi women, Fateema included, had nothing but gossip to fill long, empty days. The slightest hint from Fateema to Nura, and every *hareem* in Jeddah would buzz, the phone lines to Taif and Riyadh busy with speculation as sisters and cousins, mothers and daughters indulged in their daily hours of gossip. Abdullah would not be happy if word of his intention to take a foreign wife drifted to the king's ear before he was ready.

''I can't tell you that until I have told him that I will marry him,'' Liz said finally, ''and I'm still thinking about it.''

Fateema glanced at her mother, widened her eyes and shrugged, then turned back to Liz. ''What can you tell us about him?''

"Well, I can tell you that he is a fine man, educated in the United States, and that you will be very happy for me."

Sakeena questioned Fateema sharply. Fateema answered, nodding as Sakeena replied. Then she said to Liz, "You will be the only wife?"

"Yes. Of course."

"And how can you be sure?" Fateema asked. "He has promised you a written agreement, perhaps? You think that would hold up in an Islamic court?"

"Fateema!" Uncomfortable, Liz gave a half laugh. "We're not even married, and you're talking about Islamic court! He is an educated, modern man who loves the West, and who wants a companion, not a toy. I told you about him because I wanted you and Sakeena to know what was happening in my life."

"Have you discussed this with your family?"

Liz smiled. "Well, I thought that was what I was doing."

"Your real family, in America. Your mother and father."

Liz felt the words like a slap of reality. "I spoke to them last night to wish them a happy Christmas."

"And told them you are thinking of marrying a Saudi?"

"No. That's not something I could do on the telephone." In fact, she hadn't ever mentioned Abdullah to them. "But they'd want only what would make me happy."

"A Saudi husband would do that?" Fateema asked.

"Why not? There is so much to be done here, in this society. With my training, I could help in that."

Fateema smiled and explained to Sakeena what had been said. Sakeena answered impatiently.

"What, Sakeena wants to know, could you do here?"

"As I said, practice medicine, for one thing. And be a voice for women. God knows, they need an advocate."

"For an educated woman, you are very naive, my Liz."

Stung, Liz answered sharply. "I could perhaps raise a

voice to protest the mutilation of young girls. How is Butheina Hamsa's daughter?"

"You mean the daughter of Ahmed Hamsa by his third wife, do you not?"

"Fateema, you are quarreling with me," Liz said. "Yes, that's who I mean."

"She will recover, *insh'allah.* You know *insh'allah*? God willing?"

Liz nodded. "A child you know is mutilated with no one to speak for her and you don't think women and girls need a voice in this country?"

"They do. But not yours."

"As the only wife of a prince, Fateema—"

"Ah, a prince. Well, you would not be untouchable, my Liz. The *mutawain* are more powerful than you suspect. Who, I ask, is this prince who has captured you?"

"Fateema, no one has captured me. I will make a decision, a free choice. As soon as I have made up my mind, I will tell you. Give me your telephone number and you will be the first to know."

"My telephone number has to remain one of the secrets of the *hareem.*" Fateema smiled.

"Don't give me that Thousand and One Nights routine." Liz said teasingly.

Fateema laughed. "Why not? I have been well taught." She spoke to Sakeena. Sakeena put a hand on Liz's arm, and shook her head. "You see?" Fateema said. "Sakeena agrees with me. Nassir's life, Sakeena's life, my life. We cannot burden you with the knowledge of my telephone number."

"What you mean is," Liz said, "you don't trust me."

"What I mean is I will not burden you with this knowledge," Fateema insisted. "You understand the wisdom of this since you, too, choose not to burden me with what I have asked to know. Now, enough of this talk. We have a gift for you. A Christmas gift.''

Fateema went into the hall and came back bearing the package left there by the Sudanese driver. It was wrapped in red Christmas paper decorated with robins sitting on branches of holly thick with snow.

''Oh, what have you done?'' Liz said, delighted. Her own gift for Fateema was books smuggled into the kingdom by a friend of Mary Lou Tibbets. For Sakeena, her love and gratitude, and she knew that would be everything to her grandmother.

Slowly Liz removed the ribbons and paper, savoring each moment, smiling up at Fateema and Sakeena watching her. The last of the drugstore wrapping was torn away to reveal a filigree box, gold, incredibly beautiful. Liz opened it and lifted out a bundle wrapped in silk—red silk and new, unlike the old ivory-colored silk, yellowed with age, that Tess had kept for her for so many years. Carefully she unwound the silk then held up a gold incense brazier, exquisitely worked, encrusted with semiprecious stones of jade, amethyst, peridot, amber. She looked at the two women smiling at her, sharing her delight.

''This is incredible,'' she said. ''It must be very old.''

''It came with Sakeena from her home,'' Fateema said. ''From her mother, and from her mother, back into the past many years. Somehow, Sakeena's mother managed to keep it safe for the daughters to come, even through the civil war and the years of famine that came after, when Sakeena was sold to the caravans to save her from starvation. She was already with child then but her husband, her father and her brothers were all dead in the fighting.''

So much terror lay in those few sentences. The revolution in Russia, the famines created by Stalin to bring the Caucasus under control, the untold millions dead from disease and starvation and war. Liz put her arms around Sakeena sitting next to her, burying her face in her grandmother's neck. She felt Sakeena's hand on her hair.

"Thank you," Liz whispered. "I will treasure it."

Sakeena murmured a few words, and Fateema translated.

"Sakeena says you must keep it for your daughter." A silence, pregnant with who, what, that daughter might be. Then Fateema said, "Come, we will light it." She reached into the gold box, retrieved a second silk-wrapped bundle and handed it to Liz. Unwrapping it, Liz found a box that matched the one containing the brazier, filled with incense and matches.

"Once it would have been flints to strike a spark, but we are modern now." Fateema lit a tiny wick in the bowl of the burner, sprinkled incense over it. Sweet-smelling smoke drifted toward the ceiling. Fateema swung the brazier on its gold chains in front of her mother. Sakeena wafted the smoke into her hair, then, laughing, lifted her skirt to capture the scent, insisting that Liz do the same.

They were still laughing when Siti announced dinner, as traditional a meal as Liz had been able, with her own limited skill, to show the two Indonesian maids how to prepare. Afterward, Belle was allowed in, but as usual she watched the strangers warily from her place at Liz's side, refusing any overtures.

The evening passed too quickly. The coming war was not mentioned, and the two women refused to be drawn into talk of their own lives. They wanted to know of Liz, her life in the United States. Her education. Her family. Judd.

It did not escape Liz that she was being reminded of all that she would give up to marry a Saudi. Even a prince.

21

Liz glanced impatiently at her surgical nurse. "Amina!"

Startled, the nurse brought her wandering attention back to the incision. Liz kept her eyes on the layer of muscle she had just exposed, cutting deeper, preparing to remove a section of the muscle tissue of the patient's back so that she could use it to repair her damaged face. "Someone, please go outside and tell those men shouting and banging out there to be silent. This is a hospital, not a circus."

She felt the nurses slide uneasy glances at each other.

"I don't care that they are men. You are nurses, professional women, and they are orderlies. Now, Patrizia, go outside and tell them to stop that noise."

The young circulating nurse moved toward the door. Inside the O.R., the silence was disturbed only by the hum of equipment and the soft voice of the nurse anesthetist murmuring verses from the Koran. Somewhere a door banged. Outside the room, excited voices increased in volume. Someone had turned on a radio adding to the tumult. The nurse eased back into the room.

"Dr. Ryan. There is great excitement—"

"Is the hospital on fire?" Liz kept her concentration on what she was doing.

"No—"

"Then it can wait. If I can't get peace outside, I will at least have it in this room."

"Yes. Excuse me." Quietly, the young Filipina took her place behind the anesthetist.

The disturbance outside faded from awareness, and for the next three hours, Liz heard only the answers to her questions, the responses of her surgical team. At last the final suture in place, Liz stepped away from the table to allow the patient to be prepared for the recovery room.

The nurses were subdued, none of the laughter that was usual in the letdown following completion of a difficult surgery.

"I'm sorry I snapped," Liz said to the room at large. She had been short-tempered for the past few weeks, ever since the phone call from Judd. It hadn't helped that Abdullah had not been able to get away from Riyadh. "I thank you for your work, and when she finds what a terrific job we've done for her, Mrs. Salamah will also thank you. Patrizia," she said to the young nurse. "What was that racket all about?"

"The war, Doctor. The radio says United States airplanes are attacking Iraq."

"So it's started." And Judd was in it, somewhere on the east coast.

Quickly, she showered, changed into slacks and shirt, and slipped on a fresh white lab coat crackling with the starch used by Siti and Megawati. In her ground floor office she called Bob at King Khaled Clinic. She'd seen him last at a rather dismal party on New Year's Eve at his house, but not since. She guarded her time now in case Abdullah found a few hours to spend with her. When he answered, she said, "Bob, have you got CNN?"

"Yes. The air war has started," he said. "Aircraft are pounding the hell out of targets in Baghdad and Kuwait. CNN's coming in clear. Come on over."

Her thoughts flew to Judd. "No, I've still got rounds to do before I can leave, and then it's home for me as early as I can make it. I'm exhausted.'' The Bosnian surgeon Bob had found to replace her had stayed only until Liz had returned from Yanbu, claiming, with justification, that her contract was with the Scandinavians at King Khaled Clinic, and she was not interested in transferring to Jeddah General Hospital, no matter how great the need. ''I keep thinking about Judd. I got a letter from him, but he didn't say where he was. He could have still been at sea.'' It had been a love letter which she hadn't been able to answer. How could she tell him? ''He must be somewhere on the east coast by now—''

''Don't worry about him, Lizzie, it doesn't help.''

''Easy to say.'' She said goodbye and put the phone down. Then, after a moment's hesitation, she punched out another number.

Abdullah's recorded voice answered. ''I love you and regret that I am not here to tell you so in person.'' He'd put the line in for her use only in case she needed him, and only he answered it. She hung up without leaving a message.

When she got home, the black Jaguar was parked behind the tamarisk trees.

Liz ran up the front steps, threw her briefcase onto the hall table. No Siti to greet her. No Belle—the girls must have locked her up. She raced down the hall to her bedroom, threw open the door.

''What are you doing here?'' she exclaimed. ''At this time of the day? You are going to get me beaten by the camel whips, deported as a woman of easy virtue—''

Abdullah swung her around. ''Who would dare even a glance at the wife of Prince Abdullah bin Talal bin Abdul Azziz Al Sa'ud?''

''Abdullah, I don't know—''

''We'll have a quiet ceremony.''

"How can you even talk about this now?" she asked. "In the middle of a shooting war?"

Abdullah tumbled her onto the bed. "I have only an hour. Not even that. I must be mad. I have to be in Riyadh in an hour—"

"Then I'd better get you some coffee. Some food to refresh you for your journey." She pretended to struggle to get upright.

"Are you crazy?" He slipped a hand inside her clothes, down her belly, between her legs. "Yes. You are. As crazy as I am."

She lifted her hips, helping him to slide off her pants. Then he was inside, filling her. A few powerful thrusts and she felt the brink of climax, the quivering deep in her belly. Abdullah groaned with the final flooding push and Liz clenched her muscles. Then control left her, and she bit into his shoulder, every nerve shuddering a release.

As their heartbeats slowed, Abdullah sat up. "Call your family. Tell them you are to be married."

"I can't do that, Abdullah."

"Then how can you behave like this with me?"

The sweat on her body felt suddenly chilled. "What do you mean?"

"I mean you cannot behave like this with a man who is not your husband."

Liz got off the bed and bent to retrieve her clothes. This was not possible, she thought. Their worlds were too different.

"I am not another of your possessions and I will behave any way I please," she said sharply. "If that offends your sense of moral order, please, feel free not to join me in my depravity."

"You are going to drive me mad with this. I cannot continue in this way."

"That's your decision."

Abdullah seized her by the arms, held her in front of him. "Look at me." Liz turned her head away. Abdullah shook her. "Look at me." She turned her eyes to him. "I am in the middle of war plans. The king needs me, and yet I am here, with a woman who will make love with me, but refuses marriage. Can you tell me what I should do?"

"Go to Riyadh," she said. "You are needed there."

"But not here. I am not needed here."

"Abdullah, I will not be bullied into marrying you. I said I would think about it, and I will. I am. If you are offended that I am a Western woman who uses her body as she chooses, not as and when she is commanded by a man, I can't help that."

Abdullah released her and reached for his *ghutra*. He settled the *arghal* in place, picked up his *bisht*.

"This cannot go on."

Liz did not answer.

She heard the door close, then the sound of the Jaguar leaving the courtyard. She opened the sliding door into the garden. Belle came bounding into the room, tail wagging, giving little whimpers of joy.

Liz ran a bath, lavishing rose-scented bath oil into the water. From the depths of her being, a chill that had nothing to do with the cold of the desert at night spread through her veins. Every movement was an effort. The chasm yawning between them was almost more than she could bear.

Two hours later, the phone rang. Liz picked it up and wasn't surprised to hear his voice.

"Sometimes I forget that you are a woman of a different culture."

"Abdullah, I think it would better if we called this off, now, before it goes any further." Judd was always on her mind now—that had to mean more than she wanted to know.

"No, listen to me," he said. "I've told many women that

I love them, never meaning it beyond the requirement of the moment. Now it is different, and I cannot have what I want. I am told I must wait. Try to understand. It is a new experience.''

He was trying so hard, she thought. Why didn't she just tell him that she would marry him? It seemed almost preordained. Why else had the current of her life brought her here? She heard muffled voices in the background and Abdullah answering in Arabic. Then he said, ''I must go. Good night.''

''Abdullah.''

''Liz, I must go now—''

''I love you. You know that.''

''If you do, call your parents and tell them.''

''All right,'' she said. ''I will.''

But he had hung up. He hadn't heard. She thought of calling him back on the private line, but decided against it. It wasn't the sort of message to leave on an answering machine.

The days were filled with rumors and counterrumors. The Iraqis had attacked Dhahran, Jubail, Khobar. They had fired the storage tanks at Ras ta Nura in the east. They had invaded, they were asking for negotiations, Baghdad was in ruins, they were using nuclear weapons.

CNN was heavily edited, broadcasting days later than the events depicted. Nothing was sure.

On Saturday, after work, Liz had Yousef drop her off at Bob's, just to hear a rational voice among the confusion. The door stood open and young Americans milled about. Bob had started to open the house and swimming pool to the military, for showers and a swim, a meal. Word spread quickly, and now it was a rare day that the house was empty.

''Liz.'' Bob caught her eye, calling above the hubbub of young voices singing around the piano being played inexpertly in the next room. He beckoned, and Liz made her way through the crowd of kids in desert fatigues, a few seasoned warriors among them but most looking as if they should still be playing high school football, or twirling batons at the head of a marching band.

"I'd like you to meet Captain Hannah Stone, U.S. Marine Corps." Gould smiled at the young woman standing next to him. Like the others, she wore desert fatigues, somehow managing to look well turned-out and elegant. "Hannah, this is Dr. Elizabeth Ryan. Known to her friends as Liz."

"Captain Stone." Liz held out her hand. "Welcome to Saudi Arabia."

The marine's handshake was firm, brisk. "Thanks," she said. "Hell of a strange place. Have you been here long?"

Liz laughed. "Long enough." She took a drink from the tray offered by Gould's houseman. The level of noise had picked up—some of the Cokes and Sprites were obviously not as innocent as they looked. "Seven months. Sometimes it does seem longer. When did you get here? Or is that a military secret?"

Captain Stone laughed. "Hardly. I arrived two weeks ago."

"Captain Stone runs a field hospital out near the Kuwaiti border," Gould said.

"You're a doctor, Captain Stone?"

"Trained at McGill," she said. "Did my residency in the Marine Corps, though. I'm a Marine Corps brat. My dad was a thirty-year man."

"Captain Stone knows Judd." Bob dropped his bombshell.

"Really?"

"Sure. Good man. Terrific with the troops. They love him." A softness invaded her voice. Captain Stone, obviously, could count herself among his admirers.

Liz glanced at her with new eyes, suddenly seeing someone who could tease Judd about his crooked nose, laugh at his jokes with the cheap wine, talk about the kids he saw in the emergency room. Feel his body next to hers.

Judd with another woman.

"Well, when you see him again, would you ask him to call?" Liz kept her tone easy, friendly. She had no right to be anything else. "We're old friends, and we worry about him." To put Captain Stone's mind at rest, she added, "And I know you'd like to hear from him, Bob."

"Sure would." Bob took a deep gulp of his Pepsi, raised his eyebrows defiantly when he saw Liz's questioning glance.

"Colonel Cameron has several field stations under his command, mine's only one of them, and this is a war, so I don't know whether he'll be able to call you," Hannah said. "But I'll pass the word when I see him."

Colonel Cameron. He'd been promoted. Once she would have been the first to know. Now that information came from a woman she hadn't even known existed before today.

"How are you holding up?" Liz looked at the young doctor with new eyes. Hannah's coffee-colored skin looked soft, cared for. Her almond eyes fringed with long dark lashes, her hair cropped close to her well-shaped head. Strong, capable hands were well tended. Twenty-eight, maybe thirty.

"Okay. Good," Hannah answered. "Our main worry is the chemical weapons, the biological stuff. But we're trained and we've got the equipment. We can handle whatever Saddam throws at us."

Slim and fit, she looked as if she could deal with Saddam Hussein single-handedly, Liz thought, and come off the victor.

"Well, perhaps I can show you the sights of Jeddah while you're here," Liz offered. "It's quite an interesting city, supposedly the burial place of Eve."

"Eve, of Adam and Eve?"

Liz nodded. "So they claim."

"Wow. I'll have to take a rain check, though, if that's okay? I've got a ride back on a cargo plane tonight. I only came to look at the Red Sea."

"Well, take my number. Call me any time you can break free." Liz pulled a card from her wallet, handed it to the marine.

For the next few minutes talk turned to the war—no, the storage tanks had not been fired; no, nuclear weapons had not been used; Jubail, Dhahran, Khobal were not under attack, and Iraq had not asked for negotiations. But Israel had announced that it would respond in kind to any attack by Iraq, and the United States had carried out more than twelve thousand bombing missions over Iraq and Kuwait.

A young sergeant interrupted. "Captain. If you're ready, ma'am, we're moving out."

The two marines saluted, thanked Bob. Throughout the room glasses were drained, plates replaced on tables, cigarettes crushed. Within minutes, the room was empty.

"Well." Bob rubbed his hands together, satisfied. "Let's go get some dinner. These guys have cleaned us out."

Liz glanced at her watch.

"Oh, for God's sake, Liz. What's so important on a Saturday night you can't get out for a bite at a restaurant?"

"I might get a phone call—"

"So, if you're on call, we'll leave the number of the restaurant."

"Not the hospital. I'm expecting Abdullah to call me."

"Oh." Bob picked up his glass, replacing it on the table without drinking. "This is just plain Pepsi, you know. I'm not drinking. There's an AA group in Jeddah, and I joined it."

"Oh, Bob, that's great," Liz said. "I'm so glad. But

thank heaven you waited to find one in Saudi Arabia and not in Santa Monica. I'm going to marry him, Bob.''

For a moment her words seemed not to register. Then he ran his eyes over her face—she knew her uncertainty showed as she waited for his reaction.

"Jesus, Liz."

"Don't look so shocked. It's good news I'm telling you."

"Have you told Fateema?"

"Well, just that I was thinking of getting married to a Saudi.''

"What did she say?" he asked.

"I can't say she was exactly jubilant."

"I bet.''

"She doesn't understand, that's all," Liz said. "As soon as she knows who it is I'm marrying, she will be happy for us. I'm sure of that. He's a terrific guy."

"What about Judd Cameron? And have you told your mother? I mean Tess?"

"I haven't spoken to Judd since that call before Christmas. I don't know where to call him, and it's not something I can do by letter. That's why I wanted Hannah to... Well, anyway, I only made up my mind a couple of days ago."

"Liz. Honey. I think you should think about this."

"I have thought about it, Bob," she said firmly. "Why the long face? I'm going to marry a man who loves me. A man I love. Come on, be happy for me." She knew what Bob was thinking. She was abandoning herself to a closed, medieval society, where women had value only as chattel. Where she couldn't drive, or check into a hotel without producing written permission from her husband, or take a plane trip without a male guardian. Where she couldn't even hold her own passport. But that wouldn't be her world. Abdullah was a man of two cultures, his own and hers, and he would never try to force her into that mold. Bob just didn't know Abdullah as she did.

"Anyway," she said, "I haven't told Abdullah yet, so don't call Melly with the big news."

"What do your parents say?"

"I haven't told them yet, either. I thought Abdullah should be the first to know, not my parents. But now, you're the first. It just jumped out of my mouth."

"Well, you have to let me buy you dinner to celebrate. After all, I was there at the beginning."

"No, I'm sorry, I'll take a rain check, too. Abdullah should be calling—"

"So, let him call you later," Bob insisted. "These Saudi princes have a thing or two to learn about the real world. Be good for him not to find you there, hanging on the phone."

Liz laughed and picked up her bag, finally giving in. They decided on the Al-Alawi Traditional Restaurant off *Suq* Al-Alawi Street in the old city, Moroccan food not Saudi, but the best Arab dishes in Jeddah. The screens shutting the women's section off from the main dining room were decorated with desert scenes, so the "family" tables were not so bleakly isolated.

They went in separate cars. The presence of foreign troops in the kingdom, with female soldiers driving army vehicles and working side-by-side with men, had outraged the *mutawain*. They were cracking down on Westerners even more heavily lately, watching for the smallest infraction of Islamic tradition. At best the guilty could expect a harangue in Arabic lasting hours in a tiny room off some mosque or other; at worst…who knew?

Hisham Badawi's execution was never far from Liz's mind.

After dinner, Yousef was waiting to drive her back to Al Fatayah Street. Pewter paths stretched across the road, turning the street into the negative of what it would be in daylight. Gray palms moved against the huge disk of moon, silvery bougainvillea cascaded over luminous white walls.

The gates to the house were open. The maids must have opened them.

Liz's heart started to dance with excitement as she pictured Abdullah's face when she told him she would marry him. She forced herself not to urge Yousef to hurry.

Abdullah's car wasn't in the courtyard; he must have driven to the back of the house, she thought. As she opened the door, Belle raced to greet her, nails clicking on the marble floor of the foyer. Liz grabbed her collar, irritated that Siti had not put her outside in the garden, wondering why Abdullah hadn't given the order. It wasn't like him. Could he be getting used to her?

"Liz? You're home!"

It was Fateema's voice that came from the sitting room. Liz released Belle's collar, held up her hand to command the dog to stay down.

"Hi!" she called. "What a lovely surprise."

The saluki sat in front of her, staring up, fringed tail sweeping the marble floor, body trembling with joy, soft whimpers of welcome in her throat. Liz stroked the animal's chest, avoiding the long red tongue trying to plant wet kisses on any patch of exposed skin, taking a moment for her disappointment to fade. She wouldn't hurt Fateema for the world.

"Have you heard anything?" Fateema's usually measured voice was high. Tense. Frightened.

"Okay," Liz said softly to the dog. "Come on."

Fateema was standing in the middle of the room, looking as if she hardly dare move. On the table were untouched plates of dates, cookies, halvah, a pot of tea. The tiny cup was unused.

"What about? What's happened?" Liz put her arms around her. Fateema's body was cold and trembling.

"Oh, Liz. Liz." Fateema clutched Liz's arms. "I thought you'd know from the Americans. Riyadh has been attacked by Iraqi missiles."

"What?" Liz couldn't believe it. "How do you know? There's been nothing on CNN."

"No. No. They're all blacked out. All the foreign news broadcasts. The BBC. Voice of America. Everything."

Bob had tried CNN before they left for dinner, without success. They'd thought nothing of it.

"Fateema, it's a rumor," she said. "You know what they're like. Nothing to be frightened about."

"Not this," Fateema insisted. "I know. This is different. My husband knows, he said a missile, but he will tell me nothing more. You must find out for me."

"Your husband?" Liz said. She'd never thought of Fateema as being married, but why not? She was always richly dressed, chauffeured in a Mercedes, she mixed with highborn women, had a respected position, not that of a concubine. But when she referred to him, it was always as her master.

Fateema had obviously not heard her question. "My son is there, but he will tell me nothing. You must find out what is happening."

Liz sat on the arm of the sofa closest to her. She held Fateema's hand, tangible flesh and blood, seeing behind her the shadowy figures of a whole life about which she knew nothing. "I don't know how I can find out anything, Fateema—"

"Yes, you can. You can. The man you will marry is close to the king, you say. He will tell you. You are a Western woman, educated. He will talk to you. That's what you said."

"But he's in Riyadh, too." My God. Liz heard her own words. Suddenly she was frantic to hear Abdullah's voice. "I can call him."

"Yes, call him. Call him."

Liz half ran to her bedroom, heading for the phone she always used when speaking to Abdullah, Belle racing ahead of her, Fateema trailing behind. Her fingers felt clumsy as she punched out his number.

"I love you and regret…"

Impatiently, Liz waited for the message to end, then said, "Abdullah, please call me the minute you get this message. I have heard a rumor that Riyadh has been attacked by missiles and I'm frightened." She lowered her voice, hoping that Fateema would not overhear. "I love you. Abdullah, I do want to marry you. Call me." She replaced the receiver and turned to Fateema standing in the center of the bedroom. "He's not there, but he'll pick up the message and he'll call me back."

Fateema was pale, locked in her own anxiety, clearly deaf to everything Liz had said on the phone. "Samir is flying with the American Air Force," she said. "He loves America and Americans, but he has to spend a lot of time in Riyadh. But even if he is not there, his life is always in danger, proving himself to the Americans. He's wild and brave, too brave."

Liz stared at her. "Samir?"

"Samir, my son. I am so frightened for him."

Liz picked up the phone, tapped the number for the kitchen, waited until she heard Siti answer.

"Siti, please bring fresh coffee. Strong American coffee, a large pot." She hung up, then picked the phone up again, punched the redial button. "Siti, bring the bottle of Scotch, too, and some ice and water. One glass." Fateema was not a Muslim but she would not drink alcohol. Carefully Liz replaced the phone, turned to Fateema. She already knew what she was about to be told. "I have to know who he is if I am to find out if he is safe. His rank. His name."

"Prince Samir bin Bandr bin Talal al Sa'ud. He is a major in the Royal Saudi Air Force."

"All right. Okay." Liz wasn't sure if she spoke the words aloud or whether they filled a space in her brain so that she wouldn't think of Abdullah. "Prince Samir bin Bandr al Sa'ud is the other baby born on the *Murphy* in 1958? He's my brother?"

Liz saw Fateema nod, saw her lips move, but all she could hear was her own voice in her head.

Then her father, too, was Prince Bandr. And Prince Abdullah, the man she loved, the man she planned to marry, was related to her by blood. Her father's brother. Her uncle.

Suddenly she was locked in a nightmare.

22

How could she tell him? *What* could she tell him? Liz stared up into the darkness, the questions a drumbeat, the answers no clearer than they had been hours ago.

When Samir was born, Fateema had told her, the young Prince Bandr already had two wives and many daughters, but no sons. He was not told that Fateema could bear no more children, so in his delight, his anticipation of the sons she would continue to give him, he'd made his beloved Circassian concubine his third wife. Since then, more daughters had been born to his other wives, but no sons. Eventually Fateema had been taken to Europe for medical attention, to no avail. She bore no more children, as she knew she would not. As *umm* Samir, the mother of Samir, the only son, her place in Prince Bandr's household was forever secure, and Sakeena was respected as Samir's grandmother.

Daylight filtered through the branches of the tamarisk. Liz got up, let Belle out into the garden, then showered and brushed her teeth. When she came out of the bathroom, Megawati had brought coffee and some fruit. Liz poured herself some coffee, then hit Bob Gould's number, listening to it ring while she drank.

"Good morning, Bob. Hope I didn't get you up."

"Of course you did," Bob said. "What's the time?"

"Early. Bob, I want you to reinstate my application for

an exit visa. I've decided to leave Saudi Arabia. Do you think you can get the paperwork started today?''

''This is pretty sudden.'' His voice told her that he had snapped awake. ''What's happened?''

''Nothing's happened,'' she said. ''I just want to go home.''

''Give me credit for a bit of brain left after my years of boozing. Something's happened. Does Abdullah know you want to leave?''

''I'm going to call him later.''

''Lizzie, you can't do that. You can't break that kind of news on the telephone. The poor guy's hoping you're going to marry him, not go out to dinner.''

''Oh, Bob, please,'' she said wearily. ''Don't lecture me. Did you hear anything about Riyadh being hit by SCUDs?''

''All we're getting are the local Saudi stations with the usual glorious victories. What've you heard?''

''Fateema was here last night. Her husband let drop that Riyadh was hit but wouldn't tell her any more. She's frantic with worry about her son. She thought I'd have more information because I'm an American.''

''Fateema has a husband?'' He sounded as surprised as she'd been. ''Who is he?''

''I can't tell you anything, Bob. She didn't want me to know, she doesn't want anybody else to know. This whole country seems to me to be a morass of secrets, tribal laws, religious madmen, God knows what else. I can't tell you anything, Bob. Please don't ask.''

''Must be the young guy who took her to Tess's house,'' he said. ''How does Nassir fit into all this? Abdullah's not your father, Lizzie, if that's what you're thinking. He's too young. Your father must be twenty years or more older than Abdullah.''

''I know. Can you get the paperwork on my exit visa going? Call me if you get any news about Riyadh.''

She hung up, then sat staring at the telephone. She put out her hand, then jumped when the phone rang as she touched it. She picked it up.

"Yes."

Abdullah's voice said, "Liz, you have made me very happy. I shall come to Jeddah as soon as I can. I have told the king I am taking a Western wife. He is pleased and will come to our wedding. His wives will be with you at the women's celebration."

"Abdullah." She stopped, then tried again. "Abdullah—"

"Yes. Yes, I'm here. What is it?"

Liz couldn't say what she knew she must. Instead she said, "A friend called me last night, the wife of Prince Bandr. Fateema, *umm* Samir. Prince Samir. She is very worried about him. There has been a report that Riyadh has been hit by Iraqi missiles. Are you all right?"

"How do you know *umm* Samir?"

"We met at one of those women's functions, a fashion show or a tea or something. Are you all right?"

"How did she hear this?"

Liz wanted to scream, the interminable questions. What did it matter? "I don't know. She's frantic about Samir."

"No one must know of this until the attack has been officially reported. Tell *umm* Samir not to gossip."

"She won't talk to anyone, Abdullah, but she's frantic. Just tell me. Have you been under attack?"

"One SCUD. Samir is here with me. Tell *umm* Samir that he is well."

"Thank you. I will."

"Liz, we won't wait to marry. Your father and mother—"

She had to do it. Now. Do it. "Abdullah, I'm sorry. I should not have said…" Oh, God, she thought. "Abdullah, forgive me, I cannot marry you. It was a mistake to say that I would."

"What are you saying? I have already told the king, my brother Bandr. Arrangements have been started—"

"I'm going home, Abdullah. I'm sorry. My exit visa should be through within a few days."

The line hummed, then he said, "This is foolish. I will come to Jeddah today. We'll talk."

"Please don't come. I have a very heavy day—"

"Then I will come to the hospital."

"Abdullah, don't—"

She heard the dial tone then dropped the telephone into the cradle, too disheartened to feel anything.

Iraq had attacked Riyadh, Taif in the mountains, Rafha in the north. Chemical warheads. No chemical warheads. The hospital buzzed with rumors that changed hourly. Knots of men gathered, dispersed, reformed. The evening prayer passed without word from Abdullah. Perhaps, Liz thought, he had accepted that her decision was final.

When the Mercedes turned into the courtyard on Al Fatayah street after her day at the hospital, the black Jaguar was in front of the house. Without comment, Yousef got out to open her door. Liz watched him as he came around to the passenger side, and wondered what he knew. He opened gates, closed them. Saw everything. Reported to whom?

Liz handed her briefcase to Siti without speaking and the maid scurried away to the kitchen. Abdullah stood, watching her as she came down the shallow marble steps into the sitting room. She stopped, keeping the sofa's soft bulk between them. She studied his face—the heavy, straight eyebrows above long, dark eyes, beard and mustache touched with silver, framed today by a brilliantly white *ghutra* kept in place by the black *arghal*. A handsome face and, suddenly, absolutely unknowable.

Love? Was that what she felt? Lust? A call to lead the disenfranchised into freedom, a female Martin Luther King? She no longer knew anything, except that she had retreated into the safety of nonfeeling.

"Are you all right?" she asked. "Was the SCUD close? There's been nothing on the news."

"Not close. You spoke to *umm* Samir?"

"Yes. She is only interested in her son's safety. She will speak to no one else."

"Liz—"

She interrupted. "Abdullah, I have made up my mind. I cannot marry you. Nothing you can say will change that. I am going home."

"No. You are not."

"Don't do this. Please."

"You are nervous, I understand that. I will wait and that is not something I am used to doing." He smiled at her. "I will be a Western man very soon."

Liz returned his smile with an effort. "I don't think so."

"Well, maybe not. Liz, the king had already been told of my plans, and has given his permission. And Prince Bandr, the head of my family. That wasn't easy, a Western woman, you understand? But I got his approval. Friends are already congratulating me. This marriage must take place now."

Or he would lose face. She understood what that meant, but there was no other way. "My exit visa will be here in a couple of days—"

"We shall see."

Liz turned her head to look away from him, her glance taking in the room, the flowers. Did he want her to plead?

"Please, Abdullah. Let me go home." She would plead if she had to.

"Why? Why do you want to leave me?"

Liz gripped the back of the sofa, held on fast. "When I heard that SCUDs had fallen on Riyadh, I was frightened that something might have happened to you and I called you, left that message. But I've thought about it since, and I realize I cannot live with the restrictions of a Muslim wife. I don't have to explain, you've lived in the West. You know what you are asking me to give up. I'm sorry, Abdullah. I just can't do it."

He made an impatient gesture with his hand, brushing away her words. "You can be as free as it is possible for any woman to be—"

"I'm sorry. Abdullah, I cannot talk about this any more. I'm very tired." Only hours ago the future had glowed—a wonderful man in love with her, and she with him, the land of her birth reaching out to her, claiming her. It had seemed so right. There was so much to do, enough to last a lifetime. All that had shattered with Fateema's words, and she couldn't tell him why without endangering people she had come to love. "I think you should leave now," she said.

Abdullah looked as if she had delivered a body blow. Liz knew that in his entire life, no one had ever spoken to him in such a manner. If she were the daughter of a Muslim family, such words would never be spoken, or even thought.

Abdullah picked up his *bisht* from the back of an armchair, threw it over his shoulders.

Liz didn't look at him as he passed her and went up the steps to the front door. A scent, faint and familiar, drifted in his wake. But it could have been her imagination.

Both maids wept when Liz told them she was leaving. For days the atmosphere in the house was heavy, lifting only slightly when she promised to try to get them jobs in Santa Monica and visas to work in the U.S. when their contracts in Saudi Arabia came to an end. Liz didn't hold out much hope, but in their youthful optimism, they grabbed the crumbs she offered.

Dr. Mukarek unbent enough to smile and thank her for her work at the hospital, accepting her offer to continue working until the day before she left—whenever that might be.

"They're stonewalling," Bob said on the telephone. "I have to go through the same rigmarole every time I speak to them. It's as if every time I call it's the first time they have heard your name. I've sent a written request three times already, so I think someone's behind it."

"You mean Abdullah?" She couldn't keep the alarm out of her voice.

"Maybe. Liz, why don't you talk to him."

"I can't. I can't see him again, or speak to him."

"Why not?" Bob asked.

Because he's the brother of my father, she wanted to shout, and she still did not trust herself to be with him.

"Leave it, Bob. Please."

"All right," he conceded. "But if you're really determined to go home, you'd better think of some strings to pull. As far as the Saudis are concerned, you can kiss your exit visa goodbye until they're good and ready."

Liz disconnected, then dialed the number Fateema had finally given her, running through in her mind the names of the women she had met at Princess Iffat's house. The phone rang a dozen times then a woman answered in Arabic. Liz replied in English, asking to speak to Princess Fateema, repeating the name slowly. The woman answered in Arabic, then put down the phone. Liz could hear the wailing music that always made her think of Egyptian belly dancers. The sound was cut off abruptly, then a woman's voice said in English, "Who is this?"

"Dr. Elizabeth Ryan. I'm a friend of Princess Fateema. Is it possible to speak to her?"

"Princess Fateema is not here, Dr. Ryan." The voice sounded strained.

"Oh. Well, would you give her a message?"

"Wait, please."

The phone clicked. She'd been put on hold. Two minutes later, the woman came back on the line. "Dr. Ryan. Are you there?"

"Yes."

"Princess Fateema wants you to come."

"Is she all right?" Liz asked, concerned.

"She is. But—" The woman stopped. Liz heard a shaky breath, then, "Please, you should come to the palace of Princess Riata." Riata was a name Liz did not recognize. The woman gave directions to Prince Bandr's palace compound, just off the Corniche. "Please, now if you can. Princess Fateema says that a doctor is needed. The guards at the gate will be told to expect you."

Liz grabbed her medical bag, called Yousef, then, sick with anxiety, waited for him to get to the front of the house to pick her up. The drive across the chaos of Jeddah took forever, every traffic light red, every car muscling ahead of the Mercedes.

The Corniche blazed with light, as families strolled along the sea front, men holding children by the hand, shepherding shrouded women who pushed baby carriages. Out at sea, several U.S. naval ships could be seen riding at anchor; and outside Abdullah's compound, half a dozen soldiers in uniform, M-16s over their shoulders, strolled back and forth in front of closed gates.

A mile further on, Yousef stopped at a gatehouse that faced onto the Corniche. Men wearing the khaki *thobes* of the National Guard, red-and-white checked *ghutras,* bandoliers of bullets across their chests, emerged from the small building. They looked fit and young, more like the men who had died in the courtyard in Mecca than the elders of Yanbu.

Liz sat back, unseen behind the closed, tinted courtesy window separating her from the driver, allowing Yousef to explain the presence of a Western woman at Prince Bandr's gate. Finally, they were waved through.

The road to the house was long, brightly lit, heavily landscaped. The massive three-story building was pale peach, Italianate, with curved pilastered balconies, fifteen-foot-high doors and a tiled roof—a Beverly Hills transplant. Yousef drove past the steps leading up to the front door, then followed the graveled courtyard around to the back of the house, an exact replica of the front down to the last balustrade.

As if someone had been watching for her arrival, the right side of the enormous double front doors opened, dwarfing the tiny Indonesian maidservant who stepped out. Above her veil her eyes were puffy, bloodshot from weeping. She beckoned urgently with both hands, then went back inside.

"Wait for me," Liz said to Yousef. She picked up her medical bag and ran up the steps.

Two staircases curved at each side of the marbled entrance. The entire place blazed with light, yet was as silent as a graveyard at midnight. The sound of her heels on the marble floors sounded like gunshots as Liz followed the maid across the foyer then up the right-hand staircase, along a wide hall, stopping in front of a set of white doors. The girl tapped and one side cracked open.

"Liz, you're here. I'm alone with her, her family is still in Cairo." Words tripped from Fateema's tongue. She clung to the door as if she needed its support to stay upright. "Maimona phoned me, she knew I had been calling you, but the line was always busy." She did not explain who Maimona was.

"I was talking to Bob Gould," Liz said. "Are you all right? What's happened?"

A woman moaned in the room behind her and Fateema's

face crumpled. Her voice shook. "Oh, Liz. He is going to kill her."

"Kill who? Who's going to be killed?"

"Safeya, Riata's daughter. Bandr is going to behead her."

The bedroom was enormous, gauzy curtains billowing with the cool breeze coming through the open windows. Liz looked over at Riata, quiet now from the sedative Liz had given her, exhausted from weeping. She was not yet thirty, dark haired, hazel eyed, probably lovely when her face was not swollen with grief. Young to be the mother of a fourteen-year-old.

"Take me to see the girl," Liz said to Fateema. "Where is she?"

"In her room." Fateema had aged ten years since Liz had last seen her. Dark smudges beneath her eyes, deep lines between nose and mouth, even the brilliant hair was dull. She looked in shock, pale and shaking.

"What did the doctor say about her?"

"She hasn't seen a doctor!" Fateema looked horrified. "She hasn't seen anyone. We couldn't publicize her shame. Anyway, it doesn't matter. His honor has been destroyed by this. He must kill her—"

"She's had no medical attention?" Liz was outraged. "Where is she?"

"Locked up."

"Fateema, an examination can prove she has been raped. I must see her right away. When he knows what happened, her father will understand she's not at fault—"

Fateema interrupted, suddenly angry, her voice raised. "Your lives in the West are so simple. It is not like that here. A man's honor depends upon the virtue of the women of his household—"

Riata started to wail again. "She wouldn't listen to me."

She was tossing her head from side to side, banging against the pillow, building hysteria. "I warned her that what she was doing was dangerous. She wouldn't listen." Riata took a handful of her dress and screamed as she struggled to tear the fabric. Fateema went to her, grabbed her hands, holding them close to her chest, murmuring in Arabic.

Liz felt a cold rage spreading in her own chest.

She'd been told that Safeya's marriage to one of her cousins had already been arranged, a young man ten years her senior, suitable in every way. But Safeya had always been high-spirited, daring, always the one to evade the servants whose job it was to make sure the women were out of the garden when her brothers' friends came to visit. Sometimes Safeya managed to cross the young men's path before fleeing into the women's quarters, shooting mischievous glances over her veil, her mother said, sometimes even answering the young men when they called after her.

Then yesterday she had spent the day at the house of her friend Alia, a girl she had known all her life. There Safeya had given the servants the slip, allowed herself to be persuaded to linger and to drink orange juice with Alia's brothers and their friends.

She had only a distorted memory of what happened next. She had been passed from boy to boy, intimately examined, violated, raped repeatedly. Just after midnight, she had been found on the terrace of her own home, outside the women's entrance, drugged, wearing only her *abayah* over her naked body.

This time, the *hareem* had been unable to keep the secret.

Liz bent over the exhausted woman on the bed. "Riata. Listen to me. I have to see your daughter. She needs help. Can you get into her room?"

Riata shook her head. "He won't let me see her. He blames me." Her sobs increased hysterically. "He will divorce me now."

Her daughter had been raped, her husband was going to kill her, and she worried about divorce? Liz wanted to shake her.

"For God's sake, Riata, the man's a monster."

"Life is so easy for you in the West," Fateema said again. "Riata is disgraced. She will have no life now."

Liz remembered Nura's panic, realizing again that what little value these women had was nonexistent outside of marriage.

"*Umm* Samir can get in to see Safeya," Riata said. "Bandr allows his favorite to do whatever she wishes. She is never punished."

Even through Riata's pain, genuine though it was, Liz recognized the jealousy. My God, she thought, who could comprehend this world?

Fateema shook her head. "I can't do this," she said. "Bandr will allow no one to see her—"

"Fateema, you're going to have to try," Liz said.

Fateema allowed seconds to pass. Then she nodded. "Wait." She slipped through the door and shut it softly behind her.

Riata reached out a hand and Liz took it, sitting quietly beside the prostrate woman on the bed. Half-formed thoughts whirled through her brain. Abdullah might be able to help. Or Samir. Someone had to try to talk Prince Bandr, someone he would listen to.

Fateema came back into the room holding up a key. "The majordomo is at prayer so I took it from his office."

Prayer call had sounded fifteen minutes ago, the *isha* prayer, the last observance of the day. Liz squeezed Riata's hand, then rose and followed Fateema out of the room, hoping the key would not be missed. The house was silent.

"Where are the servants?" Liz asked.

"I sent the maids to their rooms, and the menservants are in their own part of the house. They won't come here.

There's no one else. A man may have four wives, but the Koran demands that they be treated equally. Only Riata lives here."

"You have a house like this?"

"An exact replica at the other side of the compound," Fateema said. "Down to the last piece of furniture."

Fateema led the way up a broad flight of stairs, stopping in front of double doors directly above Riata's suite. She slipped the key into the lock, turned it, then pushed open one door. The suite was a duplicate of the one below it but dark, curtains drawn across closed windows. Fateema turned on a light. The sitting room was empty. She crossed to the door leading to the bedroom.

"Safeya?"

Silence. Fateema spoke again in Arabic. She turned on a lamp next to the bed.

The bed had not been slept in.

Liz opened a door, flipped a light switch. An enormous, luxurious bathroom came to view. In a corner, a small naked form huddled on the marble floor.

"Safeya." Liz knelt beside the girl. She was cold, her eyes squeezed shut. "Fateema, she's here. Grab that robe and wrap her in it. I'll run the bath. We need to get her warm."

Liz fiddled with huge gold-and-green taps until the tub started to fill. She could hear Fateema murmuring to the girl.

"She won't speak to me," Fateema said.

"Help me get her into the tub."

Safeya gave neither resistance nor help. It was as if she had left her body. Automatically, Liz ran her eyes over her checking for injuries. Toothmarks on both breasts, already a deep purple, her thighs and abdomen covered in bruises of the same color. Deep scratches on both buttocks. Between them, the two women lowered the girl gently into the water, cradling her limp form to prevent her from slipping beneath the surface.

"Whoever did this to her should be punished to the full extent of the law," Liz said grimly. "*Shari'ah* law condemns rape—"

"Nothing will happen to them! What do you think would happen? Who will even know? Her honor has been destroyed! Don't you understand that?" Fateema trembled, again on the edge of hysteria. "Her honor, not theirs. Her family's honor. Her father's honor. Not that of the boys. She tempted them by her loose behavior. No one will blame them. She is to blame for this."

"Fateema! My God, you don't believe that!"

Fateema's hand stopped moving, water from the sponge in her hand dripping onto the girl's bruised body. Then she shook her head. "What does it matter what I believe?" She dipped the sponge into the water, resumed bathing Safeya. "No. But it is our way."

The girl's eyelids moved as her eyes rolled back in her head, and she went on murmuring in Arabic, the same phrase over and over. Fateema murmured soothingly to her.

"What is she saying?" Liz asked.

"She says she wants to die. She wants us to let her die."

"Well, she won't die. I'll go to see Bandr myself as a doctor. If that doesn't work, we'll think of something else."

She'd have to go to Abdullah, ask him to intercede with his brother.

It was midnight when Liz left. She had examined the girl, found her torn and still bleeding from forcible entry, but the physical damage would heal in time. Her mental damage was another question. Liz had given her a shot of diazepam, then she and Fateema had tucked her into bed and left her alone. For the next few hours, at least, there was no danger of suicide. Riata, too, would sleep until her family arrived, her mother and sisters and cousins now on their way back from Cairo where they had gone, with suitable male guardians, to wait out the war.

For a moment, Liz's heart lifted when Yousef turned into her own courtyard. Abdullah's car was where he always left it, discreetly hidden behind the tamarisks.

He would listen to her, help her deal with this, speak to Bandr for them.

Yousef stopped in front of the steps and Liz climbed out, realizing her imagination had created a black Jaguar out of a blue Mercedes.

"I've been romancing your dog," Bob called as she entered the house. Belle padded across the entry to greet her and Liz pulled her ears. "Won't have anything to do with me, though. You're going to have to take that dog with you when you leave, you know, she hates everyone but you. Pretty deficient in the charm department."

Liz dropped into a chair and kicked off her shoes, running both hands over the saluki's warm, silky flanks. "Yes, I've been thinking about that. I'll have to talk to the airline.... What are you doing here at this hour?"

"Thought I'd drop by, tell you the latest—"

Liz barely heard him. All she could think of was a small form curled into the fetal position on a cold marble floor.

"I've just come from Prince Bandr's palace." She cut across his words. "Or rather one of the palaces in his compound, the home of his fourth wife, Riata. His daughter by Riata has been gang raped so he's going to kill her on Friday, after the noon prayer, in the garden of her mother's house." She couldn't stop the flow of words from pouring out. "He is going to cut her head off, and he's going to wield the sword himself. The girl's fourteen, she's traumatized physically and emotionally, and she's locked up alone. The boys who did it won't even have a blot on their reputations, and her punishment for being gang raped is death by her father's hand, to protect his fucking honor. His *sharaf.*"

"Liz! My God!" Bob put a hand to his temple, his eyes wide with horror. "There's no trial, nothing?"

"Prince Bandr will not allow it to be brought before a court. And before you say I can't get involved, it's too late. I'm going to try to see Prince Bandr, tomorrow if I can. There's no time to waste. The kid's got seventy-two hours left."

"How do you think you are going to get to see him, a Saudi prince?" Bob demanded. "What good do you think you can do if you do manage it? A female? A Westerner? Bandr's the powerful voice of the traditionalists." Bob stopped speaking, the shock deepening on his face. "I bet that's it, Liz. He's seized on this as a test of the king's willingness to listen to them." Bob held up a hand to prevent Liz from speaking before he had finished. "There's more at stake here than the life of one girl, Lizzie. A lot of Saudis think American troops are the camel's nose under the tent. Once in, the rest of the camel will follow. If an execution like this is planned, you can bet the king himself has given his permission, a show of unity with the leader of the fundamentalists. It's a political matter, easy to do, no cost. Prince Bandr is not going to back off."

"Well, equally this country can't afford to offend the West, the Americans and Europeans. They need us."

"And how would the Americans and Europeans know about a private little beheading in the garden after church?"

"Because I'd blow the whistle, Bob," she said. "Loud and clear. First, though, I'll try to see Prince Bandr, and I'll talk to Abdullah. He'll help."

Gould shook his head. "Lizzie, you can be so naive. Prince Bandr would not take an action like this without the support of the male members of his family."

"You're wrong. Not Abdullah. I know he doesn't know

about this. He'd never support such a terrible thing. It's barbaric and he's not that."

"Then why do you think your paperwork has been miraculously found? That's what I came to tell you. You can leave any time you like. It looks to me as if Abdullah wants you out of the way."

"That's a stretch. Your paranoia is showing."

"If he knows that Fateema is a friend of yours then he knows that as a doctor you're already involved."

Liz got to her feet and opened the glass door into the garden, breathing deeply of the fragrant air. "I have to see Bandr. I couldn't live with myself if I didn't at least try."

"So, what are you going to do?" Bob asked from behind her. "Call for an appointment?"

She turned. "No. I'd never get through even if I knew his number. No. I'm going to attend his *majlis*."

Bob stared at her, then started to laugh. Even through her pain and anger, Liz had to laugh with him.

23

They were in good time, Liz thought, the crowd was still milling about outside Prince Bandr's gates. The prince kept up the old Bedouin custom of a daily *majlis* when he was in the kingdom, as did his father, Prince Talal bin Abdul Azziz, and as his grandfather, King Abdul Azziz al Sa'ud, had done before him, even sharing his midday meal with as many as a thousand men after he had heard and settled disputes. A good politician nurturing his political base.

Liz leaned forward. "Yousef, I want you to take this note to Prince Bandr."

Yousef took his eyes off the road, turning his head. "What note? What is it, this note?"

"Yousef, just do as you are asked, please."

"I cannot just give a note to a prince," he argued. "I am merely a driver, I brought you here as you demanded. More I cannot do."

"Any man has the right to claim an audience with a prince during his *majlis*. You are a Saudi, you know that. Anyone can petition him for what they need, for alms, for legal help, his intervention with authority."

"So what is this to do with me? I have no petition for this prince."

"But I do," she said. "This is my request for an audience with Prince Bandr during his *majlis* today."

Yousef slammed a foot on the brake. "You cannot do this. A woman cannot—"

Liz braced herself with a hand on the back of the seat in front of her. "I have the right of the stranger, by tradition, to petition the prince. He will see me."

"You are a woman—"

"I am a doctor, a stranger and a petitioner," she cut him off. "Now, get this car tight against the gate so that we'll be first in line, then give my note to the guard."

"I cannot."

"Yes, you can. Just keep driving and they'll give way, they'll have to."

The car remained stationary, Yousef silent.

"Okay, then I'll walk." Liz's heart thumped against her chest as she reached for the door handle, gambling that Yousef knew that his employer, whoever he was, would not be pleased if he allowed her again to be swallowed in a crowd of men, even though this was a less inflammatory occasion than the day at Chop Square.

The door gave and Liz made much of trying to push it open. Then, "Madam," Yousef said. "Give me the letter."

Men gave way as the Mercedes inched forward until the front bumper touched the gates. Yousef shoved the dark courtesy window closed before he got out, then swiftly slammed the door behind him before the curious could peer in. Liz watched him talking with the National Guardsman and almost smiled at the shocked expression on the guard's face as he turned to stare at the car. A heated discussion followed between the guard and Yousef until the intervention of a superior officer and a telephone call from the guardhouse. Liz looked at the faces pressed against the windows of the Mercedes as men tried to see who was inside, grateful for the one-way glass protecting her, realizing this was how Saudi women felt about the veil.

Yousef got back into the car.

"Will he see me?"

"No."

"Then why are we waiting here?"

"We wait for the guard to let us through."

"Then he will see me."

Yousef didn't answer. Poor Yousef, Liz thought. He didn't want to be part of this, and couldn't bring himself to say Prince Bandr would see an infidel, a woman at that. Time dragged on in silence. Ten minutes. Fifteen. Then the gate swung open. Yousef turned on the ignition and jerked the car forward. Men surged through the gates, the Mercedes with them.

Just inside the gates a small lane led off the main road which she had used the night before when going to Riata's, and the crowd of petitioners turned into it. Three hundred yards in, a white building appeared on the far side of a rush-lined body of water, the sweeping curves of the roofline reminiscent of the curves of a series of Bedouin tents. Tall date palms surrounded both the building and the man-made oasis, the fronds of the trees casting moving patterns against the white stucco in the breeze. Sleek racing camels wandered freely around the oasis, browsing and drinking or couched for rest.

Yousef drove past the building.

"Where are you going?" Liz asked.

"You cannot enter where men enter. There is no door for women. You will enter by the kitchen." He stopped in front of a door, remained seated stubbornly behind the wheel. Liz waited a moment for him to open her door, then opened it herself and climbed out.

A Saudi emerged from the building. The ends of his *ghutra* were wrapped around his face as though facing a sandstorm—or a visitation from a demon—leaving only his eyes visible. Without looking at her, he motioned Liz to follow him.

They entered through the kitchen, vast, white tiled, redolent with the smell of roasting lamb and baking bread and the fresh sweetness of mint. Pans clattered as Egyptian chefs shouted orders to an army of Sri Lankans who poured mounds of chopped cucumbers into minted yogurt, slid *khubis* from traditional brick ovens, manhandled great metal pans of rice and basted whole sheep turning slowly over spits. Silence fell as Liz followed her guide between the wooden worktables. No one looked up as they passed, but Liz felt the examination of a hundred pairs of curious eyes.

The Saudi opened a door, allowing it to swing closed behind him, leaving Liz to catch it or be caught by it. She followed him into a wide white corridor that appeared to run through the center of the building. They walked for five minutes in silence, turning corners, passing through arches and reception halls, before her escort stopped at a door. He tapped, listened to the voice from inside, held up a hand commanding Liz to wait, then uncovered his face and entered.

Liz adjusted the long black scarf wound around her head to make sure no strand of hair had escaped, then smoothed her full-length black caftan, chosen because it revealed only her hands and the tips of her black shoes. The man returned, motioned Liz forward. She took a breath and entered the room.

Briefly her eyes took in the surprising scene—Louis Quatorze furniture, white-and-gold tables, heavy overstuffed chairs and couches lining the walls, the sumptuous Oriental carpets—then settled on the dark figure silhouetted against the window.

He was seated behind an enormous empty Louis Quatorze desk, bare even of the fancy desk sets beloved of Saudi officials. Standing behind his right shoulder was the tall robed figure of Naif, his bodyguard from Mecca.

Her heart gave a thump, sped up, then slowed. She hadn't given Naif a thought. Too late now, she had to rely on the circumstances being so different, trust he would not recognize her out of the context of battle wounds and blood.

Liz waited for an invitation to come closer, but the prince remained silent and still, so she walked forward. When she was ten feet in front of the desk, he held up a hand without speaking. Liz stopped. She ran her eyes over his face, for the first time able to see up close the results of the work she had done in Mecca. The scars were smooth and fine; he'd healed well. She'd done a good job. His face was set in stern, heavy lines, his untrimmed beard was a grizzled white and gray. He wore a simple white *thobe,* black-and-white checked *ghutra,* his rank proclaimed by the heavily embroidered edges of his black *bisht.* The watch he wore would be platinum, not white gold—the wearing of gold by men was forbidden by the Prophet, a commandment this man would take seriously.

Her father. His large, dark eyes were fixed on her and Liz felt the power radiating from him. Her skin rippled as if someone had walked over her grave. He filled her with horror, and she was sick to think his blood ran in her veins.

When Prince Bandr did not speak, she said, "Thank you for seeing me, sir."

No answer. The eyes did not waver, seemed not even to blink.

Liz took a breath. "I am Dr. Elizabeth Ryan. I am an American surgeon. I came to the kingdom to work at King Khaled Clinic in Jeddah, but at my own request was seconded to Jeddah General Hospital where I have worked for eight months among the women and children."

No answer. Not a flicker even that he had heard.

She went on. "Your piety and your justice are well-known, sir, so I have come to you to plead for the life of a girl who was viciously raped. I know that once you are aware of the violence that this innocent child has suffered at the hands of her attackers, you will find it in your heart to offer her mercy.''

Liz stopped to draw breath, waited for a response. He gave her nothing. She searched his face for a glimpse of the young man who, for the love of his concubine, Fateema, had broken the strongest taboos of his race and religion. She could find no trace of him.

''I speak of Princess Safeya bint Bandr al Sa'ud,'' she went on. ''I have examined this girl, and it is my medical opinion that she was used brutally and against her will. Her injuries show that she fought hard to protect her honor and the honor of her family. I bring this to your attention, sir, knowing that you will show the same mercy the Prophet, blessings be upon him, would show to an injured child.''

Prince Bandr stared at her with the cold, implacable gaze of a Muslim elder. For the first time, he spoke. ''How was it possible that you saw this girl?''

His English was flawless.

''I was called by women of the household. As a friend, initially, but it was my duty as a doctor to impress upon them the urgency of medical attention in a case of rape.'' Deliberately she used the word again. ''This was my professional responsibility, sir, and no fault should attach to them.''

''What exactly is it you are asking of me?''

She phrased her request carefully. ''I understand the child, Princess Safeya, is to be executed after the noon prayer on Friday. I come to plead for her life.''

Prince Bandr leaned back in his chair, turned his head toward Naif. Naif bent, listened, then straightened and walked to the door and left the room. Prince Bandr motioned Liz toward one of a pair of chairs in front of the desk. Surprised, she sat. Silence hummed between them.

The image of Fateema rose in her mind's eye, strong, brave, still finding ways to resist the oppression inherent in

her life. Love for her, for Sakeena, and gratitude for their
courage overflowed from her heart. Gratitude for Tess, taking the risks she'd had to take. If she'd been allowed to live,
if she'd been raised in this man's household as Safeya had
been, would he have treated her any differently because he
loved the girl who bore her? Saudis adored their children.
Liz let her eyes slide over his face, careful not to catch his
eye in case it should be interpreted as a challenge, or im-
pertinence, anything to hurt the cause she was pleading.

This man looked incapable of affection, even for children.

Naif reappeared. Behind him, another Saudi bore a silver
tray. He placed the tray on a small table beside Liz and
poured tea from a silver pot into a delicate porcelain cup.
Liz accepted the offered cup without smiling and took a date
from the dish he held out to her. He replaced the dish on
the tray and retreated through the door from which he had
entered.

She felt foolish, at a complete disadvantage under the
watchful eyes of the prince, holding a tiny cup of steaming
mint tea in one hand, a date in the other. For the first time
she realized the celebrated Saudi hospitality could also be
used as a weapon of negotiation. Her heart sank. This man
would never unbend enough to see anything beyond his own
narrow view of the world.

She sipped the tea, took one nibble at the corner of the
date, then replaced both cup and date on the tray.

Prince Bandr turned his head again toward Naif. Naif
bent, nodded, and once more left the room.

Prince Bandr looked at Liz. "In the name of the Most
Merciful, blessings be upon him, your petition is granted.
The woman will not be executed. Word has been sent to the
household."

Liz felt heat swelling in her chest, expanding, threatening
to rise into sobs. She looked down at her clenched hands,

took a deep breath, knew that her face was still and would show nothing to this man. She rose to her feet.

"Thank you."

She turned to leave and heard Prince Bandr's voice behind her.

"Dr. Ryan."

She turned in front of the door, waited for him to continue.

"It is time for you to leave this kingdom. Go back to the United States. We have no need of you here."

"My plans to leave are already in hand, sir. I shall be gone within a week." Never to return, thank God.

She looked for a moment at her father. Suddenly all she could think of was Jim Ryan, puttering about his study at home in Santa Barbara in the old gray sweater her mother had been trying to throw out for twenty years. She had been so lucky with her parents. She nodded, turned her back on Prince Bandr bin Talal bin Abdul Azziz al Sa'ud, and left the room.

The same shrouded Saudi led her back through the kitchen, out into the clean air. Yousef sat behind the wheel of the Mercedes, staring ahead as if she did not exist, and Liz opened the door herself and climbed in, then leaned back against the soft leather. Her entire body was shaking and tears were close; she wasn't sure why. If ever there was a moment for jubilation, this was it. She pulled the yards of black chiffon from her hair, wadded it into a ball, and threw it on the floor of the car, then leaned forward and tapped on the closed courtesy window. Yousef slid it open without turning.

"Drive to Princess Riata's palace," she said to the back of his head. "You know the way, we were there last night."

Smiling, she stopped outside the tall double front doors, listening to the celebrated ululation of Arab women. Then she felt the smile on her face gradually fade. These were not the voices of women raised in thanksgiving.

She banged on the door with both fists.

No one answered. The doors remained tightly closed. Inside she could hear shrieks. Her blood was suddenly ice.

Frantically she ran along the terrace, around the corner to the side of the house. Every set of French doors she tried was closed, the drapes drawn. Inside the house, the shrieks continued rising and falling, unabated. Liz ran as far as she could, banging on every window without response, until the wall that stretched across the terrace to separate the *hareem's* terrace from the rest prevented her from going farther. She turned, ran back and raced down the steps to the car.

"Take me to the front of the house," she shouted to Yousef.

"That is the men's entrance—"

"Get out of this goddamm car. Get out." She opened the door, pulled the startled Yousef out, then climbed behind the wheel. As she drove back down the road, around to the front of the house, she saw the startled faces of an army of gardeners turned toward her, a woman driving. She slammed the car to a stop and jumped out. She ran up the steps to the main entrance to Princess Riata's palace, banged on the door.

It opened to a tall, stout Pakistani barring her way. Chin elevated, he stared down at her through narrowed eyes.

"This is not the entrance—"

Liz pushed past him. "Get out of my way."

She ran inside—as she guessed it was the flip side of the women's quarters, the tiled floor, the double staircases on each side. From somewhere deep in the house she could hear the wails of women. She turned to the majordomo.

"Where is the entrance to the *hareem*?"

"You must go around to the other side of the palace—"

"Don't play games with me!" She advanced toward him. "Tell me how I get into the *hareem* from here."

The man backed up, pointed with his chin. "Through that door."

Liz flung open the door he indicated. The cacophony of grief that poured out almost stopped her own breath. She raced through the house, following the sound, opening doors, peering into empty rooms. A small maidservant hurried from a kitchen and Liz grabbed her. The girl looked up with huge eyes, the tray of tea in her hands tilting dangerously.

"Princess Riata. Where is she?"

The girl shook her head. Plainly she was terrified.

Liz forced herself to speak slowly, without panic. "Princess Riata? Princess Fateema?"

The girl nodded, and started away, looking over her shoulder for Liz to follow. Down a broad corridor, up an inner stair, through a door that opened onto the hall containing Riata's suite. The girl opened one of the tall double doors, and the source of the grief was suddenly deafening. The girl stood back to allow Liz to precede her.

The sitting room was crowded with women. Clothes torn, hair torn, cheeks bleeding from the deep scratches they had inflicted upon themselves with their own nails, eyes blank, sockets black with smudged kohl. Liz felt battered by the wall of perfumed heat that greeted her, by the voices, the shrieks and moans.

Quickly she searched the room for a familiar face. None of the women seemed to be aware of her presence, each wrapped in her own hysterical misery. Then she saw Fateema and could hardly believe it was the woman she had come to know so well.

Her eyes were glassy, her face scratched, the beautiful red hair stood out from her head in a tangled mess where she had torn at it. Like the others, she was rocking from side to side. Liz crossed the room and stood in front of her.

"Fateema. What's happening? Did she kill herself?"

Fateema did not answer.

Liz placed her hands on Fateema's shoulders and shook her.

"Stop it," she ordered. "Stop this right now. What has happened?"

Fateema's frame was shaken by a deep breath as she suddenly came back from wherever it was her anguish had taken her. "Liz. Liz. You've heard."

"Did she kill herself?"

Fateema shook her head. Tears started to well from her eyes, but they were tears of grief not hysteria.

"Then what? Riata?"

"No. It is Safeya."

"It's all right, Fateema. I saw him, I just came from there. He said her life would be spared. He told his bodyguard to send word. She will not be executed on Friday. She's safe—"

Fateema started to rock. "No, the building is to be started—"

Abruptly, Liz shook her again, then hustled her out of the door, closing it behind them, cutting off the noise.

"What are you saying?" she asked. "I just saw him, I just came from seeing him."

"She is to be walled up. Walled up without light, without sound."

"What?" Liz sagged against the wall, her legs suddenly too weak to support her. "That can't be true—"

"It is, it is." In anguish, Fateema started to rock back and forth. "She is not to be killed by the sword, they called the majordomo to tell us. Safeya will not be executed, she is to be given food and water. But she will hear nothing, see nothing."

Bile rose in Liz's throat, and she swallowed convulsively.

"Oh, Liz, first she will go mad, then she will die. When no sound has been heard for seven days, the wall will be broken open. Her body will be left in the desert for the wild dogs."

Liz swallowed again, but her mouth filled with vomit. She put a hand to her mouth, waved the other frantically, hoping Fateema would understand. Fateema grabbed her, opened a door to a powder room. Liz stumbled to the toilet and dropped to her knees, her body wracked with spasms.

When it was over, her stomach empty, Liz leaned back against the cool marble wall, her legs stretched in front of her. She felt a wet cloth against her forehead, and closed her eyes. Fateema cleaned her face with a damp towel, then touched a glass of water to her lips. Liz nodded her thanks, took a few sips. Then she looked up.

"I need a toothbrush. And some mouthwash." It was all she could think of. She had to keep her thoughts narrowly focused, or she'd start to wail like the women in Riata's bedroom.

Fateema nodded. "I'll send a maid for them." She slipped through the door, closing it softly behind her.

She'd made it worse, Liz thought dully. By her interference, she had doomed Safeya to a death that was unimaginable. This was her fault. The grief and suffering in the next room was her fault. Tears coursed down her face. She started to retch again, but there was nothing left in her stomach.

A knock came at the door but she could not raise a voice to answer. The door opened. Fateema's head appeared. "Are you all right?"

"No, I'm not all right. Are you?"

"I've got a toothbrush and some toothpaste."

Liz got to her feet, made her way to one of the opulent

sinks, and turned on a gold tap. Solid gold, probably. Solid gold plumbing fixtures and death by sensory deprivation.

What a fucking monster.

She brushed her teeth, rinsed her mouth, gargled. After spitting into the fancy dark-green glass bowl, she glanced at herself in the mirror. She looked like hell. And so did Fateema, standing behind her.

One monstrous human being was doing this to them. One power-crazed, self-righteous, religious fanatic. To them. To the other powerless women in the room next door.

She had not done this to Safeya. She would not take on the sins of this man.

She met Fateema's eyes in the mirror.

"Is Safeya still here, in her room?" she asked.

"Yes."

"Is this where is he going to do it, in her mother's house?"

"Yes. Here. A small room will be prepared with a metal slot for food and water." Fateema started to shake. "This is never done now even among traditional people—"

"We'll get her out of here before that," Liz said. "Do you think you can help?"

Fateema took a step back, her head shaking from side to side.

"What are you saying? That is not possible."

"Yes, it is possible. If we are ready to do whatever we have to do." Liz thought of weapons. Bob would know about that. Maybe he knew someone in the military. "Your part will be to get her out of this house. I'll do the rest."

"How?"

"I don't know yet. But I will." Liz felt the blood beginning to move again in her veins.

"There is no time, Liz. No time. Nothing can be done. She is to be walled in tomorrow at noon—"

"Can you get her out of this house?"

"No. I don't know. I don't think so."

"Get hold of Nassir. Ask him."

"Nassir?" Fateema looked bewildered.

"He will help, I know it—" Liz stopped. "Prince Abdullah. Does he know what Bandr is doing?"

Fateema shook her head. "I don't know. Not this, perhaps. But certainly, he knew Bandr was going to execute Safeya by the sword. He came from Riyadh yesterday."

There was no time now for grief or anger, Liz thought. When she was back in Santa Barbara, she'd think about Abdullah, the man she knew, the man she didn't. "Nassir must have come with him. Well, don't ask him for help. You will have to do it alone somehow. What about her mother? Can she help?"

Fateema shook her head. "She is prostrate. You saw them. They will be like this for a week."

"Then we will do it alone. And you will have to come with us, Fateema, otherwise he might do the same to you in revenge. Will he punish Sakeena?"

"She is in Taif, not here. No, Samir will protect her."

"Okay. I'll need a four-wheel drive. Can you get one?"

"I don't know." Fateema suddenly looked frightened, as if the realization of what Liz planned was only now becoming clear. But she nodded. "I think so. There are cars and vans, hundreds of them, here. Samir alone has more than he can count."

"I'll leave that to you as well, then." Liz looked at her watch. Two in the afternoon. They hadn't much time. "Is there a guard on her room?"

"This is the *hareem*. There are no men here."

"Do you think you can pull the same trick with the keys?"

Fateema nodded again.

"Have Safeya ready, dressed in black, heavily veiled. And be ready yourself, also heavily veiled. I will be back during the *isha* prayer."

She was committed.

24

Bob Gould shook his head. "Lizzie, honey. This is crazy. You'll never pull it off."

"Yes, I will. Anyway, I have no choice now, Fateema is expecting me when the menservants are out of the way for the evening prayer. I'm only telling you so that when Siti starts looking for me you'll know what's happened. You'll be the first person she'll call."

Bob got to his feet. His agitation took him on a tour of his office. "Maybe we can get some help from the U.S. Army."

"That was the first thing I thought, but I can't involve those young kids, and no one of any rank would risk upsetting the Saudis. We need them." She watched him pace and tried to contain her impatience. "If Bandr carried out his threat and it got out, sure, even in the middle of a war there would be newspaper publicity, notes of protest, calls back and forth. But it wouldn't do Safeya any good, she'd already be dead in that brick coffin. The Saudis would deny everything anyway. No. I have to do this myself. I do need you to do a couple of things for me, though, if you will."

"Sure. What?"

"I have a gold incense brazier Fateema gave me. Her mother brought it with her from...from her home." Now was not the time for long explanations. "Can you collect it from the house and take it home with you when you go?" She told him where she kept it.

"Sure. What else?"

"Will you send Belle home for me? Dr. Mackay will give her the shots she needs."

He nodded. "I can do that. Don't worry about her."

"Thanks. And one more thing. Is there any way you can reach Hannah Stone?"

"I can try. What do you want me to tell her?"

"Be careful how you say it, but tell her I'm making for her area—she told me about where she was. Tell her, if she can, to get hold of Judd. Once I get to the American line, he'll help get us out of the country. I can get fatigues and lose myself in the army, and Safeya can pass as a Kuwaiti woman without papers."

"What about internal identity cards?" Bob asked. "Saudis can't move casually around the country, they have to have identity cards. Have you thought about that?"

"Fateema is getting them—"

"How in God's name is she going to manage that?"

"I don't know, but she'll do it. Steal them from someone I suppose."

"And that's your plan?" Bob looked stunned. "You are going to drive to the American lines?"

"Can you think of anything better? I can't fly out of here without an exit visa for Safeya and signed permission from her father for her to travel, plus a Saudi male escort. Your thoughts on getting any of that would be welcome."

"What about the roadblocks? They're all over the place now."

"A man with his women in the back of the car usually gets waved through, nine times out of ten. You've seen that yourself. I know I have."

Bob tried a laugh. "You're going to look very cute with your hair chopped off, wearing a *thobe* and *ghutra*." His voice cracked. He brushed a hand over his eyes. "Christ,

Liz, why didn't you listen? I warned you not to get involved in the politics of this country—''

"And I never have," she cut in. "This is about a girl, Bob. It's always been about one girl, the kid in front of me who needed help. Let's not argue about it. I'm doing it." She looked down at her hands. The hands of a healer. What she might have to do was so terrible, she couldn't find the words that would give it substance. "Is there any way you get your hands on a gun?"

"I don't know, the penalty for owning firearms is pretty severe. I could probably prowl around, make some inquiries, but by seven tonight?" Bob shook his head. "Don't bank on it."

"Don't do anything, then. I don't want any suspicion to come back on you. And don't speak to Abdullah, no matter what he says. You were right. He knows what Bandr is going to do. He hasn't tried to stop him." Liz rose to her feet. It was time to go.

Bob came around the desk. "You know what will happen if you don't get away with this?"

She tried a grin. "It will be one hell of an international incident."

He put his arms around her, pulled her against his chest. "Honey—" His voice failed him. He swallowed and tried again. "I'd give anything, anything, if I could go back and do this over. I should never have asked you to come here."

"No, don't say that," she said, hugging him. "I found Fateema and that means so much to me. No reason for you to be sorry about anything if I'm not. It's okay."

"Bandr will never let this get as far as an international incident, honey. You understand what I'm saying?"

"Yes, I know." They could have been talking about the death of strangers, not her own and Fateema's, not that of the young girl Safeya. That was good, she thought. Her brain was ice-cold and she needed that to get them through the next couple of days. Liz leaned her head against his. "I'll call when we're safe. If you don't hear from me, tell my mother what happened. Tell her and Dad I love them. And Judd. Tell him, too."

He raised a hand, rested it on her head, a benediction without words, his prayer for her. "I'll wait to hear from you, then."

"This is not politics, Bob," she said softly. "This is a kid sentenced to death in a particularly horrendous way. Not just any kid, not that it makes any difference. Prince Bandr is my father, too. He's Fateema's husband. I'll never let him take Safeya back to what he plans for her." Her voice caught as the unthinkable surfaced, was given substance. "I'll kill her myself first."

She slipped out of his arms. The door closed behind her before he could respond.

Liz checked her medical bag for the fourth time. Simple supplies—diazepam, ampoules of penicillin and morphine, plenty of salve for sunburn, sterile gloves, alcohol, gauze, bandages, tourniquets, stethoscope. A *thobe* and *ghutra* belonging to Yousef filched from the laundry room. She'd have to get an *arghal* from Riata's house, maybe a gun if she was in luck, and plenty of water.

She'd given the two maids some of her clothes and a load of makeup, told them to take the night off, stay in their room and try everything on. They'd been thrilled. She looked at her watch again. In ten minutes she'd call Yousef to bring the car so she could get to Riata's in time for him to join the other men at evening prayer.

She went into the television room, turned on the set. No CNN. A lot of pictures of damage in Baghdad. No word ever on Saudi television about the recent SCUD attacks on Israel, or their threatened retaliation. She turned off the set, went back into the sitting room, filled as usual with flowers. They still came twice a week, without a note.

From the kitchen, she heard Belle give a single bark. She barked again, this time a warning.

Liz went to the front door to see Yousef opening the gate and an olive drab Range Rover drive into the courtyard. A Saudi was at the wheel.

She turned blindly, thinking to run, then stopped. Where was there to go?

The Range Rover drew to a stop at the bottom of the steps. The driver climbed out. She recognized him and alarm bells clanged in her brain.

She forced a smile, then went down the steps calling a greeting. "Prince Samir. What a nice surprise."

Without looking at her or answering, Samir opened the passenger door so that Liz could see inside. Fateema leaned forward, the eyes over her veil wide and dark, unreadable in the overhead light.

Yousef hovered in front of the Range Rover and Liz's eyes moved from Samir, to Yousef, back to Samir, half expecting one of them to make a move to grab her. Samir barked a few sharp words and Yousef shot a last surreptitious look in Liz's direction, then turned to leave for his own quarters, reluctance in every step.

"Get in," Samir said.

"No, I don't think so."

Fateema leaned forward. "Liz, it's all right," she said. "Come."

Liz hesitated, and Fateema beckoned sharply. "Quickly."

Still uncertain, Liz looked from face to face, still didn't move, but knew she had to. Something was happening, and whatever it was, she couldn't let Fateema face it alone.

"Wait. I have to get my bag." She went back into the house and picked up her medical bag from the kitchen. She looked around once, then walked back to the courtyard.

Samir stood by the open door of the Range Rover where she had left him. Liz climbed in, the door slammed.

As the Range Rover slowed for the turn into the street, Liz glanced back at the house for a last goodbye. A dark shape hurled itself out of the front door, across the courtyard.

"Dammit, I left the door open! Wait! Samir, wait! My dog's following us."

He did not answer or slow the Range Rover. Liz raised her voice. "You have to stop." Belle raced after them down the center of Al Fatayah Street. The Range Rover turned into Al Batala Street and Liz twisted to look out of the rear window. The saluki was at full stretch but she was falling behind.

If she left her, Belle would be lost once more to the indifferent cruelty of boys with stones.

Hisham Badawi had died for that dog.

Liz slammed her fist into Samir's shoulder. "Stop, goddammit." She wrenched at her door, managing to push it open against the rush of wind. "I mean it. Stop." She hung half out of the moving vehicle.

Without answering Samir stood on the brakes. Liz lurched hard, clung to the door, and stumbled into the street. Panting, Belle reached her, then jumped into the Range Rover at her urging, Liz behind her.

"Okay. Go."

The vehicle jumped forward, steadied. Liz put her hand reassuringly on the animal's head. What was she going to do with her? She couldn't take her to Bob without pulling him into this, and she couldn't abandon her.

"That creature makes this even more impossible." Samir echoed her thoughts, the first words he had spoken.

Liz pushed the panting Belle down onto the floor, beneath her legs. "Makes what impossible?"

"Don't play games, the time has passed for that."

"Why are you here?" Liz asked. "Where are we going?"

Samir did not answer. Fateema groped for her hand, squeezed it and shook her head, warning Liz not to speak. Samir hurtled through the streets of Jeddah, turned onto the Corniche.

Liz could hardly breathe. The next turn would be into Prince Bandr's compound, the ugly peach-colored house where Safeya waited. And then what?

Samir spun the wheel. The Range Rover turned sharply. Samir leaned out of the window, shouted to the guards in front of Abdullah's gates. The men jumped to open them and Samir gunned the Range Rover through as the gates swung shut behind them.

"Where are we going?" Liz moved her tongue around in a mouth so dry from fear she could barely speak. She turned to Fateema. "What have you told them?"

"Only that you are very brave, and that you need help. Samir also is very brave."

Samir said a few sharp words in Arabic. Fateema answered with the same sharpness, then turned to Liz. "Be patient."

"Fateema—"

Fateema put a hand to Liz's lips.

The Range Rover turned off the main compound road, then turned again, onto narrow maintenance roads now, foliage brushing the windows on both sides. They passed several large buildings, only glimpsed through the trees, before stopping at the side of a large building surrounded by a deep limestone terrace. Liz had lost all sense of direction, but the building looked much like the one she had visited with Bob for the reception for General Readhead, this time approached from the rear.

Samir opened the passenger door. Fateema got out, and Liz followed, Belle pressing close to her leg. Samir strode ahead of them, up several wide shallow stone steps, along

the terrace. Light came intermittently from inside as they
passed closed glass doors, but the house was silent.

Liz's heart lurched from beat to beat. All she could think
was: this was the end. No one about. No servants, only a
sinister emptiness in a culture where an excess of servants
was part of the scenery. They'd never leave this place. No
one would even know they had been here.

At a wall across the terrace, Fateema stopped. She turned
and put her lips close to Liz's ear.

"I leave you here. Go with God, Dr. Elizabeth Ryan."

She put a key in a door in the wall and opened it. Turning,
she deliberately removed her veil so that what light there
was from one of the glass doors illuminated her face. She
touched her fingers to her forehead, to her lips, then put her
hand against her heart.

The exact gesture of Sakeena on the dockside thirty years
ago, saying goodbye to Tess Ryan.

Fateema slipped through the door and it closed behind
her.

Liz's body was ice. "Fateema!" Liz seized the doorknob,
twisted it, shook the door.

"That leads to the *hareem*," Samir said. "It locks from
within. You will not open it. Now we must leave here."

Liz looked at the closed door through a haze of tears,
searching for a way through it, although she knew Fateema
was gone now from her life. Samir called again, and Liz
put a hand on Belle's collar, turning to follow him through
one of the glass doors and into the house.

"What is going on? Please, Samir, speak to me—"

"You know what you have done? Never before—" Samir stopped midstride, turned, his face tight with rage.
"You, *aznabi*, have started something that now must be
finished." He threw open a door. "Wait in here."

Liz looked into the face of her twin brother, and a sense

of loss seemed suddenly to split her heart. He'd called her foreigner. And he was right.

Liz stepped toward the doorway, Belle at her side.

"Leave the animal," he said.

"Only if you promise she will be safe here."

Samir locked eyes with her, daring her to threaten him.

Liz looked away, told Belle to wait, then entered the room. It was small, luxuriously furnished, unlike every other room Liz had seen in the house. Bookshelves weighted with leather-bound books, an antique desk, its surface tooled in gold and green, deep leather armchairs and sofa, oriental rug. A masculine room reassuringly comfortable and Western, even to the fireplace. In a corner was an enormous illuminated globe.

Liz stood in the middle of the room. Whatever was coming, she'd face it on her feet. She told herself nothing could be known. Fateema had been the only other person who knew what had been planned, and Fateema would never betray her.

A section of the bookshelves suddenly swung back.

Prince Abdullah stood in the doorway.

His first words astonished her.

"You have cut off your hair! Why have you done such a thing?"

Liz studied him warily. She felt no desire to throw herself into his arms, no urge to plead for Safeya's life. It would be useless—he'd known about the girl's impending execution and had done nothing to stop it. All she felt was an almost overwhelming fear. He had power of life and death over her, over Safeya, over Fateema.

"Oh, Liz." Abdullah shook his head. He was not prepared for such a change in her. Without the mane of red hair, she was still beautiful but very different, the strong cheekbones more evident, the slant of her eyes more pronounced, the green even more startling. "This is not exactly how I'd planned our next meeting."

"Why have I been brought here?"

Abdullah almost laughed aloud. There was no give in her. No weakness. She had to be uncertain, frightened, yet she allowed no sign of it. Abdullah crossed the room to stand behind the desk. "I am told that you examined Princess Safeya bint Bandr?"

"Yes, that is true."

"You say that she fought her attacker?"

"Attackers. More than one. Yes, she did."

"That does her credit. But you must understand it makes no difference. She has dishonored her family—"

Liz's voice rode over his. "You are an educated man, Abdullah. You know how ridiculous that is."

"Prince Bandr is the head of this family. He has the right, the duty even, to maintain the honor—"

"You think he has the right to wall up a child until she goes mad and dies?"

"He has the right to take her life. He gave her life. He takes her life. Such is the will of Allah." He paused, then said, "*Umm* Samir has told Prince Samir what you propose to do. She then asked for his help to plot against his father."

Liz felt the saliva dry in her mouth. She swallowed, fought for words. "For God's sake, Abdullah! What plot?" Desperately, Liz improvised. "I said I'd need a four-wheel-drive and asked her to ask Samir for the keys to one of his. An open request. Where's the plot in that?"

"And then you involved her in a scheme to abduct a daughter of this family."

"No. To help save an innocent child from a cruel and unjust death."

"The ground war started twenty-two hours ago," he said abruptly. "The whole border area is under fire, tanks and artillery."

Liz felt as if a chasm had opened at her feet and she had just stepped into it. She could never save Safeya by driving her into the middle of a desert war being fought with biological and chemical weapons. She kept her face still, trying not to give him an inkling of the panic sweeping through her.

Abdullah opened a drawer, took out a map, spread it across the desk. "Look." He looked up, saw her standing in the middle of the room and beckoned impatiently. "Come. Look."

Liz went to the front of the desk, bent to look at the map. "Liz, you must come around to this side of the desk."

She stood beside him, leaned over the map. As she braced herself against the desk her arm felt too weak to hold her.

"Look." Abdullah placed a hand on the northeast. "This is known as the Anvil of Allah—a misnomer, we have no iron, no use for anvils. But it was named by Lawrence, the Englishman who liked to dress up as a Bedouin. It is deep desert, no minefields. You may run into American patrols there."

Liz heard his words with an excitement she was careful to hide. Hannah Stone's field hospital was somewhere in that area. Without taking her eyes from the map, she said, "Why are you telling me this?"

"Shall I say it is because I love you?"

She looked at him. "Then prove it by flying Princess Safeya out of the country. It would be so easy for you."

"That is something I cannot do—"

"Of course you can," Liz urged. "You got two infidels, one a woman, in and out of Mecca. You had the power to do that, this is much easier."

"Look at me." When she didn't move, he put his hands on her shoulders, turned her toward him. "What would you have me do? Kill the pilot and mechanics to keep their silence? Or perhaps have Prince Samir fly the plane—"

"Yes, why not?" His hands felt heavy on her shoulders, and she was careful not to step away, unsure of where this was going. If it secured Safeya's freedom, she would lie down here, now, on the carpet, open herself to him. "That's a great idea. Samir would be perfect."

Shaking his head, Abdullah took his hands from her shoulders. "You know so little. Already Prince Samir is humiliated because he is not with the Americans, fears they will think him a coward."

For a Saudi, loss of face was tantamount to loss of honor. Samir had to be in anguish. "So what? This is about a life, the life of an innocent girl."

"I cannot ask this of Prince Samir."

"Why not?" she demanded. "Why are his feelings more important than the life of this girl?"

Abdullah lifted a hand. "Stop! He is too deeply involved as it is."

"Why is he involved? There was no need for it."

"Be grateful that he is. Opposing his father is so foreign to everything in Samir's blood and culture, there is no frame of reference for him to even consider such a thing."

Liz opened her mouth to protest, to bring him back to Safaya, to her life or death.

Abdullah stopped her. "Listen to me. We Arabs have a saying, 'Paradise is beneath the feet of a mother.' Prince Samir is sacrificing his honor so that he can ensure *umm* Samir's life. Show respect for him, be grateful. Safeya's disappearance will cause grave consequences. As his father's only son, Samir's presence, his involvement with *umm* Samir, will be her protection. But, Liz," Abdullah dropped his voice to a quiet, more ominous tone, "the mother of Samir is not the mother of Abdullah. *Umm* Samir remains here in the kingdom. Her safety depends upon you."

Unwavering, Liz kept her eyes on him. He was keeping Fateema as a hostage.

"Why are you doing this, Abdullah?"

"I gave my support to the execution, but not to this," he said. "I have urged Prince Bandr to reconsider, to use the sword, but he will not now listen to my counsel."

He had spent an hour pleading with Bandr, explaining that such an ancient form of execution would infuriate the Americans—they were already queasy about the recent public beheadings. If their newspapers got wind of this, and they certainly would through the American doctor, it would be a public relations disaster. The argument had proven to be oil for the flame. There was nothing Bandr wanted more than to infuriate the Americans.

"Not one word to newspapers or television or magazines," Abdullah said. "You understand? Should a breath of this matter come to my ears, *umm* Samir will die in Safeya's place." He looked at her. "By the sword. You have my word on that, she will die. You understand?"

"I understand that you are keeping her hostage," Liz said. "What will happen to the other women? Riata and her family? They know nothing, they were out of their minds with grief."

Abdullah put a hand against Liz's cheek. "Riata will be banished but she will live. The others—" He shrugged, dismissing them as unimportant. "Nothing. If you were reasonable, none of this needed to concern you."

He put his hands on her waist, bent his head and brushed his lips against hers, feeling her body stiffen in resistance. His own flesh surged. Did she realize he could take her now with no one to stop him, or know, or even care?

He released her, folded the map and handed it to her. "When you are in your home in Santa Monica, think of this night. Remember that I have asked you to marry me. Send me a message and I will come. I think my actions prove that my feelings for you are deeper than you know."

Liz looked down at the map without taking it. "What if I don't get to Santa Monica, Abdullah? What if I'm caught?"

He shrugged. "We all are moving toward our destiny, Liz. Nothing can change it. Yours, like mine, is already written."

She had loved this man, lain in his arms, laughed with him, shared her heart. "You would not prevent Prince Bandr from ordering my death, is that it? A few questions easily answered, an official letter or two, you close ranks with your brother?"

Abdullah placed the map in her hand, curling her fingers around it. "You will reach safety, *insh'allah.*"

If God wills it.

Abdullah pressed a button beneath the desk. The door to the hall opened and Samir entered. Belle hovered in the doorway. The two men exchanged a few words in Arabic, then Abdullah turned to leave the room.

"Abdullah," Liz said. "Did you really try to find out who was behind Hisham Badawi's death?"

He turned. "No. It was important only to you. His destiny, too, had already been written. But as I promised, blood money was paid."

He opened the door that appeared to be a solid bookcase and was gone.

Liz shivered. The night air was cold, made colder still by the wind tossing the palm fronds. They had not passed through any gates, had not been challenged, so she knew they must still be inside the walls of Abdullah's compound.

Samir turned the Range Rover toward a single-story utility building, stopping tight against its wall. Beyond the building were rows of vehicles—trucks, vans, wheeled equipment of all kinds. He got out, abruptly signaling Liz to follow. He stopped by another parked Range Rover.

"This is equipped for long-distance desert driving, extra gas tanks. It will get you where you want to go, *insh'allah.*"

He opened the passenger door and Liz leaned in. A figure shrouded in black was slumped in the corner.

"Safeya?" No answer. Liz spoke to Samir. "Tell her to take off her veil so that I can see her face." She wanted no surprises, no Indonesian maid passed off for a princess. Samir spoke a few curt words, and the girl did as she was told. Her face was bruised and swollen, but it was Safeya. Satisfied, Liz straightened, turned to Samir.

"Samir, I want to thank you. I know how difficult this is for you—"

"You know nothing, *aznabi.*"

He turned, beckoned, and a tall heavy figure emerged from a doorway of the utility building. Belle rumbled a growl. Liz quieted her, and could have cried with relief when she saw the man's face, realizing it was Nassir, the former slave whom even Bandr trusted with the secrets of his past. The man at the gate, she knew suddenly, who'd protected her from the *mutawain.*

Without greeting her, or even looking in her direction, Nassir got behind the wheel. Liz urged Belle into the back of the Range Rover and climbed in after her. Samir slammed the door, the force of metal connecting with metal rocking the vehicle.

No one stopped them at the gate. Liz shrank into her corner, glad for the anonymity of the *abayah* and *gutwah,* and the voluminous black dress Samir had shoved into her arms and made her put on before leaving the house. Prayers were long over, but the usually crowded streets of Jeddah were deserted. A strange silence hung over the city. The rumor machine had been busy. Even without the news, everyone knew the ground war had started.

Nassir did not speak, and Liz was content to be silent, collecting her thoughts. Several times she glanced at Safeya but the girl seemed to be sleeping, and Liz wondered if she had been drugged.

They turned onto the freeway to Riyadh, weaving through the column of army vehicles in desert camouflage moving north. A few of the brightly colored Mercedes trucks that hauled goods throughout the kingdom kept pace with the column, the drivers happily exchanging shouted threats to Saddam. The number of private cars was minimal, a lot fewer than before the war started.

Lights and buildings gradually gave way to desert scrub, and Liz started to breathe for the first time since leaving Abdullah's compound. With the immediate danger receding, the problems she had pushed into the back of her mind now clamored for attention.

"Nassir, I think that Yousef could be a problem," she said. "I don't know who he works for. I was never able to find out, but he knows everything that happened in that house, who came, who went, when. I never trusted him."

"What is there to know?" Nassir replied. "Nothing. But be free of worry. Yousef was to watch to see that no harm came to you. He is to be trusted."

"What makes you think so?"

"He is the brother of my wife and he has many daughters. Allah has been good to me, and I have been able to assist him with dowries. Some daughters remain unmarried...they, too, will require dowries. He knows nothing."

"He worked for you?" Liz suppressed a mad urge to laugh, fearing she wouldn't be able to stop. "I never even considered that. I wish I'd known." She hesitated then said, "Nassir, are you armed?" She met his eyes in the rearview mirror, glanced at the girl slumped in the corner, then back at him. Understanding flashed between them. Safeya could not be taken alive. He nodded.

Liz leaned back. Sometime she would have to spell Nassir at the wheel, he could never make the entire journey. Now she had to rest....

The Range Rover braked, light and shadow alternating in the interior of the vehicle. Liz sat up, her heartbeat suddenly pounding in her ears. Ahead of them, army trucks formed a blockade across the freeway. The colorfully decorated Mercedes trucks jockeyed with the few private cars, inching forward.

"Identity cards!" she said, panicking. "Do you have them?"

"Those of my wife and one of my daughters, but pray that we do not have to show them. Keep veiled and silent. Cover the animal."

A small whimpering came from the other corner of the Range Rover, and Liz glanced over to see wide, terrified eyes above Safeya's veil. She took Safeya's hand, smiled reassuringly.

"Don't worry, we're going to be all right." Liz kept her voice low and soothing as she would with a frightened child. "I wish I could speak Arabic to tell you—"

"I speak English," Safeya whispered.

"Quiet," Nassir said softly. He reached behind him, closed the curtain between front and back seats.

Liz nudged the edge of the curtain back. The army trucks rumbled on; goods vehicles and civilian cars were being routed into different lanes. They were two car lengths from the blockade.

Nassir leaned his head out of the window to see what was happening, lit a cigarette and tossed the match: a citizen with nothing to hide. A century passed. Voices called back and forth. Someone laughed. Under the layers of cloth she was wearing, Liz could feel the sweat run down her body, and she knew that if she opened her mouth, her teeth would rattle against each other. She squeezed Safeya's hand and smiled at the frightened girl.

Then they were at the blockade, and gently Liz eased the curtain back into place. A few curt words, Nassir's helpful answers, then the engine picked up, regained speed, passing the lines of trucks rumbling north.

They were through.

Twice more during the night, army trucks blocked the road. Each time the soldier on duty waved them on without stopping, and in spite of herself and her fear of hoping for too much, Liz began to think it might work. She'd been right—they never stopped a man with his women behind drawn curtains in the back of the vehicle. But thank God for Nassir, she doubted she could have passed for a man, not without a beard, and she hadn't given that a thought.

Liz jerked upright and glanced at her watch. It was 4:00 a.m. She was instantly alert, every sense in high gear, a gift from fifty-hour stints of duty as a surgical resident. Safeya's head bumped uncomfortably against the window, but she did not stir.

"What's happening?" she asked Nassir. They had left the freeway.

"Another road block. Keep silent. It is not the army."

"Who is it?" The words crept past lips suddenly stiff with fear.

"The National Guard. There is a base here, at Unayzah."

"Unayzah! That's near Buraydah." The town where the Canadian women had been beaten by *mutawain*. Liz leaned forward, grabbing the back of Nassir's seat to steady herself, suddenly terrified. She stared at his reflection in the rearview, trying to read his eyes. His loyalty to Bandr went back deep into their boyhood—Fateema told her he served both houses, traveling with Abdullah because of his fluency in languages. "Why have you brought us this way?" she asked.

"Two roads only lead toward the Anvil, and the other is even closer to Unayzah than this one. They will know nothing yet. Princess Safeya's absence will not be discovered until after the dawn prayer, *insh'allah*. Keep silent."

Cold with sweat, Liz peered through the curtain. Safeya opened her eyes, and Liz took her hand, then put a finger to her own lips, commanding silence. Safeya's eyes widened, terror etching lines on her child's face.

The dark enclosed space was suddenly hot with fear, Belle's panting breath clearly audible. Liz put a hand over the saluki's mouth holding it closed. The outline of a male figure—*thobe* and *ghutra* instead of the sharp line of an army uniform—appeared against the curtains, slowly moving to the driver's side of the car. The voice was curt. Nassir protested, and was answered with a sharply raised voice that brooked no argument. Grumbling under his breath, a citizen unfairly delayed, Nassir drove the Range Rover out of the line of cars, stopped, killed the engine. He turned, barked a few words through the curtain.

Safeya put her mouth to Liz's ear. "He says we have to get out. They want to search us."

25

"How can they do that?" Liz breathed.

Safeya shook her head. Hands shaking, Liz pulled at Safeya's *abayah,* making sure she was totally covered, twitched at her *gutwah,* then adjusted her own. She bent and softly ordered Belle to stay, glad that Abdullah's dislike had forced her to take the time to train the saluki to immediate obedience.

Then Nassir was opening the passenger door.

Liz climbed over Safeya to be first out, her eyes taking in trucks, the vapor lights flooding the road, the darkness of the desert beyond. The air was filled with the sound of car engines revving impatiently; exhaust from the cars waiting to pass through the barrier wreathed upwards into blue clouds under the lights. Maybe they could run, weave through the cars, get into the desert—

Nassir spoke sharply in Arabic, and Liz could only guess it was a husband's instruction to hurry. Liz lowered her eyes submissively, turned to await Safeya climbing out of the Range Rover. Safeya, a dutiful second wife, nodded at Nassir's words, then started toward the edge of the road. Liz kept close, conscious of the automatic weapons slung casually over the shoulders of the National Guardsmen lounging by their vehicles, smoking, fingering worry beads.

A female voice called imperiously, and a large shrouded woman emerged from behind a black tarpaulin stretched be-

tween two posts along the side of the highway. She beckoned, calling again in Arabic.

"Egyptian," Safeya whispered. She picked up her pace,
and Liz held on to her arm as if she had difficulty walking.
Immediately, Safeya put an arm around her and together
they made their way across the road.

Chatting volubly, the woman hustled them behind the
tarp. A couple of hurricane lamps hung from the posts, casting a harsh but limited light. Safeya murmured a few words,
and the Egyptian clucked her tongue against her teeth,
barely pausing to take breath. Carelessly, she ran her hands
down Liz's body, then turned and did the same to Safeya.
She gestured to the veils, and Liz pulled hers aside. Then
Safeya uncovered her face, revealing bruises that had deepened to violent color, purple and green, the edges already
turning yellow. Shaking her head, the Egyptian drew Safeya
closer to a lamp, took her chin, and turned her face from
side to side. She rattled off a stream of rapid Arabic.

Safeya started to answer, but the woman held up a hand
to silence her, and turned to Liz. Her questions had been
addressed to Liz, and it was from Liz she wanted a reply.
Her voice louder, she repeated her words, frowning, her eyes
darting from Liz to Safeya and back.

Safeya was visibly shaking. Liz reached a hand to her
and the girl moved closer until Liz could lean against her
as if she needed support to stand, hoping the Egyptian would
see that any conversation was beyond her. For an interminable moment, no one spoke. Then Safeya, voice barely
discernible, broke the silence with a few stumbling sentences.

Her scowl deeper, heavy dark brows drawn together over
her prominent nose, the woman gestured abruptly to them
to wait, then adjusted her *gutwah* and disappeared around
the edge of the tarpaulin. The sound of male voices stopped

as if cut off in midword, and only the female voice could be heard.

Liz grabbed Safeya's arm, tried to drag her toward the open desert. "We'll make a run—"

Safeya was rooted, lost in her terror.

"Safeya, they're coming for us! You have to move!"

The crunch of feet could be heard just beyond the tarpaulin. Liz pushed Safeya behind her. A hot wave of adrenaline pumped through her body. If it was now, she would not make it easy for them. The tarpaulin swung back, the Egyptian reappeared.

She was alone.

Liz felt the feigned weakness become reality as adrenaline drained from her bloodstream. She raised a hand to cover her mouth so that the Egyptian would not see her lips shake, but her hand shook as violently, and quickly she tucked both hands away in the folds of the ugly black dress.

The woman clucked her tongue against her teeth, her head bobbing from side to side while she unscrewed the top from a small yellow tube. She pushed Safeya toward a lantern, then squeezed a liberal amount of cream onto a grubby finger. She took Safeya's chin and gently smeared her finger across the bruises, then replaced the cap and pressed the tube into her hand. She patted Safeya's shoulder, stared at Liz, then waved a dismissal.

Liz held the girl's arm, forcing them to walk slowly toward the Range Rover. Three of the Guardsmen, shaggy beards henna-stained, watched every step, making no attempt to disguise their scrutiny.

Belle's tail thumped a welcome against the floor. The dark interior of the Range Rover gave an illusion of safety, but no one spoke until Nassir had swerved back onto the road and the lights of the roadblock were fading into the distance behind them.

Liz took several deep breaths, a hand on Belle's head.

"Thank God they didn't search the car, too. What were they looking for?" she asked Nassir. "I've never heard of women being subject to that kind of treatment at a roadblock, only at airports."

"They said they're searching to see that Iraqi terrorists are not lurking under the veil." Nassir sought Liz's eyes in the rearview mirror, raising his eyebrows in silent suspicion. "That is what they said," he repeated.

Liz tore her eyes from his, picked up Safeya's hand and squeezed it. "You were very good with that woman. What did you say to her?"

"I said that you were my mother and you had just miscarried. Then I said you were too frightened to speak, that I had refused the husband my father had chosen for me which was why I had bruises."

"That was quick thinking." Thank God for the resiliency of youth. Safeya hadn't been drugged, merely scared to death—her brain was working just fine. All the same, the Egyptian had drawn attention to them. They had not passed anonymously through that roadblock.

From the front seat, Nassir said, "Egyptians! They don't know how to behave. She demanded medicine from their medical kit, and would not leave until they gave it to her." He clicked his tongue in disapproval, then said, "We shall be off this highway before dawn, then we cross the desert to the northeast. There will be no more roadblocks, *insh'allah.*"

If God wills it. But Prince Bandr would tear them out of the desert with his bare hands rather than let them escape his concept of justice.

The eastern sky was opalescent when they turned into a tiny gas station, just two pumps and a vending machine for bottled water. They had decided it was worth the stop—

using the auxiliary gas tanks was not wise with the Anvil still to be crossed.

Liz lifted the curtain an inch, watching Nassir stretch while he spoke to the skinny Indian pumping the gas. A battered Toyota pickup drove in, a camel couched in the back, and two gray-bearded Saudis got out, exchanging greetings with Nassir and the attendant. Nassir counted out a handful of crumpled *riyals* into the Indian's palm—not many as gasoline cost less than bottled water—then he held up a hand in farewell to the men with the camel and started to climb back into the Range Rover.

The tinny recorded voice of a *muezzin* sounded and re-sounded, calling the dawn prayer. Nassir hesitated, then got behind the wheel, slipping the Range Rover into gear. "I must join my brothers for the dawn prayer," he said in a voice only just audible. "Not to do so would raise suspicion, but keep silent. I have told them I travel alone."

He parked out of the way of the gas pump, got out and took his turn at the trickle of water from a hose to rinse his face, nostrils, ears and hands. He slipped out of his sandals to wash his feet, then joined the other men at the side of the road for the dawn prayer. Twenty minutes later, prayers over, he climbed behind the wheel, drove leisurely on to the small road.

Liz stole a glance out of the rear window. As the Indian pumped gas into the Toyota, the two Saudis stood at the edge of the road, staring after the retreating Range Rover.

"Can they read?" Liz asked. "Will they know the license plate is not from this province?"

"They are old men, *Wahhabis*. It is unlikely that they can read, but this is the fundamentalist stronghold of the country. They know that I am a stranger."

Gradually the gas station dropped into the distance and he increased speed.

It had been a long arduous night and no one spoke. The

heat was already rising uncomfortably. Then Safeya nudged Liz's arm, whispering a request. The girl was pale, and Liz leaned forward.

"Nassir, we must find a place to stop soon. You understand?"

Nassir switched on the air-conditioning. "In an hour we leave this road to start across the desert," he said. "Then we will rest until nightfall. A vehicle crossing in the heat of the day will not go unnoticed. But here it is impossible to stop."

The hour dragged by, then Nassir swung onto a goat track that intersected with the paved road. Immediately dust rose, filtering into the Range Rover. The smell of drying sweat and the odor of the dog filled the enclosed space, and every bump under the wheels was agony to bladders unrelieved for more than twelve hours.

The sandy terrain started to break up and shallow channels appeared in the surface of the desert. Nassir turned off the track into a small gully.

"We stay here until the heat has passed."

"Are we safe?" Liz asked. She already knew what he would say, and if she'd had the spirit left, would have smiled when he proved her right.

He shrugged and said, "*Insh'allah.*"

A goat nosed at her feet and started to nibble at the fabric of the hot black dress. Liz struggled upright, every bone aching, her mouth foul and dry. Belle lay motionless by her side, her eyes riveted upon a point beyond Liz's right shoulder. Liz looked around. Fifty feet behind her were three Bedouins, two men hunkered in the rocky shale, and beyond them a woman, standing, surrounded by a scattered flock of black goats.

On the other side of the vehicle, Nassir called a greeting to the Bedouins and got to his feet. He barked a command at Safeya, sleeping like the dead in the darkest spot of shade thrown by the vehicle, then, nudging Liz with a sandaled foot as if to rouse her into action, he passed to speak to the two men.

Liz grabbed her veil, covered her face and the chopped remnants of her hair, then picked up the thermos of water. She nodded wordlessly at Safeya to get into the Range Rover, then went around to the far door out of sight of the Bedouin before climbing in herself, with some confused idea that they would not see Belle jump in after her.

Liz looked at the sky streaked with red, the dying sun reflected from the base of a bank of black cloud. The hour of Safeya's execution was now long past. Without any doubt Prince Bandr knew she had escaped him. Liz sent a prayer toward Fateema, then turned her thoughts away, but not before thanking God for Samir's love for the woman who bore them both.

Nassir hunkered down with the two Bedouin, accepted a handful of dates and a chipped white enamel cup filled with water. Ten minutes passed in conversation, the woman waiting patiently thirty feet behind them. Then he rose and returned to the Range Rover.

"I told them I was on my way to see kinsmen, but they are suspicious."

The goats scrambled leisurely out of the way as Nassir backed out of the gully. He called a farewell to the Bedouin, then returned to the track that led into the Anvil, and beyond that to safety.

Insh'allah.

They drove without stopping for the last prayer of the day. The sky darkened into night. Liz gave Safeya some Tylenol for cramping pain, and the girl dropped into a restless doze. Liz found herself drifting into a fugue state, not quite awake, not asleep, the desert mesmerizing in its monotony. Nassir must be exhausted, she thought, she should have insisted on driving at least for the first part of the night....

The Range Rover slid, the shale beneath the wheels moving as the vehicle surged forward.

"Nassir, what is it?"

The headlights picked out a landscape riddled with *wadis,* broad fissures carved out by the rush of ancient floodwaters, eight and ten feet below grade, with sheer walls of ocher rock that made Liz think of the Navajo country of Arizona and Nevada.

Nassir kept a heavy foot on the gas. "We've picked up headlights. I don't trust them—"

Liz looked out of the rear window. Two sets, following across the desert. "How long have they been there?"

"Moments only. But they are driving very fast and will soon overtake us."

"They could be Bedouin on their way back to their tents—"

"We shall see." Nassir spun the wheel hard, taking the Range Rover over the shallow edge of the *wadi.* The vehicle tipped, dropped precipitously, then righted itself on the rock-strewn floor of the streambed, hidden from any pursuer by the rocky walls. He killed the headlights. The moon was in its final phase, but the stars threw a tenuous light, enough to avoid collision with the sheer walls closing in on each side.

Safeya sat up, her voice panicky as she called out to Nassir. In English he said, "Maybe nothing. Maybe Bandr's people." He spoke to Liz. "There is a compartment beneath your feet. Uncover it."

Liz pulled up the carpet, tugged at the small ring set into the floor. A panel gave way revealing a fitted compartment—a small arsenal of handguns, machine pistols, silencers. She picked up an AK-47, slammed a clip home with the heel of her hand, then handed it across the back of the seat to Nassir.

Suddenly headlights played on the walls of the *wadi,* piercing the Range Rover, holding them in the glare like bugs on a pin. They had been followed into the maze of watercourses.

"Not Bedu," Nassir said. The Range Rover leapt forward.

"How could they have found us so soon?" Liz asked, panicked.

"Who knows? The Bedouins gossiped with the National Guard at the road block, and the Guard questioned the Egyptian? Who knows?"

A stream of bullets kicked up fountains of pulverized shale ten feet behind their rear wheels. The gunmen found their range and the back window exploded, then the windshield. Nassir grunted, and the Range Rover veered sharply to the right, then straightened. He tossed the AK-47 across the seat to Liz. "Fire! Fire at them!" he shouted.

Liz shoved the glass-covered saluki closer to the floor, then threw herself across Safeya, screaming at her, "Get down, get down." She pushed the stub nose of the gun out of the shattered rear window, pointed it toward the pursuers, and pulled the trigger, sweeping the weapon from side to side in the way she had seen on television.

Behind them, a small Jeep swerved, then slid into the rock wall of the *wadi.* Overcompensating, it fishtailed against the opposite wall, the motion deepening with every swerve as the driver fought the wheel. The vehicle behind it jammed on its brakes, barely avoiding collision.

Driving without lights, Nassir jerked the Range Rover into a short hard turn, then another and another, the scream of metal scraping rock adding to the cacophony of gunfire and roaring engines. The noise bounced from wall to rock wall, reverberating through the connecting watercourses, until it seemed to fill the night, a blessing and a curse—they could hide beneath the blanket of sound, but so, too, could their pursuers.

"Can you get out of here?" A nightmare vision rose in Liz's mind: trapped in a labyrinth of gullies, its walls becoming deeper and narrower.

The Range Rover grated along the wall of the *wadi*, trailing fountains of sparks, then failed to make a turn and slammed to a stop.

"Nassir! Go on! Go on! What is it?" He didn't answer.

Liz's door was too tight against the rock, she had to clamber over Safeya to get out. The gun still in her hand, she wrenched Nassir's door open. "Nassir! Are you hurt?"

For a second the Saudi sat motionless, both hands on the wheel, staring through the splintered windshield. Then slowly, his body crumpled like a doll with the sawdust draining from its limbs.

The engine was roaring and Liz reached across Nassir to turn off the ignition, praying to hear silence. Instead their pursuers seemed closer.

"Safeya! Quickly!" Liz heard the edge of panic in her voice. They couldn't stay where they were, the dark green Range Rover was a cutout against the light-colored wall of the *wadi*. "We have to move him. Get into the front."

Safeya climbed over the back of the passenger seat. "Is he hurt?" Her voice broke into small whimpers.

"Pull him! Pull him toward you!"

Liz pushed at the heavy body. The noise from their pursuers was deafening, coming from everywhere, nowhere, vibrating from wall to wall in the narrow watercourses. Between them, somehow they got Nassir into the passenger seat, panic lending them strength they didn't have.

Liz slid behind the wheel, shouted to Safeya. "Hold him!" She turned on the ignition, gave a short prayer of thanks when the engine fired the first time, then turned the wheel, jamming a foot on the gas. The Range Rover careened forward. She could see clearly even without the headlights—dawn was breaking, the sun edging into the sky. They had to get into hiding, she knew. She couldn't hope to outrun the men hunting them. She turned, then again, taking every turn she could, until the stone walls pressed in, and she barely had room to keep the vehicle scraping forward.

A declivity appeared in the wall ahead, a rock fall that had left an overhang, not much but something. Then suddenly there were more, a number of them deepening into caves hollowed out by the force of water that raged through the *wadis* during the rare but torrential rains of the desert.

An opening appeared, large enough for the Range Rover to enter and she took it, blinded by the sudden darkness of a cave that was low but very deep. She turned off the engine and for a second sat, ears straining for the sound of their pursuers. She heard only silence. Could they have stopped for the dawn prayer? Or to listen? She had no hope they'd given up the hunt, but the noise was no longer vibrating through the maze of the *wadi*. They had breathing room, a little time at least to give Nassir attention. She reached over to slip her hand beneath the *ghutra* wrapped around his face and throat, feeling for the carotid pulse.

He was cool, and her fingers slid on his blood.

Liz got out of the Range Rover, remembering the first time she had seen him, that night at the Beverly Hills Hotel, standing regally behind Prince Abdullah. She thought of Fateema, the love of his life.

"Is he hurt?" Safeya had climbed out and stood uncertainly peering at Nassir.

"Nassir is dead."

Safeya's voice rose, giving wordless tongue to grief and fear, sounding like her mother and her aunts, her cousins.

She swayed, tore at already bruised breasts, her eyes rolling in their sockets.

Liz grabbed Safeya's shoulders, forcibly turning her so that she couldn't see Nassir's body, then shook her. "Stop it! Safeya!" A dead man, a hysterical girl, hunted like animals in an alien landscape—she couldn't do this. "Stop this noise." Liz shook the girl harder, fighting the hysteria, fighting, too, her own fear. "Stop it!"

Safeya opened her eyes, shaking, panting through her open mouth, but silent and cognizant.

"There is no time for this now," Liz said urgently. "We have to concentrate on getting away. We can do it, but we have to stay calm." Liz spoke with a confidence she did not feel. "We'll stay here for—"

"We must bury him," Safeya said.

Engines had started up again, the sound drifting, hard to pinpoint as if deflected by the maze of gullies. They could be in the next canyon, or searching miles away.

"He must be buried by sundown," Safeya said. "It is our way."

In the *wadi* outside, heat already rose in wavering lines, and fingers of sun were feeling their way into the shadow of the cave, their only refuge until Liz could figure out what to do. How to do it. Before long, the temperature would be 120 degrees in the shade, maybe more. There were good reasons for the Muslim custom.

"Yes. You're right," she said. "Help me."

Liz got into the Range Rover, for the first time realizing that the black dress she wore was heavy with Nassir's blood and clung to her legs with every movement. She took his shoulders, struggled to drag him across the seat. His *ghutra* caught on the wheel, slipping drunkenly across his face, and Liz removed it, anxious to maintain his dignity even in death. His hair was a grizzled nap, and without the *ghutra*, suddenly he looked younger.

Between them they dragged him out of the Range Rover. Liz straightened his limbs, rigor had not yet set in, then gently wrapped his head in her *abayah,* the one that Fateema had given her—he'd like that, she thought.

The floor of the cave was hard, impenetrable, deep in animal droppings—goats, camels, sheep—and patches of what looked to be dried human excrement.

"Get rocks, large ones," Liz said to the girl. "We can't dig, we haven't time, and there's nothing to dig with, anyway. Keep listening for their engines, we mustn't let them sneak up on us."

They dragged the body deeper into the cave. Liz changed into Yousef's *thobe*—she'd put it into her medical bag after Samir made her change—and used the black dress to clear a patch of ground of animal droppings. They braced his head with large stones, one on either side, then slowly, painfully, covered his body. Finally, Liz uncovered his face. She paused, gave thanks for what he had done for them, then rewrapped his head in the black *abayah* that still bore the fragrance of the woman he had loved so dangerously and for so long. Then gently she lowered the last stones in place.

When she got home—if she got home—she'd let Abdullah know where he lay.

Safeya murmured words from the Koran over Nassir's resting place, then collapsed against the rear wall of the cave. A few feet from her, Liz leaned back, legs spread in an effort to find what coolness there was, her breath shallow.

The sun was approaching its zenith, the temperature inside the cave barely tolerable, and outside the relentless white light drained the world—sky, rock, sand—of color and sound. The hunters were at the noon prayer now, Liz thought, but then they'd wait, listening for the sound of the Range Rover starting up.

The stone cairn over Nassir was the best they could do, but it wasn't adequate. Before long, the stench of putrefying flesh would start to escape from the grave.

They had to get out of here. And silently. But how?

26

Liz crawled to her feet. Something had to be done. Safeya was drifting into despair—even in the punishing heat she turned her head away from the water Liz held to her lips and remained curled into the fetal position against the sloping wall of the cave. And Belle had had no food, she'd merely nosed the dates Liz had offered her. Since leaving Jeddah, she'd had nothing but a few cups of water.

The *wadis* had to lead to an oasis. If she could get a rough idea of their position, she might find a way to American lines. It was their only chance.

Liz climbed into the Range Rover, stretched across the seat that was stiff with Nassir's blood and searched the glove compartment for maps. There had to be at least the one that Abdullah had given her. Then the steering wheel started to vibrate against her ribs, increasing rapidly until it was hammering her body.

A Californian, she knew instantly. Earthquake.

Liz grabbed the wheel, tongue cleaving to the roof of her mouth, heart pounding with the primitive fear of the uncontrollable earth. She started to back out. The Range Rover was dancing a mad fandango, and the belt Safeya had given her to hoist Yousef's *thobe* to a wearable length caught on the gear. Panicked, Liz fought to free herself, dislodging the Beretta she had thrust into the belt. She grabbed at it, shoved it back—no matter what happened, she had to stay armed.

The entire cave was shaking, dust and chunks of sandstone falling from the roof. Through the grinding rumble of moving rock, Liz could hear Belle howl.

Somehow she got to Safeya, the girl's mouth wide, her screams lost in the increasing roar, and dragged her out into the murderous heat of the *wadi,* a maelstrom of swirling dust and thunderous noise, the air throbbing with shock waves.

But not an earthquake, she realized. Low-flying jets sweeping through the sky just above them.

The United States Air Force.

Dragging Safeya with her, Liz raced back into the murk and din of the dust-filled cave. She threw open the door of the Range Rover, shoved Safeya in—Belle needed no urging—then grabbed up their meager supplies, a gallon thermos of water, some dates. Fingers shaking, Liz turned the key in the ignition, the sound mercifully lost in the roar overhead, backed out of the shaking cave, ramming into the wall of the *wadi.* Cursing out loud, she crashed into first, twisted the wheel, pushed on the gas as hard as she dared, the rock walls barely inches away from the Range Rover as it moved forward. Each time she had a choice, she turned toward the northeast, toward the Anvil of Allah, the direction from which the jets, already faded into the south, had come.

Every few minutes she had Safeya put her head out of the window to listen. Each time, the girl shook her head. No sound of pursuit. Liz watched for signs of water to give her a direction to an oasis, but there was nothing—no hint of moisture in the air, no green threads of hardy saltbush, no camels grazing.

An hour later, the watercourses were wider, the walls shallower and they were out of the system of *wadis.*

A leaden despair filled the Range Rover.

Against all odds, they had stumbled out of the maze—

only to find themselves surrounded in every direction by a barren trackless world of sweeping dunes of golden sand.

The Anvil of Allah.

The engine sputtered, died. The depth of the silence was a palpable presence. No sound, no smell. Nothing but a vast terrifying emptiness.

Liz glanced at Safeya, knew the horror in the girl's eyes mirrored the horror in her own.

"Abdullah said the Americans patrol this desert regularly," Liz said. Her voice was lost in the immensity of their surroundings. "We'll find them."

"I think Prince Abdullah intended that we die out here," Safeya whispered. "My shame would die with me and no one would know of it. His hands would be clean of my death." She looked up. "And of yours."

Liz fought the urge to rest her head on the steering wheel and howl like a dying beast. "Well, that's a thought."

"I want to thank you," Safeya said. "You have given your life for me—"

"Not yet, I haven't," Liz said grimly. She twisted off the cap on the thermos jug, poured half a cup of water and handed it to Safeya. The girl drank, an improvement—action, any action, was better than lying down waiting for death. "We'll keep going. Northeast."

Liz poured water for herself, allowing it to trickle into her parched throat. She hesitated, then gave the same amount to Belle, holding the cup so that the Saluki would get every precious drop. She screwed the cap back on the thermos as tightly as she could to prevent evaporation, stowed it out of the reach of the sun, then smiled with as much reassurance as she could manage. "Don't worry. Sooner or later, we'll get to a border." Or die in the attempt—the most likely end to this journey, a fear she kept to herself.

"But we have no gasoline—"

"Yes, we do. I forgot to switch on the auxiliary tank, that's all."

She put the Range Rover into four-wheel drive and made her way carefully across the packed sand, threading through the sand dunes, keeping an eye on the sun to keep them on course. Silently, she feared that Safeya was right, that Abdullah had pointed them into the deep desert so they could meet their goddamn destiny.

The thought of Nassir kept her sane. Nassir, who had loved her mother so devotedly, would never have been a party to that.

If he'd known.

Wavering in the heat, towering hills of sand stretched in every direction. Liz drove with the *thobe* hiked to her thighs, parched eyes narrowed against the sun and the rush of searing air pouring through the smashed windshield.

At three, she stopped in the shadow of a dune that rose above them for a hundred feet, and turned off the engine. Nothing in the landscape had changed. It looked as if they were back exactly where they had started, but they couldn't be. The sand dunes were pristine, no tire tracks. No vehicles had passed this way. Their own, or any others.

So, she must have been mistaken.

For the past several minutes, she'd thought she was hearing a sound coming out of the great, deep silence.

Safeya opened her eyes. She looked close to death. Weight had dropped from her already fragile body, and in spite of the salve Liz had applied, her lips were cracked and bleeding. In a face drained of all color, the bruises were livid, her dark eyes red-rimmed and bloodshot.

"What is it?" Safeya said.

"Nothing. I just need a break."

Nausea swept through Liz in waves, without the cold sweat that usually accompanied sickness. Dehydration, she thought, and exhaustion. She was beyond hunger. Safeya

had to feel even worse, raped and traumatized as she had
been before this nightmare journey had started. Liz poured
water, handed the cup to Safeya. "Drink slowly, then eat
some dates. You need the sugar."

She heard it again. A distant hum.

Heart lurching unsteadily, she fumbled with the ignition,
swollen fingers refusing to obey. To a Western eye, one
sand dune might look like another, but Bedouins could read
these dunes like a city street, see tracks in the faintest shift
of sand.

Safeya tried to sit up, almost too weak for the effort. "I
hear engines."

"Let's hope it's Americans." Liz glanced at the AK-47
she had already loaded and placed on the seat beside her
with an extra clip, then checked the Beretta in her belt.
"Safeya, hold on to Belle. She's frightened."

A roar swept from the southeast, increasing, deafening,
drowning all other sound. The jets, low over the dunes, returning to base. Lightheaded, suddenly elated at the sight of
American planes, Liz shielded her eyes to watch until they
faded into the immense blue sky. She pressed a foot on the
gas, following them.

She turned to smile at Safeya. Over the girl's shoulder
she caught movement at the top of the wall of sand above
them, a vibration, then a break along the edge. As if in slow
motion, sand ran down the face of the wall, gathering volume and force—a trickle, a slide, an avalanche.

Liz gunned the engine. Then they were slipping, slipping,
riding a wave of sand as the side of the dune collapsed.

Liz opened her eyes. The sky was darkening, a deep-blue
still streaked with pink. She put a hand to her face and found
it sticky with blood. Exploring gently, she discovered a cut
in her scalp. It had stopped bleeding so she must have been
out for some time—either that or sand had clogged the

wound. Gingerly, she turned her head from side to side. No neck injury. Her body was intact. No bones broken.

But why was she lying in the sand?

The sound of a groan reached her and everything came back. Safeya. She had survived—they must have been thrown clear. Liz sat up, fighting nausea, every muscle in her body screaming protest. She crawled toward the sound, her legs hampered by the *thobe,* the automatic in her belt pressing painfully against her bruised belly. She came to the thermos jug, half buried, and she pulled it free. It was cracked, its precious contents leaking into the sand.

Safeya was a small heap of black about ten feet from the Range Rover. Her eyes were open, she was dazed but conscious. Liz ran her hands over the girl's limbs, relieved to find her bones intact—even if she could find it, the medical kit contained no splints.

The girl's whisper sounded like paper rustling in the stillness. Liz lowered her ear closer to Safeya's lips.

"Are we there?"

There. She meant safe. "Not yet," Liz said. "We overturned, but the Range Rover must have rolled, it's upright now. We'll get it started as soon as you can move." If the keys were not buried, if the engine wasn't clogged with sand, if the gas tank hadn't ruptured. "Here." She held the last of their precious water to Safeya's lips. "Do you hurt anywhere?"

"I think I am just shaken."

Liz looked around for Belle, but she was gone. Sadness gripped her. No way could Belle survive alone in this desert. Liz hoped that death would claim her quickly, if it hadn't already. Grief would have to come later—if they lived. Right now she had to get them both through the night, hypothermia was a real threat and tomorrow, without water, the sun could kill them. There was no shelter among these dunes.

Or Bandr's men could find them first.

"Can you stand?" she asked Safeya.

The girl nodded, and Liz helped her to her feet. She swayed, then got her balance. Tears had dried, leaving streaks on her bruised, grimy face. She looked like a child who had been beaten.

"I wish Fateema were here," Safeya said. "What will happen to her?"

"Nothing. Don't worry about her." Liz felt her own throat tighten. "Prince Samir will protect her."

Incredibly, the keys were still in the ignition. Liz scooped out as much sand as she could, closed the door gently on Safeya, fearful of starting another avalanche, then slid behind the wheel. With luck they could make a few more miles before it became too dark—she couldn't risk turning on the headlights.

Safeya grabbed Liz's arm, eyes wide. "Listen! Listen!"

Liz held her body motionless, not breathing, straining to hear. The sound was clear in the thin silence, and getting louder. This time it wasn't American jets.

A small Jeep rounded the base of the dune, traveling fast on the packed sand untouched by the avalanche. Another followed.

The men in them wore khaki *thobes,* red-and-white checked *ghutras.*

Frantically Liz turned the key in the ignition. The engine ground, turned over without catching.

"Come on, come on!" She slammed her foot against the accelerator, again and again. The engine ground uselessly and the stink of gasoline filled the vehicle.

Safeya's eyes bulged with terror. She clutched Liz's arm. "Don't let them take me—"

Liz dragged the hysterical girl out of the vehicle, shoved her down behind the front wheel, then knelt in front of her. She took the Beretta out of her belt.

Both Jeeps stopped. A bearded figure climbed out of the passenger seat of the lead vehicle and stood behind the open door. His English was heavily accented but clear.

"Dr. Ryan. Safeya bint Bandr must be returned to her father's house. No harm will come to you, Dr. Ryan, you are free to leave the country."

Like hell no harm would come to her. Liz shot a quick glance up at the wound in the sand dune, then holding the Beretta with both hands she aimed at the lead Jeep and fired.

And missed.

Men leapt out of both vehicles, crouching in the sand.

Six. Jesus, Liz thought. Six men.

A spray of bullets struck the Range Rover. Cautiously, Liz reached across the seat, dragged the AK-47 toward her, and the extra clip. Another burst kicked up sand well short of the Range Rover. A different gunman. A slow stream of sand at the edge of the avalanche moved twenty feet, then stopped.

Safeya fell to her knees, her voice dagger thin, a keening polyglot of Arabic and English. "I want to die...kill me...."

Liz shoved a hand over the girl's mouth to quiet her. Another burst of fire and the Range Rover sank onto its rims, the tires shredded.

Bandr had won, Liz thought. They were not going to survive this.

She stood, arced a burst from the AK-47. A man screamed. He staggered to his feet, his hands clutching his belly, his life's blood spreading across the front of his *thobe*. He collapsed against the Jeep and hung there, his *thobe* caught on the door. Liz thought she had to be weeping, her lashes were sticky with tears that dried in the heat before they could fall.

The rustle of moving sand was clearly audible in the silence following the gunfire. Liz could hear the voices of the men—they were planning something—and she replaced the clip. Then two of the men were running, firing as they raced toward the Range Rover.

Suddenly she couldn't draw breath, in the same instant found herself on her back in the sand, and knew she had been hit. She felt nothing, no pain.... Struggling to her knees, she fired at the running men, praying she could cut them down, then saw them fall.

Safeya's screams broke through the gunfire. She pulled at Liz's hand, trying to turn the gun toward her own head. "Kill me...you must...kill me...they're coming for me...."

Liz could feel the edges of her vision clouding, knew she was slipping into darkness. If she was going to do it, she could wait no longer. Three men still lived....

She dropped the AK to the sand, grabbed the Beretta, placed it against Safeya's temple. She could hear herself sobbing.

Dear God, she was a doctor, she'd vowed to protect life. How had she come to this?

27

"What the fuck's that?" Corporal Andy Ruiz focused his glasses on a spot in the desert. "You see that, Marty?"

Sergeant Martin Uhlmeyer raised his own glasses. "Yeah."

"Give it a burst—"

Uhlmeyer raised his M-16, sighted, frowned. He lowered the weapon. "No, wait a minute—"

"Bullshit, man. That's some Iraqi out there."

"Christ's sake, Ruiz. We're miles from the fucking Iraqis."

"Yeah, well, like to see you tell that to my old lady when they ship me back in a body bag."

"Get closer," Uhlmeyer said.

"No way—"

"Jesus, Andy. Get closer. It's a dog."

"Man, that ain't no dog. What the fuck's a dog doing out in sandland?"

"I tell you it's a dog."

"Who gives a shit, man? If that's a dog, you bet your ass some fucking Iraqi got it booby-trapped—"

"Jesus! Slow down. I'm going to check it out—"

"Man, you crazy?"

Sergeant Uhlmeyer looked at his driver in disgust. "Don't you got no dogs where you come from, Andy?"

"What you think, man, we got no culture? Sure we got

dogs. My barrio's full of fucking dogs. Pit bulls. And no one mess with them, man—"

"Well, that's no pit bull out there," Uhlmeyer said. "That's some kind of hound, a hunting dog. Cover me. I'm gonna check."

"Jesus, Marty, you're one crazy motherfucker, you know that, man? Fucking dog—"

Sergeant Martin Uhlmeyer of Tonville, Wisconsin, opened the door of the humvee, jumped down onto the sand, his M-16 ready. Cautiously, he walked toward the dog.

"Hey, boy. Come on. What's the matter, you thirsty?"

The dog got up, moved away.

"It's okay, buddy, come on," he said soothingly. "I got water here. You want water?"

The dog stood waiting until Uhlmeyer got within twenty feet, then moved away, looking back. Uhlmeyer followed warily, eyes checking every foot of ground, although this area was supposed to be clear of mines. The dog moved on, staying out of reach, watching to see if Uhlmeyer followed.

"Hey, Andy, he's trying to tell us something."

"Nothing I want to hear, man." Corporal Andy Ruiz of East Los Angeles, California, kept the humvee moving slowly, following his colleague, eyeing the dunes for signs of ambush.

The sound of scattered gunfire blasted through the silence of the desert. Ruiz thrust his head out of the window to shout a warning, but Uhlmeyer was already racing back to the humvee. He jumped aboard the moving vehicle. "Go, go, go, go, go."

Ruiz swung the humvee around the base of the dunes. "Who the hell else is in this sector?"

"We're it."

"Shit! Then who's firing?"

"Not our guys. Sounds like a private firefight."

"Jesus, man, we don't want to get ourselves stuck in the middle of some fucking Arab gangbangers' turf war."

"Get us to the top of that dune," Uhlmeyer said. "Sounds as if the action's right on the other side."

Ruiz put the humvee at the dune. The vehicle chewed the sand, stopping at the top. Below them the scene was spread like a tableau, a fight between toy soldiers.

"Jesus, Marty, that's a woman. Look at that."

"They sure as shit ain't getting out of there in that vehicle. That mother's history."

"Christ, he's going to blow her away! Look at that! Jesus, Marty! Put one over his head—"

Sergeant Uhlmeyer loosed a prolonged burst. Ruiz poured on the gas, taking the humvee over the top of the dune, down toward the tiny figures below, muttering curses as the humvee slid, fighting to maintain control. "*Madre de Dios! We're slipping!*"

Under the wheels, the sand was giving way.

Gunfire was coming from another direction, Liz realized, from the top of the dune, above Bandr's men. She looked up. A humvee, sliding, a plume of sand rising behind it. Fighting the darkness driving the edges of her vision ever closer, she lowered the Beretta from Safeya's head.

"They're ours! Safeya, they're Americans!" Using the Range Rover for leverage, Liz pulled herself to her feet, the Beretta still clutched in one hand, ducking as a burst of fire from Prince Bandr's men fell short. Then bullets were arcing erratically, smacking into the sand, striking the Range Rover as the gunmen turned to look behind them at the humvee and saw instead the sand, moving, gathering speed.

Liz pulled Safeya to her feet, screaming at her to move, move. Holding the girl's arm, she started to run, dragging Safeya with her.

The men from the Jeeps threw down their weapons, tried

to escape. Too late. The sand moved on, tipped each vehicle, poured around, over, in them. Sand caught the legs of the running men like mud, slowing them, immobilizing them. One by one, the men went down, and the sand moved onward mercilessly. Gradually, the thunder slowed to a rustling movement, then came to a stop. The surface of the sand settled smoothly as if the men buried beneath it had never been.

Safeya fell, a dead weight too heavy for Liz to drag upright. She turned, searching for the humvee, saw it emerging like a mirage, slowly taking form in the cloud of dust. She waved, shouted.

"I'm an American—"

A burst of fire answered her—she felt her hair move as bullets passed low over her head.

"Drop your weapons," a voice commanded. "Raise both hands."

Liz opened her hand, allowing the Beretta to drop to the sand. "I'm an American—"

"Okay. Keep your hands up."

"That's a woman dressed in one of those nightshirts," Ruiz said. "Marty, Jesus, that's not a guy, it's a woman, two women."

"Who the fuck are the other guys""

"Dead meat, man, whoever." Ruiz wrapped both arms around the wheel, shaken in spite of himself. "Fucking sand just rolled over 'em, man. Just rolled on over. Jesus."

"Cover me." Uhlmeyer jumped out, crouched by the wing of the humvee.

Liz supported Safeya, slumped against her legs. "I'm an American doctor," she called, her voice a croak. Her strength was going fast and Safeya seemed beyond effort. "Dr. Elizabeth Ryan, from Los Angeles, California."

"Hey, I'm from L.A." Corporal Ruiz put the engine into

idle, climbed out. Cautiously, the two Marines advanced, weapons ready, eyes sweeping from side to side.

"Hey, guys. Are we glad to see you. Do you have any water? Safeya." Liz stroked the girl's head. "It's okay. You're safe. We've done it. We're both safe."

"Babe, no way are you going to get that girl out through Kuwait." Judd Cameron leaned forward, elbows on his knees, clasping Liz's hand in both of his. "The fighting's already over but it'll be weeks, maybe months, before commercial flights start up again. The Iraqis fired the oilwells before leaving, and the First Division of the Iraqi Guards was wiped out there, just annihilated, one hundred thousand men... It's a mess, the dead not buried, military materiel still burning, survivors turning themselves in. You can't go that way."

She was thin, dehydrated, her creamy skin blotched and peeling, green eyes bloodshot...and her hair, her glorious hair was gone, but she was alive. An inch higher, the blow to her temple—probably a piece of the Range Rover blasted off during the firefight—could have killed her. Silently, Judd thanked whatever power it was that sometimes took a hand in human affairs. Miraculously Ruiz had known where to look when she'd told him who it was she was trying to find—he'd treated two of Ruiz's brothers for gunshot wounds less than a year ago in the E.R. at USC County General in Los Angeles, and they'd met again at Pendleton before shipping out.

"So how are we going to get her out?" Liz asked. "I can't let go now, Judd." She leaned back on the pillows he'd propped on the cot, her hand in his. In spite of the Marine buzz cut, he was still Judd, dearer than she thought possible. She didn't know how long she and Safeya had hunkered down in the humvee while the two young Marines had driven around searching for him—the hours had become a blur of passing images and voices, questions and answers, light and dark, in and out of consciousness. Then Judd was carrying her into his tent, while Hannah Stone took charge of Safeya. He'd stripped off the filthy *thobe,* bathed her from a tin bowl—it wasn't possible to use the field showers, too many eyes he'd said, and besides, she couldn't stand up alone—then put one of his own military issue T-shirts on her.

In the hours since, every time she awoke, he was there. He'd listened when she'd told him about her mother Fateema and Prince Bandr bin Talal Al Sa'ud, and the terrible journey across the country. He'd held her when she spoke of the men she'd killed and the death of Nassir. He'd stroked her hair while she cried because she had doubted Nassir outside Unayzah.

"You'll get out okay, something I've been working on," Judd said. "It's kind of bizarre, but if you're up for it, it will work—"

A knock on the canvas door of Judd's tent interrupted him. "Anyone home?" a female voice called.

"Come in, Hannah," Judd said.

Liz slid him a glance.

Dr. Hannah Stone ducked into the tent. In her combat gear she looked as trim and elegant in the desert as she had in Bob Gould's guest house in Jeddah.

"How are you feeling?" she asked Liz. "You look better."

"I'm fine, Hannah, thanks." Liz swung her legs over the edge of Judd's cot and sat up. She ran a hand over her head, still surprised to find a rough pelt instead of a smooth fall of hair. It was matted and filled with sand and featured a bald patch that Judd had shaved so that he could repair the wound. "How's Safeya?"

"Okay. Sleeping," Hannah said. Judd pointed to the other camp stool in the tent, and she sat. "She's safe in my tent, no one goes in there without an invitation. That kid desperately needs some downtime.''

"Not yet," Judd said. "They've got to leave tonight."

"For God's sake, Judd, give them a day. They need to rest," Hannah said.

"It's too dangerous," he said. "I've got to get back to Safaniyah, I can spare only another day at most, and you've got no security here. Saudis are all over the place, nobody seems to know who they are even. Anybody could get in here."

Hannah looked at Liz, shaking her head. "These people can't seem to get it that American women fly choppers, work on ordinance and trucks. The Bedouins constantly try the perimeter with their goats, pointing the female Marines out to their relatives. Even the Saudi army personnel keeps making excuses to come over to stare. It's spooky."

"We're a shock to their systems," Liz said. "Anyway, I don't need to rest and Safeya can rest all she wants in Santa Barbara. My mother—" Liz thought of Fateema, and her voice pinched in her throat "—my mother will see to that."

"Give the kid another hour," Judd said, "then get her up. Dress her in these." He picked up a set of folded fatigues, tossed them to Hannah, and put a set on the cot next to Liz. "You, too, Liz. Compliments of Corporal Ruiz, the great liberator of military equipment." Ruiz knew how to keep his mouth shut and would convince the other guy, Uhlmeyer, to do the same. In any case, it was a chance they had to take. When the two women were gone, it didn't matter. Rumors could fly. "I've got some final arrangements to make. Hannah, have them in the hospital tent by 4:00 a.m.—"

"You mean 0400 hours, Colonel?" Hannah said.

"Hannah, please. I'm a civilian in drag. Don't break my balls."

"What about Belle?" Liz asked.

At the sound of her name, the saluki thumped her tail. The two young Marines had retraced their steps until they'd found her lying in the desert. Judd had rehydrated her with a saline solution under the skin, and she'd staggered to Liz's side. She hadn't moved since except to take food from Liz's hand.

"Don't worry, we'll get her out," Judd promised. "Jarheads have been smuggling their unofficial pets stateside since the beginning of the Corps." Judd pulled back the door to his tent revealing a night sky filled with stars. Cold air rushed in and with it the sounds of the camp became strangely more insistent, as if the canvas had kept noise out: helicopters landed and took off, voices called back and forth, mess tins clattered. "'What the brass don't know don't hurt 'em,' is an old military axiom. Isn't that right, Captain Stone?"

"If you say so, Colonel."

The hospital tent was silent, dimly lit. Empty beds, neatly made with tight hospital corners, lined the canvas walls—the fight hadn't got this far south. Liz shivered with anticipation and anxiety, a sick sort of horror at what was to come. The edge of the cot pressed against her thighs and she moved, adjusting her grip on Safeya. They'd decided to keep her drugged, and the shot of diazepam was working; she was barely conscious. Belle was out completely. After some discussion, they'd decided to reduce the amount of drug to match the dog's weight and pray the canine reaction was the same as the human and that it didn't kill her.

Hannah Stone, standing by the door, turned and beckoned.

"They're here."

Judd entered the tent. "Corporal Ruiz is driving. We're in safe hands." He picked Safeya up, Liz and Hannah lifted Belle between them. The ambulance was backed against the open door of the tent and within seconds, they were inside. Hannah jumped out. They heard her fasten the doors, then slap the side of the ambulance in farewell as it moved off.

Judd slid Safeya into the bottom bunk, straightened her legs, lifted an eyelid.

"She'll be out until—"

"She's in love with you, Judd." She was exhausted, frightened and there was no barrier between thoughts and words. Still Liz wondered why she said such a thing with so much else on her mind.

"Who, Princess Safeya bin Bandr—"

"Bint Bandr. It's bint for a woman. Princess Safeya bint Bandr," Liz said. "No. You know who I mean. Hannah Stone."

"Hannah Stone is in love with the Marine Corps, Liz."

"But you had a thing going—"

He hesitated, then said, "Yeah, a few weeks. It was nothing really, for either of us."

The glass panel slid back. Ruiz's voice said, "Get ready, Colonel."

"It's over?" Liz said.

"Liz, it barely even started."

For the first time, Liz looked at the dark-green body bags piled on the top bunk. She got up, braced herself in the aisle but it wasn't necessary. Ruiz drove carefully, and the sand was flat.

Outside the ambulance, she could hear the sound of a chopper idling. She took the top of one of the bags, held it while Judd slid down the zipper. Between them they wrestled Safeya into the bag, leaving a space through which she could breathe. Then Belle. Judd unzipped the third bag. Liz slid into it.

"Liz, sure you don't want a shot?" he asked.

She looked up at him, shook her head. The bag was

clammy and smelt of rubberized plastic. "You won't leave us?"

"Not for a minute," he said. "The body bags will be put into transfer cases before they're loaded onto a C-130. I've squared it with the Graves Registration guys, they'll pass you over without logging you in. I'll be with you until you take off, and I'll make sure the cases are not fastened down. You'll be able to breathe. As soon as you're airborne, the guys onboard will open the cases and you can move around. While you're refueling in England, you just stay onboard, out of sight."

"You're sure about my dad?" They'd already discussed it, but suddenly she wanted reassurance.

"I called him on a secure line, Liz," he said. "He'll be at Pendleton when you arrive. He's got some pretty influential friends at State. He'll get you off the base."

"Colonel," Ruiz's voice said. The ambulance stopped.

"It'll be okay, Liz." Judd bent and put his lips gently on hers, careful not to press the damaged tissue, the old thrill running through him as he felt her lips move in response. "I'll be right here."

The sound of the heavy zipper seemed deafening. She wanted to struggle against the cold plastic enclosing her into the darkness. She felt the stretcher being lifted, the voices above her muffled. The stretcher bumped as it was secured in the chopper. She could barely breathe and wondered about Safeya and Belle. In an hour they'd be placed into metal coffins, relying upon others to see they didn't suffocate. The thought made her flesh crawl.

But Judd would be there; he'd see to it that they were kept safe.

He hadn't mentioned Abdullah, hadn't asked the obvious question even when she told him that she was holding a Beretta to Safeya's head when the sand dune collapsed.

Would she have done it? she wondered. Would she have pulled the trigger?

The powerful Allison engines whined and caught, the noise increasing in volume, reverberating through her body. Liz closed her eyes, took several deep breaths and thanked God for the Marine Corps.

She was going home.

Epilogue

"You know, I kind of like your hair that way, Lizzie." Jim Ryan reached across the redwood picnic table and touched a strand curling against Liz's neck.

"Really?" Pleased, Liz put a hand to the cap of waves that hugged the shape of her head. It still felt strange to have her neck so naked and vulnerable.

"Looks a hell of a lot better than it did when you stepped out of that plane at Pendleton."

Liz laughed. "Anything would look better than that, Dad." The bald patch was growing in, and her hairdresser had tidied up the rest. "I think I'm going to keep it short, less trouble. Mom doesn't like it, though."

"Well, you know your mother, she doesn't take easily to change. Truth be told, she'd like to see you still in pigtails."

"Dad, hate to tell you this, but I never had pigtails."

Jim laughed. "You know what I mean. She should have had half a dozen kids, your mother, spread a bit of that love and attention around instead of concentrating it all on you."

"Well, looks as if she's getting another daughter, at last," Liz said.

For a moment they watched Tess and Safeya on the other side of the garden, carrying easels and canvasses, palettes and boxes of oils out of the studio, stepping over Charlie stretched across the doorway in a patch of sun. The gear set up on the patio, Tess buttoned Safeya into one of Jim's old dress shirts which she used as a smock, stood back and nodded her approval.

The spring sun was warm, drifting through the fresh green of the sycamores and dappling the lawn with gently moving pools of light and shade. The air smelled of new roses, moisture from the flowing creek at the bottom of the empty paddock, a breath of eucalyptus from the trees along the road. Liz imagined the subcutaneous layers of her skin drinking in the moisture, smoothing away the dryness she thought would be there forever.

"How's Safeya doing, Dad?" she asked.

"Okay, I think, considering," Jim answered. "Kid's had more to deal with than anyone should have to, gang rape, loss of mother and homeland. To say nothing of the father's role in all this." Jim kept his eyes on his wife, his new daughter. "Your mother's got her talking to a woman, a psychiatrist. It'll take time, but we've got plenty of that."

"What about school?"

"We're going to see how she is in a couple of months, maybe enroll her in summer school if she wants, get ready for the fall term. Or she can go to private school if she likes. We don't have to make that decision now." Jim smiled at his daughter. "She says she wants to be a surgeon, can't think why. Still, it sounds good, so we're encouraging that idea."

Liz laughed. She let her hand drop to Belle's silky ears— the dog still wouldn't leave her side—content just to sit in the sun with her father, enjoy the warm Sunday in spring in Santa Barbara, watch her mother and Safeya laughing and talking. Jim broke the silence.

"So what about you, honey? How are you?"

"Good. I'm in good shape, Dad." She glanced at her father, knowing he was worried. "Talbot brings me in whenever Bodessian isn't available. You know, he never did offer Armin a deal. I've got some private patients, too, so

I'm about back to where I was when I left. Better, in fact. I really did learn a hell of a lot there. Thanks to Hisham Badawi.'' A familiar cloud of sadness settled over his name. She didn't resist it, knowing it would pass, at least for now.

"Well, I'm glad to hear it," Jim said. "But I didn't ask about your work, honey. How are you?"

Liz stared at the garden for a moment. "Sometimes I think I lost something out there in that desert. I killed three men. I might have killed Safeya. I probably would have." Liz gestured to the lively girl dabbing oils on the canvas. "Look at her."

"Did you have a choice, do you think?" Jim asked gently.

"No, I didn't. I know that. I had to do it, and I guess I'm not sorry that I did. But still, I'm a doctor. I've seen death, a lot of it, but I've never put a bullet into anyone."

"You need to talk this over with someone, Liz."

Liz turned to smile at him. "I am, Dad, don't worry. It's going to be all right." Her nightmares were less frequent now, still dreamed in black and white. Only her memory of the people remained vibrant—Fateema, Sakeena, Nassir, Samir, Hisham. Abdullah.

Jim reached over and squeezed her hand. "So you're going to stay in Santa Monica. This will make your mother happy."

She hesitated, then said, "I don't think I'll be here for long, Dad. I worked a lot with kids when I was in Saudi and I've decided to go into pediatric work. I'm applying to the NIH in Bethesda. Bob will put a word in for me."

"Oh. So what about Judd? His practice?"

"Well, trauma specialists are in demand in every urban center in the United States. He says just point him in the right direction. We're going to talk when he gets home."

"And that will make you happy? To have Judd home?"

"Daddy, I can't tell you how much."

Jim let a moment pass, then said, "I got a phone call couple of days ago. Prince Abdullah. He's in Washington."

Liz stiffened at the mention of his name. "I hope you told him I wouldn't press charges of attempted murder by sand dune."

"He seemed concerned for you—"

"Oh, bullshit, Dad. If he was so concerned, why didn't he just get us out of there? What did he want?"

"He seems to have been reading up on Western ways, but he's a few years off. He all but asked my permission to pay court to my daughter."

Liz shook her head. "What did you tell him?"

"I played the heavy father, what else? I said that you were unavailable, you were not interested in living in Saudi Arabia, blah, blah, and as your father, I forbade it, anyway, your family needs you here. He might listen to that. And he might not. Who knows."

"It doesn't matter, that's history now." A fantasy about a man she didn't know and a way of life she could never have embraced. "Did you ask about Fateema?"

"I didn't have to. He volunteered information. Told me to tell you that she was safe and well, even that, given time, she might be able to travel again outside the country. He didn't exactly say so, but I got the impression that her husband is pretty much enthralled by her, always has been."

"Isn't that strange?" Liz said in wonderment. "Fateema really seems to be the only human passion that monster of a husband of hers has ever had. From the beginning when she was only thirteen, maybe even twelve." Liz shook off the shadow of the terrible story of her and Samir's birth. "Did Abdullah mention Nassir?" She had written to Bob as soon as she got home—the telephone seemed unwise— and told him roughly where Nassir's body could be found, asking him to get that information to Abdullah.

"No, honey. And I didn't ask."

Liz nodded. "I can't reach Fateema on the phone, I tried. The number I had isn't available anymore. I guess Sakeena's okay."

"No reason to think otherwise."

"Hey, you two, how about some tea?" Tess's voice sailed across the garden. "I'm putting on the kettle. Want some scones?"

"Absolutely," Liz called back. "I'll come and help." She got to her feet. In passing she bent, pressed her lips to her father's cheek. "You're such a good guy, Dad." He'd even started to look into the possibilities for Siti and Megawati.

"While I had him on the phone, I talked to Abdullah about Safeya," Jim said. "If we want to adopt her, they won't rock the boat if we don't. She's safe."

"Oh, Dad." Liz leaned against his back for a moment, her arms around him, her chin resting on his head. Then she straightened and walked across the lawn to the kitchen door, Belle at her heels. The saluki gave a low growl, raised her upper lip as Charlie attempted a friendly overture. Tess finished filling the teapot with boiling water and spoke over her shoulder.

"What's Judd going to do about that dog, Liz? She hates everyone but you."

"I wondered how long it would take you to get around to Judd today, Ma."

Tess laughed, put the teapot on the tray. "Oh, you."

"Where's Safeya?" Liz asked.

"In her room. It's about the afternoon prayer time. She goes to her room then, and at sunset. Prays at dawn, too, shouldn't wonder." Tess busied with cups and saucers. "Your father would prefer a martini, I'm sure. Sunday afternoon, he's entitled. Get the gin would you, darling?"

Liz got out another tray. "It's a problem, isn't it?"

"What, Daddy's gin?"

"No, Ma. Safeya's religion."

"No, not really. There are a few Muslim families in Santa Barbara. I've talked to them, only generally, of course, nothing specific. But if Safeya chooses, they'll be available."

"You really are something, Tess Ryan." Impulsively, Liz put her arms around her mother. She found herself doing that a lot lately. "Did Dad tell you about Abdullah?"

"That he called? Yes." Tess banged the lid back onto the kettle she'd just filled. "Let's talk about Judd."

Liz laughed. "Okay. He'll be home in a couple of weeks and we've got a lot of talking to do." She loaded her father's tray with gin, vermouth, ice, olives, a bowl of peanuts. There would be time enough to break the news to Tess that she was leaving when she was sure of an appointment at the NIH.

"Well, I knew he was coming home. Bob told Melly on the phone last weekend."

"Did she mention what Bob plans to do when he gets back?" A wealthier man than when he left, no doubt, Liz thought silently.

"He's not going back into practice, that's for sure. Melly said he intended to do research, some writing. He joined AA in Jeddah, did you know that?"

Liz nodded. "He was looking pretty good, too. Twenty years younger."

"Melly's going to Al Anon. She says she doesn't know why she resisted it for so long."

"It's called denial, Ma. We were all guilty of it."

Tess broke a scone in two, fed half to each of the dogs. "I imagine Judd will be going back to his E.R. practice. So what about you two? When are you going to get married?"

"Ma, what you need to do is learn to be more direct. Did anyone ever tell you that?"

"Yes, now that you mention it. Often. So that's what I do when I want an answer to a question. I ask."

Liz laughed, put the plate of scones on the tray with the butter and jam, cups and saucers and teapot. She picked it up, leaving the tray she'd prepared for her father for Tess. They made their way across the lawn, the two dogs trailing behind.

Tess put the drinks tray in front of her husband. "Jim, did your daughter tell you about her plans for the future? Or am I going to be the last to know?"

Jim looked from one to the other, leaned back and raised both hands in mock alarm. "Girls, whatever it is, I don't have a dog in this fight."

Liz poured tea, handed the cup to her mother, and said sweetly, "Ma. Judd is coming home. We are going to talk. A lot has happened, and as it stands right now, I still don't want to get married. He still does."

Tess smiled. "Oh, so nothing's changed."

The last year flashed through Liz's mind—people loved, blood spilled, bitter lessons learned, about herself, about the world. "Ma, everything has changed."

"Yes, but you and Judd are still arguing. That's a good sign."

Liz caught her father's eye, and they laughed.

She really was home.

Let **DEBBIE MACOMBER** take you into the **HEART OF TEXAS.**

Let her take you back to...

PROMISE, TEXAS

Dear Reader,

In Promise, Texas, people know that family, home, community are the things that really count. They know that love gives meaning to every single day of their lives.

Some of the people in Promise are from old ranching families—like the Westons and the Pattersons, who first came to the hill country more than a century ago. And there are newcomers like Annie Applegate, who agrees to marry a widowed veterinarian for the sake of his children...and discovers that this marriage can lead to a great deal more.

MDM502A

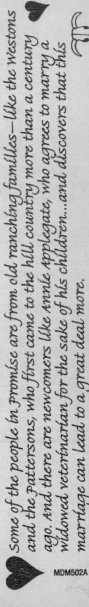

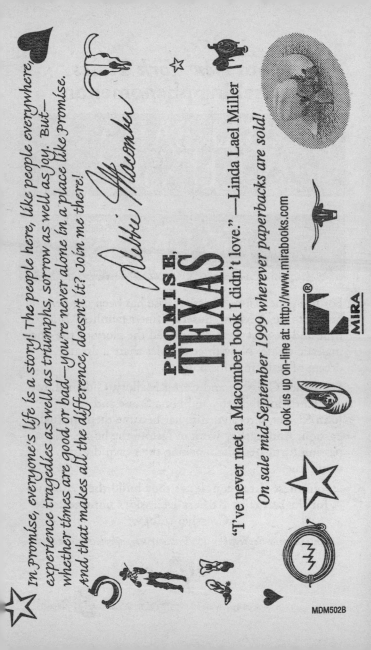

In Promise, everyone's life is a story! The people here, like people everywhere, experience tragedies as well as triumphs, sorrow as well as joy. But— whether times are good or bad—you're never alone in a place like Promise. And that makes all the difference, doesn't it? Join me there!

Debbie Macomber

PROMISE, TEXAS

"I've never met a Macomber book I didn't love." —Linda Lael Miller

On sale mid-September 1999 wherever paperbacks are sold!

Look us up on-line at: http://www.mirabooks.com

MDM502B

From *New York Times* bestselling phenomenon

BARBARA DELINSKY

DREAMS

For five generations Crosslyn Rise has been the very heart of one of Massachusetts's finest families. But time and neglect have diminished the glory of the once-majestic estate. Now three couples share a dream...a dream of restoring this home.

For Jessica Crosslyn and Carter Mallory, Gideon Lowe and Christine Gillette, and Nina Stone and John Sawyer, Crosslyn Rise has become their mutual passion. And as they work to restore the house, that passion turns personal, making their own dreams come true....

Join these three couples as they build their dreams for the future in Barbara Delinsky's unforgettable Crosslyn trilogy.

On sale mid-September 1999 wherever paperbacks are sold!

MIRA

By the bestselling author of
KISS THE MOON

CARLA NEGGERS

In a tragic accident, world-famous oceanographer Emile Labreque's research ship went down, killing five people. Emile, his granddaughter, Riley, and the captain barely escaped with their lives.

A year later, the captain turns up dead and it looks like murder...and all evidence points to Emile. When Emile disappears, Riley enlists the help of John Straker, a burned-out FBI special agent. But one of the things they discover as they work to clear Emile's name is a passion too big to ignore....

ON FIRE

"When it comes to romance, adventure and suspense, nobody delivers like Carla Neggers."
–Jayne Ann Krentz

On sale mid-October 1999 wherever paperbacks are sold!

Old Money. Older Sins.

ELIZABETH PALMER

In the world of stiff upper lips and martinis before dinner, bachelor Morgan Steer is the perfect catch— except he's completely broke. To escape the financial control of his ruthless, manipulative grandmother, Morgan must marry a fortune.

In desperation he proposes to the very chic, very icy, very, *very* rich Chloe Post. The impending nuptials rekindle old passions, stir bitter furies and shift family loyalties. And the havoc that ensues will crack the thin veneer of barely contained civility in the Steer household.

For old money is worth any cost— even murder.

old money